The Chastened Heart

The Chastened Heart

A Novel

Robert Crooke

THE CHASTENED HEART
A NOVEL

This is a work of fiction. All of the characters, names, incidents, organizations, and dialogue in this novel are either the products of the author's imagination or are used fictitiously.

This book uses excerpts from previously published material:

Dante Alighieri's Divine Comedy: Volumes 1 & 2, Inferno, Italian Text with Verse Translation, Notes and Commentary by Mark Musa. Published by Indiana University Press. Copyright © 1997 by Mark Musa. Used by permission.

The Portrait of a Lady, by Henry James, first published in the Atlantic Monthly and in Macmillan's Magazine, 1880-1881, in book form by Macmillan (London) and Houghton, Mifflin (Boston), 1881, revised and republished by Scribner (New York), 1908.

The works of Henry James are in public domain.

iUniverse books may be ordered through booksellers or by contacting:

iUniverse
1663 Liberty Drive
Bloomington, IN 47403
www.iuniverse.com
1-800-Authors (1-800-288-4677)

Because of the dynamic nature of the Internet, any web addresses or links contained in this book may have changed since publication and may no longer be valid.

ISBN: 978-1-4917-4988-3 (sc)
ISBN: 978-1-4917-4987-6 (e)

Library of Congress Control Number: 2014918197

Printed in the United States of America.

iUniverse rev. date: 10/20/2014

For Sean

"But you must journey down another road,"
he answered, when he saw me lost in tears,
"if ever you hope to leave this wilderness;"
                    —*Inferno*, Canto I, 91-93, Dante Alighieri

There were lights in the windows of the house; they shone far across
the lawn. In an extraordinarily short time—for the distance was
considerable—she had moved through the darkness … and reached
the door. Here only she paused. She looked all about her; she listened
a little; then she put her hand on the latch. She had not known where
to turn; but she knew now. There was a very straight path.
                    —*The Portrait of a Lady*, Henry James

One

May 2007

Tom Winslow smiled as he remembered tossing his gym shorts on the floor. Rising to slip them on again while Alice slept, he padded to the window for a glimpse of their meadow and the distant ridge marking the western boundary of Connecticut. The ridge-line had been pristine when they'd moved to Trent, 25 years ago, but a row of expensive homes now adorned its craggy face. In earliest sunlight the houses were blanched, white squares, like sheets hung out to dry.

It was the third Friday in May, and from what Tom could see, the weather would be splendid for Alice's book event this evening at Shelby College.

He glanced as she rolled toward the vacated side of their bed and grew still again. A spasm of grief clutched in his chest as he followed the graceful line of her body beneath the sheet, and admired the girlish effect of her long hair splayed against bare shoulders.

On the night table near her outstretched hand lay his worn copy of her novel, *The Chastened Heart*, which he'd read three times, not counting the manuscript drafts. In his opinion, it was a magical work—a story of love and sorrow that cast a spell when you opened its pages. People were reading it by the thousands. Friends were recommending it, book clubs were discussing it, and a *New York Times* reviewer had offered perhaps the best description of its unique power—"Enter this fictional world and you will feel that its author has appropriated your life, that somehow she has conjured her narrative from your own experience."

Even Tom had succumbed to this strange alchemy. Alice's story, which was *their* story, more or less, had changed not only with each new draft, but again with each new reading of the published version—until he could no longer find the threads of truth from which her tale had been spun.

Now, as the sun came up full and strong on the distant ridge, the white houses vanished in the glare. Tom felt himself floating, as if between two worlds bridged by memory. He recalled a romantic young man with a beer in his hand, jammed into the crowded living room of a Beacon Hill brownstone in 1967. On a stereo somewhere in the room, Richard and Mimi Fariña were singing *Pack Up Your Sorrows*.

There was a girl talking with someone in the kitchen, at the opposite end of the house, and she was beautiful, with rich, brunette hair flowing to the middle of her back. He was unable to stop watching her until she caught him at it. Then, sufficiently embarrassed, he turned away to re-engage the party he and his buddies had driven from Providence to attend. But he asked about the distant pair engrossed in their private conversation.

"Some guy from the Harvard *Lampoon*," he was told. "Don't know the chick."

Later that night, he noticed that the Harvard guy had left, and the beautiful girl had come into the main room of the house. She stood alone by the fireplace, not quite aloof from the party, not quite embracing it, as if someone so beautiful could be uncertain of anything.

He angled through the frat-party crowd, determined to reach her before anyone else did. She noticed his urgency and smiled. Her face was more beautiful the closer he got, and he could see the blonde highlights in her hair now.

"What are you doing?" Alice asked from bed, dispersing his memories.

"Just looking." He turned from the distant mountains to see his wife sitting up and smiling. Her face was still beautiful, a slightly older version, perhaps, of the face that had smiled curiously in a Boston brownstone. That was the face he'd fallen in love with, but he'd come to love this older version better. It had the look of honesty.

"Come back to bed."

"Don't you want coffee?"

"I want my husband."

He started toward her, as pleased as she seemed by this latest renaissance in their sexual life, which had undergone many phases of intensity and reversal over time. As he drew near, slipping off his gym shorts again, she laughed, sliding back down and pulling the covers open for him on her side.

When he pressed in against her, she kissed him and pulled him on top. He felt her thighs tighten around him.

The phone rang.

He was chilled, dead weight.

"Don't answer it," she whispered.

He stopped moving into her.

"Come on," she urged, holding the back of his neck and pulling.

But the phone's insistent ringing broke her concentration now.

"Maybe we better," she conceded. "It might be Peg Harvey ... or school."

He rolled off.

She grabbed the receiver. "Hello? Will!"

She turned away and sat up, with the sheets around her waist and her legs dangling off that side of the bed. Tom sat up too, listening to her end of a conversation with their son, who was in London on business with his wife, Nancy.

"Yes," Alice said. "They came yesterday. No. Your father. I was still at school. Yes. They're beautiful. I love them. Oh?"

And as Alice listened to some juicy bit of London gossip, Tom again pondered the sleek curve of her bare back, and the sweep of her hips, half-covered in bunched sheets. He kissed her shoulder through tumbled hair, then propped a pillow behind himself.

She glanced at him while listening intently to Will.

"Ask him when they'll be home," Tom said, gazing across the room at a window now glorious with sunlight.

Alice hung up and sat very still, noticing his copy of her book near the phone. "They're flying back Sunday."

"How's business?"

"Huh? Oh. Good ... he says." Abruptly she stood, pulling that side of the bed sheet up to herself and facing him. "It's later than I realized. Peg's due in forty minutes."

"I'll make coffee."

She nodded pensively.

"Is everything okay?"

She leaned over and kissed him. "Yes."

Dropping the sheet, she hurried to the bathroom. The shower came on.

He reached across the bed for the book. Leafing through a few pages, he found his favorite scene—in which her two main characters decide to marry. Reminiscent of events in their past, the scene expressed its own truth about love's enduring sorrows.

"Aaagghh!" she muttered in apparent discomfort.

The book closed in his lap. "What's wrong?"

"Nothing's wrong! A stomach cramp."

"You're sure?"

"Coffee! You said something about coffee?"

"Yes."

But still he lingered, contemplating her picture on the book's back cover. The photographer had captured the calmness of her smile in elegant black and white, but also a chilly tension in her eyes; a sign, perhaps, that literary success on her scale had its burdens—except that he'd seen this tension in her eyes before.

On a bright, May morning very much like today, he recalled, Alice had traveled down from Boston for his graduation weekend—after which she was to leave for a Columbia University fellowship earned on the basis of several respectably-published short stories.

As he took her bags and guided her from the train station to his rickety Volkswagen that morning, he noticed her face was sullen and pale. He wondered if she had the sense, as he suddenly did, of their lives diverging. On the way to his apartment, she mentioned feeling car sick. When he suggested, in obtuse helpfulness, that she visit his campus nurse, she glared. He turned on the radio. Tuned to the Aquinas College station, whose signal carried barely beyond campus, his Blaupunkt threw a blast of static. She groaned. He lowered the volume while she gulped fresh air at her open window.

The static faded in the middle of *Pack Up Your Sorrows*, and Tom remembered their disagreement over Richard Fariña's novel the night they met. Published in 1966, days before its author was killed in a motorcycle accident, *Been Down So Long It Looks Like Up to Me* had been a brief, counter-cultural sensation. But she'd been right to argue, he now thought, that its blend of Kerouac and Pynchon was more cute than radical.

Arriving at his place on Exton Street, she quickly excused herself while he handled her luggage. Twice more that afternoon she locked herself in his bathroom, and he could hear through the door as she retched. Finally grasping what this was, he tried to discuss it. She refused. The cold tension in her bloodshot eyes told him they'd become strangers, somehow, in the same mysterious process which had made them lovers.

Then, on the evening before his commencement, as they finished dressing to meet his mother for dinner, he held her hands, kissed her, and asked her to marry him. She was shocked into silence.

"I'm serious," he told her.

"I know." She stared at the quiet street outside his living room window.

"You don't want to?"

"You knew I was dating someone when we met."

Though they'd never spoken clearly about this, Tom had harbored assumptions.

"You know what," he said. "I need some fresh air."

"Wait. I'll go with you."

"No." He started for the door. "I won't be long."

"We have to be downtown in less than an hour," she reminded him.

"I'll be right back."

So he left her in his apartment and walked quickly along Exton to a part of campus that had been cleared for expansion. Picking his way through a desolation of construction rubble, he came upon the skeletal frame of a dormitory high-rise being readied for next fall's freshman class.

Without its skin, the structure was a cut-away puzzle of rooms, stairways and halls, behind empty window frames. He'd been to the top once before in a burst of boyish curiosity. Now, with more purpose, he entered again through an open door frame.

As he climbed a central stairwell of echoing concrete, a dizzying view emerged of the leafy streets and fieldstone houses around his school. On the 20th floor, he stepped out across a concrete promenade to the edge of the building's southeast side, from where he could see the greater part of downtown Providence—its neoclassic state capitol building, its gilded bank domes and white church spires—clustered at the basin of seven hills. He could see the red-brick Biltmore, where his mother would be waiting for them.

Standing near the edge of the concrete promenade, he stared out beyond Narragansett Bay to the thin blue distance of the Atlantic. Everything at this height was silence and stillness. He felt as if his life had slipped away, moved on without him.

Having come to Aquinas thinking of himself as a novelist, he was heading home to a more prosaic job as Long Island reporter for the *Daily News*. His stellar running career had ended in a bitter dispute with his coach after not quite three years here.

And five months ago Colonel Arthur Winslow, his spit-and-polished father, had kissed his mother and driven the short distance from their Bayview home to Deep Meadow State Park on Long Island Sound. There he parked, hiked up into the hilly woodlands, where the old cross-country course was, and blew his brains out with his service pistol. A man walking his dog the next morning found the Colonel's frozen body on the trail.

"Tom?" said an edgy voice behind him.

He turned toward her. "You shouldn't have followed me."

"It looks dangerous." Slowly she approached, holding out her hand. "Step back a little."

He did as she asked. They stood together silently as the sun began setting.

"It *is* a beautiful view," she said.

"This Harvard guy," Tom said, clinging to one part of his past that hadn't yet vanished in a hopeless future. "I thought he wasn't your boyfriend."

"Did I *say* that?"

"A 'friend' is what you said."

She nodded gravely. "All this time, you never thought to ask any more about him?"

"I'm sorry. I must have thought, 'Alice would never let me make a fool of myself.'"

She turned her head with a snap and looked at him. She was crying.

"I suppose he's working on some big-time magazine by now," he ventured.

She looked away again. "*The New Yorker*," she said bleakly.

"Maybe you want to marry *him*."

"Shut up," she hissed.

"You still haven't said 'yes' or 'no.'"

She stared out on the city, apparently embarrassed by his insistence.

As he waited, Tom considered the wisdom of plans made in the wake of failure and betrayal. He accepted that honesty meant different things to different people, but assumed he knew the truth about himself. And, at least, she was starting to say what she really thought, even if he'd had to trick her into it.

Finally, she spoke. "What about your novel?"

"What does that have to do with anything?"

She pressed him, searching in his eyes. "Will this newspaper job give you time to finish it?"

"Have you seen him lately?"

She looked away again.

"Just say 'no.' I don't care if it's true or not."

"Oh, Tom."

"Can you promise not to see him again?"

"Can you promise *me* you'll finish your novel?"

"I don't get why that's important."

"And that you won't throw this up to me later? That you still want to do this with me, and it's not just some challenge for you now?"

"Challenge?" he said in disbelief.

"*Promise* me."

Alice turned off the shower with a snap that sent a tremor down the pipes of their rebuilt farmhouse. Roused again from distant memories, still clinging to her book, Tom decided her version of the past was better than his.

"How's that coffee coming?"

She stood in the bathroom doorway now, a damp towel around her body, beads of moisture on her beautiful face.

Yes, he thought, the photographer had gotten her perfectly.

Peg Harvey was running late when the argument erupted. She'd surprised Peter two months ago with her plan to spend their summer vacation alone. And he'd grown increasingly sullen, until this morning, when real anger flashed in his voice.

"That goddamn book," he shouted, before retreating down into his carpentry shop behind a slamming cellar door.

Perhaps he'd been expecting her to change her mind? That would be just like Peter, she thought, mistaking determination for caprice. Peg also wondered which book her husband had meant, Alice's, or her own unpublished manuscript. Perhaps it was both, except that she didn't quite believe he'd read Alice's novel.

Peg, on the other hand, admired *The Chastened Heart* almost beyond reason. She'd already hosted a book-signing for Alice here at her home, had organized a reading at the Trent Public Library where she served as a board member, and had arranged tonight's private dinner for four, just prior to Alice's appearance at Shelby College. But in its immensity, the success of Alice's novel had overwhelmed Peg, upsetting the balance of what she'd felt in common with a friend, neighbor and teaching colleague.

Naturally, Alice had been wonderful throughout the past months. She'd taken time from her own increasingly harried life to read the latest drafts of Peg's work, and to offer gentle, useful commentary, while showing some of the best pages to her literary agent, who'd rendered sound, market-based advice. Yet, even her friend's suggestions had felt condemnatory, since Peg would never have found solutions of such simple beauty herself.

"Just keeping writing," Alice had urged. "All I know, I've learned by trial and error."

Peg had followed Alice's advice and applied for a fellowship at the Long Valley Writer's Conference in Vermont. She was still waiting to hear back. But with or without a fellowship, Peg knew, she was going to the conference next month—during the time she and Peter always vacationed—and even if she had to use half their vacation budget to pay the fees.

Staring at the silent, cellar door at the far end of her kitchen, Peg felt a flutter of compassion for her confused husband, remembering

9

a moment last week when it appeared he might simply ask to come along with her to Vermont.

"There's a lot of trout in those mountain streams," he'd said.

But the last thing Peg wanted was to have her husband hanging around in a motel room, or in one of the writer's cabins at the conference, waiting there every night like a dark cloud of judgment— the embodiment of her fear that nothing changes.

When she ignored Peter's open-ended reference to fly-fishing in the Green Mountains, something became fully alert in him.

"This Vermont thing," he'd said this morning. "It's not just about writing, is it?"

"No."

"Are you even coming back after the conference?"

Shocked by his directness, she whispered the words, "I don't know," and revealed an unbearable sadness to herself.

The Harveys' moment of insight, then, was shattered by Peter's angry retreat to the cellar. But now, Peg ran her coffee cup under the hot water faucet in the kitchen sink, and tried to recapture the clarity.

Why should it be so important to her what he thought about Alice's novel anyway? Yes, he'd claimed to have read it, even though his unabashed preference was for histories and biographies, which he called "the real facts of what happens." Was he not allowed what she'd spent a lifetime demanding for herself—his own opinion, the space to form it?

It wasn't that he lacked appreciation of creativity. Peg considered him an artist in his own right, a successful building contractor with a keen eye for real estate, as a result of which they owned the nicest home in the oldest section of Trent—a pre-revolutionary Georgian— grabbed up cheaply in foreclosure, and refurbished, as he'd done with the Winslows' Victorian farm house.

Finally, she realized how late it was. She called to him through the closed cellar door.

"I'm going to work!"

Waiting, briefly, for a husbandly response that didn't come, Peg gathered her things and hurried out to her white Toyota parked in their pea-stone driveway.

She got in, tossed her bags on the seat beside her, and turned the key. But nothing happened. The engine was silent. For several moments, she stared at the quiet solitude of their beautiful house, which the early sun began fully to embrace.

At first, she thought it some trick of sunlight playing on the front door, an optical illusion. But no, it really was Peter, coming out of the house and walking briskly down toward her car, with a look of—what—satisfaction?

He was nearly on her now. She could almost feel the air outside her air-tight Camry moving in the wake of his purposeful gait. That look on his face—what was it exactly?

"Might be the starter." He stood close outside the car. Looming over her, he cast a cold shadow where, moments earlier, sunlight had begun warming the metal and glass of her useless vehicle. "Or the battery," he added.

As Peg sat perfectly still, staring at her house, Peter softly wrapped his knuckles on the driver's side window, inches from her ear.

Instead of answering, or even looking up at him, she reached for the electronic button and pressed. She heard the coordinated snap of all doors locking. Then she leaned forward, rested her head against the cold steering wheel, and wept.

Tom poured two cups of coffee near the kitchen window and watched for Peg Harvey's Camry. According to the girls' arrangement, Peg drove to Shelby with Alice every Monday, Tuesday and Wednesday. Alice drove them in the Winslows' Range Rover on Thursdays and Fridays, when Tom worked from home on his column. But Tom needed the Rover today. *The Hartford Chronicle* had been acquired by a media conglomerate, and the new owners were sending a financial guy from Manhattan to meet with senior editors.

"These are beautiful!" It was Alice, calling out from the dining room. "Aren't they?"

He joined her at the dining room table on which her best vase brimmed with roses. "Very nice," he said.

She took a steaming cup from him. "Are you worried about your meeting?"

"I survived the *other* cutbacks."

"What does Bill Sanchez think?" she said, referring to the *Chronicle*'s editor-in-chief.

"That it's just the newspaper industry."

She took a sip and checked her watch. "Peg's late."

"That one didn't make it." He pointed to a single rose, which had drooped so low overnight its head appeared ready to fall from its stem. Several petals already had.

Alice reached for the note that Will and Nancy had sent with their gift.

"Read it again," Tom urged.

"Okay." She held the note up and read aloud, slowly, without her glasses. "Dear Mom, we spent hours in Covent Garden yesterday, walking from bookstore to bookstore. And everywhere we went, your novel was on display. Most of the stores are carrying it in their front windows, and the newspapers are filled with wonderful notices. Your publisher has started running ads, and everyone is talking about it. Our new client even mentioned your name the other day. Mother, you are famous."

Tom peered over her trembling shoulder. "That's your best review so far."

Moments later, wiping her tears, Alice removed the dying rose and cleared the fallen petals. She was tossing it all in the kitchen trash bin when the phone rang.

It was barely nine o'clock, but Tom tensed as Alice answered.

"Hi Peg! Oh. No problem." She hung up. "Her car won't start, so, we're going in Peter's pickup. They'll be here in 10 minutes."

Pouring himself a little more coffee, Tom noticed Alice's pensive stare. "What?"

"*Your* health insurance is so much better than the college plan."

He touched her shoulder. "We'll be fine."

"Something may be happening with that thing on my uterus."

She was talking about a growth, which her gynecologist had monitored for years but resisted excising, since it was benign, and because its removal would have damaged the uterus itself. This had seemed like reasonable advice when they were trying for a second child. But they'd given up on that after two miscarriages.

"Dr. Coben thinks it's gotten larger. I'm expecting her to call with biopsy results."

"Why didn't you tell me?"

"I didn't know anything yet." She spoke with a nervous edge. "You're worried enough about the paper."

Tom accepted the irony of feeling excluded by her reticence on his behalf. After all, he had his own secret—the disturbing phone calls of the last few evenings, each at precisely five o'clock, with no response when he picked up.

Alice moved toward him and rested her head on his shoulder. He could hear her deep, steady breathing, and could smell the warmth of her hair.

"Life's been good," she whispered. "Overall."

"You sound like you're putting your affairs in order."

"Don't be silly." She lifted her head and stepped toward the window again. "I'm just saying ... we've reached the age when things start to happen."

"Things *always* happen."

"We run out of time to make them right." Alice stared at the quiet street in front of their house. "We have to keep these jobs as long as we can."

Watching her from behind, Tom kept his own fears to himself. The industry that had employed him since boyhood was in decline. Worse yet, his calm second life with Alice felt threatened by the secret he'd been keeping—unexpected wreckage now washing in from their stormy first marriage. The earth felt like liquid again beneath his feet.

Peter's blue truck pulled into their driveway and Tom came to his senses.

Alice grabbed her briefcase.

Tom walked with her to the front door.

"Don't forget," she said. "Five o'clock at The Shelby Inn."

"I'll be there."

"It's very important to Peg."

They kissed.

She hurried down the walk. Tom followed slowly behind her.

Peg got out on the passenger side of the pickup, allowing Alice to squeeze in. Then, she called out to Tom with obvious irritation. "Car trouble!"

Tom waved to Peter, who waved back, but otherwise sat rigidly behind the wheel.

"Reminds me of high school," Tom said, approaching the passenger side.

"What do you mean?" Peg asked.

"The boys with the trucks always got the girls."

Peter heard the joke and smiled briefly.

Alice shook her head.

"This old thing?" Peg got in and slammed her door. The truck gently backed into the street. "See you at dinner," she reminded him from her open window.

Over many months, while writing *The Chastened Heart*, Alice had grown accustomed to imagining her life in the third person. Even after finishing the book she'd clung to this objective frame of mind, and the comfort of processing the world at a safe distance. As a result, the gravity of real things had been subverted—cramps, biopsies, job security and health insurance had come to feel like weightless concerns in someone else's story. Or so she'd thought until this morning, when the sound of Will's voice brought her back to earth.

"How's Will?" Peter asked, his truck speeding along Route 12 toward Shelby.

"Good," she fibbed. "He called this morning … from London."

Peter nodded with interest. "London?"

"He and Nancy landed a new client."

"A good trip then," he said, watching the road.

"He says it was. They're coming back Sunday."

"Too bad they can't be here tonight," Peg said, smiling briefly before turning her gaze on the passing greenery.

Alice had noticed the heavy makeup around Peg's eyes—she'd been crying, apparently. And Peter's manic grip on the steering wheel, his burly hands clenching and unclenching, evoked the image of a fidgety prize fighter. There must have been an argument, Alice thought, sitting in the edgy silence between them, estimating that 10 miles had gone by without the Harveys uttering a word to each other.

She was familiar with the subtleties of marital tension, and unsurprised by the cold silences of her neighbors. But her son's marriage troubled her.

Will's distress had something to do with Nancy, his beautiful, talented, but distant wife. Alice felt sure of this. She'd never entirely believed that Nancy loved her son as he deserved to be loved by a wife. There always had seemed something held in reserve about the girl—something not quite given. It was no less horrible to feel this way about your own daughter-in-law, Alice thought with a shudder, than to be reminded of yourself as a young woman.

Of course, Will had raised no such issue. There'd simply been the sound in his voice. And it was possible—indeed likely—he hadn't heard it himself. But Alice knew the sound of despair. She'd heard it in Tom's voice on a day long ago, when she'd followed him to the top of an unfinished building in Providence, frightened enough of his intentions to change the course of her life by embracing the mysteries of his.

"Yes," she finally said to Peg. "It would have been nice to have them here."

Peg smiled again as the Trent River flashed beyond the foliage outside her window.

Peter dropped Alice and Peg at the academic building and watched until they disappeared inside. Then, slowly, he drove his pickup back toward the main entrance.

He liked being here on the rustic campus of this small, liberal arts school in the tiny hamlet where he'd grown up. As troubled as he was with his wife, and his looming financial pressures, Peter could remember who he was in this place.

The college and town were named after Isaac Shelby, who'd moved here from Rhode Island in 1832. Having rejected his ship-owning family—though not his share of their slave-trading fortune—Isaac

Shelby fell in with local abolitionists who ferried runaways up the Trent River. As he'd written in an old diary, recently published by the Shelby College Press, "we must endeavor to save these souls or lose our own."

Peter thought the college had done a great service bringing out the Shelby diary, and he admired Peg's role in editing it for publication. But some of her colleagues had disliked the intensely self-critical narrative of the school's founder. And the diary's merits had been lost in a nasty academic skirmish over the wisdom of having published it.

As he passed the gates of the Shelby estate, just down the road from the college, Peter thought fondly of his old high school friend, Virginia Shelby Porter. She was Isaac Shelby's great, great, granddaughter, and was a formidable woman, who continued overseeing her family's good name and its endowment of the college. Virginia Porter often had Peter to her mansion for tea—to ask his opinion about structural problems with the old house, or to get advice about land use and development on the adjoining campus.

It was during one such visit, several years ago, that she'd mentioned wanting to publish her ancestor's diary.

"I've shown the manuscript to an agent in New York," Virginia confided. "He said it has no commercial appeal, but might be just the thing for an academic press. What I need is a good editor to work with."

"I wonder if that's something Peg could do," Peter said.

"*Your* Peg?" Virginia rose from her plush parlor sofa. "I need to look at my cuttings, Peter. Do you have a few minutes?"

"Of course." He followed her into a long, paneled hallway leading to a large solarium.

"Would she be interested?"

"She might."

Virginia nodded as she opened the solarium door and showed Peter inside.

"These belong to my family." She examined a row of pots containing sickly roses. "I've been a poor caretaker."

Peter knew she'd been experimenting with miniature roses grafted from samples Isaac Shelby had imported from Italy and planted here

150 years ago. Each of the new hybrids—a red, a white, a pink and a yellow—had been named for Virginia's four grandchildren.

"Are you using fungicides?" he asked.

"In the soil …"

"Try misting a little on the buds and petals."

"They'll tolerate that?"

"Roses are hardy."

"I'll speak to my landscaping man about it."

"You're still using Jack Washburn?"

"Yes."

"Tell Jack I mentioned putting some anti-fungal into your spray-water. He'll know the right mix."

"Thank you, Peter." She glanced over her roses again. "How *is* Peg? Has she published anything lately?"

"A few articles in academic journals," he said, "to maintain her tenure."

Virginia listened as she troubled over her pallid roses.

"She's been trying to write a novel too."

"Oh?"

"I don't think it's going well. She keeps starting and stopping."

"I'm no expert," Virginia said. "But I've heard you need a block of private time to launch yourself into a serious book. Does she have a sabbatical coming up? Maybe she should take a summer off and just write."

"I hear you. But this novel has become a frustration for her. It's making things worse."

"What do you mean 'making things worse'?"

"Honestly, Virginia, she's just … I don't know … unhappy."

"I see." Virginia stopped examining her flowers and faced Peter. "We all have the creative spark. We can't all be novelists, but we do have that same creative drive. It needs expression."

"I suppose you're right."

"I know I'm right." She turned again to her flowers. "For me, it used to be riding." She paused. "Do you remember?"

"Of course." He said it with fondness.

"Speak to Peg. Ask her to come see me. I'll show her the manuscript. Maybe she'll agree to help with my project."

Now, heading toward the site of his own latest project, he wondered if Peg's undiminished frustrations were somehow related to his blunt intercession on her behalf.

Cruising on the rustic sections of Old Route 12 in Connecticut's northwest corner, Peter rolled down his window and inhaled the sweet bouquet of field and farm. This had been the heart of a dairy region once, but there was a history of textile production here too. And now that the farms were few, and the mills silent, developers had their eyes open for opportunity. Peter, in fact, had recently joined an investment syndicate hoping to convert three old factory buildings on the upper Trent River into condos.

But he was a restoration man, a preserver of fine old properties. And though it was worthwhile doing something with those derelict factory shells, the job was replete with contradictions, emotional pitfalls. He needed the work, and the small profit-share that his partners had granted him. Yet increasingly, it seemed, his survival depended on the slick gentrification of a region which, like his marriage, was changing for the worse.

Hurrying toward a destination he didn't want to reach, Tom challenged the antique speed limits along twisty Route 12, tracing the river north through villages sleepier than Trent. Soon after turning east into open farm country, where the road was straight, he felt the momentary solace of unhindered motion. But then, he thought of Alice.

The sudden force of her stomach cramp in the shower had surprised her, as if *she'd* forgotten the biopsy she'd kept from him. That this could happen to her now upset him too. Yes, he knew it was childish to feel singled out by life's untimely disappointments. But sometimes anger was spontaneous, like love.

This morning's meeting at *The Chronicle* would be another disappointment—though hardly unexpected in an industry obsessed with its own demise. Senior-level editors and columnists with Guild seniority would file meekly into a conference room and be told that more needed cutting from already thin budgets. The word "efficiencies" would be invoked. A slaughterhouse silence would descend on the room as the plan for culling was revealed, sacrifices mainly to be found among younger staff reporters—talented kids who'd placed their careers in the hands of frightened men like himself and Bill Sanchez.

The traffic around Leicester Village wasn't bad this morning, so he cut through town, behind the old court house, past the Wilton Leicester homestead, and on toward Hartford.

Moving freely again, his thoughts drifted to a night, thirty-seven years earlier, when Alice's mother had reached him at the *Daily News* bureau on Long Island. "You have a son," Mrs. Prescott had said in her flat, Brookline accent. "You should be he-ah."

Even before hanging up, he'd started weeping for this unsuspecting new soul.

That first marriage with Alice was a disaster of angry break-ups, lonely separations and mutual betrayals. But he marked its end at a particular moment, during their final separation, when she'd swallowed her pride and reached out one last time.

She called to say there was a nice little house they could rent together in Quakers Meadow near her mother.

"Maybe," she offered, with tentative grace, "if you did something about the drinking?"

Only weeks earlier, he might have welcomed her proposal. But the tides had changed. He'd just met a woman he intended to sleep with, and Alice's call felt like one more bitter irony. Hadn't she just spent months dating an unfortunate Columbia colleague, who'd moved to Hawaii in heartbreak because she wouldn't marry him?

Tom told Alice about the woman.

"Oh," she whispered, her voice so wounded that it pierced his cold resolve for a moment, sparking a memory of her frantic retching in the bathroom of his Providence apartment. This time, though, his compassion was for himself.

So, she accepted a job offer in Chicago and moved there with Will.

He was approaching West Hartford now. The traffic was heavier again. He thought of the evening ten days ago, when Alice had been teaching her late class, and the phone had rung.

"Is this Mr. Winslow?" said the voice of a young man.

"Yes," he said, frustrated with the interruption of his solitary, five o'clock dinner.

"You knew a person named Sally Hayes?"

Tom was stunned to hear the name of the woman he'd lived with after Alice left for Chicago—the woman he'd told her about that day on the phone.

"She was my mother," the young man said. "She died last month."

"Oh, I'm sorry."

"It was a stroke. She was a heavy smoker."

Tom replied nervously. "Yes …"

"She was in AA," the young man quickly added, as if in vindication. "Almost fifteen years."

"I'm glad to hear it."

"She spoke highly of you."

"What's your name?"

"People call me Dec … middle name's Declan. My first name … well, it's Tom."

The young man paused. Tom felt the fear on both ends of the line.

"She told me you were my father." Dec's voice was unsteady now. "She made me promise to call you." He sighed. "So we could meet."

Tom was rigid, silent.

"Now to me, I have a father … a man who lived with Mom most of my life. They split, but, we've kept up. I consider him family."

"I understand. You say you want to meet?"

"I promised."

"Right. And you believe her?"

"She wasn't a liar, Mr. Winslow."

"I didn't mean …"

"Let's get this over with, okay? So we can go on with our lives."

"You think we'll be able to? Go on with our lives, I mean."

"Don't worry, Mr. Winslow. I don't expect nothing from you."

"Maybe you should."

"Well, I don't."

"Why didn't Sal ... your mom ... have you contact me before?"

"She never wanted to ruin things for you. She'd heard from some of her AA friends how you'd made a good life with your former wife ... in Connecticut somewhere."

"Trent."

"Yeah. She was friendly with some people I think you know in the Program. That's how I got your phone number."

Tom stopped resisting. "All right, Dec. What are you doing next Saturday?"

"I'm free."

"Is that Friendly's still there in Bayview?"

"It's a Starbuck's now."

"Oh. Well, do you want to meet there? Say noon?"

"Okay. It shouldn't take long. I think we'll know."

"You have your own doubts then?"

"I only know what my mother told me."

"Of course. By the way, Dec, how old are you?"

"Twenty-eight."

Tom remembered the day he'd moved out of the house that he and Sally Hayes had shared. She hadn't felt well that day, and hadn't said very much as he'd packed his things. It had all been said in the horrible week preceding that day of silences. Now, he feared, there was one last thing she could have mentioned.

"And what do you do for a living?"

"Used to be a pretty good clammer," Dec said. "Most of the beds around Long Island are shot now. I *had* been working for a guy at Bayview Fish & Shell."

"That's a nice store. What happened there?"

"He's out of business. So, I'm tending bar at the Crow's Nest, until something better comes along."

For days after that phone call, Tom had wrestled with self-loathing—what would he tell Alice? What would Will think? How could they not be unsettled, as he was, by this reminder of old betrayals?

He'd decided not to tell them until he was absolutely certain. But when the agreed Saturday had come, he'd failed to keep his appointment on Long Island—a decision that had stopped feeling like relief the moment he'd made it.

Then, as he'd considered the sin of standing up his own son, or at least, a polite young man whose poor mother had told him he was, more calls had started coming in at five o'clock each evening. Tom had made the connection slowly, reluctantly, holding the secret in his heart with equal amounts of resignation and denial.

Now, as he entered the dreary precincts of central Hartford, Tom wondered how he'd become so afraid of life. It had been easy to feel brave in the midst of disaster, he thought, when every last thing was gone. But his sober, second chance with Alice and Will had created a false sense of entitlement. Happiness had made him a coward.

Bill Sanchez appeared at the doorway of Tom's 10th floor office. "Ready for the meeting?"

"I'll be a little late." Tom scrolled through a draft of his Sunday column. "I can't find that quarter-million dollars you want me to cut."

Bill's face blanched. Quickly, he stepped inside and closed Tom's door. "Keep it down." He glanced back through a glass panel at the young reporter working just outside. Then, stepping behind Tom, he stared at his computer screen. "Land use in the northwest corner?"

Tom nodded as he looked up into his boss's blank gaze.

Bill backed against the ledge of a window with a panoramic view of downtown Hartford. "Anyway ... it's not 250 any more. It's 500,000."

"From *my* budget?"

"I have new figures from corporate."

Tom laughed bitterly.

"I can help with at least half," Bill said. "*If* you'll move to the fourth floor and take a desk in the bullpen area."

Tom listened carefully now.

"We have this floating lease option. Once a year, we can adjust our total rent, based on the square footage we actually use. I can squeeze more bodies into an open format." Bill glanced out on the city view. "Plus, the square-footage downstairs is a lot cheaper."

Tom recalled how the *Chronicle* had sold its grand, old building several years earlier for a cash infusion. It was a deal which made them renters in their own home.

"I'll move," Tom said. "But where do I get the other 250? I can't lay off any more people, Bill. I just can't do it."

Bill came off the window ledge and stood over Tom's desk again. "Management is about choices, Tom."

"What does that mean?"

Bill frowned. "The new CFO, Carl Fervor, turns out to be a reasonable guy. We met for breakfast this morning and went over everything." Bill raised his hands in an almost priestly pose. "The Tri-Art people believe most of the *Chronicle* Building will be unnecessary in a few years. I mean think about it. You don't even come in any more on Thursdays and Fridays."

"Uh-huh."

"At some point," Bill said, "the paper itself becomes obsolete."

"This is your solution?"

"Digital, Tom. We'll be a digital news service, with more than just print-and-pictures. We'll be video and sound and interactive stories … interactive advertising. Our readers will get us on all sorts of devices."

"They do that now."

"Not enough of them. Besides, all they're getting now is an online newspaper. We're planning something brand new." Bill nodded toward the reporter outside. "That's where kids like Lev Gellman come in. They were *born* in the digital age. The world you and I come from makes no sense to them. It makes less and less sense to the corporation."

"It's a TV and broadcasting group," Tom said. "They're not about the printed word."

"Look at your screen. I believe those are words. But it's 2007. We don't have to print words on paper any more. We certainly don't have to be sitting in this office-space to write them. Do you see what I'm saying?"

"It's very clear."

"Good." Bill glanced at his watch. "Now, I'd like you to consider releasing Lev, and your other reporters, to the digital edition."

"Really."

"They'll still report to you. But we'll pay them from digital revenue."

Tom laughed. *"Is there any?"*

Bill shrugged. "This is how I save you another $250,000."

"Oh. I see."

"We'll move *you* over, at some point," Bill added.

"All you're really doing is pushing costs around."

"There'll be cuts as well. Be thankful you're not one of them."

"It's not a Guild shop on the digital side," Tom reminded him. "They won't like it."

"Let *me* worry about the Guild."

"I'm not sure *I* like it," Tom said. "But I don't care anymore, as long as my kids keep their jobs."

"They will."

"For how long?"

"This is the future, Tom, the *only* future." Bill opened the office door and smiled. "Oh, by the way … Arts & Leisure reviewed your wife's book for Sunday. They *loved* it."

"Thanks, Bill. I'll tell her."

"No problem."

Bill paused outside to talk with Lev Gellman as Tom finished composing an email to Lev, asking him to make a phone call for his column, a draft copy of which he attached.

"I'll see you down there!" Bill called out as he started toward the elevator.

Tom waved and sent the email. Then he grabbed a yellow pad and stepped outside to Lev's cubicle. The young man was already reading the message.

"That number is Peter Harvey's cell phone," Tom said over the cubicle wall.

Lev smiled as he turned to speak. "Nice column."

"Maybe you can improve it. I've been told, off the record, that those Trent River condominiums are getting state tax abatements and subsidies."

"They're pretty high-end developments," Lev said.

"Exactly." Tom nodded. "Our readers would probably like to know what the taxpayer gets in return. Tell Peter you work for me. He's my neighbor, and he's told me a lot about the project. He knows all about development in that part of the state. Just say we need a comment on the subsidy issue, either from him, or any of the other partners."

"I'll call him right away."

"I'd do it myself, but I have this damn meeting."

Lev frowned, as if he knew what might be happening downstairs. "Mr. Winslow … is my job safe?"

"Yes, it's safe."

Lev turned back to his screen. There was a small, framed photograph of his wife near his computer. It was a recent photo, showing her seven or eight months pregnant.

"How's Carol?" Tom asked.

"It's been hard." Lev reached for his telephone and punched in Peter Harvey's number. "Thanks for asking."

"I'll be back soon," Tom said, in an almost fatherly voice, noticing a copy of *The Chastened Heart* next to Carol Gellman's photo.

Eleven editors sat quietly at a conference table in the semi-darkened boardroom as Tom slipped in and took the last available chair. Bill Sanchez stood near a video screen at the head of the table, and conferred in soft tones with a man in his mid-30s, dressed in a pin-striped, English suit—Carl Fervor, CFO, presumably.

Bill nodded at his secretary, who closed the door and sat in a chair near the wall.

"Ladies and gentlemen," Bill began. "Let me formally introduce Carl Fervor, chief financial officer for Tri-Art Media, our new corporate parent."

Spontaneous applause rippled along the table.

"Carl's going to lay out a new strategy for the *Chronicle*. As we know, times are tough in our industry. And Carl comes to us with quite a record of print turnarounds. So, please, let's give him our complete attention."

As Bill sat near the head of the table amidst more formal applause, the new CFO smiled politely and pressed a button on his laptop, which suddenly projected the Tri-Art Media logo on the screen behind him. Then, in a practiced, theatrical flourish, he gestured toward the screen.

"This is our logo," he said. "It represents who we are as a corporation. It's a brand that says we're in the *media* business, not the newspaper business, the radio business, or the television business. It says that news is one of our products. It says that talk, music, and filmed content are other products. And it says that our future will be in offering *all* these products in the newest formats and most exciting combinations."

There was silence around the table.

"When you came in this morning, you were working for *The Hartford Chronicle*," Carl said. "But ladies and gentleman, that entity no longer exists."

Feet shuffled beneath the table.

"No, no. I don't mean we're closing you down." Carl smiled broadly. "I'm saying this—*The Hartford Chronicle* is not a newspaper any more."

Abruptly, Carl tapped another button on his laptop, and projected *The Hartford Chronicle*'s familiar logo. But Carl Fervor's version did not include the well-known tagline calling it America's oldest, continuously published newspaper.

"*The Hartford Chronicle* is a brand," he said. "Let's talk about ways of making it work harder for us."

As midday sunlight glowed against classroom windows, Alice confronted the bleak faces of her writing students and felt the chill of failure.

She'd started class by returning corrected drafts of their final short-story projects. After waiting for them to digest her written comments, she'd coaxed them into a group discussion of common flaws.

"Don't approximate and don't equivocate," she'd urged. "Say what you mean. Use specific details. Be compassionate with your characters. Most importantly, admire other writers, but don't hide behind them. A serious writer finds his *own* voice."

But these bright honor students of hers remained children in their hearts—still so unfamiliar with failure, hungry for approval.

Now, as they gathered their things, anticipating the bell, Alice knew it was her job to pull them back from disappointment.

"This was a good start," she said.

Tim Sheehan slowly raised his hand and posed an earnest question. "What are you looking for? I mean … what do you want from us?"

"*Honesty*," she said.

Tim frowned and leaned back in his seat.

"You're saying we're dishonest?" Florence Alvarez asked.

"The topic is writing," Alice reminded her.

"Who decides what's honest?" Tim asked.

"Each writer decides that for himself."

"What does that even mean?" Florence countered.

"How can *you* judge whether someone's writing is honest?" Linda Bellows added. "You just said everyone has their own conception of truth."

"I did." Alice paused to gather her thoughts. "Let's say Tim writes something that Florence doesn't feel is honestly rendered. Florence's reaction might come from the fact that she hasn't had the experiences Tim is describing. Maybe she *has* had those experiences, but came away with a different idea about them. Or maybe, Florence would simply rather not re-live those experiences. Readers do have preferences, and there's nothing we can do about it.

"*But*," Alice continued. "If Tim writes something that Florence can clearly see *Tim* doesn't believe, or even understand, *then* … that writing probably *is* lacking in truthfulness. Artistically, I mean. And that *is* Tim's fault." Alice looked around the room, hoping she was starting to break through their injured feelings. "Writing is about choices. The goal is to find the appropriate choice, for a character,

27

a situation, a bit of dialogue. The easiest choices are tempting, but they're usually imitations of the truth. In *my* experience, it takes hard work to find the best choices ... the most truthful choices." She paused again. They were listening now. "When we look honestly at our own writing, we know which parts sound true, which parts sound fake."

"And which parts are just crap?" someone groused, evoking titters of recognition.

Alice smiled. "What was the first thing we discussed at the start of semester?"

"*Write what you know!*" they all replied.

"Exactly!" Alice joined in their laughter. "And that means we start in here." She tapped her breastbone. "When our writing expresses the truth, as we know it, we can't help but touch on something truthful about *all* human experience."

The bell rang, signaling the end of class. But her 15 writing students, mature and respectful seniors, resisted the impulse to jump up like a bunch of sophomores.

As they waited for her to make a final point or dismiss them, Alice thought of sharing something from her own career. In her youth, she'd written a number of pretty good stories, which magazines had published and readers had admired. But it had taken her almost 40 years to write a halfway honest story. And even now, she wasn't entirely sure how she'd done it—a life lesson she decided to save for another day.

"So," she concluded. "I can't wait to see your new drafts."

"Neither can we," Tim said, as the class rose to leave.

"And will I see some of you tonight?"

"*Yeeeessss*," they said in unison.

"Because I'm *very* nervous ... so, I'll look for your beautiful faces in the audience to calm myself!"

They laughed affectionately at their teacher's honest expression of her own truth.

Jennifer Yi and Rick McDougall were at their desks when Tom returned to the 10th floor. Lev Gellman's laptop was on. His jacket was slung over the back of his empty chair. It was two-thirty.

"Lev got your statement," Jennifer said, looking up from her work. "Check your email."

"Where is he, lunch?"

"His wife called with terrible pains. Her doctor's meeting them at St. Francis de Sales."

"Is she *in* labor?"

"I don't think they know for sure."

"If he calls, let me speak to him."

Jen nodded gravely.

"Do *you* have anything for tomorrow?"

"I was at the Assembly this morning," she said. "Speaker Dolan told me he's moving a health insurance bill."

"Again?"

"No mandate this time. It does have the market network, with private and public options. He says he has the votes, which means some Republicans are on board."

"That *is* news." Tom nodded. "The Assembly breaks for summer-recess soon."

"They're bringing something to the floor next Tuesday," Jen said. "Dolan wants a bill on the governor's desk by the end of the week. Of course, she's on record saying she'll veto any health insurance bill they send her."

"Are Democrats just forcing her into an embarrassing veto?"

"They wouldn't have a bill without Republican support in the Assembly."

Tom agreed with Jen's political assessment. "Do you have a statement from the governor?"

"I'm waiting for her spokesman to call back."

"What about the insurance industry?"

"I have Bethlehem Mutual, Deerfield Health-Net, and Connecticut Life & Health, all on the record."

"Saying what?"

"That they're concerned, without a mandate. *And* surprised ... they thought it was a dead issue this session."

"Sounds like a good story, Jen. Why didn't the speaker give this to our political guys? No offense ..."

"I didn't see any of them over there."

"Okay, keep me posted." Tom glanced at Rick McDougall, who was whispering into his phone. "Does *he* have anything?"

Jen glanced at her colleague and shrugged, before getting back to her own story.

In his office, Tom discovered a hastily-scribbled Post-It note from Lev Gellman. It directed him to his email, where he found six neatly crafted paragraphs.

—Trent River Associates, a Hartford-based investor consortium, has filed a $35 million plan to develop residences in three dormant factory buildings on 27 acres along the Trent River in Shelby. Each of three refurbished buildings would house 20 condominium units, priced from $350,000 to $600,000.

Peter Harvey, a contractor from Trent and a consortium member, acknowledged several obstacles: "As tough as bank financing has become, the major stumbling block on this project is river pollution."

According to Harvey, who was born and raised in Shelby, water contamination is a legacy from "a half-dozen textile factories built along this river in the mid-19th century." The factories produced blue jeans, and clothing dyes got in the runoff, he noted. "Then, the factories were refitted to make US Army uniforms during the Second World War, and there was more runoff. Pollution just wasn't a priority like it is now."

Harvey said it would be "a shame" to lose an opportunity to retrieve "dead and defunct" property over the issue of who pays for river-bed remediation. But since the State Department of Environmental Conservation has demanded a cleanup in return for its approval of the project, he said, the Trent River consortium believes the State ought to pay, "or at least share," the cost.

Charles Babcock, Deputy State DEC Commissioner, confirmed the agency's provisional approval of the project, to which the State has already attached a generous package of development incentives.

"The pollution issue needs to be worked out," Babcock stressed. "We encourage projects like the Trent River development. But we think investors and developers have a responsibility. These will be

high-end condominiums. You can't expect taxpayers to subsidize developers and shoulder all the cost of cleaning that river too. It's not government's role to provide public housing for the rich."—

Tom smiled as he cut and pasted Lev's copy directly into his column.

"Perfect," he whispered, admiring Lev's flair for old time journalism.

Scrolling down to the bottom of the column, he added: *Chronicle Staff Reporter, Lev Gellman, contributed to this article.*

Tom saved the file and sent it to Bill Sanchez with an email explaining Lev's contribution.

"The governor wants to see me!" Jen was almost breathless, peeking into his office.

He leaned back in his chair.

"I'm heading over now," she added. "Can we get this in for tomorrow?"

He glanced at his watch. It was nearly three o'clock. He was supposed to be in Shelby for dinner at five, but realized now that he wasn't going to make it. What he wanted to avoid was missing Alice's event at six-thirty. "How much have you written?"

"Most of it," Jen said. "The governor might send it in a new direction."

"Then you'll have to go back to the speaker, too."

Jen frowned in agreement.

"Interview the governor," he said. "Get back here as soon as possible. We might put the story to bed tonight, but, it's starting to feel like a Sunday piece to me."

She smiled broadly.

"Front page, maybe."

"Oh my God!"

"I'll talk to Bill Sanchez."

Jen's expression hardened. "There's a rumor going around that we're moving."

Tom smiled. "You *are* a good reporter."

"Rick told me."

"So *that's* what he's working on." Tom sighed in frustration. "Yes, we're moving to the fourth floor. It's a cost saving."

"I hear there may be layoffs."

"It looks okay for *us*." He glanced out and saw that McDougall had just left. "We'll have to make adjustments about which division pays us. When I get more details, I'll sit down with you and Lev … and McDougall, if he ever comes to work."

"I'm getting married in July."

"I know that, Jen. You invited me."

"I need this job."

Tom got up and walked to his office door. He looked into Jen's troubled eyes. "Get a good interview."

She pressed her lips together and nodded.

"Go," he urged.

She raced to the elevator and was gone.

Tom took a moment to look out across the 10th floor, where a dozen good journalists once worked and reported to him. Now, only three cubicles showed any sign of habitation. Soon enough, this would all be shut down.

He went back to his desk and marveled at the unexpected relief of being off his feet. He'd been getting tired lately, every day, at this point in the afternoon. It even happened when he worked from home. But it was worse here. He checked his watch. It was three-fifteen. The pressure of getting to Alice's book event was building—his life wasn't cooperating.

Jen's desk phone rang. After two more rings, the call jumped to his extension.

He picked up and heard Lev Gellman's agitated voice. "They can't stop her pains, Mr. Winslow! They don't even know what's causing them."

"Okay, Lev. Slow down. Carol's in the right place."

"Yes." Lev's voice shook with uncertainty.

"Is it the baby?"

"They don't *know*!" Lev sounded desperate.

"Who's there with you?"

"My dad's coming. Carol's parents are in Boston. They'll be here later."

"So you're alone." Tom was concerned. "Can *we* help?"

"Send someone over, maybe, with my computer? I won't be back tonight."

"Don't worry. I'll get somebody."

"Mr. Winslow, I have to go. Carol's doctor is coming out."

They hung up. Tom tried to reach Alice and got voicemail. He left a message—explaining that work was running late, that the wife of one of his reporters had been rushed to the hospital, that he would not make dinner with the Harveys.

"I'll do my best to be there by 6:30," he promised.

Moments later, Bill Sanchez called.

"This is a good column," he said. "Gellman knows his stuff."

"He's great." Tom agreed. "My other star, Jen Yi, is with the governor."

Tom explained the legislative news she'd gotten. He pitched it as a Sunday piece.

"When do you expect her back?" Bill asked.

"I assume within the hour."

"Let's see what she gets."

Tom told Bill about Lev's wife. "The kid's all alone at St. Francis de Sales, so, I'm going over there. I'll be back as soon as possible."

"No, that's all right." Bill sighed. "I'll wait in your office for Yi. You've got that thing at Alice's college, don't you?"

"Yes."

"Then just go," Bill told him. "I have your column. I'll handle the rest."

"You'll square things for Jen at the Political Desk?"

"Don't worry about them."

"**I**t's Bonnie at Jeffords-Blaine," said the bright young voice in Alice's phone. "Can you speak with Mrs. Lavan?"

"Of course."

"I'll patch her through from Los Angeles."

Alice stared at the banks of the Trent River not far beyond her office window until an older, deeper voice spoke her name in the phone.

"Judith!" she replied. "How's the West Coast?"

"We're having good meetings about your book," her agent said. "Yesterday, I met with Fox Searchlight and DreamWorks. I'm seeing Ron Howard and Brian Grazer in an hour. They've just bought Claire Messud's latest novel. This afternoon, I'm seeing the Weinsteins. I worked with them a few years ago when they bought *The Shipping News* for Miramax."

"I remember that film," said Alice, amazed by Hollywood's interest.

"I've missed Sam Mendes on this trip. He's in London, working on a screenplay with Ian McEwan. But his people here say he loves *The Chastened Heart*. I'll fly over to meet him soon."

"Sales are still up?"

"Up isn't the word, my dear. Farrar Strauss just told me the second printing is almost gone. Bookstores can't keep it on shelves. I've never seen a literary project quite like this." Judith paused. "I'm sorry I won't be there tonight."

"Me too."

"Everything's set for your Midwest tour. FSG hired a top PR agency in Chicago to handle you. Just remember what we talked about ..."

Alice laughed. "No politics, no edgy opinions, no criticisms of anyone or anything!"

"And no sarcasm," Judith said. "Just be your sweet, appealing self. This beautiful book has broken through the culture-noise. Don't give anyone reason to make it a target."

"A target ... me?"

"Success brings out the nastiness in some people."

"You remind me of my mother."

"On this project, I *am* your mother." Judith slid into her own brief laughter. "Look, honey, just let your book sell itself and enjoy the ride. I'll call you next week."

Alice hung up as another voice spoke from her office door—it was Delia Radcliff, chair of the Shelby English Department.

"Have you seen the new proposal from Cathy Maldonado?"

"I've read it." Alice nodded. "Is she serious?"

"You know her mantra: 'students are clients.'"

"But she's talking about posting final grades a month before the end of semester."

"A group of students and parents complained about our schedule." Delia shrugged. "Final exams and term papers are hitting them just when they're looking for summer jobs and internships."

"I see."

"*That* got Dick Emerson's attention," Delia said, referring to the college president. "He wants the faculty board to vote on Cathy's plan."

"But how do we motivate students, even *our* students, for a month after exams?"

"I'm meeting Cathy in a few minutes to talk about it," Delia said. "*I* think we should create a job-sourcing program in *her* office. She's dean of students, after all. If she got our kids connected with employers sooner each spring, we wouldn't need to perform radical surgery on the calendar."

"This is another reason the college needs to hire an academic dean … or a provost."

Delia nodded. "Cathy does seem to be overstepping her authority again."

"Power vacuums are just too tempting for some people, Delia. They can't help themselves." Alice paused. "Anyway, good luck."

Delia smiled warmly and changed the subject. "Are you nervous?"

"A little, yes."

"We'll have a great discussion. It's a wonderful book and people love it. You're sure you don't want to see the questions in advance?"

Alice shook her head.

"It's not a doctoral exam or anything," Delia said.

"I hope not!"

The women laughed together.

"Hearing questions for the first time in front of the audience might add some snap to the interview," Alice said.

"Never thought of that." And with a final wave, Delia hurried to her meeting.

Alice admired Delia, an African-American woman half her age ascending the arc of a brilliant career. Delia had already published two well-received books—one, about the influence of Transcendentalism on Hawthorne and Melville, and the other, about common elements of Modernism in Fitzgerald and Hemingway.

Five years ago, during her own tenure as department chair, Alice had been surprised to find a bright, young literary prospect like Delia looking for work at little Shelby College—until a report from the search firm offered an explanation.

"Getting her would be a coup," Alice had confided to Tom. "But it's complicated."

Swearing him to secrecy, she explained: Delia had a doctorate in American Literature from Johns Hopkins, where her thesis about Hawthorne and Melville had just been published by the university press. She'd also spent nine months in the doctoral program of another major college, several years earlier, but had been asked to leave in the wake of a plagiarism charge. Delia had volunteered nothing about this, hadn't even listed the other college on her CV.

"You've discussed it with her?" Tom asked.

"She said she'd been young and foolish … overwhelmed by a deadline to present her master's thesis."

Tom was skeptical. "Overwhelmed?"

"She was caring for her dying mother. I know what that's like."

"I remember when we had our problems," Tom said. "You moved halfway across the country for a new job. You raised our son, dealt with our divorce … paid for *your* dying mother's health care. Did *you* plagiarize?"

Alice didn't respond, because he was right.

"Why are you doing this?" he asked.

"I understand youthful mistakes. I understand mothers and daughters."

Tom listened.

"What would *you* do?"

"Who else knows?"

"Dick Emerson," she said. "And we had to tell Virginia Porter. She said it wouldn't hurt having another African-American on the faculty."

Tom stared at her. "Is that why you're doing this?"

"There are many reasons to hire this person, *including* our founder's complex legacy. I'm asking what *you* would do."

"Plagiarism is serious," he said. "On the other hand, how wrong can forgiveness be?"

Alice smiled in relief. "This is why I love you."

"Plus, you'll have someone on-staff who owes you a big favor!"

"I never thought of it that way."

"That's why I love *you*."

Tom parked in a tow-zone near the front doors of St. Francis de Sales. Hurrying inside with Lev's laptop and jacket, he informed a security guard that the Range Rover with press plates was his. Then, he jogged to the elevators.

On the ninth floor, he approached the Obstetrics desk.

"Any news about Gellman?" he asked the duty nurse.

"They're with the doctor now," she told him.

"Mr. Gellman works for me."

She nodded and pointed across the hallway to a large, sunny lounge. "If you'll have a seat, I'll let them know you're here, Mister ..."

"Winslow ..."

The nurse spoke his name as she wrote it on a pharmaceutical pad. "I'll tell them," she promised, while picking up a ringing phone.

Choosing a seat near the lounge windows, he waited with Lev's jacket folded over the adjoining seat and the laptop packed in its travel case at his feet. For several minutes, he accepted being a captive of protocol in an oversized, faux living room.

Now, standing to ease his tension, Tom glanced out on the Asylum Hill section of downtown Hartford. To his right was Bushnell Park and, beyond the park, the Capitol Buildings, which sprawled along the crest of a high greensward. He assumed Jennifer was hard at work questioning the governor up there. Or maybe she'd already finished and gone back to the *Chronicle* Building, whose face, darkened by ancient railroad soot, was nearly hidden by the newer high-rises on his left.

As he gazed across the urban panorama, with the reflection of his own aging face on glittering glass, he noticed someone entering the lounge behind him. He turned and saw an elderly man with brilliant white hair, dressed in an impeccable blue suit, holding a dark fedora. The man sat on the edge of a small chaise which allowed him a view of the hallway. He sat very still, his fedora on his lap, watching nurses come and go.

"Mr. Gellman?"

The man looked up. "Yes."

"I'm your son's boss at the *Chronicle*." Tom walked toward the man who stood to greet him. "Tom Winslow."

"David Gellman."

They shook hands and then stood together in awkward silence.

"Please." Mr. Gellman indicated a chair facing his. When they were seated, he smiled politely. "My son speaks of you in *heroic* terms."

"Oh no."

"Oh yes." Mr. Gellman's voice was urgent as he glanced down the hallway. "What is happening here? Do you know?"

"Lev said Carol had terrible pains. That's all I know."

"Poor girl."

"I just got here myself." Tom pointed back across the lounge to where he'd been sitting. "I brought Lev's things from the office."

Mr. Gellman nodded and glanced into the hallway again. Several moments passed before he broke the silence. "I was against my son's career choice."

"I wasn't aware of that."

"Journalism," he said in disgust. "It's a dying business. Wouldn't you agree?"

"It's seen better days. But I wouldn't say ..."

"The boy went to Williams College," Mr. Gellman said. "He has an MBA from Harvard."

"Yes, we know."

"And he goes to work for $65,000 a year, at a newspaper."

"He'll be getting a raise soon."

"A raise." The older man chuckled. "Next year, he'll have no job at all."

"That isn't true."

"Agh!" Mr. Gellman waved his hand in disgust. "The boy could write his ticket. He's being foolish."

"You think finding the truth and putting it in the paper is foolish?"

"What I'm saying, Mr. Winslow, is that newspapers are a dying business even if they had truth in them."

"I mean no disrespect, sir. The news business is *not* dying. There *is* a transition going on."

"Transition?" Mr. Gellman spoke caustically. "What kind of word is that? It means nothing. It's the sort of word you're apt to find in a newspaper article, which is why no one with any sense reads newspapers any more."

Tom liked this man. "What do *you* do for a living, sir?"

"Please, call me David, considering the circumstances." The old man sighed wearily. "I was a corporate attorney for many years. I'm retired now."

"Well, David, I'm sure you've seen changes in the corporate world. The newspaper industry is part of that corporate world."

"Which means?"

"That our fates are in the hands of men like you."

Mr. Gellman stared at Tom for a long time. "Then, I pity you."

"The *Chronicle* is changing," Tom conceded. "In a few years, the whole thing may be a web site or a digital news service accessed on screens … smart phones, iPods, digital tablets … whatever."

Mr. Gellman nodded. "This is what Lev tells me."

"But there will be a *Hartford Chronicle*. There will be newspapers around the country. If they stop publishing in a paper format, so what? Does it matter, as long as good work gets published?"

Mr. Gellman glanced down the hallway. "I wish they'd tell us something about this poor girl."

"Would you like me to check with the nursing station again?"

"They don't know anything. They wouldn't tell us if they did."

Another silence passed between them. Again, the older man broached it.

"Do you have children, Mr. Winslow?"

"We have a son. Will is his name. He's a few years older than Lev."

"And what does he do?"

"He and his wife started a small public relations agency in Boston," Tom said. "It's done very well. They have clients around the world."

"Good for them."

"You know … David. We didn't kidnap Lev. Frankly, we hadn't even pursued him. *He* came to *us*. Of course, when we saw his background, his education, his writing ability, it didn't matter that he hadn't gone to journalism school. We were only too happy to have him."

"In the *news business*," Mr. Gellman said with sarcasm.

"Yes." Tom laughed. "I understand your concerns. Lev could be making a lot more money in another profession, I'm sure."

Mr. Gellman smiled pensively. "May I share something with you, Mr. Winslow?"

"If you call me *Tom*."

"All right, Tom." The old man took a moment to gather his thoughts. "Many years ago, when I was a boy like Lev, a family friend got me a position in the legal department at a major film studio. I went out to Hollywood thinking I was going to work in the motion picture business. I knew it was a business. And I knew it was about entertainment. But I also knew that the studios had produced some worthwhile films over the years. A few had even touched upon the truth … *your* word."

Tom smiled as Mr. Gellman continued.

"It didn't take me long to realize I was kidding myself. My work wasn't even connected to the films in a direct way. I was more of a fixer. When a top director or valuable actor was arrested for drunk driving, domestic violence, or much worse … I was to make the problem go away."

"I see."

"I did this for as long as I could." Mr. Gellman paused as if remembering something he preferred to forget. "Finally, I asked to be placed on something like contracts, or acquisitions of good books and plays. But, apparently, I was too skillful at this dirty work. I became unhappy. My superiors lost patience with me. The studio chairman called me to his office. He asked what the problem was. I told him. He said, 'David, these people are assets. We make money with them, and, like any other corporate asset, they need to be protected, at least as long as they continue being assets.' I asked him to find a more dignified way for me to help the studio."

"You were a brave young man," Tom said.

"He laughed at me. But he did say something, which I never forgot. It's the point of my dreary story. He said, 'this is a carnival we work for, David, in a carnival town. We try to keep the clowns and trapeze artists happy enough, and sober enough, and out of jail long enough, to make our customers laugh, or cry, which is what they want from us. David, we work for the circus. And the circus makes its money selling popcorn, crackerjacks and frankfurters. So, come back down to earth.'"

Tom laughed.

"This was the 1950s," Mr. Gellman recalled. "The tail-end of the studio era … the talent agencies were already moving in on the business of packaging properties with stars and directors. It was an industry in transition … *another* word of yours."

"Yes."

"I resigned, right then and there. I walked out of his office. I went back to New York and found myself a real job."

"You didn't want to be in the carnival business," Tom said.

"I wouldn't have minded the carnival business. If a carnival knows what it's doing, it puts on a good show. A movie studio that puts on a good show is at least honest. But a movie studio that thinks it's a hot dog stand … that is not a good business. Nobody wants to see movies made by short order cooks."

Tom nodded in sad agreement.

"When a business doesn't know what business it's in, it's already dead," Mr. Gellman said.

"Papa!" It was Lev bursting into the lounge.

"How is Carol?" His father stood abruptly.

Lev smiled and let out a long sigh. "They did a caesarian. Carol's okay. She's sleeping now. Papa, we have a son."

"A son," his father whispered in awe.

"Yes!" Lev touched his father's hand and glanced at Tom. "Mr. Winslow, how long have *you* been here?"

"Not long." He pointed across the room. "I brought your things."

"A son," Mr. Gellman repeated.

"Papa, you haven't been annoying my boss with your business theories, I hope."

Mr. Gellman looked at Tom with a stony expression. "Have I annoyed you, sir?"

"Certainly not," Tom said. "We've been chatting."

"About what?" Lev pressed.

"What it means to be a father," Tom said.

Lev was confused.

Mr. Gellman's eyes glistened as a subtle smile softened the angles of his dour expression. "Your boss is an intelligent man," he told his son.

"Yes, Papa, I know."

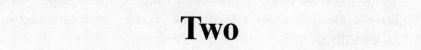

Two

It was past six when Tom drove through the ivied campus gates and followed signs to Shelby Hall. So many people had come to hear Alice speak about her novel that he was forced, like other last-minute arrivals, to search the perimeter of an immense parking lot outside the theater. Squeezing his Rover between an oak tree and another SUV, he struggled out and hurried through a maze of vehicles whose just-stilled engines ticked like overheated clocks.

Inside the busy lobby, he ran into Vanessa Beasley and Perry Miller, who lived several houses from each other on West Street in Leicester Village.

Vanessa was an increasingly popular author of romance novels, which her publisher described as "uplifting historical fiction." She and her husband, Richard, a pediatrician, had four children.

Perry recently had established full-time residence in Connecticut, after cutbacks at Random House ended his 30-year career as a book editor. He now hosted a book-chat radio show from the sun room of the 1759 Georgian restoration he'd bought as a summer retreat, and shared with an investment banker named Allan Sloan.

"What a nice crowd," Tom said, feeling grateful to have arrived with 15 minutes to spare.

"Isn't it something?" Vanessa agreed.

"How are you, Tom?" said Perry, offering his hand.

"I'm very proud of Alice," he said. "What do you think of her book?"

Vanessa's face went still. "I need to pick one up."

"You're in luck." Tom nodded casually at a table where copies had been laid out by the college bookstore. "I hear they're selling them tonight."

"I hear it's *literary.*" Perry's tone was faintly admonishing. "Who is Alice's agent?"

"Judith Lavan."

"Well, Judy did a great job getting a first book like that to FSG," Perry said. "They normally prefer a track record."

"*Sales,*" Vanessa added gravely.

"Oh, it's selling," Tom assured them. "There's been a second printing. It hits the *New York Times* best-seller list on Sunday."

Vanessa and Perry nodded in perfect unison.

"Is Judith here tonight?" Perry scanned the lobby. "I haven't seen her."

"No, she's in Hollywood ... talking to film producers about the book."

Vanessa smiled. "I better get my copy."

As she started away, Perry called after her. "Get one for me!" Then, he looked at Tom with a pensive smile. "Do you think Alice would come on my show? It isn't NPR. But we have a following in the county, folks from the industry, book critics, reporters ..."

"We love your show, Perry. She'd be thrilled, I'm sure."

"Which means I better do my homework." Now, Perry hurried toward the book table.

Tom stepped inside the auditorium and searched the buzzing audience.

"Over here!" It was Peg Harvey waving from six rows down.

Tom waved back and moved slowly along the center aisle. As he struggled in toward the seat that Peg and Peter had saved, he begged forgiveness for missing dinner.

"Alice said you left a message," Peg conceded, reclining in her seat.

"One of my reporters got a big story for Sunday. By the time I finished helping her, it was already late."

"I spoke to that Gellman kid," Peter said.

"My column ... yes ... thanks for doing that."

"We talked about bank financing and real estate. Kid knows his stuff."

"Harvard MBA," Tom said.

Peter was impressed. "Is that right?"

"After he spoke with you, he was called to St. Francis de Sales. His wife was in labor. There were complications and no one knew what was happening at first. I was concerned, of course, so I ended up at the hospital too."

"Are they okay?" Peg asked.

"Everything's fine. Their doctor did a caesarian. They've got a beautiful little boy."

"Nice," she said.

"Lev's a fine young man," Tom said, "great family."

Peter smiled and Peg nodded as the house lights dimmed, hushing the audience.

Moments later, the stage lighting came up. Alice and Delia Radcliff appeared from the wings and walked to center stage. The audience clapped as the women sat in big, comfortable chairs.

Alice looked nervous, Tom thought, while Delia was almost preternaturally calm.

The audience kept up its applause as Delia reviewed her questions on a clipboard, and Alice sipped from a bottle of spring water. Tim Sheehan, the earnest young man from Alice's writing seminar, helped the women clip on their live mics before vanishing into the back-stage shadows.

The applause subsided.

Tom noticed Alice searching beyond the stage-glare. He raised his hand and waved until she caught sight of him and smiled.

"Good evening," said her boss. "I'm Delia Radcliff, chair of the English department here at Shelby College. My dear colleague and mentor, Alice Winslow, has published a stunning debut novel entitled *The Chastened Heart*. She's here with us to share her thoughts about this lovely book. Ladies and gentlemen … Alice Prescott Winslow."

The enthusiastic audience clapped again. Tom glanced around, observing that many people had copies of the book. Down in front, a group of Alice's students watched her with admiration.

The applause settled and Delia began.

"Alice, if I may," she said, holding up her own copy. "How did you decide on such an evocative title?"

Alice smiled, as if relieved by this opening question. "I don't have my Webster's handy. But, from memory, it defines the word *chastened* as … having learned from sorrow."

"A heart that has learned from sorrow, then," said Delia.

"That's right."

"Made humble or restrained," Delia added, reading from her notes. "Through suffering or punishment ..."

Alice smiled again. "We have the same dictionary!"

The audience laughed.

"The characters in my story find humility in heartbreak," Alice said. "They learn the meaning of love."

"It's a *beautiful* love story. Which leads me to ask you this: if your characters could be enticed onto our stage tonight, what would *they* tell us about love?"

Alice stared out beyond the stage lighting into the shadows of the audience. Tom leaned forward in his seat, sensing her searching again for his face.

"That love is a blessing," she said. "A gift we can't possess until we've given everything else away."

Tom heard sighs of recognition in the auditorium.

"Your characters even give love away," Delia observed.

"Sometimes, love isn't understood until it's lost."

Delia nodded as she turned through the first pages of the book.

"There's great tension in the story," she said. "Your characters are clearly in love, yet, they struggle with honesty."

"They do."

"I wonder if you would read us a short excerpt that illustrates this ... it's right here in the first chapter." Delia handed the book over and pointed to a particular page.

"Oh, all right!" Alice smiled when she saw the section Delia meant. "This is a pivotal scene early in the story." She kept a finger on her place while looking up at the audience. "My characters have been lovers for several years. They're graduating from college and starting careers. But they're confused about what they mean to each other. They've each harbored unspoken assumptions while holding back something of themselves."

"Perhaps because they're just so young," Delia suggested.

Alice smiled in agreement. "And it all leads to this moment of decision about their future."

"They want to be writers."

"Yes," Alice said. "Though, that means something different to each of them."

"I just love it when the boy takes the girl up, up, up, through the guts of that unfinished high-rise at his college, until they reach the 20th floor, where they look out on the city of Providence. It's such an inspired scene."

"Thank you."

"Almost like a dream, yet real," Delia said. "Would you read it?"

"Of course." Alice put on her reading glasses and held the book in two hands.

"As they stood below the unfinished building, the girl became frightened. This large, imposing structure—like an empty dollhouse without its skin, each of its rooms, staircases and halls, cut away and open—exposed a nauseating emptiness within her. Yet, she followed the boy inside, up the stairwell, flight after flight. And with each step, she understood more clearly what he would say when they reached the top.

On the 20th floor, they crossed a dizzyingly open promenade. And there, as she'd feared, he asked her to marry him.

With difficulty, she told him she'd been seeing someone else the whole time they'd known each other. But he was steadfast, as he'd been for days in his apartment, watching her get sick each morning, declining to ask for the vaguest of stipulations.

She began feeling sick again, queasy in the stomach, weak-kneed. Was it this height, she wondered, or the feeling of what it meant to bear someone's heart within your own? She looked at him and waited, hoping for a harsher question, something firm and suspicious about finding herself pregnant, though she knew—as perhaps he did—there could be no honest answer.

The girl felt herself crying. The boy wrapped his arms around her, too tightly, as if promising to embrace even her doubts. In that moment, she let his certainty be hers."

"And on that hopeful, yet ambiguous, note," Delia said, "a tragic love story begins."

Alice nodded as the audience applauded.

"We learn soon enough that the young man isn't honest either," Delia added.

"No, he isn't."

"Would you say they're consciously deceiving each other up there?"

"They deceive themselves," Alice said. "That's where their hope comes from, the idea that a future can be made from your own imagination. Of course, nothing works as we expect when the truth is unspoken. There will be difficulties ahead."

"How does it feel to write such tragic lives for your characters?"

Alice glanced away from Delia and thought for a moment.

"Tragedy is our *common* experience," she said at last. "There's nothing unique about my characters where that's concerned."

"But there *are* unique examples of tragedy," Delia said. "Things *I* might experience that *you'd* never understand … and vice versa."

"I think that's more a political premise than a philosophical one."

Tom now sensed an abrupt change in the audience's mood. This remark about tragedy had struck a dissonant chord, something which people hadn't expected. Perhaps they weren't sure they agreed, or, even if they did, hadn't liked hearing it.

Delia was shaken by the silence. For the first time tonight, Tom thought, she was nervous.

She tried to regain her balance with a subtle change of focus. "I would say that your characters are sympathetic and admirable … *because* of what they endure for each other."

The audience rebalanced itself, too, with polite applause.

"They are to me," Alice said. "I'm glad that came through."

"And yet in the final scene, when they've been reunited after that horrible argument that comes out of nowhere, there's the implication of a secret … of something still unspoken between them. You get a sense that they might actually divorce a *second* time, as they sit together staring out on the meadow. They barely speak, and the mood is *almost* as ambiguous as the feeling in your opening scene at the unfinished building."

Alice laughed. "There was a big row about that with my editor."

"Really."

Alice turned to the audience. "She was afraid readers would feel let down if things weren't tied up with a nice, neat bow. She wanted me to show that they'll definitely stay married. But, I sensed she was wrong."

People laughed.

"The truth is: married people argue." Alice smiled as the audience laughed louder. "And what they might do in the future is much less dramatic than what they've come to understand about their past. We debated the structure of the scene for a long time. She kept asking whether things were clear enough. I kept wondering if things were too clear. Our main disagreement involved just how much or how little the characters should say about their feelings in the scene. I made some changes ... not as many as she wanted. It was an instructive process."

"You would have preferred something *more* ambiguous?" Delia asked.

"I wanted the final scene to echo the opening scene," Alice said. "And by keeping my characters as silent as possible, chastened by their experiences, I counted on people seeing and feeling how *different* this moment really was from the earlier one."

"Well, I think you struck the right note," Delia said. "And your readers agree."

People now roared in approval.

Alice acknowledged the compliments with a firm nod.

Delia asked her to read and discuss two more passages from the book. Then she invited audience questions—one of which came from a middle-aged man, who stood up in the center of the crowded auditorium and spoke nervously into a microphone handed down the aisle by Tim Sheehan.

"Were you consciously emulating Dante in this book?" he asked.

"That's an interesting question," Alice said. "What made you think of Dante?"

"That wonderful scene about climbing the staircase, for one thing," he said. "But more generally, I would say that this young couple follows a journey which reminds me of *The Divine Comedy*.

It's a journey from the agonies of youthful passion, a kind of inferno, to the disappointments and cynicism of betrayal, purgatorio, and finally to the enlightenment of maturity, an understanding of love, paradiso."

"I see."

"There's something about the narrative voice as well," the man said. "A kind of duality almost; it's a voice arguing with itself, almost as if *two* people were telling the story."

Alice nodded calmly in the silent auditorium. "Your commentary is elegant, and flattering, but a lot of this wasn't obvious to me as I wrote my story. I can't disagree with your insights. I'll admit to the influence, but not to any real comparison of my work with Dante's masterpiece."

"Well, I really enjoyed your novel." He smiled as he sat down.

"Thank you, sir. You're very kind."

"I'd like to follow up on what the gentleman was suggesting," said a young woman near the front. "The woman in your story writes a successful novel based on her life with this man. It takes her a long time to accomplish this. And, as I read it, her ability to see and to write clearly depends on her ability to forgive her husband. That's why I loved the way you did that final scene. It didn't need to be more specific, because the novel she was able to write says everything we need to know about their relationship."

"I think that's true," Alice said.

"The wife has grown more sophisticated in her writing as she's learned how to love her husband … I mean *really* love him."

"That's an important connection."

Tom heard soft whispering in the audience.

"So, you *are* making a connection between love and art?"

"Yes." Alice held the book up. "Consider the title again for a moment. A second definition of *chastened* refers to a thing having been refined or pruned of falsity and pretense."

"Oh! I see!" The young woman was excited. "That could mean love *or* art."

"Or both *together*," Alice said, "if we think of art as a form of love, as a gift, seeking nothing in return."

"Nothing?" Delia asked. "Surely, a writer wants appreciation and applause. In fact, isn't *that* a form of love too?"

Alice appeared unconvinced. "I think fame might be more like *sex* than love."

Tom heard nervous titters in the crowd.

Delia's eyes widened in alarm, as Alice completed her thought.

"And, at my age, it's just so humbling to get a little."

The crowd roared with laughter.

"Good girl," Tom whispered beneath his breath.

When the event concluded to generous applause, Alice and Delia stood and embraced. Tom worked his way into the center aisle and pushed—with the Harveys close behind—against the growing tide of a slowly exiting audience. Finally reaching the base of the stage, he called out to his wife. "You were great!"

She turned toward the sound of his voice and smiled.

Peg waved intensely until Peter's piercing whistle sent her into mortified stillness.

"See you outside!" Alice shouted over the buzz.

As she and Delia left the stage, Tom and the Harveys moved back up the aisle with the crowd as it squeezed into the lobby and swarmed the book table. A wine bar at one end of the lobby, and a bank of coffee urns at the other, attracted growing attention. Student waiters moved in the throng with trays of chardonnay in plastic goblets.

Spontaneous cheers greeted Alice and Delia who emerged from the stage door and started toward the book table.

"I have to tell her something," said Peg, pushing away from the men.

A waitress paused to offer wine, and Peter looked at Tom. "Want one of these?"

"No thanks. How was dinner?"

Peter took a slug and leaned closer. "I could have used you there, buddy."

Tom smiled and watched Peg struggle toward Alice. "Is she upset that I didn't make it?"

"No."

"*Something's* bothering her. Am I wrong?"

"Don't worry about it." Peter drained his goblet in time to stop a passing waiter, deposit the empty, and grab another.

"Is that stuff any good?"

"Good enough."

Tom laughed. "Thanks again for speaking to Lev. It really helped us."

"It helps me too. Good publicity."

"I should tell you. We interviewed the Deputy DEC Commissioner."

"Charlie Babcock." Peter nodded and sipped.

"The State wants your group to clean the river."

"I told your kid we're willing to help." Peter paused to glance across the room at his wife. "My partners won't pay the whole thing though. Why should they? I mean ... that part of the Trent River is a dead zone. If the State wants it to stay that way, they can keep treating investors and developers like they're doing *us* a favor."

Hearing the edge in Peter's voice, Tom recalled the doubts Peter had admitted more than once about the relentless transformation of Leicester County. Tonight, however, he seemed annoyed by the idea of this particular project being stalled.

"Have you folks planned your summer vacation yet?" Tom asked him.

"Peg wants to spend our summer vacation at a writer's colony in Vermont."

"I love Vermont. You'll have a great time."

"I'm not invited. She wants to write the great American novel without distractions." He finished his wine. "Damn waste of money, if you ask me."

"I've been to summer colonies. Alice has too. They can be useful."

"For what?" Peter scoffed.

"Learning it's *hard* to write the great American novel ... for one thing."

"I think Peg already knows that." Peter leaned close again. "I hear a lot of other stuff goes on."

"What do you mean?"

"*Affairs*," Peter said, almost spitting the word.

Tom shrugged. "I suppose." Then, with a laugh, he contemplated the crowd whose excitement seemed almost as erotic as Alice had implied earlier. "You don't have to go to a writer's colony for that."

As Peter frowned and stared into his second empty wine goblet, Tom realized he'd made precisely the wrong joke at the wrong moment.

"Peter, I'm sorry …"

"She wants a separation."

"Oh." Tom looked into Peter's glassy eyes. "Alice and I were separated."

"I know. I read the book."

"Don't go by that. It's fiction."

"Sure."

"A separation isn't the end of the world, Peter. Sometimes it helps."

"She's not coming back."

"She hasn't left yet."

"I think she has someone." Peter glanced around, as if looking for the suspect or the nearest wine tray.

"Maybe you've had enough cheap wine for one night. Why don't you go get your wife and tell her it's been fun, but now, it's time to go home. And she's driving."

Peter laughed sourly.

"I'm serious."

He stared at Tom without speaking. "Okay," he said at last, apparently grateful for Tom's concern. Then, abruptly, he turned away.

"Don't forget! Give Peg the keys."

"No," Peter promised. "I will."

Tom watched him move unsteadily toward the table where Alice signed copies of her book for a long line of fans. Peg hovered, saying something that drew smiles from Alice, while Delia entertained the queue. As Peter approached them, Alice and Delia looked up brightly. Peg frowned.

The lobby's electric buzz became a whisper as the crowd thinned out. Tom again felt the chill of his doubts, the isolation of old sins. Relieved to see the Harveys making their exit, more or less peaceably, he headed to the coffee bar. As he poured himself some fortification for the long drive home, he felt a tap on his shoulder.

"What did you think?" asked Delia.

"Great interview." He sipped the strong, black brew. "You were kind to set this up."

"A nice event for the college and community," she said. "So, when do we get a novel from *you*?"

"I'm just an old journalist." He laughed at himself. "Alice is the artist in our family."

"It's such a good novel." Delia paused. "Do you think people understood some of the things she said?"

"What ... that joke about fame and sex?"

"No, that was funny. I meant the other thing—all human tragedies being more or less the same."

"Did she say that?"

"Some people thought she did."

"Then they weren't listening."

Delia nodded.

"Is there a problem?"

"I don't think so. It's just ... you know how touchy people can get."

"Yes. In my business, it's called Letters to the Editor."

"Someone asked if I thought a wife like the one in Alice's book, whose husband leaves her, had experienced the same tragedy as a wife who'd lost her husband on 9/11."

"Someone actually asked you that?" He was stunned. "Who was it?"

"It doesn't matter."

"Does Alice know?"

"I told her a concern was raised. We'll have to address it."

"*Address it?*" He laughed bitterly. "It's crazy."

"I know it is."

"Delia, as far as I understand it, all she said was that tragedy is our common fate."

"But when someone loses her husband on 9/11, we don't have a right to assume we understand. Do we? That's dismissive."

"We were *all* attacked on 9/11, Delia. People who lost loved ones that day deserve compassion. But they weren't *targeted* and they don't own the copyright to what occurred."

Delia frowned. "That's a bit harsh."

"I'm sorry, but it's the truth. That day and the tragedy of it belong to all of us."

"Forget it," she implored. "It's not that big a deal."

"It sounds like it is for someone."

Delia changed the subject. "You're still coming to my expository writing class next week, I hope."

He forced himself to be polite. "How *are* they this year?"

"We have some budding essayists, but it's a struggle." She sighed. "It's always a struggle."

"A perfect description of writing," he said with a painful smile. "Of course, I'll be there. Always glad to help."

"Thank you." Delia kissed his cheek.

"Listen, I can't speak for Alice, and I shouldn't. But I know she wasn't saying what this person heard."

"We'll resolve it," Delia promised. "And we'll get a novel out of *you* soon. I can feel it."

"What makes you say that?"

"You've got what a novelist needs ... secrets you're dying to tell."

Delia smiled and headed back toward the book table where Alice relaxed with a glass of wine, sharing a bit of private conversation with Tim Sheehan, Florence Alvarez, and several more members of her creative writing class.

Except for this impromptu colloquy, now joined by Delia, only a few other professors and administrators still lingered in the quiet lobby.

Tom started toward his wife, concerned about the conversation he'd just had with her boss. Delia's controlled objectivity and slightly phony camaraderie had troubled him—even more than had her presumptuous message, conveyed from an unnamed party. Maybe she was a bit unsure of herself, he thought. She was a young woman, after all.

Driving home, Tom told Alice he was proud of her. She maintained an odd stillness, as if embarrassed by his compliment. He knew that answered prayers were sometimes harder to bear than unanswered ones, but he sensed something else in her silence—was it something to do with the issue Delia had raised? He asked if this was bothering her.

She nodded silently.

"I didn't notice anyone *particularly* upset in that audience," he told her.

"It wasn't an audience member." Alice spoke softly. "It was Cathy Maldonado."

Tom cringed when he heard the name of Shelby College's officious dean of students.

"Her sister's husband died at the Trade Center," Alice reminded him.

"I know. Did she speak to you, or just Delia?"

"The three of us talked in Cathy's office while you were getting the car." Alice paused. "Did you notice a reporter from the *American-Leader* hanging around?"

"Jack Daly. Why?"

"Cathy said *he* mentioned my comment. Will he make trouble?"

"If he didn't ask *you* anything, he probably won't."

"I hope not."

"Delia's got your back, right?"

"She told Cathy my comments were misunderstood."

"That's all she could say?"

Alice replied with an open-ended shrug.

"That girl wouldn't have her job if not for you."

"She said the audience loved me."

"Big deal; anyone could see that."

After a moment's silence, Alice conceded his point. "Delia could have been stronger."

"What exactly did Maldonado say?"

"'Be aware of sensitivities in the future.'"

"Oh, Jesus!" He sighed, offended for his wife. "Who are these people?"

"They're my bosses, Tom."

"Your book is a *New York Times* best-seller! If those two don't realize what that means, I'm sure other colleges would."

"Stop."

"I mean it. If this issue is raised again, tell them you're leaving for Yale."

"I like where I'm teaching," Alice said. "I love my students. They need me. If I went somewhere else ..."

"Yale!"

"First of all, there *is* no tenured position available at Yale, or most other places, for someone my age."

Tom knew she was probably right about this. It would be the same in his profession.

"I don't need a visiting professorship, not even at Yale," she added. "I need health insurance. And my students need me."

"I understand."

"Putting up with Cathy Maldonado is ... nothing."

"I respect what you're doing at Shelby. I do."

They were silent for miles until Alice offered a sad observation.

"The Harveys are having trouble."

"Peter confided some things," he said.

"Try to help him. Be a friend."

"He's convinced she's leaving him."

Alice kept silent now.

"She's apparently obsessed with writing a novel," Tom added. "Peter sounds very confused."

"They're *both* confused." Alice stared at him briefly. Then she gazed straight ahead into the dark highway, and whispered. "I hope things are all right between Will and Nancy."

"What do you mean? Has he said something?"

"No," she admitted. "I just have a sense ..."

"He told you it was a good trip, didn't he?"

"He didn't sound like a man on a successful trip. He sounded disappointed."

"It's the sound of his voice you're going on?"

"Not just that. I wish I weren't running off on a book tour before I see them again."

"It's probably nothing," he said. "Anyway, you won't be gone *that* long."

"I suppose." Abruptly, she gasped. "Tom, I'm so sorry! How was your meeting this morning?"

"Oh, that." He laughed and outlined what had happened.

"That's a lot of change all at once," she said with compassion. "Are you okay?"

"I'm fine."

"How is your staff? They're just kids."

"They're very nervous. But they have their jobs. I still have a job ... and a health plan."

"For how long?"

"We'll be all right."

Apparently too tired to question him further, Alice slowly fell asleep.

Tom drove on into a strangely welcoming night.

When he pulled into their driveway and eased into the garage, she awoke and sat up. He turned off the engine and looked at his wife. He felt the overwhelming urge to tell her about the phone calls.

"What is it?" she said, putting her hand in a familiar place on his thigh.

He considered the way in which a well-deserved evening of praise for her beautiful book had been cheapened by the literal-minded foolishness of disloyal colleagues. He could not cheapen it further just to relieve himself.

"I'm proud of you, Alice. And I love you."

"Something's bothering you," she whispered. "What is it?"

"Nothing," he said, aware that his secret now had come perilously close to being a lie.

As Alice waited for him to say something more, he tried to make sense of the silence in which they sat, and the darkness which gave her face the look of girlish longing.

Alice hung up the kitchen phone as Tom returned from his Saturday morning jog.

"Did someone call?" He heard the tension in his own voice.

"The lab report was inconclusive."

He leaned against the counter in his shorts and damp sweatshirt. "What does that mean?"

"Coben wants another biopsy." Alice made a note on the calendar. "We'll do it when I'm back from the Midwest."

"What does *inconclusive* mean?"

"The lab screwed up. Why is your face so pale? Are you all right?"

"I'm fine. Don't change the subject."

Alice stared at him. "Apparently, labs have a 20% failure rate."

"I never knew the rate was that high. It's a bit frightening, when you think of it."

"I'm going to stay positive. Are you sure you're all right?"

"I'm *fine*, Alice."

"You're as white as a ghost."

He frowned dismissively. "I'm a little tired. That's all."

"I was thinking ... of having the Harveys over."

"Tonight?" He allowed his disappointment to show.

"We could have a little dinner party."

She was leaving tomorrow morning and would be gone for a week. He'd hoped to spend this last evening alone with her.

"If that's what you want," he said sadly.

"I want you to stay close to Peter. He'll need support."

"So it's definite. Peg's leaving him?"

"I just think it would be ..." Her voice trailed off as she turned and appeared to contemplate the phone on the counter near the humming refrigerator.

"What?" he asked.

"Don't you think we should replace that old thing?"

"Oh. That's a good idea, actually. We could get a new *wireless* phone for the house. Maybe even an unlisted number?"

She shook her head. "I meant the refrigerator."

Sitting in his underwear at the French-Provincial desk in their London hotel room, Will Winslow tapped out a message on his laptop. Nancy opened the bathroom door and emerged with fluffy white towels around her body and her head. Their room now smelled of the subtly perfumed soap from her shower. Pausing before finishing his email to their newest client—a British insurance group with US expansion plans—Will smiled at his wife.

She sat on the edge of their unmade bed. "Do you mind if we don't go out for lunch?"

"No." He clicked the send button and turned to face her. "I don't mind."

She stared past him to the window, where transparent, linen curtains were animated by midday sunlight. "We could call room service."

"Are you feeling all right?"

"I just want to rest, Will."

Detecting annoyance in her voice, he allowed a bit of his own to show. "Okay."

"I'd like to finish your mother's book and probably get to bed early."

"It's been a long week. You were great with the new client. You really sold them."

Frowning as she stood again, she glanced at her copy of *The Chastened Heart*, which lay face down near her pillow. "I think they were impressed by your mother's notoriety."

Will watched as she unraveled the towel around her head and disappeared behind a half-closed bathroom door. The hotel's satellite radio service, which he kept at a low volume as he worked, played Laura Nyro's haunted, 1971 recording of *It's Gonna Take A Miracle*.

He hadn't heard this version of the song for years. But as he listened, he remembered it playing on the stereo in Nancy's college dorm the first time they'd made love. Later that same night, they'd gone to a pub near Harvard Square and she'd played it again on the jukebox.

"It's surprising," she'd whispered.

"What is?" he'd said, leaning forward in their booth.

"A lot of boys start drifting away … after."

He nodded in recognition.

"They don't mean to," she said. "But …"

"Girls drift away too."

She smiled. "So, here we are."

The bartender put two beers down in front of them and walked away.

"I had a dream about us last week," she said.

He sipped beer and listened.

"We made love."

"That's nice."

"But then, you told me you were sorry." Her voice tightened.

"Sorry? I don't understand."

She waited a moment. "You said it was a mistake." She tasted her beer. "That you'd confused me for another girl."

He leaned toward her again, reaching his hands across the table. "That's crazy."

Orange flames licked the sizzling steaks on his ancient Weber grill. Like an oracle reading the burnt entrails of a calf, Tom saw the future and shuddered.

"I hear steaks are on the menu!"

It was Peter Harvey with a drink in his hand, coming through the screen door to join Tom on the back patio.

"Get a look at these," Tom said.

"Nice." Peter leaned toward the grill. "Peg likes it medium-well."

"Okay." Tom turned the steaks with his long grilling fork.

"I'm a rare man myself."

"That you are, Peter."

After a moment's confusion, Peter laughed and gulped from his Old Fashioned.

"How are things?" Tom asked, inviting his guest to choose the subject and level of disclosure.

"Oh, same, you know." Peter gazed at the Winslows' meadow. A fat, yellow sun was poised above the distant ridge. "Peg's hot for the writer's colony."

"In Vermont."

"Um hum." Peter mumbled over another sip. "Early June."

"Alice will be on the West Coast, then, selling books."

Peter nodded at the distance. "Do you ever use it?"

Looking up from the steaks, Tom followed Peter's gaze to the refurbished shed at the farthest reaches of his meadow. "Oh. Sometimes, I go out there to think."

"Not to write?"

"No."

Peter stared at the shed.

"You did a great job on it," Tom said. "It's just … I don't know."

"It's what?"

"Lonely, I guess."

"So where do you write your column?"

Tom laughed. "Usually the kitchen … sometimes the bedroom."

Peter turned his back to the meadow and watched the steaks crackle.

"With the girls away, we'll have an ironclad alibi," Tom proposed.

"What's the crime?"

"Golf! What else?"

Peter smiled. "Haven't played in a while."

"I still belong to that little club in Cranwell. Come out as my guest. We'll get our games in shape."

"Maybe …"

"No maybes. When are you free?"

"Next Saturday."

"I'll get us a tee time," Tom promised.

Peter shrugged and finished his drink. Tom gave his steaks another turn and pulled Peter's out to the relatively cool perimeter.

When the kitchen phone rang, Tom didn't need to check his watch. It was just after five. Two more rings and Alice answered. He could hear her through the screen door.

"Hello?" Her innocent voice carried into the quiet evening. "Hello?" she said again with more urgency. Moments later, apparently having hung up, she spoke to Peg. "No answer. Some one was there, but they wouldn't say anything."

"Oh, I hate that," Peg said. "It's so rude."

"Those look done," Peter said, rousing his host from distraction.

"Right!" Tom shoved a platter at his guest. "Hold this, will you?"

Peter balanced the plate in his strong right hand as Tom lifted steaks one by one from the fire, and then covered the grill with a dusty, black dome.

"Another Old Fashioned?" Tom asked.

"You read my mind."

After dinner the couples took their coffee to the living room.

"Listen, you guys," Peter said. "I have to apologize ... for getting smashed last night."

"Don't be silly," Tom said.

"No, I drank too much. Forgive me, Alice. It was your night."

Peg grabbed Alice's hand. "We're sorry we had to leave early."

"Will you stop," Alice pleaded.

"Did we miss anything?" Peter asked.

"Actually, you did." Alice explained the issue raised by Cathy Maldonado.

The Harveys were stunned, silent. Finally, Peg added something of her own.

"That reporter you mentioned ... from the *American-Leader* ... he's close to Maldonado's family."

Tom frowned. "Jack Daly?"

Peg nodded.

Alice looked at Tom. "Were you aware of that?"

"No."

The couples sipped their coffee until Peg broke the silence again.

"Last term, Cathy had me in her office for an hour, questioning my lesson plan for *Atonement* and *A Farewell to Arms*. Alice, you remember."

"Yes. She thought you were teaching kids to question the idea of war."

"I *was*. I told her—that's the point of those novels."

"She seems to poke her nose into *everything*." Peter shook his head gravely. "The way she attacked the Isaac Shelby diary—it was nuts."

Alice agreed. "She didn't like hearing that the college was endowed with slave-trade money, even if Isaac Shelby became an abolitionist later."

"But telling the press I'd made it up?" Peg sighed bitterly. "By the time I was able to show the original text to reporters, the accusation became the news." She glanced at Tom. "*The Chronicle* did a wonderful story, but the damage was done."

"That whole thing was so unfair to you," Peter said.

Peg shot her husband an accusatory glance. "At least *Alice* has Delia running interference."

"I don't know," Tom said. "Delia could have been tougher with Maldonado last night … instead of trying to finesse the whole thing."

"She's in a tough spot," Alice said.

Tom shrugged. "Someone told me yesterday that management is about choices."

"Maybe I *was* a bit insensitive."

"Alice, there was nothing wrong with what you said."

Peg sighed in disgust. "Delia's young. You know how kids are. Don't get between them and their ambition."

"Let's not go overboard," Alice cautioned. "It amounts to nothing probably."

Peg reached again for Alice's hand. "You do seem concerned."

Tom lost control of his anger. "That girl owes you."

"I thought I asked you never to …" Alice's voiced trailed off.

"What's this?" Alert to a marital confidence, Peg glanced back and forth at her silent hosts. "Oh, it's a secret. Well, I know what *Tom's* secret is."

He smiled nervously.

"No really." Peter chuckled. "Peg thinks she figured it out."

"Figured *what* out?"

"Why you've been so distracted lately."

"I've been distracted?"

Alice nodded gravely at Tom. "Yes."

"Well, maybe it's just these changes I've been dealing with at *The Chronicle*. The new corporate owners are shaking things up. It *has* been on my mind."

"You said you were all right."

"I *am*."

Peter cut in. "Peg thinks *you're* writing a novel *too*."

"Oh." Tom laughed. "Delia said the same thing."

"You see?" Peg smiled broadly.

"But I don't know why anyone would think that."

Alice shifted uncomfortably on the sofa as Peg pressed the issue.

"You *are* a writer, Tom."

"I'm a journalist, Peg."

"Tom was working on a beautiful novel when we were in college," Alice said. "A love story, with some of the best writing I've ever seen."

"So?" Peg persisted. "What happened?"

Three sets of curious eyes now focused on Tom.

"I tried going back to it after we graduated." Tom stared sheepishly at his wife. "But the story just … it stopped speaking to me."

"You could have finished it." Alice's voice had an edge now. "And you should have."

The room was silent again.

Will watched the Strand from the hotel window. It was just past noon on Sunday. Nancy had left 15 minutes earlier and he was about to leave too. Below him the growing traffic jostled, but Nancy's taxi would be well beyond the city crush now, speeding on the M4 toward Heathrow. She was catching a plane for somewhere on the Continent. But where, exactly, she'd claimed not to know. His three o'clock from Heathrow was the flight on which they'd both been booked until last evening, when she'd told him she wasn't coming home yet.

Early this morning, in the darkness of their bed, she'd suggested something more devastating: that they'd used up the hope which kept married people together.

Now, remembering the dream she'd shared with him that long-ago night in the Cambridge pub, he felt as if their actual love affair and marriage had been a dream too. Had he simply confused his own hopes with love, he wondered? What more could he have done? What more did she want? Their marriage had given him everything *he* could have wanted, except children—an absence he now sought to accept as a form of blessing.

They'd made love this morning in this anonymous hotel room, furiously, almost angrily. It had seemed like playing out the last stages of the dream. And when they were finished, they lay quietly in each other's arms, waiting to awaken and become strangers again.

Finally, glancing at the clock near the bed, she'd whispered to him. "It's getting late."

"You always knew it would come to this."

"I did?"

"I should have listened to what you tried to tell me."

She kissed him and stared with forlorn confusion. "It's time to go."

"I know it is."

Stepping back from the window now, he worked his way around the empty hotel room, making sure that nothing valuable had been left unpacked. And the satellite radio station softly played the Laura Nyro song again.

A lice watched for the airport limousine, thankful to be escaping the pettiness of campus politics for a week. The trip might even soften her annoyance with Delia, she thought.

It had been hard enough admitting disappointment with her young friend's response to Maldonado's posturing. It was even harder to admit that Tom was right—that she had gone out on a limb to hire Delia, and then to nominate her as department chair when she'd given up her management duties to write *The Chastened Heart*.

She recalled how everyone at Shelby had seemed to support Delia's nomination—even Peg, to whom she'd spoken first about the position.

"I'm too old for that now," Peg had said. "And I'm busy with the Isaac Shelby book."

But when Alice brought her formal nomination to the faculty board, she was shocked to learn that John Woodward—a Shelby alumnus recently hired from the Harvard doctoral program—had been nominated by Cathy Maldonado. In the end, Delia won by a few votes.

Yes, Alice thought, this Midwest book tour will be a relief.

Tom looked up from his dismembered Sunday *Chronicle* and reached across the kitchen table. "I'll miss you."

"Me too." She took his hand and smiled. "What are you reading?"

He held up one section. "It's a front-page story by one of my kids."

Alice recognized the by-line of that intense young woman, Jennifer Yi.

"The State Assembly is pushing a health insurance bill," Tom said.

"Good."

"The Governor will never sign it. The Assembly would need to override her veto."

"Oh." She glanced out the window.

"Are you feeling all right?"

"Show me your column."

He pushed the Ideas Section over and she quickly read his piece.

"It's pretty strong," she said, passing it back. "Especially that headline."

"I know." Tom turned the page around and stared at the header:

Public Housing For The Rich?
State Subsidies Sought in Luxury Home Development

"Did you suggest that?" she asked.

"I left it with Bill Sanchez."

"Peter may not understand."

"I already told him we had comments from the DEC." Tom looked at her and sighed in frustration. "I'll talk with him again."

"He did this as a favor to you."

"The headline is a bit strong."

"He's under *enough* pressure." She turned to watch a car drive by on their quiet street. "You saw how much he drank again last night."

"They *both* seem miserable."

"They wanted children, but it didn't happen. Something about his sperm count."

"Jeez, you girls talk about everything."

Alice frowned and sipped at her coffee. "Peg suggested adoption. Peter didn't want that. At first, she was disappointed. Now, she's angry."

"Then why does he think it's about some novel she wants to write?"

Alice sighed. "Because he's clueless."

"Is he supposed to read her mind?"

"Maybe—or get honest with himself."

Tom shrugged and looked down at his newspaper again.

"You promised to look out for Peter."

"I know."

"Can you keep an eye on the *American-Leader* for me while I'm gone?"

"They'll call if they're doing anything."

"There's the car," she said.

As they rose, he stepped closer and held her for a moment. She was grateful for his steadfast affection.

"Don't forget this." He gave her the folded Arts & Leisure section containing *The Chronicle*'s review of her novel and a *Publisher's Weekly* best-seller list, on which her book had debuted at Number 6.

"I'll read it on the plane."

She tucked the folded newspaper into her carry-bag.

"I checked the *New York Times* website," he said. "You're Number 7 on *their* list."

"Can you believe I forgot about the *Times*? I'll pick one up at the airport."

Tom hefted her travel luggage out the front door and turned it over to the limo driver.

Alice stood nearby, waiting to kiss her husband one last time.

"Let me know if you hear from our son," she said.

"Of course," he assured her. "Sell lots of books."

"I'll call you from Chicago. Don't forget your promises."

She stepped to the car and got in. Moments later, as the limo backed into the street, she lowered her window and waved. Her heart always ached when she saw his earnest smile.

Tom stepped back inside and picked up the ringing phone. It was Peter Harvey.

"I just read your column," he said. "What's with the headline?"

"I'm sorry, Peter. I didn't write that part, though it *is* what the DEC told us."

"You couldn't make a headline from what *I* said?"

"What would you suggest?"

"I don't know. 'Trent River Associates to revive dead zone'?"

"I see your point. It was a judgment call."

"I guess that's what *I'm* saying." There was a brief silence on the line. "What's wrong with government helping the winners a little?"

"The thing is, Peter, *everybody* wants a chance to win."

"I've got a minority share in this Trent River thing. My partners won't understand this headline, and they'll blame me."

"What did they expect … a PR handout?"

"I told them you're a friend."

Tom didn't know how to respond.

"I'm only *in* this deal because somebody owed me a favor," Peter said. "I need it to go through."

"What do you mean?"

"I've had three refurbished homes on the market for a year now, Tom. I can't get a nibble at the price I need. There's something happening in the real estate market and it worries me. It's worrying a lot of people. I've got all my own money, and a lot of bank money, tied up."

"I didn't realize, Peter."

"Some of the senior partners were skeptical about me to begin with. They're a bunch of MBA types from Hartford and Boston. I was trying to help my cause with these guys, you know, by getting some good publicity."

"I'll do another column," Tom promised.

"Why don't you come meet the partners? Tour the site; get to know the project."

"That makes sense."

"Can I tell them you're coming?"

"Sure. Tell them I want to learn more. So I can tell my readers more about it."

"I appreciate it. Listen, Peg's awake. I better go."

After hanging up, Tom poured another cup of coffee. He considered Alice's parting admonition about promises, knowing very well which ones she'd meant. But there was a promise he'd made to a stranger almost two weeks ago. And it was time he'd kept it.

It was one o'clock as Tom reached Bayview and ignored the turn that would have taken him into the downtown harbor area. Instead, he drove another mile east on Route 7A before turning into the leafy grid of Chapel Hill, the old residential neighborhood above the village. From there he made his slow descent to the waterfront.

Two and three-story buildings on each side of Main Street evoked the 1950s and his boyhood. The Bayview Cinema, Gramma's Sweet Shop and the Shipwreck Diner were still operating. These few holdouts were scattered among newer stores and restaurants that somehow seemed familiar—even if old Mr. Klein's book shop had become a health food emporium, and the wide, grey building that for years had been Hengstenberg's Department Store now housed an art gallery.

There'd always been apartments on the upper floors of these buildings. But many now seemed expensively refurbished. Their wide, street-facing windows allowed stunning glimpses of antique, copper ceilings retrieved from beneath layers of naval paint.

Most of the stone and brick buildings had been refaced and painted—pink, blue or sandstone white. Some had names like Harbor House or The Asharokan. Others were identified by stenciled, black street numbers on glass panels above their doors.

Cars were parked head-first, at a 25-degree angle to the curbs, and every space was guarded by a chrome parking meter.

Even the tracks running down the middle of the street looked as shiny as they must have been in 1902, when a horse-drawn trolley started operating between the village and the East Bayview train station. Except now, these glistening rails supported a weekend trolley ride for tourists.

Tom decided there was something a bit theatrical about all these formal preservations. Their perfection overwhelmed his memories, and seemed less about the past than some implicit comment on the present.

At the Crow's Nest, Tom sat in a row of empty bar stools and ordered a Coke. He hoped to find Declan on duty or get enough information about him to arrange another meeting.

The bartender, a balding man roughly Tom's age, placed the Coke down.

"Be back in a minute," he said. "Someone comes in, just holler."

"Okay." Tom took a sip.

As the man disappeared into a storage room, Tom noted the TV above the bar was tuned to FOX News. Behind the bar there was an old black and white photograph of a handsome, young Jack Kerouac, with his hands on his hips, standing outside Klein's Book Shop. It would have been 1958 or '59, Tom guessed, the height of his fame, a year or two after *On the Road* was published.

Kerouac had lived in Bayview on and off in the late 50s and early 60s, and had been well liked in town. He'd given some jittery public readings from *On the Road* and *The Dharma Bums* at Klein's. But he'd become increasingly known for bitter, rambling interviews given to reporters who'd tracked him down here at the Crow's Nest—his favorite haunt, aside from the library, and the house he'd purchased for Memère on Sea Spray Avenue.

The bartender reappeared, lugging a heavy cardboard beer-case, which he slid onto the zinc-coated lid of a cooler in front of Tom.

"How's your Coke?"

"I'm fine."

The barman ripped the cardboard case open with a single, practiced gesture. "You look familiar. Are you from Bayview?"

"I was raised here."

"Is that right?" The man started pulling bottles of Budweiser from the case and placing them carefully into the cooler.

"My name is Tom Winslow."

"Mel Hoffman," the man replied. "Used to be a *Daily News* reporter named Tom Winslow."

"That's me."

"No shit!" Mel chuckled. "I haven't seen your by-line in ages. Still working?"

"Just barely." Tom laughed. "I've been with the *Hartford Chronicle* almost 25 years now. I've survived three rounds of layoffs and a corporate acquisition. I probably won't survive what happens next."

Mel glanced at the TV. "I guess it's pretty tough for newspapers."

"Anyway, I'm almost at retirement age."

Mel's voice warmed in recognition. "You used to be a runner."

"A long time ago," Tom admitted with a rueful laugh, watching the man work.

"I saw you win the state cross country championships at Deep Meadow in … 1965."

Tom nodded.

"I did a little running in high school myself. *You* were amazing."

"Like I said; it was a long time ago."

Mel slammed the cooler shut and tossed the empty beer case on the floor. Then, he leaned across the bar and spoke with the formal gravity of a wake visitor.

"We all had a lot of respect for your father."

Tom smiled politely.

"A real, old-fashioned war hero," Mel said. "Quite a man and people admired him, regardless of …"

"Yes." Tom was uncomfortable. "Thank you."

Mel checked his watch.

Tom glanced around at empty stools and booths. "Things seem pretty slow today."

"Weather's too nice. People get a late start Sundays. There might be some action this afternoon … a few tourists."

"Right."

"I go off duty at two, so …" After a shrug, he pointed at Tom's Coke. "You're still okay there?"

"Yes. Could I ask you something?"

Mel stared.

"I'm looking for a young man who works here. His name is Declan."

"What do you mean 'looking for'? He's not in trouble, is he?"

"No, no." Tom laughed. "It's nothing like that. We have friends in common, which I only learned a few weeks ago. We were supposed to meet here in town, but … it didn't work out."

"Dec's a good kid," Mel asserted, as if giving legal testimony.

"I know. Would you be willing to help me with a phone number or an address?"

"You can ask him yourself," the bartender said. "He'll be here at two."

Tom waited in a window booth, glancing now and then at the public marina across Bay Street. A few Saturday night stragglers came and left. An elderly couple from Manhattan stopped in for directions to Deep Meadow State Park.

"Get back on 7A heading east, about five miles," Mel told them. "You'll see signs for the park."

"Is it true they have a boardwalk two miles long?" the wife asked.

"Absolutely," Mel replied. "You folks brought your roller blades, right?"

The couple enjoyed the laugh and moved on.

Then, at a few minutes after two, Tom noticed a young man hurrying up the near side of Bay. He wore jeans and an open jacket of tan cloth or suede. He had Sally Hayes' sandy blonde hair and intense gaze. With his hands in his pockets and shoulders hunched he looked like Bob Dylan walking up West Fourth Street.

Moments later, he burst through the saloon door.

"I'm sorry, Mel! Kerry's Ford broke down again, so I had to walk …"

The bartender frowned and shook his head to indicate that time was not an issue. When the young man reached the bar, Mel whispered something and cocked his head toward Tom.

The young man briefly glanced. "That's him?"

"I'll be here," Mel said.

With a bemused smile, the young man approached Tom's booth. "This is a surprise."

Tom stood to offer his hand. "Better late than never?"

"Story o' my life."

They sat across from each other. Neither knew what to say.

The bartender came to the booth. "Another Coke, Mr. Winslow?"

"Do you have any coffee?"

"I can make some."

"I'll have one too, Mel."

"Sure, Dec."

When the bartender left, Tom spoke purposefully. "Have *you* been calling my house at five o'clock every night?"

The young man shrugged. "A promise is a promise." He glanced out the window at the sun-drenched marina.

"Don't you think it's kind of hostile, making calls like that?"

Dec didn't reply.

Tom leaned back and sighed as the aroma of brewing coffee began sweetening the dank, boozy air.

"Look, sir ..."

"*Tom.*"

"It's very nice you drove out here today. Maybe you're not as much of a jerk as I thought."

"Okay."

"I need to start work in a minute. Mel's having Sunday dinner at his sister's."

"That's fine. I only came down here to ... uh ..."

"Keep your promise?"

"Yes, keep my promise."

Dec nodded graciously.

They went silent again.

Mel approached and placed two large, white coffee mugs on the table.

"This won't take much longer," Dec assured him.

"Barb knows I'll be late," Mel said. "You guys finish your talk."

"Nice man," Tom said when they were alone again.

"Yeah."

Tom broached the subject. "So, what do you think?"

Dec laughed. "Damned if I can tell."

"You have hair like your mother's."

"I heard that somewhere."

"Ask me whatever you want. Maybe you'll tell me a little more about your mom's life ... *your* life."

Dec sipped his coffee and stared at Tom. "She loved you. That much, I know. I mean she *really* loved you. It wasn't the same for you, though. Am I right?"

"No. I guess that's right."

"She got caught up in whatever was going on between you and your wife."

"It had nothing to do with ... it was between your mom and me. Unfortunately, we were both drinking."

"But *you* stopped." There was something accusatory in Dec's voice.

"You told me that *she* stopped too."

Dec sipped more coffee and stared.

"It's all right if you want to blame me."

Beneath Dec's edgy politeness, Tom sensed a well of kindness. This, more than looks or his own guilt, reminded him of the boy's mother.

"Do you have a girl, Dec?"

"Her name's Kerry. We rent a house on Valley Road. We'd like to *buy* a place some day."

"That's good."

"We have our eye on a little house down near Asharokan Inlet." Now, his expression blossomed in a broad smile. "It's expensive."

"You'll get it."

"Right. So listen, I better get to work."

"Don't you think we should talk some more? When do you finish?"

"I don't know. Like I said before, I have no expectations." Dec glanced out the window at a group of tourists passing by.

"It was wrong of me to stand you up."

Dec took a big gulp of coffee and stared intensely at Tom.

"All I'm saying, Dec, is that I'm here. I don't have to rush back home."

"I get off at seven."

"Why don't we have dinner? Bring Kerry. It's on me."

"You don't have to do that."

"But I'd *like* to. Why don't you say yes?"

Declan glanced out the window again. Then he laughed, as if relieving some inner pressure. "All right, that's very nice. I'll tell Kerry."

"Do you have a favorite restaurant in town? I'll make reservations."

"Just meet us here at seven."

Two miles east of Bayview, Tom turned off 7A and followed North Beach Road to Long Island Sound. Another turn took him into the small community of North Beach, where he'd lived with Sally Hayes.

The older houses to his left had spacious lots backing on a marsh called North Beach Pond. These properties dated to the 1850s, and their weathered clapboard was consistent with the rustic, summer cottages they'd once been—before electricity, indoor plumbing, and carports.

On his right were bigger structures built in the early 1960s by a politically connected developer with a suspiciously favorable zoning variance. Tightly bunched along the beachfront facing the Sound, these newer houses had effectively blocked the older residents' water view.

A class action lawsuit, and various counter-suits, had worked through the courts for nearly a decade. But by 1970, when Tom was covering the story as a young reporter, the North Beach litigants had achieved little more than a stalemate.

The big beach houses were there to stay. Those on the marsh were exempted from a strict, new zoning law which the developer's lawyers had hoped would drive them out entirely. A bitter silence settled over two distinct communities living on a single street.

Near the west end of the strand, on the right, Tom came to the place he and Sally had rented for several years—one of the newer, modern beach structures. He paused in the street with his motor running and looked at the place. It was a white, two-story shingled house, with a slanted green roof, and lots of windows on the ground floor.

There didn't seem to be anyone home—no cars in the driveway, no open doors behind screens, not a single jalousie window cranked out to catch the breeze.

Impulsively, he turned into the driveway and parked.

After picking his way along a slate path between the house and its proximate neighbor, he reached the front patio at the edge of a 40-foot beach. The north shore waves were falling almost silently on this brilliant day. There was no haze on the water. But there were sailboats and fishermen. Southern Connecticut was clearly visible across the bluish-gray horizon.

And when he caught a brackish whiff of marsh on the southeasterly breeze, memories flooded his brain.

"Tom! Is that you?"

Turning toward the house, he saw Sally descending wooden steps from the deck. A loose, embroidered blouse, unbuttoned at the top, displayed the sensual amplitude of her breasts. Her long, blondish hair was pulled back, tied behind her head, and her pale but pretty face looked tired. Her dark eyes burned more intensely than the sun.

"What are you doing out here?" she asked with a nervous laugh. "You've been staring into space for half an hour!"

"We need to talk."

Her eyes narrowed. Her lower lip quivered subtly.

She spoke in a falling voice. "You're going back to your wife."

Instead of answering, he looked out on the water.

"Don't act so surprised," she said.

"She's not my wife!" He turned to look at her again. "We're divorced."

"Uh huh."

"There's nothing going on."

"No," she whispered. "It's worse."

"I've been seeing more of Will since they came back east."

"So, it's your son you want to talk about?"

This silenced him.

The expression on her face was incredulous.

"What I mean is: we should sit down and agree …"

"On what?" she scoffed.

"What you need. How you'll manage, financially, I mean."

As he struggled to find the next right words to say to her, she stepped closer and abruptly slapped his face. Then, she turned and went back up into the house, slamming the door behind her.

Looking out on the water again with his cheek tingling, as if sunburned, he realized she'd finally brought tears to his eyes.

"Tom! Is that you?"

Again, he turned toward the house, but this time Sally wasn't coming down the steps. There was no one there. He heard the soft waves. A distant motorcycle engine revved.

"My God, it *is* you," said the female voice, which he now realized was coming from the upper deck of the house next door.

Tom was surprised to find Dawn Harper still living in North Beach. During the early 1970s she and her husband, Ted, had hosted weekly parties here for a raucous group of teachers, actors and writers, to which the Winslows had belonged. In those days, Dawn was the drama teacher at Bayview High School. Ted was Alice's colleague at Columbia.

Following an awkward embrace on her doorstep, Dawn gave Tom a quick tour of rooms filled with shabby furniture decades out of fashion. The walls were covered with sea shells and driftwood, and photos from their wild old days. Though instantly familiar, the Harper house felt odd to Tom in its utter coldness, as if it were frozen to a single moment long past.

As Dawn brewed a pot of green tea, Tom waited at her kitchen table, recalling how she'd helped him lease the neighboring house during that final bleak separation from Alice. He and Dawn had shared the blunt camaraderie of people whose spouses were sleeping together.

"Who lives next door these days?" he asked.

"A nice family owns it." Dawn poured the tea and sat. "I don't know them very well. The husband's a dentist with a practice in Queens. The wife sells real estate or something. They have two young daughters. I see them in the summertime. They're rarely out here otherwise."

He glanced at their silent house.

"They'll be here next weekend," Dawn said, "for Memorial Day."

He nodded. "Ever hear from Teddy?"

"He's got prostate cancer," she said gravely.

"That's too bad. Is he still in Hawaii?"

"Yes, but we've been speaking again." She sighed wearily. "After all these years and everything that happened … it's strange. I even talk to his wife, the surfer girl. She's no girl any more, I guess."

"Remind me how they met?"

Dawn laughed. "She worked at a surf shop on Waikiki, when Teddy first got there."

"Oh, that's right."

"She was 18 or something. Teddy was, what … 27, 28? Sort of a teacher-student type thing … you'd think. But she told me that *he* seemed like the student to her … like a lost kid she had to take home." Dawn chuckled ruefully. "Anyway, they've been together in Honolulu ever since. They have three children. It turned out they loved each other."

Tom smiled politely. "Sounds like it."

"He made his choices," Dawn said. "I made mine. After he had that thing with Alice, he didn't have a leg to stand on. And he knew it. That's how I got this place free and clear."

"And he got the surfer girl in Hawaii."

She nodded. "And *you* eventually got Alice back."

"Yes."

"She's getting great notices for that novel of hers."

"Have you read it?"

"I just finished … very impressive." She paused. "We all basically ended up doing what we were supposed to do, I guess."

Tom thought of Sally again as he glanced around Dawn's oversized beach house.

"It's funny," Dawn said. "The amount of drinking we all did … you and I never got it on."

"Well. I was either married to Alice or living with Sally. Our lives were lurid enough, don't you think?"

"I suppose." She frowned and sipped tea. "You were never my type anyway."

"No. I know." He glanced out onto the Sound. "Did you keep up with Sally … after I moved out?"

"She stayed next door another three months maybe. We used to talk now and then, but she stopped coming to my parties. Trying not to drink, I guess. She was having money troubles … couldn't make the rent on that monstrosity."

"She wouldn't take anything from me."

"I know. Foolish girl … always was."

"She was foolish to be with me. But she was a nice girl."

"The day she left here she told me she was pregnant. Did you know that?"

"No." Tom shifted uncomfortably in his chair. "Not at the time."

Dawn stared, as if not quite believing him. "Bearing that burden by yourself is tough."

"I'm sure it is." Tom blew into his tea cup. "There was no one else living with her?"

"Not that I ever saw, why?" Dawn's eyes grew large. "Oh! I see."

He nodded. "Did you know she recently died?"

Late that afternoon, Tom found Sally's grave where Dawn had sent him—the cemetery behind The First Presbyterian Church of Bayview. Sally hadn't been religious when they were together, but it comforted him to know she was here. Perhaps she'd found church more to her liking in sobriety, he thought, smiling to observe the placement of her stone beneath an ancient oak—something he was certain she would have loved. Although he could easily read the inscription in the dappled evening shadows, he knelt to be closer to something words rarely express.

Dawn told him she hadn't seen Sally in decades, and hadn't thought much about her, even though her haunting face appeared in several party photos on her walls. But hearing of Sally's death had set her thinking again.

"A neighbor told me he'd seen an obituary in the *Bayview Observer*. He knew she'd lived next door to me years ago. I guess he thought I'd want to know. I was so surprised to hear her name. All I could do was thank him. Of course, later, everything hit me."

"I understand," Tom said.

"I started thinking about the day she moved out. How sorry I was we never saw each other again. I remembered her telling me she was pregnant. And then … I thought of *you*."

"We *were* together for three years."

"Apparently, she'd gotten a nursing license and worked at the VA Hospital. But you know, my neighbor never mentioned anything about children or a husband. I didn't ask. I only thought of it later. Then, I just forgot. I'm sorry."

"I don't believe she ever married. Apparently, she lived with a local man for a while."

Dawn nodded and seemed curious that he would know this.

"And she had a son," Tom added.

Dawn poured more green tea into their cups. "So, *this* is why you're back."

Now, as Tom knelt close to Sally's grave, reaching out to touch her stone, he wondered about Dec. The kid didn't look anything like him as far as he could tell. But he seemed like his mother's son. And maybe that was all that mattered at the moment.

Heading back down into the village past St. Matthew's Catholic Church, Tom observed that everything but the Bayview Cinema and a few of the restaurants had closed for Sunday night. As he passed the shuttered health food store, he thought fondly of Reuben Klein, the old bookseller, who used to let him hang out in the musty stacks for hours on end, the way most teenagers hung out at Gramma's Sweet Shop. He remembered a day in 1964, when Klein introduced him to Jack Kerouac, who seemed painfully polite and uncomfortable. Kerouac was losing his grip then, but Tom was too young to appreciate what that meant.

Kerouac finally had left Bayview, fleeing the reporters who crowded him here, inciting his rage about hippies and draft-dodgers. It was a strange irony that his early books had embodied so much of what he'd come to hate about the revolutionary 60s—especially the "flower children" whom he had such difficulty acknowledging as his own.

Stepping inside the Crow's Nest at seven o'clock, Tom found things eerily quiet. There were no customers. The TV and most of the lights had been turned off. There was no one behind the bar. Then, he heard the mumble of voices coming from the back room. As he walked along the bar, the voices became more distinct—one was Dec's, the other was a woman's. Tom was about to call out when something in the woman's voice made him swallow his words and listen.

"Will he give you something?" she asked.

"I don't even know this man," Dec replied. "He doesn't know me."

"But he's here."

"He was pretty pissed off about those phone calls, Kerry. I told you not to do that."

"I don't understand you, Declan."

There was a long silence.

"We need help," she said at last. "The car is shot. We owe back rent ..."

"I'm aware of it," he muttered.

"You make hardly anything in this stupid gin mill."

"I said *I know.*"

Tom softly backpedaled to a stool at the opposite end of the bar. From this vantage point, he could seem innocently oblivious while gazing out at the harbor lights coming up in growing darkness.

Moments later, Dec and his girlfriend emerged from the back room and were surprised to see him sitting there.

"Tom!" Dec said. "You been here long?"

He shook his head. "Just walked in."

Dec put his arm around the girl. "This is Kerry."

Tom stood up. "Hello, Kerry."

"Hello," she said, with more sweetness than her disembodied voice had implied.

She was attractive. Tom would have said she resembled the boy's mother in some way, but that was too obvious. Her blonde hair, bleached almost white, was feather-cut. She wore a long black sweater over a short black skirt, with knee-high black leather boots and black tights. Her face was pretty, a little puffy for a young woman. But that might be explained by the most prominent thing about her appearance—she looked very pregnant.

Three

On Monday morning, the East Loop was a glitter of headlights on rain-dappled bridges far below Alice's hotel window. When she'd checked in yesterday afternoon, Lake Michigan had sparkled with sunlight and sailboats, and she'd seen the Marina and Lincoln Park filled with springtime revelers. Now, pulsing beacons at the north and south ends of the promenade were all but smothered in lake mist, reminding her that she disliked being here.

Contemplating the long journey which had brought her back to Chicago as a celebrated novelist, Alice felt nothing like the "brave author of an honest and hopeful book" so many critics and readers were praising. She felt something closer to guilt—as if life had given her things it had taken from others.

Her fitful night's sleep had ended early this morning with a dream about Will and Nancy splitting up. And she knew that Tom had serious doubts about his future employment, no matter how bravely he'd explained things. He hadn't even answered when she'd called him last night. Now, she longed to comfort him in the hotel bed where she'd slept so restlessly.

The phone rang and she hurried to answer it.

"Good morning, Mrs. Winslow." It was Eileen Vachon, the young PR executive assigned to the Midwest leg of Alice's tour. "Did you sleep well?"

"Not really."

"You must be so excited!" Eileen paused. "I thought we might get together at the Green Briar Room in your hotel. Have a bite and discuss our day."

Alice chuckled. This thoughtful, 28-year-old girl had met her yesterday at O'Hare, and had ridden into town with her—giving up the better part of her Sunday. Now, apparently, she wished to ensure that Alice started her tour with a good breakfast.

"Don't we have a TV show this morning?" Alice asked.

"Good Morning Chicago, at 10 o'clock."

"Which gives us an hour."

"I like to orient my authors. I find it helps to go over the schedule and make sure there aren't any questions or doubts. We can take a look at the whole week, if you like. Most authors prefer one day at a time."

"One day at a time sounds sensible, Eileen. I know we have two signings here."

"Yes. The first one's at noon at the Barnes & Noble on Jackson. That's in the business district, and the store-manager expects a big lunch-hour turnout. He's got a hundred pre-orders."

Alice recently had learned this was an extraordinary response to a book.

"We do the Barnes & Noble on State Street at 5:30," Eileen added. "That's the high-end shopping district. Of course, there, we'll pick up commuters, folks heading home … maybe some on their way out for the evening. I'm also working on an NPR slot for this afternoon."

"Well, Eileen, it sounds like we've covered everything."

"I have some other ideas I'd like to share. Things you might consider mentioning during your talks and interviews."

"All right. How long will you need to get here?"

"I'm downstairs now."

"Goodness." Alice glanced at the digital desk-clock. "Give me 15 minutes?"

"Of course, Mrs. Winslow."

"That should be enough time to practice calling me Alice."

After a long silence, Eileen laughed. "Oh, Mrs. Winslow, that's a sketch."

Alice hung up and the phone rang again. She grabbed the receiver. "Eileen?"

"It's me," said Tom.

"Where have *you* been?" The urgency in her voice embarrassed her.

"Long Island," he said. "I stayed overnight in Bayview. I just got home."

This stopped her cold.

"I saw Dawn Harper. She told me Teddy's got prostate cancer. It sounds serious."

Alice couldn't speak. Her lungs felt like stone.

"But I should start at the beginning."

Pressing the receiver tightly to her ear, Alice slowly sat at the edge of her bed.

"Almost two weeks ago, I got a phone call ..."

As she listened to her husband describe a reluctant journey into his past, the discomfort she'd felt in her gut for weeks exploded in a storm of nausea and cramps. Perspiration covered her body like cold rain.

Pulling her complimentary terrycloth robe tight against her chest, Alice felt the weight of her own responsibility for Sally Hayes, the woman in whose broken life Tom had taken thoughtless refuge years ago. She felt responsible, too, for poor Teddy, with whom she'd conducted her own callous affair, ending the Harpers' marriage—even if it had set Teddy free to find a woman who actually loved him.

When Tom had told her everything about Dec and the pregnant girlfriend, on whose living room couch he'd slept overnight, Alice finally chanced a question.

"Do *you* think he's your son?"

"I don't know. I don't think *he* knows. But he's *her* son."

"I think we can say her name."

His voice trembled. "You're angry." He was clearly nervous.

"Yes," she admitted. "That it took you so long to tell me."

"Only that?"

She paused to consider what she actually did feel. Apparently, Tom had expected embarrassment, jealousy—even moral judgment. It never failed to surprise her how differently men and women responded to the same crises.

"Mostly ... I'm grateful," she said, breathing out hard. "I know what's been bothering you now."

"What is Will going to think?"

"Our son is a grown man. You must know we're with you. You have a generous heart, Tom. That's why we love you." She paused. "The truth is, you and I *both* took people into our lives and selfishly discarded them. I'm in no position to judge you or anyone."

He said nothing.

"What are you going to do?" she asked.

"Help them, if I can."

"It sounds like they need money."

"They're months behind in rent ... about to be evicted. I convinced them to pack up this morning and come with me."

"You brought them to Connecticut?"

"I put them in the shed."

"Our shed?"

Now, she was upset—disoriented—by the rapid movement of events he'd spent weeks getting used to. It wasn't his kindness that unsettled her, his willingness to proceed in this way from moral abstraction to human imperative. It was more the resistance she'd detected in her own voice; it had sounded like her mother's voice.

"Alice, I'm sorry. I didn't know what else to do."

"I know that. It's just a little sudden for me."

"I walked away from this boy's mother. I can't walk away from *him*."

"We don't really *know* these kids."

"They're not bad people. And they do need help."

"I understand." Alice struggled to say the right thing and put her own heart at ease. "But that shed ..."

"If you don't want them there, I'll put them up at The River Inn."

"Tom, stop!"

"I should have told you sooner. I'm sorry."

"Stop apologizing and let me speak, will you?"

"All right, I'm sorry."

"I'm just wondering if that old shed is really designed for people to live in. Shouldn't we ask them to stay with us ... in the house?"

"Don't go overboard," he said. "They'll be fine out there. I'll ask Peter Harvey about some temporary construction work for Dec. He and his girlfriend can have a roof over their heads while they figure something else out. Maybe save a little money, head back to Long Island with enough to start over ... get a new apartment ... a car."

"When is this girl due?"

"About a month ... she thinks."

"She thinks?" Alice scoffed. "What does her doctor say?"

"Apparently, she doesn't have a doctor. She goes to some woman's center in Bayview. It sounds like a midwife service. They'll help deliver the baby."

"So, she hasn't even *seen* a doctor?" Alice asked in disbelief.

"This place she goes to has doctors on referral," Tom said. "She told me she's seen one a couple of times ..."

"In eight months?"

"Apparently, yes."

"I think you should get her in to see Coben," Alice said. "If she runs into problems with the baby, she'll need more than herbal tea and meditation. I don't suppose these kids have any health insurance."

"I doubt it."

"Take them to Coben. Have her send me the bill."

"Okay. That's very nice."

"When they get back to Long Island," Alice said, "she can probably get herself picked up by Title 19. Coben can explain that to them."

"What's Title 19?"

"It's Medicaid ... basically."

"I see."

Glancing at the desk clock, Alice realized there was no time now for breakfast with Eileen. In fact, if she didn't start moving, they'd be late for Good Morning Chicago.

"Tom, I have an interview. Can we speak tonight?"

"Where will you be? I don't have your schedule handy."

"Indianapolis ... the Marriott downtown. I'll call you when I get in, probably around 10 o'clock. That's 11 for you. Is that too late?"

"I'll be up," he assured her.

As she quickly dressed, Alice remembered converting the old utility shed into a writer's cabin years ago. She'd hired Peter Harvey to do the wiring, insulation and plumbing. She'd picked out a manly rug, bought a desk and ergonomic chair, and placed them by the picture window Peter had cut out, with its panoramic view of the Leicester Hills. She'd even put a small refrigerator and sofa-bed in the cabin, encouraging Tom to forget everything there including time. None of it had inspired him to get back to his novel. In fact, he'd rarely set foot in the cabin, whose hopeful presence on their meadow had come to represent the sadness of an un-kept promise.

But heading down in the elevator, Alice felt a surprising calmness as her stomach cramps subsided. Tom's decision to embrace this boy from Long Island, and the sound of relief in his voice, had touched her heart and set something free inside her too. She hadn't yet lost the nagging fear that her novel's popularity represented a vast misunderstanding. But there were practical reasons, now, to embrace its success—just as Tom had finally found a use for his writer's cabin.

The elevator doors parted. Alice hurried across the lobby toward Eileen Vachon, whose tense expression softened as Alice approached.

"I'm sorry, Eileen. I was speaking with my husband. Can we make the show?"

"I called ahead. They're taking you in the second segment."

The women rushed through the lobby doors to a limousine idling beneath the hotel marquee. They got in and settled themselves in the rear seat as the driver jumped behind his wheel and gave the A/C a kick.

"WMCC, Ms. Vachon?"

"That's right, Tony, thank you."

As the limo glided from the curb and edged into city traffic, rain pelted the roof. The women took deep breaths of de-humidified air, then glanced at each other and laughed. For a minute, they enjoyed the comfort of the ride.

"I heard from NPR," Eileen said. "They want you for a long segment, which they'll use on Weekend Edition. But they can't do it today. I told them our itinerary, and they suggested their Minneapolis studio on Friday morning. We can do that and still get over to St. Paul in time for the Prairie Home Companion rehearsal."

"Good."

"So, you have this afternoon off." Eileen made a note in her thick, leather-bound diary. "Or … we *could* fit something in."

"Like what?"

"There's a gentleman who reviews books and interviews authors for … a sort of counter-culture newspaper … *The Chicago Independent.*"

Alice smiled. "It sounds subversive."

"Oh no, nothing like that," Eileen said. "It's a pretty good paper, with a small readership. He *does* pick up the university crowd. And yes, it's very liberal."

"I like it already."

"He's a nice man from an old, Chicago family."

Alice felt a stirring in her gut.

"Of course, we'd be helping him as much as he helped us. He's had personal difficulties." Eileen lowered her voice and whispered in Alice's ear. "He's been hospitalized a few times." She glanced at the driver. "Psychiatric."

"I see."

"We don't have to do it."

"No, no," Alice said, fighting her own judgment. "If you think it's worth our time."

"I'm sure he'll do a great piece on your book."

"How well do you know him?"

"We met at the press club several years ago." Eileen smiled broadly now. "I was working at a small PR agency. That was my first job and I was totally lost. He took me under his wing, and we struck up a friendship … very professional. He knows a lot, and he's done a lot. He's had a … well … interesting life. And actually, he owns *The Independent*. He supports it through a family trust he inherited."

Lightning cracked above them. Thunder rolled as Alice's cramps returned in long, nauseating waves. Struggling to maintain equilibrium, she glanced at Eileen. "I trust your judgment."

"I'll give him a call, then, while you're doing the TV spot. We'll have him come to your hotel this afternoon."

"Excuse me, Ms. Vachon," said the driver. "We're here."

"Okay, Tony."

The car veered out of traffic and cruised to a stop in front of an old, sandstone skyscraper. As Alice knew, it was one of the first major office buildings erected north of the river in the early 1900s.

Even now, it dominated the wide street of skyscrapers on which it sat, overlooking the Michigan Avenue Bridge.

Eileen rested her fingers on the door handle. "He says he knows *you*."

Alice nodded gravely. "You're talking about Craig McCall?"

"Why yes." Watching Alice gaze out her window at the rain-swept sidewalk, Eileen touched her arm. "Are you all right?"

"Just nerves," Alice fibbed, feeling her stomach tighten.

They climbed out of the limousine as Tony held a large umbrella over them. Hurrying to the revolving front door of the McCall Building, the women pushed through while Tony returned to the car.

Eileen spoke to a man at the security desk; Alice waited a few steps away, noting the big Tri-Art Media logo on the wall behind him. She remembered reading about Tri-Art's acquisition of this fabled building five years ago—when they'd acquired the newspaper and broadcasting companies housed within it and, presumably, the priceless Diego Rivera mural that still covered the north lobby wall.

"They're sending somebody down for us," Eileen said, standing close again. "Have you been to the McCall Building before?"

Alice smiled politely. "Yes."

"It's really grand. It's owned by Tri-Art Media now."

Alice nodded. "They've just acquired my husband's paper."

Only moments ago, Tom's voice had calmed her nerves and balanced her senses. She admired his decision—their decision—to shelter these young people he'd found in Bayview. Even her renewed feeling of guilt about Sally Hayes and the Harpers had been a bracing dose of reality. But this city held memories of sorrow and betrayal that touched the darkest places in her soul. She'd expected it would take strength to come here again. Now, she understood she'd need to be brave as well.

Eileen's eyes narrowed. "You really do have the jitters."

"I do." Alice touched Eileen's hand.

Nancy's train approached the main station in Florence on Monday afternoon. Staring from her window as the platform eased by, she realized her conviction about leaving Will had dissolved somewhere in the distance she'd put between them. Not only that—she now feared that returning to Florence had been a mistake.

Stepping down from the first class coach, she walked with other passengers along the half-covered platform into the station concourse. Instantly, she recalled its banked skylights, the walls of yellow Sienna marble, the polished serpentine flooring. But the recent refurbishment, described in a magazine she'd read on the train, made Santa Maria Novella new again.

West along the concourse, following taxi signs, she approached *Partenze*, the new wall fresco by Giampaolo Talani. This impressive mural high above the exit doors evoked the city's Renaissance heritage and the station's Modernist design. It pictured a line of colorfully painted travelers—"…a train of mankind in everlasting departure and arrival," the magazine had said. "A journey of shadows and thoughts, not of bodies, but souls and minds, burdened with memory and hope."

Nancy passed beneath the fresco and out into the temperate, late afternoon. Now, she paused to take in the wide frontage descending on a grassy mall into Piazza della Stazione. In the distance, across the great plaza, was Santa Maria Novella Church.

Fellow passengers hurried toward smiling family members and friends waiting near parked cars. Nancy continued to the taxi stand where a dozen travelers had queued up.

Several minutes passed until a swarm of distinctive, white Renaults with Comune di Firenze seals appeared and formed a line at the curb. As people on the queue responded with charming restraint, Nancy counted down and walked to the car which corresponded to her place in line. The driver, a lean, tall man of perhaps 35, opened a rear hatch and took her suitcase.

"A dove, signora?"

"Villa Michelangelo," she replied. "Lo conoscete?"

"Si." He waited as she got in before gently closing her door. Quickly, then, he slid behind the wheel and they were off. "Siete una Americana?" he asked, turning onto the main thoroughfare.

"Sono una Americana, si."

"Il vostro Italiano è buono."

"No." She sighed. "It isn't."

"Your ear is very good, signora."

"I studied Italian in college and lived here briefly. But I've forgotten almost everything."

"La Basilica di Santa Maria Novella," the driver said, starting a wide turn at the edge of the vast plaza and pointing to his right. "The first Dominican church and school of philosophy in the city ..."

"Founded in 1219," she noted. "A dozen Dominican friars arrived from Bologna and began teaching against the Manichean doctrines of the Cathars."

"Ah! *I Catari!*" He was clearly impressed by her knowledge. "The purified ones, who split the world into good and evil, light and darkness ..."

"But gave us the great troubadour-poets of courtly love ..."

The driver glanced in his rear-view mirror. "It is said that Dante learned of their errors at Maria Novella School, in the teachings of Aquinas."

"And yet in *La Commedia* he praised Arnaut Danièl, the great Cathar poet of Provence."

He nodded. "Perhaps the greatest poets speak in more than one voice."

As they skirted the church plaza, a glimpse was revealed of late-afternoon sunlight warming the basilica's 15th Century façade of white, green and black marble.

"You lived before in Firenze?"

"The summer after college, yes."

"What do you think, now, of our station?"

"It's beautifully restored. A great work of Italian Modernism."

"It is from the Fascist period," he said, as earnestly as a museum guide describing an Etruscan vase.

"I noticed the memorial at Track 8," she said, referring to the city's confession of deportations under German occupation.

Now, he was silent.

"It *is* a beautiful building," she added.

"Grazie, signora."

Instead of driving due south toward the Arno, he seemed to be working his way east, pushing through narrow streets, cobble-stoned and crowded.

"You are here for business?"

"Something more personal; it's to do with a friend, an old college friend."

"Ah."

"My name is Nancy, by the way."

"I am Lorenzo!" His voice rose to meet her friendly gesture.

Now, he turned south and resumed his polite impersonation of a tour guide.

"This is Tornabuoni, our street of elegant shops. The great designers of Italy are headquartered in these buildings."

As he drove slowly with the traffic, Nancy saw designer logos in street-level windows of Renaissance palazzos. The street had always reminded her of Fifth Avenue in Manhattan, but seemed to have grown more fashionable in the 15 years since she'd left.

He turned east again, skirting Piazza della Reppublica, with its busy outdoor cafés. And then, Piazza della Signoria—more cafés, works of public art, a glimpse of the Uffizi Arcade.

Pushing his little Renault through a particularly crowded alley, Lorenzo paused to show her the historically-accurate building erected by the city in celebration of Dante's birthplace. Then, he turned south onto Via Del Proconsolo, heading toward the Arno blocks away now.

"There are good restaurants and wine bars in this neighborhood, signora."

"I remember," she said, taking everything in.

They approached the river and he paused again, pointing to a red-stone palazzo on their right. "Here is Museo Galileo." He turned left and drove along the embankment. "The Old Bridge is behind us now."

Nancy glanced back at the famous covered bridge and a lovely view, west, down the Arno. She could see several sculling crews working out on the river.

"We will take Ponte alle Grazie," he advised, pointing straight ahead.

"All right." She glanced back again. "The Old Bridge looks marvelous today."

"It has lived an interesting life. Destroyed by floods yet spared by the Germans."

"Weren't these bridges all bombed by the Allies?"

"No, signora. When Germans occupied the city in 1943 and '44, there was fighting here against them … partisans, anti-fascists … communists. But the Allies made the Germans leave. And as they left, *they* destroyed all bridges … except Ponte Vecchio."

"I never knew that."

"The city pleaded. It was spared."

"Why?"

"It is said the order came from Berlin." Lorenzo shrugged, turning onto alle Grazie. "Who can read the minds of monsters?"

When he reached the south bank and continued east, he pointed back across the river.

"La Basilica di Santa Croce," he said.

Nancy contemplated the famous church, which housed the tombs of Michelangelo, Galileo and Machiavelli, the empty tomb of the exiled Dante, and stunning frescoes by his close friend, Giotto. The church, convent and school complex had been founded by Franciscans during the 13th Century, just as the Dominican complex of Maria Novella was arising at the city's other end.

"St. Francis himself chose the site when he visited Florence in 1217," said Lorenzo.

"Dante attended the primary school there, didn't he?"

"Ah, si. The Franciscan outlook had great influence on him. Some even claim he was a lay member of the Order. St. Francis holds a place of high honor in *La Commedia*."

"As high as that of Aquinas," Nancy noted.

"Perhaps more profound, signora, is the influence of St. Francis on Dante's conception of that work … the idea of an ascent to heaven as a journey of enlightenment, the spiritual unity of all things, the cultivation of humility …"

"The idealization of woman," she added.

"Si, si." He agreed. "This is an Italian thing, no?"

Nancy laughed as they came to a splendid neighborhood where the street climbed steeply.

"We are on Viale Michelangelo," he said. "At the top of this hill will be your hotel."

Nancy glanced back and forth at villas and parks on both sides of the tree-lined thoroughfare. She felt encouraged by the sight of people out walking the wide sidewalks. But when she noticed the first sign for San Miniato al Monte, she felt a chill, and sat back quietly until the taxi slowed and turned in at the stone gates of her hotel.

Lorenzo parked in the cobble-stoned courtyard and jumped out to retrieve her bag. A bellman hurried toward the cab. Nancy paid Lorenzo, including a healthy tip.

"Oh, signora!" He gasped. "Grazie mille!"

"Prego, Lorenzo. Thank *you*, for showing me your beautiful city."

His face grew stern. "I hope you will find your friend, signora."

Nancy smiled politely.

Once in her room, she placed a copy of *The Chastened Heart* on the desk near her window which overlooked the villa's front gardens. She'd finished the book in London, but had begun re-reading it on her Sunday-evening flight to Rome and on the train today from Termini to Maria Novella. Its compelling narrative had had a strange effect on her broken heart, giving her the courage to return here.

Next to the book, she placed a small, leather-bound writer's diary and several new pens purchased at Heathrow.

When everything had been unpacked and hung in the room's generous closets, or placed in its subtly perfumed drawers, she called down to reserve a table for dinner in the hotel restaurant. Then, she lay on her bed and closed her eyes.

She allowed herself to embrace the difficult memory of Angelica Rinaldi, her closest college girlfriend.

Fifteen years ago they'd spent their graduation summer here, studying art history, hiking the Apennine foothills, bearing the weight of urgent Italian boys who'd never tired of making love to them. Troubled by life decisions soon to be made back home, they'd found brief respite in the city's timeless culture. But their summer idyll ended.

Nancy went back to America and married Will. Angelica stayed on in Florence. And though they'd written each other occasionally over the years, a rupture in their friendship that summer had never healed. Then, three years ago, Nancy received news that ended all hope of reconciliation. Her friend had died in this city that seemed to live forever.

Feeling the chill of her losses, as the warm May sunlight faded outside her hotel, Nancy rolled the bed covers down and slid beneath them. Pushing away a stubborn longing for Will, she focused on tomorrow. She would place flowers at her old friend's crypt in the cemetery of San Miniato, the ancient church up the street from the hotel, on one of the city's highest points which the Florentines called "the gate of heaven."

A young man in blue jeans and loafers appeared. Introducing himself as Michael Warren, "associate producer" of Good Morning Chicago, he guided Alice and Eileen past the security desk and into a key-operated elevator.

"They just started," Michael said, as the Art Deco cab soared to the 25th floor.

Once there, he led the women down a corridor whose left wall was entirely glass, permitting a glimpse of an intimate studio. The show's hosts chatted on a white couch, facing two cameras and 80 audience members in metal bleachers.

Along the right-hand wall were large, color photos of the hosts—air-brushed images of two women and a man that seemed computer-generated.

Michael brought his guests to a small "green room" with a shabby couch of orange plush, beaten through to a pale, under-fabric. The little room had a window, a refreshment station, and a TV monitor tuned to the show. The wall above the couch had been emblazoned with a bright, new Tri-Art Media logo, beneath which faded the old, WMCC brand.

"We'll call you in a few minutes," Michael advised as he left them.

Eileen turned immediately to the refreshment station. "Would you like some tea, or spring water?"

"I'm fine, thanks."

Eileen poured tea for herself as Alice stood by the window. The rain was letting up, but a thick bank of fog had come in off the lake to hide the city from itself.

"You mentioned having some ideas?" Alice said to the gloomy window—with its hazy reflection of herself—before turning away and getting a grip on her emotions. "About the book, I assume?"

"It's a fine novel." Eileen held her paper tea-cup in two hands and sat at the edge of the couch. "Your empathy was … surprising."

Alice listened, wondering where this was leading.

"You have such feeling for the *male* character, though he does some nasty things."

"My female character does horrible things too."

"You don't blame anyone." Eileen sipped tea. "It's as if your *deepest* sympathies are reserved for your characters' *worst* aspects."

"People are people, Eileen. Sometimes, I think we're the sum of our mistakes."

"I read a lot of novels by women, Mrs. Winslow. I see a lot of male characters portrayed as violent, irresponsible fools or whining babies … victims of their own masculine entitlement."

Alice smiled politely.

"Would you call yourself a feminist?"

"I believe in the feminist ideals of equality and dignity," Alice conceded. "And my characters have those concerns, the men *and* the women. But I might prefer the term *humanist*. It's far less political."

"When you go on, this is what you should talk about."

The door opened and Michael entered with a copy of Alice's book.

"Are they ready?" Eileen asked.

"They're doing two more segments with the first guest," he said. "Basically, they need time for questions and calls. We'd like Mrs. Winslow in the final segment."

"Your ratings drop off the cliff at 10:45."

The young man seemed embarrassed, irritated, by Eileen's knowledge of his business.

"It's all right," Alice assured them. "What are they so taken with?"

"You haven't been watching?" Michael glanced at the studio feed on their monitor—the hosts waited quietly on the white couch in a commercial break. Sitting with them was a woman dressed in dark, Muslim robes and a veil which hid her face—"Airport security," he said at last.

"Is that the young woman who was arrested at O'Hare?" Alice asked. "For refusing to be body scanned?"

"Yes, that's Janet Mohamed." Michael nodded emphatically. "She sued the TSA and it's going to the Supreme Court."

"Is the audience with her?"

"I'd say it's 50/50." Michael re-checked the monitor. "They're starting again. I better get back." But he lingered a moment with a sheepish grin. "Mrs. Winslow, would you sign my book?"

Alice and Eileen watched from the green room as the show began again. The first audience question came from a nervous, older woman in the front row.

"Do you think you're better than everyone?" she asked in a wavering voice.

Following some brief applause, a man in back commented. "In case you forgot, we have soldiers dying over there!"

Then, a young woman called in from home. "A lot of people have religious beliefs," she said. "But come on! We're at war with these people!"

When, at last, the young Muslim woman was given the chance to respond, she did so in a strong, unaccented American voice.

"I don't think religious convictions make anyone unique, but I do reject the premise that my beliefs threaten national security. My problem with intrusive body scanning is really a concern about the rights we *all* share." She paused as the studio audience appeared to grow more sullen. "Our government does not grant us our rights and cannot take them away. I refuse to give government security agents the power to strip-search me, even electronically, just because I wish to board a plane dressed a certain way. So I'm taking the government to court."

A smattering of applause was instantly shouted down.

Eileen answered her buzzing cell phone.

"This is Ms. Vachon." Listening to the caller, she muffled the phone with her slender fingers and whispered to Alice. "It's the manager at the Jackson Street Barnes & Noble." A moment later, she ended the call with a promise. "I'll deal with it."

"What's wrong?"

"He needs books." Eileen slipped her phone into her pocketbook and stood. "He's filled so many pre-orders, there are none left to put out for your signing."

"What do we do?"

"His distributor is sending a rush order, but he's worried it won't get there on time." Eileen looped her pocketbook over one shoulder and gripped her leather attaché bag. "I've got four boxes of review copies at my office. He can sell those if he needs to. I'll call your publisher and see if they can get us more from another distributor." Eileen glanced at her watch and thought for a moment. "I better call the State Street store. They might be in the same pickle. Can you handle this interview by yourself?"

"Of course." Alice glanced at the monitor, which showed harsh questions becoming accusations. "They might forget about me, anyway."

"They'll call you." Eileen watched the monitor briefly, then, started for the door. "I'll be at the Jackson Street store."

Alice reached out to touch her young colleague's shoulder. "You're doing so well."

"I'll send Tony back with the car," Eileen promised. "Don't forget what you said a few minutes ago."

And she was gone.

Glancing again at the monitor, Alice saw audience members arguing among themselves. The hosts struggled to maintain order. The young Muslim woman was motionless on the couch. When the hosts called for a commercial break, the studio lights dimmed and angry voices murmured in the dark.

Turning from this unfortunate scene, Alice stared at the wet fog and mid-morning darkness beyond the window.

"We're going too fast, Mom!"

"We need to see Craig." She glanced at Will's eight-year-old profile, as they drove the dark, shore-line highway between Chicago and Lake Forest.

"It dangerous!" The boy's voice was urgent, plaintive, as he stared straight into the fog beyond squeaking windshield wipers. "What's wrong with him anyway?"

She thought before speaking. "Craig has an illness ... that makes everything seem dangerous." She paused and waited for another question, but the boy only listened. "He told me once that it feels like falling, like having a bad dream about falling. Except ... he's awake." She paused again. "It feels like he'll never stop falling."

"Because no one will catch him?"

The breath went out of her for a moment.

"People are trying to help," she finally managed to say. "They're giving him medicine, trying to help him rest until he feels better."

Will leaned back in his seat, apparently satisfied. They drove on for several minutes. Then, the boy asked another question.

"Are you going to marry him?"

Alice felt her grip tighten on the steering wheel. "I don't know, Will."

"Dad stopped drinking."

She kept her gaze firmly focused on the darkness ahead, hiding her tears which always upset him. An oncoming tractor-trailer hurtled by, its glaring headlights breaking through the fog, blinding her. For a moment, she lost her bearings. It felt like falling.

Now, squinting from the sudden glare of sunlight against the window pane, Alice turned again to the TV monitor and saw chaos in the studio. Audience members had come down from their bleachers and aligned themselves on opposing sides of the stage. The hosts were caught in the middle, trapped on their couch. There was no sign of the Muslim woman.

Alice heard voices outside the green room. Opening the door, she saw chaos in the corridor. Michael Warren had placed himself between the Muslim woman and a group of audience members who'd followed them from the studio.

Instinctively, Alice stepped out and crept along the corridor, trying to get near the Muslim woman without attracting attention. When she'd gone as far as she dared, she stopped, allowing herself to blend with the angry crowd.

Several men began threatening Michael.

Alice leaned toward the public elevator button and brushed it with her left shoulder, as Michael argued valiantly with the robed woman's accusers.

The elevator doors opened, but the crowd was oblivious to anything but its righteous focus. Reaching past a screaming man, Alice grabbed the Muslim woman's arm and pulled her into the elevator as the doors began closing. Now awakened, the crowd rushed to prevent their escape.

"Go!" Michael shouted, throwing his thin body against the tide of angry people.

The doors shut tightly and the elevator descended.

Alice heard the echo of pounding fists and outraged voices grow muffled and distanced above them. And then, there was silence.

"Are you all right?" she asked.

The Muslim woman took long, labored breaths.

"I have a car and driver," Alice said. "We can take you home."

The woman began to shake. Alice heard weeping beneath the veils. As she reached for the woman's hand to reassure her, Alice was enveloped in a tight embrace.

The elevator stopped and the doors opened. Alice guided the woman out into the lobby, which buzzed with awareness. Two men behind the security desk stared at them. Small groups had gathered to gawk at several strategically placed TV monitors.

"Let's get out of here," Alice whispered.

The women pushed through revolving doors and onto the wide street, where Tony waited near the limousine. The street was wet, but the sun had broken through a rapidly thinning fog. As they hurried toward the car, Tony opened the back door.

"We need to take this woman home," Alice said.

Tony didn't look happy. "I'm not sure about this, Mrs."

The young woman got in.

Alice confronted the driver. "Do you know what just happened?"

"I got a little TV up front, Mrs. So, yes, I saw."

Alice got in. Tony slammed the door after her.

"What's your address?" Alice asked the woman.

Tony slid in behind the wheel. "Don't tell me you agree with this."

"We're past the point of agreeing or disagreeing, Tony. Can we just take her home?"

He let out a frustrated sigh, but offered no further argument.

Alice glanced at the silent woman. "Tell us where you live."

When the woman gave an address on the south side, Tony muttered and pressed down on the gas pedal. The limo jerked away from the McCall Building. Quickly, they were splashing through rain-puddled streets, beneath elevated train platforms, toward a series of river bridges, heading south.

Alice felt the woman squeezing her hand firmly.

"They act like I have a bomb strapped to my chest."

"Beliefs are as dangerous as bombs," Alice said.

By the time they'd reached her neighborhood, the young woman had introduced herself as Janet, and explained that she'd been born in Chicago, the daughter of Somali immigrants. Her mother was a physician and her father a business professor at Northwestern—and neither of them agreed with her stand.

The limo stopped in front of a two-story, red brick home, surrounded by a three foot brick wall. Immediately, a fashionably-dressed Somali woman rushed from the front door, through an iron gate, to the car.

Alice got out with Janet who introduced her mother. After a grateful kiss on each cheek from the mother, and a final embrace from Janet, Alice got back into the limo. She watched as the Somali women hurried to their house. Moments later, a small group of neighbors appeared at the gate and proceeded to the front door, which opened for them.

"I'm sorry, Tony."

"It's not your fault, Mrs."

"I don't think she knows what's happening."

"You got to figure the parents are pushing this."

"She said they disagree with her."

"I don't believe it." Tony stared into his rear-view mirror. "First of all, the lawyers must be charging a fortune for this case. Who's paying for that? Nah, the parents are in on it. They're professionals, doing very well here. Makes you wonder why they wouldn't be a little more grateful for their opportunities. This girl's a trouble maker."

Alice chose to address the least problematic of his assertions. "Maybe she's being defended pro bono, by some law firm or legal defense fund."

He sneered. "You mean like ACLU?"

"I've heard about other people who don't want to be body-scanned for religious reasons. This girl isn't the only one. Maybe she's the only Muslim."

Tony's initial silence implied that he understood her point. Then he spoke.

"Have the others made a federal case?"

Alice didn't respond. Tony's point was true enough, as far as she knew. No one else who'd criticized full-body scanning had taken such formal, legal steps—yet.

"We can't be questioning airport security," Tony added. "It's a dangerous world out there. And the danger's coming *here* by plane. Take it from someone who spends a lot of time around airports. That girl needs to learn the facts of life in America."

"I think the message is getting through," Alice said with sadness.

"Blame the parents."

Alice glanced once more at the red brick house, imagining a mother and daughter within, frightened and confused by their own angry tears, and the nervous voices of their friends.

Then, she sat back and spoke wearily. "I guess we should head over to Barnes & Noble, Tony."

"Right-O, Mrs."

Tony turned the wheel and they gathered speed on the warm, wet street.

Eileen worked on text messages while Alice sipped tea and waited for the man she'd once loved. At the far end of the nearly empty Green Briar Room, a waiter casually straightened silverware on silent tables. Nearby, a businessman nursed his mid-afternoon martini and stared at a television above the bar.

Until moments ago, the hottest story on the cable channels had been a blind item: a writer's scheduled interview on Good Morning Chicago had been cancelled due to trouble over another guest's appearance. But a FOX News report had just filled in the details, making Alice's narrow escape with Janet sound like a crime.

"We have confirmed it was novelist Alice Winslow who helped radical activist Janet Mohamed spirit herself away in a hired car," the FOX announcer said.

Alice knew it wouldn't be long before CNN and MSNBC picked up these details—as would the network news shows, whose interest in novelists normally was limited to Pulitzer Prizes, movie deals and obituaries.

Once this got rolling, she and Eileen would face endless questions at every stop on the tour. There'd already been a few during her signing at the Jackson Street Barnes & Noble. This was exactly what Judith Lavan had warned her about.

"I heard there was trouble this morning," said a man now approaching the table.

Alice smiled as she stood to embrace Craig McCall. "No comment."

He looked surprisingly youthful and fit—still quite handsome, with all of his hair, which was stunning silver gray now. It was easy to remember why she'd fallen for him at college, why he'd held a place in her life for so long.

Eileen smiled. "No introductions are necessary, I see."

Craig placed a copy of *The Chastened Heart* on the table and sat down. When the waiter had taken a drink order, Craig nodded at the TV. "Can you believe this?"

Eileen beamed with admiration. "Craig's done stories about Janet Mohamed."

"She's a courageous person," Craig said. "And a good writer."

This intrigued Alice. "She's a writer?"

"We've just received her 3,000-word essay on the case."

"For your newspaper," Alice replied. "Is that a good idea?"

The waiter was back with a beer for Craig and a Pellegrino for Eileen. Alice took another sip of tea.

Craig allowed the waiter to leave. "She has a right to defend herself."

"I hope she has a good lawyer," Alice said.

"She's got *great* lawyers."

"It seems odd to do op/ed pieces and talk shows *before* the trial."

Eileen frowned, surprised by the immediacy of their sparring.

Craig sought to change the mood. "It's so good to see you."

But Alice pressed him. "Who's underwriting her defense?"

"*We* are." Craig sighed impatiently. "The McCall Foundation, our newspaper … *The Independent*." He took a sip of beer. "Don't you approve?"

"As long as she *is* being defended … not exploited."

Eileen gasped. "Mrs. Winslow!"

"It's all right, Eileen." Craig's right hand rose, palm out, in subtle reassurance. "Alice and I have always been direct with each other. Like family … almost."

"Excuse me." Eileen stood abruptly. "I need to use the ladies' room."

When she was gone, Craig leaned back in his chair. "You embarrassed her."

"I'll apologize."

He spoke quite directly now. "What's *your* interest in Janet Mohamed?"

"Having met her, I care what happens. I understand her idealism, but she's about to learn what that means in this world."

Craig smiled. "You were never an idealist, Alice."

"No. I wasn't thinking of myself."

She glanced toward the bar as the businessman left. FOX was reporting the story again. She wondered if Tom had seen it yet. She hoped he wasn't worrying.

"Who *were* you thinking of?"

Alice waved his question away. "This girl is going to the Supreme Court. It's not a frivolous thing." She pointed to the TV. "But *that* is, and I don't see how it helps her."

Craig looked confused. "Why don't you say what you mean?"

"I thought I was. What does the foundation get by defending her?"

"What do we *get*?"

"Is there a deal ... some kind of exclusive? What?"

"We're doing a book together. Yes." He glared. "We have a publishing contract."

"So, it's PR for the book ... *and* your newspaper."

"You don't have to be so high and mighty, Alice."

"*You* weren't at that studio today. You didn't see the fear in her mother's eyes."

"Oh, please." He spoke archly. "Spare me your refined sense of morality. I'm sure *you'll* benefit from the Janet Mohamed story too."

"You sound like *your* mother now."

He leaned toward her and whispered a harsh reminder. "You let me get you a job at the University of Chicago. My parents sent wedding invitations to their friends ... *my* friends. Everything was planned. And then, you just left with your son, while I was still in the hospital. When I got out, you called me from New York and said it was over ... by telephone, Alice."

"You're right and I'm sorry." She nodded gravely. "I know I didn't handle any of it correctly. My life was a shambles in those days. I was foolish and confused, and yes, dishonest. Young women make *big* mistakes."

"Well." He tried to salvage the moment. "It's past."

But Alice couldn't let go of their painful past now. She spoke as if still seeking the moral center of their failed relationship.

"I should never have agreed to marry you in the first place."

"Who marries a crazy person, right?"

"*Stop.*" She pleaded. "I had my son to think of. He needed his father. If there was a chance to make things work with Tom, I had to pursue it. Tom was the person I loved all along. I'm sorry."

Craig seemed embarrassed by the mention of Tom in this way.

"Speaking of love, Alice, I really loved your book."

He paused. She allowed the silence to stand.

"How *is* Will by the way?"

"He's fine." She tried to hide her doubts. "He's married."

"Oh!" Craig smiled graciously.

"He and his wife run a PR business … in Boston."

He smiled again. "Boston? Good for them. Of course, I wouldn't know. I'd like to send them something, if you'll let me … have his address, I mean."

"Of course."

As Alice looked in her bag for a pen and scrap of paper, she had the inexplicable sense that Craig knew more about Will than he was admitting. Was this her guilt—an expression of old fears—or had there been something just too calm in his demeanor as she'd described Will's life in Boston? She couldn't be sure.

Finding a pen at the bottom of her cluttered bag, but nothing to write on, she looked up helplessly. "Do you have a piece of note paper?"

Craig pushed her book across the table. "Just write it in this."

She stared at him before taking the book and opening it from the back.

He watched her scribble an address on the endpaper.

"Would you sign it for me?"

"Naturally." She turned the book over and autographed the title page—*For Craig, with great affection, Alice.*

A moment later she slid the book back to him and spoke the truth.

"They may be having problems."

"Marriage problems?" Sounding surprised as he briefly examined Will's address, he looked up and waited for more.

"Yes. Their relationship has always been a bit … tenuous. What about you?"

"You mean marriage?" He smiled. "No."

"Never?"

He shook his head. "I hope Will's trouble isn't serious."

"I don't even know if it's true. It's just a feeling. I'm sorry I mentioned it."

"I wouldn't mind having some kind of relationship with him."

"Nothing's stopping you."

"You shouldn't worry." He paused and placed his hand lightly on her book. "I intend to write a glowing review."

"I'm *not* worried." Her laugh sounded false even to her. "About myself, I mean. But after 28 years, we meet again for a few minutes and I'm already worried about *you*."

He kept silent.

"Why is that?" she asked.

"I don't know." He sighed. "At least you're not confusing it with love anymore."

Eileen returned to the table as the waiter placed a fresh pot of tea down for Alice. Craig took several gulps of beer, betraying for the first time any nerves of his own.

"We have about 30 minutes to do this," Eileen said.

"Right." Craig pulled a digital voice recorder from his jacket pocket and placed it on the table near the book. He pressed a tiny button and smiled at Alice.

She was relieved to see the little red light, which meant the Record feature was on. Their conversation now, thankfully, would be framed in formalities of fiction.

The early evening flight rose above O'Hare. Alice welcomed the sensation of upward thrust meeting gravitational resistance in her solar plexus. Glancing at Eileen, who slouched in the next seat with her eyes closed and shoes kicked off, Alice felt a rush of motherly affection.

The plane continued to climb in waning daylight. Alice could see suburban communities radiating from the airport into the flat, glowing horizon. In the distance, night had fallen, and darkness rapidly approached. Communities grew smaller beneath her, becoming a pattern of glittering lights far enough below as to seem like stars—if the world were upside down.

"Please remain in your seats with your seatbelts fastened."

As if in response to the soothing male voice on the cabin intercom, Alice closed her eyes and felt the plane leveling off for its hop to Indianapolis.

She saw the lights glittering like tiny stars outside the country house.

A soothing male voice spoke to her. "Won't you sit down?"

It was late. Alice had never felt so far from home. Fog enveloped the lake and nearly smothered the lights on the McCalls' dock. Turning from the window, she smiled helplessly at Craig's father.

He spoke again. "Is William comfortable?"

"Yes, he's sleeping." She took a seat near him. "You always make us feel at home."

"You *are* at home."

"How long has Craig been suffering these breaks?"

"It started after Harvard." Mr. McCall spoke in a voice weighted by undesired experience. "You've never seen him this ill?"

"There have been times when he's struggled. And we've talked about it before. But, no, I've never seen him quite like this."

"The doctors say that people with Craig's illness are particularly vulnerable in their mid-to-late 20s." He paused. "There is a … *progression* … shall we say."

"He's so medicated. I don't think he knew we were there."

"He's safe in that hospital. And he'll come back to us … he always does."

"Yes." She found herself gazing across the room at the dark window.

"What is it, my dear?"

Slowly, she shook her head. She could not look at him. "Mr. McCall, I …"

"Oh no." He sighed. "You're not going to marry our son, after all."

Alice looked him straight in the eyes now. Unable to utter the words, she pressed her lips together as a tear fell.

"You've known each other since college."

"I know."

"We see you as part of Craig's life ... *our* lives." He paused again. "That boy has always loved you, my dear. He has great affection for William. We all do."

"I know what you're thinking. But you're wrong."

"What am I thinking?"

"That I can't deal with Craig's illness ..."

He smiled graciously and stood up. "Would you care for a drink?"

"No. Thank you."

"You won't mind if I have one." He went to the liquor cabinet and found a new bottle of Ballantine's. Breaking the seal, pouring scotch into a thick, crystal tumbler, he took a long sip with his back to her. "May I offer some advice that you might at least consider? Call it an old man's experience in a dreary world."

"Of course."

"Happiness is not fungible." Now, he turned to look at her. "Most situations are as they appear. They always will be, no matter how hard we work to change them."

He means Tom, she thought to herself. "No doubt you're right."

He sipped his scotch. "Is there nothing I can say on my *son's* behalf?"

Alice looked into the face of the fifth richest man in America and saw a father concerned for a troubled son. Dismissing an urge to say that even unhappy love could not be exchanged for less, she decided that some things were too painful to put into words.

"I'm sorry, sir."

After finishing the scotch in his tumbler, he replied in a voice resigned to its own sadness. "I am too."

Alice got to her feet. "We'll have a long day at the hospital tomorrow."

"All right, dear. I may do some reading. Or try to. I want to give my poor wife a little time to herself. When we come home from these hospital visits, she's quite ..." He stopped in mid-thought and stared into his empty glass.

"I understand." Alice put her hand on his shoulder. "I'll see you in the morning."

Moments later, climbing the great, winding staircase at the heart of the immense country house, Alice paused on the second-floor landing. Someone was crying. As she moved along the carpeted hallway, the sound of weeping grew more distinct. Stopping outside the room from which it came, Alice rapped softly on the door.

"Mrs. McCall?"

The crying stopped instantly. There was no other response. Alice waited a few moments, then, returned to the stairs and made her way to an opulent, third floor suite.

She tip-toed softly to Will's bed. Bending over to kiss him, she caught the smell of his hair and remembered lost things. Moving on through a connecting doorway to another bedroom, she left the door ajar in case her son awoke during the night. After washing her face she crawled into bed.

Sinking into soft sheets and pillows, Alice embraced the news that Tom had stopped drinking. In telling their son, surely he'd meant this news for her too. But why, since he was still living with that woman on North Beach?

Ashamed enough of the chaos in her heart, she now had to admit that this move to Chicago had been about Tom—a way of creating room for forgiveness. But in forgiving one man, she'd misled another. Yes, she loved Craig, but not in the way he deserved. And she'd known this almost in the moment when she'd agreed to marry him.

Worst of all, Alice understood the coded message Tom had sent through their son. He was planning to leave that woman. How many hearts must be sacrificed to a memory, she asked herself?

"Please fasten your seatbelts securely. Make sure your seats are in the upright position. We'll be landing shortly at Indianapolis International."

Alice opened her eyes.

Eileen closed down her laptop and glanced over. "Did you sleep?"

"I think so." Checking her watch, Alice was surprised to see that an hour had elapsed.

"I couldn't." Eileen's weary laugh was yet another sign of how much of herself she'd invested in Alice Winslow. "I'm hoping for better luck at the hotel."

"It's been quite a day."

"Those reporters at your second signing were just the beginning, you know. I have 30 interview requests ..."

"All concerning Janet Mohammed?"

Eileen nodded. "There may be reporters at the terminal, even the hotel."

Alice glanced out the window at the airport coming into view. "I should call my agent."

"We're not giving interviews until I hear back from my supervisors. My firm is talking with your publisher."

"Craig told me his newspaper website posted a statement from Janet's lawyers." Alice smiled at her young friend. "Can't we just tell reporters to look there?"

"We can certainly do that, Mrs. Winslow. But they'll want to know what *you* think."

"I know they will."

"I'm sorry about Craig. I had no idea about you two."

"How could you know?"

"You were engaged?"

"It was a mistake. We'd known each other since college and it was, well, complicated."

"I understand, Mrs. Winslow. I really do."

"Please don't worry about it."

"I hope he keeps his promise and writes a good review."

"He will, Eileen. Craig has always kept his promises, which is more than I can say."

As the plane caromed left, descending, they lost sight of the terminal for a moment. Only the blinking yellow lights tracing the outlines of their dark runway were visible.

Relieved to find no reporters waiting at their gate, Alice and Eileen hurried through an un-crowded concourse of coffee shops, newsstands and bars about to close. Approaching the glass-paneled terminal front, they could see four blue taxis waiting at the curb. And as they stepped out through electronic doors into the cool, Indiana night, a short, stocky man in a Hoosier baseball cap emerged from the lead taxi.

Pinching the bill of his cap, he reached for their travel bags. "Where to, ladies?"

"The Marriott, downtown," Eileen replied.

Moments later, speeding beneath a series of Airport Exit/ Indianapolis Business District signs, the driver spoke with welcoming interest. "Here for the tournament?"

"Tournament?" Alice noted his name—Ricardo Hermanos—and his photograph, embedded in thick plastic just behind his head.

"We have the Solway Cup this week at Crooked Stick. It's a big LPGA event. They start Thursday, but a lot of the ladies arrived today."

Eileen laughed. "Do we look like golfers?"

The driver glanced in his rear-view mirror. "Sports reporters."

"This is Alice Winslow, the best-selling novelist."

"Oh! What have you written, Ma'am?"

"A novel called *The Chastened Heart*," Alice said. "We're in town to promote it."

"I heard something about your book. And how about *you*, Miss?"

"I'm the PR person."

The cabby nodded and said no more.

At ten o'clock the cab turned in at the Marriott's half-moon driveway and stopped near the front doors. The meter read $15.

Alice reached for her wallet. "I'll get this, Eileen."

"I'll check us in then."

A bellman put their bags on his carriage and Eileen followed him inside.

Alice placed a $20 bill in the driver's hand. "Please keep the change, Mr. Hermanos."

The cabby smiled, apparently pleased that Alice had read his name on the taxi license. Leaning toward her confidentially, he whispered. "That Muslim woman in Chicago ... do you think she's being honest with herself?"

"I *think* she is." Alice smiled nervously. "It may not mean she's right. But yes. I think she's honest in her belief."

"I'll have to tell my wife about you. She loves to read novels. She'll be very impressed that I drove you tonight."

"I'm appearing at the University bookstore tomorrow morning. Please give your wife my personal invitation. If she comes, she *must* introduce herself. I'll sign a copy especially for her."

Again, he raised his fingers to the bill of his baseball cap. "I will tell her."

As he started around toward the driver's side of his cab, Alice stepped closer to her side. "What's your wife's name?"

"America!"

Alice removed her dress and glanced at the fresh bathrobe on the hotel bed. Trying to ignore the wall-mirror's reflection of an aging woman in her underwear, she called home. The line was busy. She stripped off the rest of her things, wrapped the fluffy robe around herself, and took an Amstel Light from the mini-bar.

Sipping her beer, she parted the window curtain and noticed a young woman working late on the 7th floor of an adjacent office building. Just north, a convention center and sports stadium consumed four vast blocks. To the east, the Union Station clock glowed like a yellow eye. And to the west was the Indiana University-Purdue University downtown campus, where tomorrow she would appear at a bookstore operated by Barnes & Noble.

As in Chicago, 100 copies of her book had been pre-ordered. It pleased Alice that college students had any interest at all in her writing. The idea of it seemed to promise that *The Chastened Heart*, so redolent of her life, might have some kind of life of its own.

The young woman in the nearby office building was getting ready to leave now. Alice watched as she packed her briefcase, turned off the light, and walked along a dim corridor with a cell phone to her ear. Finally, the woman disappeared—presumably into an elevator.

Concerned for a young woman's well-being this late at night, Alice told herself that the surrounding area looked safe—unlike the cabby's route from the airport past the old *Indianapolis Star* Building, whose dreary brick façade and desolate neighborhood of cut-through streets and service roads embodied the sad state of the newspaper business itself.

A few years ago, Tom had briefly pursued a job offer with the *Star*, which, by now had endured as many cutbacks and ownership changes as the *Hartford Chronicle*. How glad she was that they hadn't uprooted their lives to move out here.

Now, as she watched the street below, Alice saw the young business woman walking briskly toward a similarly well-dressed young man with his own briefcase. As they met, she leaned into him, and he wrapped one arm around her waist. They kissed. Then, he guided her across the street out of sight.

Alice turned from the window and took another long sip of beer before trying Tom on his cell phone. Her call was diverted to the message feature, so she hung up and tried him at home again. There was no answer now. In frustration, she slapped the receiver back in its cradle and collapsed on the bed.

I'll run a bath in a minute, she thought. But she closed her eyes in exhaustion as the sedative effect of a half-bottle of beer took hold. She felt herself floating.

It was dawn when she awoke, put on a robe and hurried through the suite past her sleeping son, out into the third-floor hallway of the McCalls' country house. She hurried down the staircase to the main floor and into the sitting room, where she'd made her sad confession to Craig's father the night before.

There was a telephone on the French Empire table near the window overlooking the lake on which the sun had begun to rise. She started across the room and realized she wasn't alone.

Craig's mother sat in a wingback chair, staring at the silent water. "Good morning."

Alice froze. "I was going to check on my mother back east." A half-truth, at best, since she'd awakened with an urge to call Tom, a willingness to encounter the woman he lived with if necessary, just to hear him say he had, in fact, stopped drinking. "She's been ill."

Craig's mother rustled in her seat. "What time is it now?"

"About six-thirty." Alice sat nearby in a facing chair.

"That makes it seven-thirty in the east. Won't that disturb your sick mother?"

"It's Alzheimer's, so, the time of day is almost irrelevant."

"I see."

"If she's not well enough to speak, I get a report from the homecare nurse."

Craig's mother nodded gravely. "You're a good daughter. Generous too, considering the cost of full-time nursing. Believe me, I know."

Alice replied with a weary smile.

"Richard told me that you've reconsidered your engagement."

"Yes. I hope you'll understand ..."

"I understand very well. The idea of marrying my son might give any attractive, intelligent woman pause." The older woman spoke in a deliberate cadence. "He's a good and talented man. There is this unfortunate issue of course ... his ... psychological problems. You *do* know they can be treated."

"Mrs. McCall, I ..."

"*Grace.*"

Alice looked into the older woman's eyes and saw resignation.

"Craig *is* a good man, Grace. Any woman would be lucky to have him. It would be dishonest of *me* to be that woman."

"Dishonest how?"

"I don't love him. Not as a wife loves a husband ... as he deserves."

Grace McCall smiled knowingly. "These things have a way of resolving themselves, dear. Let marriage take hold. You'll begin to see what is really important in life. Take it from a more experienced woman."

"We have different expectations of marriage, Grace."

"I doubt it. Second thoughts are quite common."

Alice sighed. "I'm very sorry."

"Perhaps you should take a little time to think about what you're doing."

"I *have* thought about it. I'm resigning my position at the university and returning to New York."

Craig's mother, whom Alice knew to be guarded and aloof, looked surprised and honestly disappointed. "I hope you're not going back to that alcoholic."

"If you mean Will's father ..."

Grace smiled oddly. "Let's be honest, shall we?"

"I thought we were being."

"I know how important your writing is to you." A shift in Grace's tone was apparent now. "As you may be aware, McCall Enterprises includes more than our newspaper chain, our radio network and television stations ... our office building in town." She paused in her odd business inventory and examined Alice carefully. "We're also majority stake-holders in McCall & Webster, the book publisher."

"I *am* aware of that."

"Then consider this: McCall & Webster would be very interested in signing a talented writer, such as you, to a book contract. We wish to publish a collection of your beautiful short stories, and take an option on your first novel."

"Oh, Grace." Alice stood abruptly. "I'm very sorry if I've given the impression of seeking your family's influence, in order to publish ..."

"There's nothing wrong with ambition. I'm simply saying that there are things I can do to help you. That there are ... compensations. It is a man's world, after all. It always has been and, apparently, always will be. Most men seem to need it that way. If the truth were told, most women do too. But that doesn't mean we gals can't stick together and get what we want from our arrangements."

Alice was stunned. "*Arrangements.*"

The older woman stared impassively. "Why don't you sit down?"

"I will not sit down. What do you take me for?"

"You're being dramatic, Alice. You're tired. We're all under stress. These issues about Craig are very draining. We'll say no more about it."

"Good." Alice spoke tersely. "Was there anything else?"

"Only one issue ..."

"Yes?"

"Your son ..."

"What does my son have to do with you?"

"Oh, my dear," Grace said darkly. "That boy has everything to do with me."

The phone rang from across the sitting room, startling Alice. Grace McCall continued sitting in her wingback chair, smiling in her vaguely threatening manner. The phone rang and rang. Alice sensed that it could be Tom reaching out to her, but she couldn't move. Her feet were embedded in the carpet beneath her.

Cold sweat covered her body as she opened her eyes. The terrycloth hotel robe was drenched. Still half-asleep, she sat up and reached for the ringing phone.

"Tom?"

"No. It's Will."

Emerging from her dark dream, Alice pressed her bare feet down into the plush carpet below her queen-sized bed and reclaimed the present.

"**A**re you all right, Mom?"

"It's been a long day."

"I've seen the Janet Mohamed stuff. It's a national story."

"Yes."

"Is your publisher standing by you?"

"They've given me a sharp PR woman from Daniels Lassiter."

"They're very good. But there's a difference between promoting books and protecting a client in this kind of situation."

"This young woman knows what she's doing." Alice glanced at the clock on the bedside table. It was almost eleven in Indianapolis. "I'll call my agent first thing tomorrow. Judy Lavan is wise about PR."

"Promise you'll call *me* if you have any doubts. I'll fly out there and help you myself."

"You're not leaving your clients in the lurch to fight your mother's battles."

"Promise me, Mom!"

Alice forced the subject away from her absurd predicament. "I've been trying to reach your father."

"He asked me to call you, about this young couple he's taken under his wing."

This surprised her. "What about them?"

"The girl went into labor. They're on their way to Leicester County General. They're probably there by now. Dad said to tell you Dr. Coben is meeting them."

"Okay." Alice struggled to adjust herself to fast-moving events. "Where are *you*?"

"Boston."

"How's Nancy?"

He didn't speak for a moment. Alice felt her fears about his marriage again.

"She didn't come home with me," he finally said. "She's taking time in Europe ... a few days, maybe longer."

"What does this mean?"

"Nothing good, I think."

"Every marriage has problems, Will."

"Sure." His voice was weary.

"She sounds confused."

"Confused," he said with a dry laugh. "Even *before* we got married, she had doubts. Maybe she just never loved me, Mom. She spent the whole summer after graduation trying to decide if she wanted to marry me. It almost didn't happen."

"You were wise to give her that time. I don't think many young men would have done that." She paused, but he kept silent. "Do *you* still love *her*?"

"It's not about that."

"It's not?"

"I just thought ... I don't know, Mom. I don't know what I thought."

"What has she said ... specifically, I mean?"

"She told me there's no hope left for us. She said I knew it too."

"Oh."

"She'll probably sell me her half of the business." He sighed. "She's unhappy, Mom. She's dissatisfied ... with everything. It's been that way for a while now."

"I know." Alice admitted her helplessness. "I'm sorry, Will."

A breakfast of Tuscan coffee and fresh fruit in the hotel solarium rebalanced Nancy's senses after a fitful night's sleep. Lingering for as long as possible in the glow of eastern sunlight, feeling heat against the windows, she contemplated the memory of a long-ago summer. Finally, it was time to go. She thanked her attentive waiter, Vittorio, exchanged smiles with an elderly German couple at the next table, and started out on her visit to Angelica's grave.

The avenue outside the hotel was busy with city-bound traffic. The tree-lined, cobble-stone sidewalk bustled with joggers, bikers and dog-fanciers. As she climbed the gentle slope, she was treated to an unobstructed view of the great city in the valley below. A thin, Apennine haze, which had rolled in overnight, glistened on the cityscape beneath the rising sun.

In minutes she reached Piazzale Michelangelo, an immense square cut into the hillside below San Miniato. Waves of tourists streamed from buses parked at the edge of the square. Armed with cameras, buzzing excitedly in a multitude of languages, the visitors thronged the square, below which the hillside fell steeply to the river and the city. Over the sounds of car engines and church bells, Nancy heard a thousand cameras click.

She pressed forward through rows of parked caravans—many still closed—several just opening for business. Within an hour, she knew, this spot would thrive as a flea-market for crafts, cheap jewelry and souvenirs. And also, as she remembered it, a little flower mart, where she hoped to find some red and yellow roses—Angelica's favorites.

"Hanno oggi fiori?" she asked a man just opening a caravan filled with leather goods.

"Fiori?" He paused to think. "Si, si." Taking her hand, he walked her down a row of caravans, stopped, and pointed. "Ci sono i fiori, signora!"

At the farthest corner of the square, there was a tiny caravan with its side propped up, exposing an abundance of colors to the sunlight.

"Li vedo," she confirmed. "Grazie."

He smiled warmly and started back toward his own caravan.

Nancy wove her way through the crowded square and approached the flower-seller, who leaned calmly against his vehicle.

"Buon giorno," she began. "Ho bisogno delle rose."

"Molto bene." He stepped toward his display.

"Un dozzina, forse. Avete il colore giallo e colore rosso?"

"Naturalmente. Sei e sei?"

"Perfetto, signore."

He pulled six yellow and six red roses from large plastic bins and placed them, dripping with water, on a small wooden table. Expertly, he cut an inch from the stems, then pulled a long sheet of purple wrapping paper from a roll and tore it off. He swaddled the roses, allowing their heads to peek from the top of the purple bunting.

She paid him 40 Euros. He handed the package to her as gently as if it were an infant. And with the bouquet cradled in the crook of her arm, she retraced her steps through the bustling square toward Viale Michelangelo. At the street crossing, she pressed the green button on a traffic-post. A red flasher briefly stopped the two-way traffic, allowing Nancy and several other pedestrians to cross on white hash marks.

The cobblestone walking path on the other side traced the curved base of an ancient stone wall covered in moss and overhanging ivy. Following the curve brought Nancy to a wide stone staircase that led from the street to the 12th century basilica, whose white-and-green marble façade shimmered in sunlight high above.

She started up. A few visitors walked behind her. Several others were coming back down. But, there was no crowd here like the great throng of tourists on the square. The first staircase ended at a terrace, which led to a narrower staircase beyond two stone columns. Finally, at the top of the second staircase, open to the sun, a wide stone piazza extended to the church front and to cemeteries on its north and south sides.

Recalling the private burial Angelica's husband had described in a letter after the fact, Nancy walked toward the north cemetery in search of the Antonini family vault.

When she stepped down into the terraced garden of gravestones and statues, Nancy quickly located the larger burial vaults in a wall overlooking the valley. Some appeared quite old and disheveled. Others were new and well-tended—like the one belonging to a famous film director.

At last she found the vault in which Angelica Rinaldi Antonini, from Providence, Rhode Island, lay sleeping for eternity. There were two stone vases attached to the granite face of the Antonini vault. One contained a bouquet of lilting daisies. The other was empty.

Nancy gently opened her bouquet and carefully placed the roses in the empty vase. She spent a few moments worrying over the arrangement, ensuring that the reds and yellows were blended. When she was satisfied, she stepped back, folding the purple paper in a flat square which she slipped into her pocketbook. Then she sat on a stone bench, staring directly into the face of the crypt, praying for her friend.

A drip of perspiration on her nose roused Nancy from contemplation, and she realized that 30 minutes had passed. The sun had risen higher. Her blouse was wet down the back. She stood and walked to the east end of the cemetery, not far from Angelica's grave but shaded by the great basilica. The melodic murmur of Benedictine monks in their service of Gregorian Chants echoed from inside the church.

As Nancy leaned against the cool granite of the church wall, a tall man holding the hand of a young girl, who was perhaps 11 or 12, stepped down into the cemetery garden and approached the Antonini vault. They walked closely, clearly father and daughter. In the girl's free hand was a small bouquet of white gardenias. The man was dressed in a dark brown business suit, the girl in a white blouse and blue skirt. A private school insignia was imprinted on the blouse above her heart.

They stopped at the bench where Nancy had been sitting moments earlier.

"Oh, papa!" said the girl. "Che belle rose!"

The man nodded.

"Giallo e rosso, papa!"

"Si, Marianna."

"Sono i colori preferiti di mama."

"Si." Stepping closer to the face of the vault, he leaned forward to smell the roses and touch them briefly.

"Che belle," the girl repeated.

The man's body stiffened. He turned his head left and right, as if looking for someone very particular. By the time he'd turned completely around, astonished to see Nancy standing in the shadow of the church, the alarmed expression on his handsome face was already softening. Nancy was crying.

Four

Will barely scanned the list of meetings prepared by his assistant, Jeanie Castro. Grateful for a few moments alone, he sipped his Starbuck's Italian Roast and gazed from his 12th floor office at Boston's Back Bay.

The brownstone he and Nancy owned was only a few blocks away on Beacon Street. Just to the south, a brilliant sunrise spilled into the green interior of Fenway Park, where the firm recently had secured a season's box near first base—choice seats for which they'd waited years. Now, he realized ruefully, he and Nancy would never use the seats—not together, anyway.

And in the greater distance, across the Charles River, were the universities, museums, and thoroughfares of Cambridge that reminded him of their first dates.

All that he could see comprised a map of his adult life. He took another sip of coffee and tried to comprehend the strangeness of this life without her.

After getting home on Sunday evening in a state of emotional denial, he'd kept himself distracted on Monday at home with client emails and neighborhood tasks—a trip to the dry cleaner's, shopping at Whole Foods—that almost made him feel as if nothing had changed.

But last night, the truth of being alone in their brownstone finally had been too much; he'd wept as their muted television flickered. Only his father's call to explain about these kids from Long Island, and to ask that he call his mother, had slowed the encroachments of grief.

And then his mother's voice when he'd reached her—lost, almost desolate, as if waiting for bad news—at the other end of their Midwest connection.

Will had tried not to burden her with the collapse of his marriage. But she'd broken through his defenses, and her own private sorrows, to embrace him in the calm assurance of her love. That's how she'd always been. That's who she was. And he was determined, now, to repay her, to do whatever was possible to protect *her* for a change— protect her reputation and beautiful novel from whatever might tarnish them.

It was unsurprising that his mother would stand immediately with the young, Muslim woman, whose case was a simple expression of personal freedom. In fact, the woman's forthrightness during an NPR interview last night had reminded him of his mother, and his father, when they were young.

But Janet Mohamed was unwise in the ways of America, Will sensed. She seemed shocked that her public statements would evoke unfriendliness from the news media or people in general. She didn't seem to know that the freedom, of which Americans incessantly spoke, was an abstraction. "Give me liberty or give me death," might be found in every 6th grade history text. But this country was an endless high school pep rally, whose motto was: "Be true to your school!" Yes, we were free, but not of each other.

Will thought that his parents' generation misunderstood this, just as the Mohamed woman did. Then again, merely contemplating the Woodstock children always made him feel uncomfortable— disoriented, by a sense of being older than his own parents. Once, he'd even mentioned this odd sensation to his mother.

She'd smiled warmly. "Each generation thinks it's wiser than the previous one."

"It isn't that, Mom. I just think *your* generation is naïve. All my friends do too."

"It's because you feel protective," she'd said. "You love us."

At the time, Will had thought of her observation as one more example of the need to declare everyone innocent of the world's cheapness. But in this moment of perspective on his own failures, he admitted there'd been some truth in what she'd said.

Sipping his coffee down to the bottom of a softening paper cup, he considered the evidence objectively.

His mother was being pilloried in the conservative press over helping Janet Mohamed, while the so-called liberal press abstractly editorialized about free speech. His father was clearly being hustled by two kids from a strange *new* generation, which honored almost no distinction between need and entitlement.

Yes, he thought, hearing several staff members coming in off the elevator, his parents did need protection. Maybe that *was* love.

Delia Radcliff knocked and entered the Dean of Students' office. Cathy Maldonado looked up from the newspapers on her desk as Delia closed the door and took a seat.

"This is unbelievable," Cathy said, glancing again at her papers. "It's outrageous."

"Thanks for coming." Cathy leaned back in her chair. "I'd like to agree on a joint recommendation, a position statement for the faculty board and Dick Emerson."

"I'm in favor of anything that supports Alice."

Cathy nodded. "You don't think she might have shown better judgment than to get so involved?"

"Involved?"

"With this young woman, obviously a radical," Cathy said.

"I'm confused. Are you blaming Alice?"

"There *is* a question of judgment. I'm concerned about the harm this does to our reputation. I'm thinking not only of our students, but also their parents and the alumni."

"Have you consulted a good PR firm?"

"No. I assume the press office is taking calls."

"You haven't even spoken to Phil Weintraub?" Delia asked, referring to the college public affairs officer.

Cathy shook her head. "Your idea about a PR firm ... that's good. We should make it part of our recommendation. Phil is a faculty board member, so he'll tell us what he thinks about the PR. He probably knows some good outside firms, if the board decides to hire one. But I mean *look* at this." Cathy indicated her newspaper sprawl. "What was Alice thinking?"

"I wouldn't draw conclusions from that nonsense." Delia then nodded at the FOX News announcer on Cathy's muted television. "Or *that*."

Cathy looked irritated. "You call it nonsense?"

"Much of the coverage has been simplistic, yes. Most of it is irresponsible ... confusing political views with good and evil." Delia paused and wondered what Cathy was up to now. "This Muslim woman might have a valid legal case and she might not. I don't know what sort of advice she's getting. Of course, she has every right

to take this stand as an American. But even that isn't the issue …
for me."

"What *is* the issue?"

"From what I understand, the girl was in physical danger at
that TV studio. Alice was there and thought she needed help …
protection, it sounds like. I might have done the same thing."

"I know you two are close. You're loyal to the person who hired
you. But I intend to bring this before the full board, Delia. I don't
take the blasé attitude that you and Alice seem to take … toward
homeland security."

"Janet Mohamed is a US citizen!" Delia sputtered. "She hasn't
set off a bomb. She's not a member of Al Qaeda. She declined to be
video-scanned, and they wouldn't let her on a flight. So, she took
it to court. If you ask me, yes, I think it's a bit extreme on her part,
but, I'm not a highly religious person. Perhaps I don't understand
her sense of modesty. Perhaps the scanning itself is a bit extreme. I
don't know. But she's made no threats, or done anything illegal. She's
within her rights."

"There are rights. And then there's judgment. What if everybody
acted this way at airports?"

"Some people have. Janet Mohamed isn't the first and won't be
the last. This level of security is new to most Americans. It's going
to take time for us to get used to it. The worst thing we can do is
overreact."

"No!" The depth of Cathy's anger now revealed itself. "This
Muslim girl is engaged in some sort of political activism."

"It's a legal matter, Cathy. It's going to the Supreme Court."

"The girl thinks she's above the rules. And Alice has become
associated with her. That's up to Alice, but she's out there representing
Shelby College. You *know* our reputation will suffer from this."

"Not with anyone whose opinion matters. Have you read some
of the letters coming in to those newspapers? They're threatening
Alice, now."

"What happened on 9/11 changed everything. For some people
more than others, I guess."

This again, Delia thought, holding her tongue in the face of Cathy's attempt to exert private ownership of a national tragedy and—for the second time in less than a week—cause trouble for Alice.

"I guess I'm not surprised," Cathy added, confirming some ongoing animus. "After that insensitive remark Alice made Friday night. She doesn't get it."

Delia felt her own anger rising. She'd seen displays of arbitrary vengeance before—had been its victim once or twice—but this stunned her. Finally, she spoke. "Who do you think you are?"

Cathy paused, as if carefully choosing her words. "I was hoping for support. Alice works for you, now, and I owed you the courtesy of this consultation. But I will raise the issue of her professional judgment. I would have thought that you, of all people, would want to distance yourself from unprofessional behavior."

This stung Delia. A shock of fear ran through her body.

"Our nation is under assault." Cathy struck her desktop with the tips of three outstretched fingers. "The age of ambiguity is over."

"This is monstrous."

"I'd be careful if I were you." Cathy glared. "There's already enough concern about the manner of your hiring."

Delia stood abruptly. "I beg your pardon."

"You know what I'm talking about, Delia. Reputation is everything in our profession."

"You and I are *not* in the same profession. I don't understand your animosity toward Alice, or me, for that matter. If it's about my being made department chair over John Woodward ..."

"Don't be ridiculous." Cathy scoffed.

"You didn't support *my* candidacy."

"It's water under the bridge."

"Fine; are we done?"

"I take it you're not with me."

"I don't like the sound of it, no. I suggest *you* be careful."

"Is that a threat?"

"It's advice. You're inviting a labor lawsuit. If you care about the school's reputation, don't associate us with a witch hunt."

"Thank you, Delia, for being direct." Cathy stood now. "I like directness. I'm not a big fan of this relativist, literary mode of thought that so many of our colleagues engage in … always trying to see a little good and a little bad in everything. That's the problem today. People can't tell the difference between right and wrong anymore."

Delia left without bothering to close the dean's door.

Back at her own office, agitated, Delia sat at her desk and riffled through her rolodex for Alice's phone numbers. It was still a little early to call her. She tried to think, to control the welling anger in her heart.

Soon enough, she understood what needed to be done.

Moments like this came infrequently in a person's lifetime, and they were disturbing. But they often came with an uncommon clarity as well. She knew this. Swiveling her chair, turning on her computer, Delia began typing a letter to Dick Emerson.

Will heard Jeanie Castro arrive at her desk.

Moments later, she leaned into his office. "Did you see the meeting list?"

"Yes, thanks!" He spun his chair. "How was your weekend?"

"Busy." She offered the harried smile of a single mother. "I helped Lina with her social studies project. Then we did a little shopping. Her class is going to New York next Saturday to see a Broadway show." She paused. "You have no idea what it's like, buying clothes for a fourth-grade girl."

"Well, I …"

"Take my word for it."

He laughed. "Okay."

"Let me know if you have questions about the meetings." She started back toward her desk.

"Jeanie, wait! Could you come in for a sec?" He stood and took two tentative steps toward her. "Close the door?"

She did so with a bemused expression.

As he stepped back and leaned against the edge of his desk, she sat in one of the large comfortable chairs nearby and watched him nervously. Oh no, he thought, she's expecting criticism—or worse—when, in fact, he and Nancy had been planning to promote her.

He spoke calmly to dispel her anxiety. "Jeanie, you know how valuable you are to us."

Her face softened in a half-smile.

He confided his plan to drive to his parents' home in Connecticut after the morning meetings. He explained why he was concerned about his mother, in particular, but shared enough about his father's situation to convey the idea of a family problem.

"You can reach me by cell," he told her. "My parents' numbers are in the rolodex."

"How long will you be there?"

"I'm guessing a day or two, but we'll have to see."

"Nancy too?"

"Nancy didn't come home with me."

"Where is she?"

"If I had to guess, I'd say Florence."

Jeanie nodded quizzically.

"Things haven't been right between us."

"I know."

"It's been that obvious?"

"Everybody's been worried about you two. You haven't seemed happy." Jeanie frowned with embarrassment. "I'm sorry. I shouldn't have said that."

"No, you're right. We haven't been."

Jeanie pressed her lips together and stared at him gravely.

"Last week, in London, we finally admitted it to ourselves."

"I'm sorry, Will."

"Things just … change sometimes." He remembered the day seven years earlier when he and Nancy had hired Jeanie, a 22-year-old girl at the time, with a three-year-old daughter, and a two-year degree from Roxbury Community College. "And sometimes you wish they *would* change, but they don't."

"Yes." Her voice, like her face, expressed compassionate recognition.

"Nancy may leave PR entirely. If she does, I'll buy her share of the business."

"What does she want to do?"

"She's always been interested in books and publishing … the arts." Will shrugged. "I'm not sure."

Jeanie said nothing.

"Would you keep this between us for now? I don't want to worry anyone about the future of the firm."

"Of course."

"We have a good roster of clients. I'm determined to keep growing this practice. With people like you working for us, we'll be fine."

"I'm sorry, Will. I'm so sorry."

He smiled at her warmly. "It's all right." He could still see uncertainty in her body language, as if she didn't know whether to stay or get up and emphatically end this personal, somewhat embarrassing moment with her employer. Abruptly, he changed the subject. "How's it going at Tufts?"

"Hardest thing I've ever done," she confessed. "It's a great MBA program. I'm so glad you and Nancy urged me to go. You've been so generous with tuition."

"You mean a lot to the firm, Jeanie. When I get back from Connecticut, I'd like to discuss some other changes."

"*Oh?*"

"Moving you over to account management. We could do it gradually, maybe have you work with Rick and Cindy's team for a few months. But you know all our clients, and they love you. You've been with us in almost every pitch meeting. You know our fee structure. You know all the Boston media."

Jeannie was shocked as Will continued.

"You have a real flair for public relations. Underneath all the razzmatazz, it's a people business. You're great with people."

"Thank you, Will."

"We'll have to hire someone to replace you. I'm sure you can help us find the right person. But … does this sound like something you'd be interested in?"

"I don't know what to say."

"You don't need to say anything. Just think about it."

She looked at him for several moments and then stood, reaching out her right hand. "Thank you, for your faith in me," she said emphatically.

As he took her hand, she responded with a firm grip.

For a moment, he felt the presence of something odd in the atmosphere between them, something not quite personal, not quite professional. It was there, just beyond the reach of his ability define, something more than the obvious confidence with which she now looked at him, a moment's clarity without a name.

"You better go," she said softly, her dark eyes glistening with intensity. "You'll be late for your first meeting."

Delia stared at her computer screen and reviewed a one-paragraph letter informing Dick Emerson of her decision to resign. An earlier draft had thanked him for his support during her tenure as department chair. She'd also deleted a line about missing her Shelby students, and another expressing gratitude for Alice Winslow's faith in her.

As she knew, it was best to be brief when saying goodbye.

"I just heard." Peg Harvey slipped inside Delia's office. "Cathy Maldonado's gone nuts about this Janet Mohamed."

"Yes." Delia saved her document before looking up. "She has."

"There's an emergency board meeting this afternoon."

"That soon?" Delia gasped. "How did *you* hear?"

"Phil Weintraub just called me. He says you wouldn't be meeting unless Maldonado already had the votes to censure Alice."

"The real problem is Dick Emerson. He won't stand up to Cathy. That makes it hard for the other board members." Delia paused to think. "Have you spoken to Alice?"

"I've left messages on her cell and her home phone." Peg glanced at her watch.

"Go to your first class," Delia said. "I'll try to reach her."

When Peg was gone, Delia re-opened her document and started printing copies. As the little machine hummed, she noticed Alice's book on her shelf. But she quickly looked away, unsettled by the question its presence evoked: what would *Alice* do if their roles were reversed? Find the truth, she might say. But, what was the truth? More precisely, which truth was right?

For Delia, the harshest truth was that a single whisper now about her youthful mistake—the plagiarism—would end not just her career at Shelby, but a life's profession. Surely, Alice didn't want that, especially if nothing she might do or say on Alice's behalf had the slightest chance of changing other board members' terrified votes for censure—votes for their own careers, in effect. That something this monstrous could take root and grow so quickly here meant that Delia had to leave.

The printer-cycle finished. In the silence, she glanced again at *The Chastened Heart*. But now, something forced her to her feet, pulled her toward the shelf where the book lay in the glow of reproachful sunlight.

As she opened the novel to a random page, she was amazed to find a passage in which the female protagonist contemplates her mother.

Back east after the failed attempt to reinvent herself, she felt chilled by her birthplace, frozen once more in the silence of her mother's house. But life had proceeded, in its strange way, through ironic reversal. She had returned to a mother whose onset of dementia now made her a kind of child—an almost-innocent—who'd fallen in a well so deep her cries could not be heard. Still, the memory of having been this bitter woman's daughter remained clear. The seed of unkindness had taken root in her heart. She, too, had grown cold, silent and unforgiving.

Delia closed the book and looked up at her sunlit office window recalling a brilliant Saturday, years ago, in Morningside Heights.

She was up early in her small, college-subsidized apartment on West 114th Street. Though she couldn't see the river from its single window, she knew the sun would be lighting spring foliage in Riverside Park, and warming the palisades on the other side.

Struggling for something new to say in her masters' thesis on Transcendentalist literature, she gazed at the uninspired prose on her dull, grey computer screen.

Someone knocked at the door. Surprised, a bit annoyed, she pulled her bathrobe tight and peered out through the security peephole. An old woman stood in the hallway.

"Yes?"

"Delia?" the woman said. "Delia Radcliff?"

"Yes. What is it?"

"It's about your mother."

"I don't have a mother."

"We all have a mother, child."

"Well, *my* mother doesn't have a daughter. Ask her yourself."

"You can't ask her anything. She's had a stroke."

A storm of conflict ripped through Delia's heart.

"That's why I'm here," the woman added.

Delia undid the police lock and opened the door.

"Don't you recognize me?" the woman asked with a nervous smile.

"Mrs. Washington," Delia said, looking into the now recognizable face of her mother's oldest friend from their neighborhood 18 blocks north. "Come in."

"Thank you." Mrs. Washington stepped into the cramped apartment and looked around at its studious dishevelment—books and papers stacked on tables, chairs, the window sill and floors.

"Please sit." Delia removed a pile of library books from the old wingback she'd bought for $10 at a street fair on Amsterdam. "Would you like some tea?"

"That would be nice." Mrs. Washington eased her considerable weight into the musty cushions.

The women exchanged a few pleasantries as tea was made. Then, Delia carried two cups from the stove and handed one to her guest. She pulled the upright chair from behind her desk and sat facing Mrs. Washington.

"All right," she said to her visitor. "When did this happen?"

"It's been almost two weeks. Your mother was alone in her apartment. I heard a strange noise and came right across the hall. She didn't answer when I called out. So I got the super to let us in, and we found her on the living room floor. We took her to Columbia Presbyterian. They thought she wouldn't make it. The stroke was pretty severe. But she hung on. And now, it seems, her constitution has responded ..."

"What does that mean?"

Mrs. Washington sighed. "The chief neurologist calls it a stalemate. Her brain is damaged permanently, but the rest of her has leveled out. She's on a ventilator, of course, but her other vital signs are strong."

"She's not dead and not really alive." Delia sipped from her mug. "It isn't much of a change."

"That's cold."

Delia sipped more tea. "Do you know why I haven't been to see her in six years?"

"I don't think your mother was happy with the way you left."

"She *sent* me away," Delia snapped. "She was honest about that much, I hope."

Mrs. Washington stared at Delia but said nothing.

"I was a 17-year-old girl, not even out of high school."

Mrs. Washington nodded gravely. "Yes."

"I appreciate that you've come. But, it doesn't really concern me at this point."

"It took four days to track you down through the university. Don't pain your heart with resentment."

"You make it sound like a silly quarrel. That woman disowned me ... kicked me out of her house. I'm thinking now about the last thing she said ... the last words I'll ever hear from her, apparently. Do you know what it's like being called a 'whore' by your own mother, Mrs. Washington?"

The older woman looked away, stung by what Delia had said.

"No," Delia whispered. "I don't suppose you do."

Mrs. Washington struggled to her feet. "I'm sorry, child."

"What did you want from me?"

"I had no idea how deep the hurt was."

Delia stared at her guest, who was uncomfortable yet clearly reluctant to leave.

"Your mother can't stay at the hospital indefinitely," the older woman said. "She could go to a special-care facility, which would be expensive. Or be taken home and cared for with a visiting nurse and the right equipment … also very expensive, but the Medicare would cover most of it."

"You've checked all this out," Delia muttered in disbelief.

"Or … another decision would have to be made."

"Oh. I see."

Mrs. Washington nodded. "A decision like the one you had to make at 17."

Delia sighed angrily. "And you think it's *my* decision?"

"Your grandmother died three years ago."

"I'm aware of that."

"No one knows how to reach your Aunt Winnie."

Delia swallowed the last of her tea, feeling the ironic weight of her mother's life pressing down on hers.

"There *is* no one else."

"Please." Delia extended her open hand. "Will you stay?"

Within 10 days, Delia had moved back home to care for her now permanently silent mother. Mrs. Washington brought food nearly every day. When Delia went to class, or visited the library, the older woman came across the hall to watch things for her.

One Saturday near the end of Delia's term, Mrs. Washington urged her to spend a little time by herself. And so, while her generous neighbor once again sat vigil in her mother's apartment, Delia took the Hudson Line north to Poughkeepsie. She did some shopping, had a quiet lunch, and spent the afternoon browsing an estate tag-sale.

It was there that she found the obscure diary of an English priest who'd known Nathaniel Hawthorne in Florence in 1858.

According to the diary, Hawthorne had confided to the priest that his willful character, Hester Prynne, had been suggested by his brief flirtation with the outspoken and progressive Elizabeth Peabody, and not based—as modern scholars assumed—on her compliant younger sister, Sophia, whom he subsequently married. Hawthorne also confessed that the character of Reverend Arthur Dimmesdale—repressed, ashamed and silent—had been a literary rebuke to himself for having retreated from Elizabeth's forthright overtures during his first visits to the Peabody household.

Privately printed in 1865, by a defunct Florentine publisher, the priest's diary astonished Delia. She bought it for $20, read half of it on the train-ride home, and the rest that evening.

Over the following days, she found no mention of this book in the permanent Hawthorne collections at Bowdoin College, at Salem's Peabody-Essex Museum, or her own university.

At first, Delia planned only to incorporate its contents—cited and footnoted—into her masters' thesis, for which she'd received a three-week extension on compassionate grounds. But as she began the final push against deadline, she decided not to mention the diary at all. Rather, to offer the priest's insight and elegant writing as her own literary speculations, supporting them with enough original research to hide her theft.

Hearing voices now, Delia watched several Shelby students hurry past her office window late to their first period classes. She envied these young people their optimism and relative innocence—how touchingly unaware they seemed of a moment's doubt that would come and break their hearts.

Her own broken-hearted moment had been the un-sourced use of the diary. It was a sin to which she'd succumbed in anger, self-pity and duress, but also, as she knew, with a sense of entitlement—to something that would make an ordinary master's thesis a work of art. Unfortunately, she now recalled, her moral lapse had been detected by one of her English professors, who owned another copy of the diary.

The phone rang. She hesitated. Angry at herself, she turned to her desk and picked up.

"Delia Radcliff."

"It is so good to hear your voice."

"Alice!" Delia collapsed in her chair. "I was about to call you."

"What's the reaction to this news coverage?" Alice's voice sounded sweetly innocent. "Do I still have a job?"

"Oh, Alice," Delia said, shaken by her daughterly love for this generous woman.

Shaken, too, by her shame, Delia reached across the desk and turned the printed copies of her letter facedown.

Gabriele Antonini ushered Nancy into his family's shop on Piazza della Signoria. As she knew, the Antoninis were renowned makers of fine paper. They had a charming design studio attached to a small factory in the northern suburbs of Florence and retail shops throughout Italy. A much larger factory in Milan served their stores in a dozen international cities.

Two fashionably-dressed young women, reviewing receipts at the sales counter, glanced curiously at Nancy.

"Ciao!" said Gabriele. "May I introduce Mrs. Nancy Winslow?"

"Signora," the women said.

"Mrs. Winslow is a friend from America."

The women smiled. Nancy guessed their ages at roughly 30.

"This is Paola," Gabriele said, indicating a woman with rich, dark hair, cut to flatter her calm, Tuscan face. "And this is Daniela," he added, referring to her blonde co-worker, also pretty, but more cautious in expression.

"What brings you to Florence?" asked Paola.

"I love your city. I came mainly to pay my respects at San Miniato."

The women stopped smiling.

"Angelica was my closest college friend."

"I met them one day at Uffizi." Gabriele beamed. "It was their graduation summer."

"*You* were there to see an exhibit of Renaissance books," Nancy recalled.

Gabriele turned to his employees. "They were like twins, those two." He laughed. "And I was speechless … muto impressionante!"

Paola and Daniela giggled.

"Yes, it's hard to imagine." Gabriele's laughter was deep and self-deprecating.

Daniela spoke softly. "They could be sisters."

"Sì." Paola agreed.

"No one was more beautiful than Angelica," Nancy whispered.

After a silent moment, the young women looked down at their receipts.

Gabriele spoke formally again. "Has my sister arrived?"

"È nel suo ufficio," Paola replied.

"Will you excuse me?" He touched Nancy's hand. "I must speak to my sister before lunch."

"Ask her to join us," she suggested, as he hurried away.

"Your blouse is lovely," Paola said. "It is not really white."

"No." Nancy glanced at herself. "I suppose it's … pearl?"

Paola nodded. "Where did you find it?"

"In New York, at Bergdorf, I think."

Paola glanced at Daniela. "Stunning, no?"

"It's *you* two who are stunning."

Paola smiled politely. "You are kind, signora."

As the young women resumed work on their receipts, Nancy examined a writing-paper display near the front window. Sample boxes were open, revealing sheaves of Antonini stationery with its watermarked *A*. Each variety of paper was thinly bordered in peach, yellow or blue. Matching envelopes were similarly colored along their rear flaps and seams.

Swaths of decorative wrapping paper were arranged against both walls. A designer wallpaper display could be seen in another room of equal size behind the sales counter.

Having started in the mid-1700s as a printing and bookbinding enterprise, Antonini published European editions of works by Byron, Shelley, Elizabeth Browning, Hawthorne, Dickens and Henry James. The firm also supplied these writers with personal notebooks and stationery. Nancy remembered seeing signed copies of special books—elegantly-crafted, private editions—which these authors had commissioned from Antonini and presented as gifts to their friends.

By the early decades of the 20th century the Antoninis' business had changed, and only the occasional book was being published. The last notable example was their work for D.H. Lawrence and his wife, who'd visited the design studio one day in 1928 with a manuscript of *Lady Chatterley's Lover.* Lawrence had written his story while living near Florence, but his New York and London publishers had demanded drastic cuts. So, he commissioned Antonini to print a first, limited edition of the unedited work.

Several customers entered the store.

Nancy glanced around, already worried that it had been a mistake getting into the car with Gabriele and his daughter at San Miniato. He'd been solicitous when they'd embraced at the cemetery, and Nancy had briefly forgotten everything—even his failure to invite her to Angelica's funeral.

All the way down the hillside, sitting in back, Nancy had answered questions about her life, and had listened to Gabriele's commentary on the city's endless maintenance and restoration. But Nancy had paid increasing attention to Marianna, who seemed so like her mother, barely able contain her youthful curiosity. Each time the girl had turned to look at her, with deep, dark eyes, Nancy had felt Angelica in the car.

When they'd reached Marianna's school, which was part of an ancient church in the Altr'Arno, the girl had embraced Nancy.

"I feel my mother in you," she'd whispered, before taking her father's hand and walking with him to the steps of the school.

Daniela approached with a white, demitasse cup on a wafer-thin saucer. "Coffee, signora?"

"Thank you."

"Prego," Daniela said in the gracious, Florentine manner that Nancy loved.

The two women stood near the front window watching the busy square. It was late morning. More customers arrived.

Daniela spoke softly. "You met Marianna today?"

"Yes. We took her to school."

"She is a special girl."

"I can see that."

"She misses her mother."

Nancy nodded and sipped coffee. "She *is* her mother."

"Gabriele is a good father. But he is wounded. Sometimes, we worry for him. This morning, when you came in, we were shocked."

"Why shocked?"

"It was a vision. For an instant, we saw Angelica with her husband. And her husband was happy."

"Has it been terrible?"

"The girl is heartbroken. But she is young and full of love. She will survive her memories and become a woman, a beauty. Her life will embrace her. But the memories are difficult for Gabriele. He blames himself."

"For what?"

Daniela paused before responding. "I know you are friends, signora. The man you see before you is a broken shell." She paused again. "You remind him. You remind us all … of her. Be careful, signora."

"I understand," Nancy assured her.

Daniela leaned forward and kissed Nancy on her left cheek. "Grazie," she whispered, before hurrying back to the counter.

Moments later, Gabriele emerged from the office at the rear of the store accompanied by his older sister who wore a conservative, navy blue suit.

As Nancy remembered, Violetta Antonini had worked hard to gain a foothold in the family business. Their father had involved both of his children in company matters, but had chosen Gabriele to succeed him. Nevertheless, Gabriele had continued his father's practice of seeking Violetta's opinion on key decisions. And when their father died, Gabriele had asked her to run the company with him formally.

Her regard for her brother was deep and enduring, yet, Violetta Antonini was neither loving nor generous in her professional demeanor. The struggle to be taken seriously had left an injury, Nancy thought. Never marrying, she'd cultivated a reputation for hard work and chilly reserve.

"Ciao, Nancy."

The women held hands and traded kisses on both cheeks.

"It's good to see you, Violetta."

"Gabriele tells me you've built a fine business with your husband." Violetta's warm smile took Nancy by surprise. "We must talk. How long are you in Florence?"

"It's indefinite." Nancy glanced at Gabriele.

"We really *must* talk."

"Can you join us for lunch?"

"Alas, no. I am showing our factory to investment bankers. They're here only briefly … from Japan."

Nancy was curious, but Gabriele and Violetta shared nothing more about their Asian visitors. Were they considering a public offering, she wondered, or an outright sale?

Violetta checked her watch and kissed her brother's cheek. "Dovrei andare."

"Call me," he urged.

"I look forward to our chat, Nancy." Violetta smiled again. "Enjoy your lunch."

It was a five-minute walk to Cathy Maldonado's office. On the way, Delia felt her gut tighten as she recalled Alice's startling advice.

"Be careful," she'd suggested, once Delia had explained what would happen at the board meeting. "You have a long career ahead of you."

When they'd hung up, Delia had put the copies of her resignation letter through a small paper shredder in her office. Rarely used, except for outdated budget presentations and personnel reviews, the little machine had seemed to offer a clean resolution to a sickening doubt.

She'd then opened her original computer document, made several quick adjustments, and printed out one new copy, which she'd placed into a manila folder. Finally, she'd called Maldonado and asked for another meeting.

The administration building was busy, now, as Delia hurried along the main hallway toward the Dean of Students' office.

Once inside with the door closed and the manila folder in her lap, Delia collected herself and spoke firmly. "I understand we're meeting this afternoon to vote on censure."

"That's correct." Cathy sounded impatient.

"Has there been any thought of letting Alice address the board? I mean *before* we vote?"

Cathy stared intently at Delia and appeared to contemplate the question.

"I'm thinking of due process," Delia explained. "How will the college community react to a resolution that some might see as untenable ... legally, I mean?"

Cathy nodded.

"It would mean a brief delay," Delia added. "Alice could be here in a day or two."

"You've spoken with her?"

"Yes."

"*She* suggested this?"

"She did."

Cathy smiled sarcastically. "And you agreed to raise it."

"I told her I would mention it."

"I have the votes now, Delia. The board is ready to censure."

"I understand."

"So, where are *you* in this?"

"I think the vote will seem more credible *after* Alice has an opportunity to explain herself."

"That's not what I meant."

"Yes, I know."

"Well?"

"I'd like to propose a delay at this afternoon's meeting. If you support my proposal, and the board agrees to give Alice a chance to speak, then, I'll give *you* what you want."

"I already have what I want."

"You have a meeting. You might have a majority supporting your resolution ..."

"Are you saying you'll promise me your vote?"

"No. But if you're right in thinking you already have the votes, you don't need mine."

"Then what are you saying?"

"That I won't vote *against* you … I'll recuse myself."

"It isn't very compelling, Delia."

"And I'll give you this." Delia stood and dropped the manila folder on the dean's desk.

Cathy opened the folder and briefly scanned the draft letter. She looked up abruptly. "You're resigning?"

"I couldn't work here after this."

"You're very foolish." Cathy closed the folder and leaned back in her chair.

Delia pointed to the manila envelope. "As it says, I'll make the strongest possible recommendation for John Woodward to replace me. He's got two years more experience now. And he'd make an excellent department head. You always wanted John in that position."

Cathy appeared to consider Delia's offer. She pointed to the folder. "It occurs to me that this offer requires a particular silence on my part. You propose enlisting me in protecting your reputation." She tapped the folder. "Otherwise, this letter is virtually meaningless and certainly worthless."

"I'm offering you the only thing of value I have at this moment. As for the future, I'll be out of your way … permanently."

Cathy leaned back again and stared at Delia. "And you won't vote against censure?"

"That's right," Delia whispered.

Cathy briefly opened the manila envelope and re-checked the letter before looking up with a cold stare.

"I'll support a delay under one further condition. If enough board members start changing their minds, or if Alice manages to sway a few when she gets back here … and it appears the final tally will be close, I reserve the right to demand your vote. And I will expect that vote to be in favor of censure."

Delia felt the nauseating rush of fear again. Cathy had gone directly to the weakest part of her offer.

"Fine," Delia said, hoping such a need would never arise. The most important thing, at this moment, was to give Alice a chance to speak on her own behalf.

"How do I know you'll keep this promise?"

"It's one thing to be a young doctoral candidate with a blemish on her CV," Delia said. "It's quite another to be a disgraced scholar and former department chair."

"We understand each other then."

When Delia had left, Cathy noticed the silhouette lengthening over the newspapers on her desk, the effect of sunlight against latticework in south-facing windows. This play of light and shadow, an almost daily occurrence, had come to represent a particular memory for Cathy—the perversely brilliant morning of 9/11.

On that morning, half-blinded by window glare, she'd sat at her desk trying to make sense of the burning tower on television. Recalling stories of the B-25 bomber that had clipped the Empire State Building in 1945, and the Park Slope airliner crash of 1960, she assumed at first this was a similar event. Her concern was for her brother-in-law, Daniel, whose banking firm kept offices in one of the towers.

But as she tried frantically to remember which tower, a second plane appeared, obviating her hopeful distinctions and historical comparisons.

Even then, Cathy didn't call her sister. Instead, sensing that Daniel was already gone, she sought refuge in childlike thoughts, convincing herself that uncertainty might keep him alive. Eventually, Laura called her. She sounded deranged.

"I can't reach Dan!"

Cathy tried to be calm. "Have you left a message?"

"There *is* no voicemail!" Laura screamed. "There's no connection, no ringing at the other end … *nothing*. Not his office phone, his cell, or the company switchboard. Cathy, it's all *dead*. I don't know what to do!"

Laura never did hear from Daniel. Nothing of him was found to bury. Nothing had been left to her, not even one of those agitated calls or voice messages so many other survivors had received. Laura had been denied even the sound of her dead husband's living voice in his last moments on earth.

In the long, sad aftermath of that day, Laura learned that her husband's floor—indeed his office itself—had been the point of impact for the first plane. No one could be sure, but it was possible that Dan never knew what had happened, that because of the way he sat at his desk with the windows behind him, a telephone headset on his ears as he spoke to clients, death had arrived without warning.

For Cathy, the truth of what she'd sensed that morning still lived—in the latticed silhouette from her windows, in the memory of her sister's shrieking phone call, in her own premonition of Daniel's death. Now, almost six years later, these memories had darkened into fears for America's future. That the country now seemed to have made its peace with that day—that even Laura had tried to move on—only heightened the urgency of Cathy's newest premonitions.

Picking up her desk phone, she keyed-in Dick Emerson's extension and waited.

"Office of the President," said Emerson's secretary.

"Hi, Dorothy, it's Cathy Maldonado. Is he in?"

"He's finishing a meeting, now, Dean Maldonado. And he's rushing out for another meeting before lunch …"

"It's about the hearing, which I've just agreed to postpone for a couple of days."

"I see. Well … he's already so late."

"He doesn't have five minutes for *me*?"

"Let me speak to him … can you hold?"

As she waited, Cathy glanced at her muted television, next to which was the framed photograph of her son, Frank, taken at school when he was 13—almost 20 years ago—just before his leukemia diagnosis. Though it was her favorite photo of the boy, it reminded her of an odd sense of loss she'd felt the day he'd brought it home from school. Frankie had already started complaining about fatigue and increasingly frequent nosebleeds. Cathy and her former husband had consulted a GP who'd recommended tests conducted by specialists.

All the doctors had been calm and procedural, their collective demeanor a flawless expression of reassurance—at first.

"Dean Maldonado?" said Emerson's secretary. "He says come right over."

"I'll be there in a minute."

Cathy hung up. After placing the manila folder with Delia's letter into her drawer, she gathered her newspapers and started to leave. Pausing only to look briefly again at Frankie's beautiful, unsuspecting smile, she opened her door and hurried to the President's office.

Built into the corner of a 14th century palazzo, which had been the meeting hall of Florence's magistrates and notaries guild, Sotto Gli Archi rested on an older, Roman foundation. But renovations for this new restaurant had uncovered the unexpected—artistically significant, Renaissance frescos lost to history.

"*Arte profana,*" Gabriele explained, guiding Nancy through the massive front door of oak and iron. "They are secular frescos of Florentine heroes … the soldiers and poets … *not* the bishops and priests."

Nancy observed the pleasant but discernibly post-modern décor of the entrance hall and main dining area just beyond. She saw brown wood and decorative metal. The bench seating in the hallway, as well as the dining-room chairs, were upholstered in grey gabardine. A bit of stone-and-mortar foundation wall lay exposed, the only hint of anything extraordinary.

"Signore Antonini!" The hostess was an elegant young woman with flowing blonde hair and a dark, tailored suit. "Ché piacere!"

"Il piacere é il nostro." Gabriele kissed the woman on both cheeks. "This is my friend Nancy."

"Signora." The hostess smiled graciously and led them to the compact dining area.

Now, Nancy was astonished.

Rising above them was a domed ceiling, supported by four mortared arches, with frescos painted in the dome, on the arches, and along the upper walls. A wooden staircase led from the dining area to a narrow balcony that tracked along each wall. There were tables set on both sides of this balcony, just beneath the dome, where the frescos would be close enough to touch. Several small sections of the paintings seemed to have been lost in the refurbishment. And their colors were slightly faded. But these flaws seemed to heighten the sense of dramatic revelation.

Reminding Gabriele to take his guest upstairs for a closer look after lunch, and to visit the Roman catacomb below, the hostess offered them a cozy corner table from which Nancy enjoyed an unobstructed view of the painted ceiling.

"This is stunning," Nancy whispered.

"Look there." Gabriele pointed upward. "You can see the earliest known portrait of Dante. It is considered the accurate resemblance of his face ... il vero volto. And just behind Dante, you have Petrarch and Boccaccio."

"What a marvelous discovery."

As Gabriele checked the wine list, Nancy listened to the jazz playing on the sound system. Moments earlier, she'd heard Nat Cole's version of *Stardust*. Now, Chet Baker was singing *So che ti perderò*.

When they'd ordered lunch and some wine, Nancy glanced at three other occupied tables before leaning forward to whisper. "She never forgave me."

"Ah, Chiara." In a voice tinged with sadness, Gabriele used the Italian form of her middle name as he'd done 15 summers ago.

"I don't blame her," Nancy added. "It *was* unforgivable."

"No, no. Do not speak in this manner."

"Had she been ill for long? The few letters we'd exchanged mentioned nothing."

Gabriele stared at Nancy for a moment, before looking off into a private distance.

Nancy pressed him. "I hope she didn't suffer much."

He began to weep. Nancy touched his forearm as he removed a white, silk handkerchief from his breast pocket and pressed it hard against his eyes.

"I'm sorry, Gabriele."

Regaining his composure, he rearranged the handkerchief in his pocket.

"I only wish you'd asked me to the funeral."

"I did think of you. But the service had to be quick. There was an issue of proper burial, even in my family's crypt. Questions were raised. Because of the church, you see."

"I don't see. What do you mean?"

He stared at her until she began to understand.

"Are you serious?"

He nodded.

"How? Oh, I'm sorry. I don't mean … I don't want you to answer that." She touched his arm again. "My God, you must be devastated."

"It is hard, Chiara. It will be difficult always."

"What about Marianna?"

Distracted by another Chet Baker song, Gabriele took a moment before answering.

"Angelica often played this lullaby for Marianna. She would sing the child to sleep with this record."

Nancy shuddered as she listened to the Italian words of the Baker lullaby—an absent father whispering to his son, whom he imagines sleeping, promising to be there when he awakens. "Oh."

"At first, the poor child did not understand her mother's death." The sadness of Gabriele's voice was now edged in anger. "She expected her mother to return. For three years, she has waited. Of course, she's older now. Still, she misses Angelica. Just today when we left her at school, she said to me, 'I think it is too difficult for mama to come back. That is why she sent Nancy to see us, papa.'"

Nancy slowly shook her head. "Gabriele …" Tears formed in her eyes.

"'She has kept her promise,'" my daughter said to me."

When they were finished with lunch, the restaurant's female chef came to their table and chatted for several minutes. Dressed in her kitchen-smudged whites, and a blue, silk bandana on her head, she looked the part of an artist, who might be as familiar with wall paintings as with a brilliant menu.

After a tour upstairs, guided by the chef, Gabriele took Nancy down to see the basement catacomb and foundation walls. But here, six tables formally set, thankfully unoccupied, struck Nancy as discomforting. This had been, in an ancient era, a place of burial after all.

Slowly skirting the empty tables, staying close to the wall, their hands brushed together. Abruptly, she gripped his hand and held it in friendship. A moment later, he turned, looked in her eyes and kissed her on the lips. Briefly she kissed him back, responding from memory. Then, she pulled away.

"I'm not Angelica." Her harsh rebuff changed his expression from concentration to disappointment. "And I'm not Chiara. I'm not even the Nancy you knew. I'm a married woman of 37, planning to leave my husband, still in love with him in some way I can't understand … a joyless love."

"And I am not Gabriele. The romantic boy you knew is gone. The world does not make us happy, Chiara mia. It challenges us to be happy in spite of itself. It forces us to find happiness with those entrusted to us. If we do not, or cannot, we lose our way … as our poor Angelica did."

"We betrayed her," she reminded him. "What good ever comes of betraying a friend?"

"I tried to love her as she needed." Gabriele paused. "It wasn't enough."

"I do understand *that*."

Gabriele sighed. "My daughter is right. It is a miracle that you came to us."

"I had no intention of meeting you."

"Still, you are here."

Nancy smiled. "I've never been one for magical thinking."

"No."

"I came to Florence for a brief visit … out of respect for my friend."

"*Our* friend."

"Yes." Now, she pulled a chair out at the nearest table and sat down. "What exactly are you proposing?"

"That you stay with us a while. Allow my daughter to know you."

"I would like to know *her*. But I'm not sure how long I should stay. Can we take it a day at a time?"

"Is there another way to live?" He shrugged philosophically as he glanced around at the ancient catacombs. "When we are young, we feel entitled to the world. But we learn the truth about ourselves. Then, it is harder to feel deserving of anything, even a bit of happiness."

"You're right about one thing," she replied. "We're no longer young."

"Una benedizione," he said with a rueful laugh. "A blessing."

Will took the Mass Pike to Route 84 and proceeded into Connecticut. When he reached Hartford he headed west on local roads, which brought him into Leicester County. Late-afternoon traffic was surprisingly light and the weather fine.

Along the way he'd tested the satellite radio service, which had come installed in the new BMW leased by the firm. One station had profiled several songwriting singers of the post-Woodstock era— Jackson Browne, James Taylor, J.D. Souther and Bonnie Raitt—and his spirits, already buoyed by the morning's successes, had been kept aloft by his inexplicable affection for tragic, 1970s music.

His morning meetings had gone well. He'd reached a lucrative, two-year agreement with a group of high tech firms working with MIT, and he'd won a cozy, one-year contract to promote the recently refurbished Franklin Park Zoo. Finally, he'd offered the Red Sox a pro bono arrangement, to help them promote their charitable work for children.

Now, on the journey's last leg, driving south on Route 12, he considered the good fortune of having Jeanie Castro still working with him. He shuddered to recall almost throwing that gift away on the day she'd arrived for her interview.

Having seen several candidates—none of whom were right for the diverse responsibilities of management assistant—he and Nancy had waited on the third floor of their Beacon Street townhouse with a late lunch of salads sent up from a local deli.

When the door bell rang downstairs, Nancy stood and pressed the intercom button.

"Is this Winslow Public Relations?" asked a female voice through the scratchy speaker.

"Yes it is. Come to the third floor, please!"

Nancy buzzed the woman in and waited as the front door opened and slammed shut three floors below. For a full minute, she and Will listened to deliberate, oddly-echoing footsteps coming up the long, winding stairway. Finally, their visitor entered the outer parlor on the third floor, but seemed to be talking to herself.

Nancy peered out from behind the partially opened door of their joint office and whispered. "There's a beautiful young woman outside … with a child."

"That can't be our two o'clock, can it?"

"I think it *is*." Nancy walked back from the door toward their partners' desk—the one she'd found for them in a Wellfleet antique shop. "She's gorgeous!"

"Really." He riffled through a thin pile of résumés on his desk.

"Like a model."

"Huh." Will got up from his side of the desk but stood there, a résumé dangling from his fingers. He was genuinely uncertain of what to do. "What's with the child?"

"It's hers, I guess … a little girl."

"Not very professional …"

"Unorthodox, maybe."

He nodded, coming around the desk and striding toward the door. "I'll get rid of her."

"No you won't. We're going to interview her and see."

He paused near the door and looked at his wife with a forlorn expression.

"I can't believe you," Nancy said. "You're ready to write this person off because she has a child?"

"No." He gestured with his right hand, urging Nancy to keep her voice down.

"Maybe she couldn't get a baby sitter. Do you have any idea how expensive child care is?"

"It just doesn't seem professional."

Nancy frowned. "We run this business out of our house."

"Okay. You're right." He turned to the door and opened it completely. "Mrs. Castro?" He glanced at the young woman's résumé

156

as he strode confidently out to greet her with Nancy following close behind him.

"It's *Miss*." The young woman held onto the child with her left hand and extended her right. "*Please* ... call me Jean."

Will took the young woman's hand. He was struck by how right Nancy had been. The woman's dark, straight hair was pulled back, tied in a bun behind her head, and held with an elegant pearl barrette. The effect was to highlight the stunning beauty of her oval face, and her pearl earrings. She had intense, dark eyes and her lips were perfectly painted an almost burgundy red. She wore what appeared to be an expensive business suit.

Only her visible anxiety, and perhaps her shoes, which looked like knockoffs of some better brand, betrayed the overall effect of a stunning and confident career woman.

Already ashamed of his churlish reaction to the idea of a job candidate accompanied by a child, Will felt the further embarrassment of spontaneous attraction. Now *that* is unprofessional, he thought to himself.

Miss Castro introduced her daughter, Lina, and apologized for having brought her. As she explained that all of her child care options had suddenly fallen through, Will glanced briefly at Nancy, who smiled.

"It's perfectly fine with us," Will assured the young woman. "Would you like to come into our office and have a seat?"

"Why don't you two go in and talk about the job," Nancy suggested. "I'll stay here with Lina, if that's all right." As the woman smiled politely, Nancy stepped forward and bent at the knees, putting herself at eye-level with the child. "Would that be all right, Lina?"

The little girl looked up at her mother, before turning back and nodding at Nancy.

Will arrived at his parents' house, parked the BMW, and started up the driveway. Fishing in his pocket for the key to their front door, he remembered the many holiday visits he and Nancy had made to this house. Even if those visits had become less frequent in recent years, there was still such a strong sense, here, of Nancy at her happiest.

And because he knew what this house had meant to his reconciled parents, Will felt their presence, too, their sense of hope expressed as a place of refuge—a promise of forgiveness so bountiful, a visitor might believe there was enough left over for him.

Peg Harvey had hoped to see a Range Rover in the Winslows' driveway but found, instead, a blue BMW with Massachusetts plates. Parking behind the mystery vehicle, she hurried to the house and knocked forcefully on the front door. After waiting several moments she knocked again. The sound of a car coming along the street sparked a fleeting hope of seeing Tom pull up. But the car vanished beyond a distant turn and she knocked once more—this time, peering into a front window. Nothing seemed amiss in the living room or dining room, though Alice's roses looked just about dead.

Finally, she made her way to the rear of the house and saw a man standing in the Winslows' meadow contemplating their writer's shed.

"Hello?" she called out.

Roused from his thoughts, the man turned and looked hard at Peg. "Is that you, Will?"

"Mrs. Harvey!" he called back, waving politely as he started toward her.

"I should have known!" She hurried to meet him. "Massachusetts plates!"

Will smiled broadly as they embraced. "It's good to see you, Mrs. Harvey."

Standing back and examining him, she was struck by the beauty of nature's transcendent purposes—the boy whose growth she'd fondly observed for 25 years was now, irrevocably, a man.

"I think it's time you called me Peg."

With a gracious nod, he acknowledged her gesture of acceptance in the world of adults. Considerate and observant—this boy was his mother's son, Peg thought. She could almost feel Alice's spirit animating him like a stream that feeds a meadow. He had his father's formal manner, too, especially with women—what the Shelby students would call "old school." The Winslows had done a good job with him.

"I suppose you've heard about my mom and this Mohamed woman."

"That's why I'm here. Have you spoken with her?"

"I reached her in Indianapolis last night."

"You probably don't know what's happening at Shelby."

"No." His face grew stern. "What's up?"

Peg described the rapidly developing events—Cathy Maldonado's attempt to force a board censure, and Delia Radcliff's temporary success in holding that off until Thursday, when Alice was to appear before them. Peg said she feared that the board's usual response to intimidation would produce a negative verdict, even after Alice had explained herself. Finally, Peg told Will how Maldonado had turned her own work on the Isaac Shelby diary into a nightmare of cultural and political mayhem.

"By the time it was over, I wished I'd never heard of Isaac Shelby."

All emotion had drained from Will's body; his warm eyes were suddenly cold. "Does my mother know about the board postponement?"

"Delia said she left a message on your mom's cell phone this afternoon. They'd spoken earlier and cooked up the idea together."

"I see."

"I'd hoped to catch your father at home and get him involved. I thought some of his media friends might help."

"That's a good idea. My father's dealing with his own problem … a long story. I think he's still in Leicester, but I expect him soon."

"How can *I* help?"

"This Maldonado person sounds like a troublemaker."

"She is." Peg sighed. "Frankly, I think she's crazy."

"We're not going to let her hurt my mother. We'll have to deal with her."

"Deal with her?"

"Rap her knuckles a bit. She sounds like a bully. You have to stand up to bullies. If no one at Shelby can do it, I will."

"I don't know. The reason so many people up there are afraid to cross her is that they've seen the way she fights, the lengths she'll go to."

"We have to do the same, then. I guess it's what they call 'hardball' in the business world. Let's go inside."

"I'll do anything I can, Will. You know that."

They walked across the patio toward the kitchen door as late-afternoon sunlight glistened against the house.

"Nancy's not with you?"

"No." He opened the screen door for her. "That's another long story."

Inside, Peg saw a business briefcase on the kitchen table and an overnight bag on the floor nearby. Will's grey suit jacket had been hung on a kitchen chair.

She pointed to the red 36 in the digital window of the counter phone. "That's a lot of messages."

"Reporters." He removed a small cell phone from his shirt pocket and placed it on the table. "I got here an hour ago and listened to every one."

"My God … it's madness."

"Exactly." He agreed. "Would you like some coffee or tea, or …"

"I'd love something stronger, but your mother doesn't keep liquor in the house."

"I know." He opened the fridge and revealed a 6-pack of Budweiser. "That's why I brought these."

"Good boy." She pulled out a chair and collapsed in it. "Don't bother with a glass."

"I like your style, Mrs., I mean … Peg."

"That's better," she said with a hearty laugh.

He grabbed two cans, popped them open, and brought them to the table.

"Okay." He sat across from her. "Tell me all you know about Cathy Maldonado."

"She's a bitch on wheels. Always has been, but it's gotten worse since 9/11."

"Oh?"

Peg sipped and nodded. "Cathy and her sister, Laura, are very close. Laura's husband, Dan, was killed on 9/11. It was horrible. Laura was devastated."

"Of course." He sipped his beer.

"Cathy took it hard, too. It's as if she's on a one-woman crusade to avenge her brother-in-law's death by keeping the world at attention. Anything that doesn't conform to her political or religious views strikes her as unpatriotic. And she lashes out."

"So, she's not really accusing my mother of bad judgment. What she really means is … *un-American*."

Peg nodded gravely. "Cathy has a black-and-white morality about the world. If something doesn't fit with that view, it isn't just incorrect. It's evil."

"And how well do you know the sister?"

"I've met her a few times socially. Laura's very nice; the direct opposite of her older sister, as far as I can tell."

A lingering sunset colored the hills of Trent as Peg arrived home and found Peter drinking beer in their kitchen.

"This is early for you," she observed. It wasn't yet five-thirty.

"I left the job-site around four." With a hearty swallow, he finished a bottle of Beck's. "We need to talk."

Peg put her school things down, opened the refrigerator, and looked for something gentle after two beers with Will. She chose a small bottle of spring water and sat down with her husband. "Is this about the writer's colony?"

He shook his head.

"Then *what*?"

"I'm sorry you aren't happy."

"Are *you*?"

"People *do* work on things. Anyway, there's something else."

Now, she was curious.

"I'm having money trouble."

"What do you mean?"

"I've got three loans out for those rebuilt houses," he said. "I can't sell the houses. And I can't repay the loans."

"List the houses lower."

"I've dropped the prices twice already. If I go lower, I make nothing. I lose money."

"At least you'll have the cash to make your payments. Won't you?"

"In theory, I guess. Peg, I can't get buyers to *look* at property in southern Leicester County. The only action now is in the northwest corner. I have a piece of the Shelby condominiums, but there's going to be a construction delay there too. I just found out today. We have binders on 20 units. Now, the bank is demanding we sell 20 more before it advances what we need to finish building out the first 20. That's impossible."

"I had no idea, Peter."

"Well, now you do. I thought you should know. Especially if ..."

"If what?"

"Aren't you leaving?"

Peg was heartened by her husband's forthright demeanor, and spoke with as much kindness as she could muster.

"I read an article, recently, about the Leicester County real estate market. It said prices had risen about as high as they could go. I hadn't realized the market was stalled."

"It's not just Leicester County. There's a correction coming in real estate prices nationwide."

She sipped her water and listened.

"But it goes deeper," he added. "It's not just builders like me being over-extended. Or investors like my partners in Shelby. The banks are over-extended. I don't know how the government let them get to this point. I don't know how the banks let *themselves* get this close to insolvency, but some of them have. I'm afraid that's the real reason the bank won't lend our condo project anything more. They're demanding we jump through a bunch of hoops, but I think they're bluffing. I don't think they *have* the money."

"Are you serious?"

He nodded gravely.

"What about another bank?"

"The partners are considering it. But Tom Winslow's latest column didn't help ... raising questions about our subsidies and tax abatements." Peter slowly turned his empty beer bottle on the table top. "I'm telling you, Peg, without that state-aid no bank will touch us. There won't be any Trent River condos. And that'll be the end of Harvey Construction."

As the gravity of Peter's situation grew clearer in Peg's mind, she felt overcome by a wave of sympathy for him. She knew that fear would come later.

"There was a *Wall Street Journal* article last month," he said. "Same thing ... banks cutting off lending in the middle of projects. It's playing out in some of the hottest real estate markets, like Florida, Colorado. Now, I guess, it's hitting Western Connecticut. That Gellman kid who interviewed me for Tom's column ... he's a very smart boy. He mentioned something disturbing about this bank in Boston that's funding the Trent River project."

"Why would he do that?"

"He said he knew that Tom and I are neighbors. I think he was trying to give me some friendly advice, off the record. He said he's been working on a big real estate story like the one in the *Wall Street Journal* ... except *his* story is about a wave of insolvencies hitting banks and mortgage lenders. The whole thing's tied to these derivatives that trade on Wall Street, mortgages packaged together, good ones with lousy ones, and then sold and resold until nobody knows what they're worth anymore. It's like musical chairs when the music stops."

He paused and stared at his empty bottle.

"One of the banks he's watching is the one my partners use. He's gone over the regulatory filings, examined the cash flow, the balance sheets. He thinks the bank is in trouble. We could see more bank failures this year than any time since the Great Depression, he says. And 2008 could be worse. It could drag the whole country down."

He stared glumly.

"I understand." Peg paused and looked at her husband. He stared back. "All right, Peter, there's something *I* need to say."

He nodded, waiting.

"I've just spent the past hour at the Winslows' place, with their son."

"Will?" A bit of brightness colored his voice. "How is he?"

"Okay, I guess."

Deciding not to mention the marital problem that Will had subtly implied, Peg went directly into Alice's trouble and Will's determination to protect her.

"I always liked that boy," Peter said. "He's got a great pair of balls."

"I'm worried that he doesn't know what he's dealing with in Cathy Maldonado."

"That blowhard?" Peter scoffed, getting up for another Beck's.

"She's dangerous, Peter."

"You expect the boy to do nothing, while his mother's being harassed? Where's Tom, by the way?"

"There's something going on with him. Will wasn't clear about it. But he seems to think his father is going to be distracted."

"The world's going to hell in a hand-basket." Peter took a gulp of beer and sat down again.

"So, I was thinking, wondering … if there was something *you* could do, maybe, to help Alice."

"Me?" He laughed skeptically. "What can I do?"

"I thought you might speak to Virginia Porter. She has a lot of influence at the college. She listens to you."

"We talk building and maintenance. We reminisce. We don't get into personnel or academics."

"She took your suggestion about the Isaac Shelby diary."

Peter slowly shook his head.

"What's going on is very destructive, Peter. Does Virginia realize that?"

"I wonder if she even knows about it."

"If not, you should tell her. This sort of thing hurts the school. Good people like Alice, talented professors, accomplished people … they'll just leave. And it won't be easy to replace them."

"I know Virginia was unhappy about that diary nonsense."

"Last fall, *I* was the target. Now, it's Alice. Who's next?"

Peter raised his bottle for another gulp, but stopped. He put it down. "So, you're asking me to speak up for Alice."

"*For me*," Peg said. "I'm asking you to do this for your wife. I'm also saying I'm ready to talk, about *us*. You implied you might be willing."

"Yes."

"Then, I am too."

"When you get back from Vermont?"

"I'm not going to Vermont."

He looked genuinely surprised.

"We can't afford it. Obviously, we'll need to tighten our belts." Peg reached across the table. "Besides, there are more important things to deal with."

Peter took her hand. As the implications of her offer settled in, his surprised expression changed into something more like confusion.

Peg smiled warmly at him until she noticed tears welling in his bloodshot eyes. Still gripping his hand, she had to look away, ashamed of her vanity and her husband's naked sobs.

Will remembered moving to Trent when he was 12. Farms abounded in those days. There were meadows and streams, woodland swimming holes and trout fishing in the Trent River. It had been a boy's paradise then. And it remained a beautiful town, in touch with nature's fragile spirit.

His mother had been happier here than she'd ever been, at least in his memory. After years of silent wandering, she'd started writing again—filling journals with thoughts and impressions from morning walks in local fields.

His father, too, had found peace in this place. Sober and calm, content with a new job at the *Hartford Chronicle*, he'd become the father Will had always dreamed of having.

And it was here that Will had finally stopped wishing for a different life. Even now, looking out through the screen door at the darkening meadow, he felt at home.

At six o'clock, still waiting for his father, he checked in with Jeanie Castro in Boston. She gave him a rundown of his afternoon calls—none of which needed immediate response. Then, she linked him to the boardroom conference phone and asked the staff to come in.

After briefly explaining his absence and thanking them for their dedication, Will talked about new clients. He listened to a report from the current-accounts team and made his recommendations. And as they all filed out again, heading to their offices, ready to leave for the night, Will waited on the line.

"Is there anything else you need?" Jeanie asked as she closed the boardroom door.

"I think we're good," he said into his cell phone. "Are you alone?"

"Yes. I want to thank you again for your generous offer."

"Don't be silly."

"I've thought about it all day, and, of course I accept."

"I'm so glad, Jeanie. When I get back, we'll sit down and work out the details."

But she was silent now.

"What is it?"

"Nothing." Her voice cracked. "I was thinking of you and Nancy, the day we met ... the day you hired me."

"That was a good day."

"It was."

"So why are you crying?"

"I don't know." She allowed a sob to emerge and become a laugh.

After hanging up, he concentrated on his mother's problem—transcribing the names and phone numbers of reporters who'd called to speak with her. He wanted to start getting back to them with a comment on her behalf. But first, he wanted to talk it over with his father, perhaps consult with his mother's agent and publisher.

At some point, he knew, reporters would learn about the faculty board hearing. The national news story would morph into a hotly-debated, and perhaps more damaging, local story. Will wanted someone friendly to his mother handling questions about her teaching career and the college's attitude toward her. Peg had assured him that the PR officer at Shelby—a man named Phil Weintraub—was an ally. Will planned to coordinate media responses with him too.

At seven o'clock his cell phone chirped. Hoping it was his father at last, calling from the car, or maybe his mother, he was stunned to hear another voice.

"How are you?" she asked.

"Nancy!"

"I'm in Florence."

"It's the middle of the night there."

"One in the morning." She sounded weary. "I'm jet-lagged … can't sleep."

"I'm glad you called."

"I saw something in the *Herald Tribune*, about your mother and a Muslim woman."

"There's a big to-do about it, and trouble at her college. I've come down to Connecticut to help her with everything."

"You're in Trent!" Now, she sounded homesick.

Will explained what his mother was facing, and his strategy for dealing with the media fallout. After briefly mentioning his father's personal crisis, he paused, waiting for his wife's opinion.

"You're a good son," is all she said.

He didn't know how to respond. He listened to empty static in the cell connection.

"I miss you," she finally said.

"I miss you too."

"I don't know how to do this."

"I don't either," he said, trying to push beyond the terrible feelings.

She told him about her visit to Angelica's grave, about meeting Gabriele and Marianna, even the unexpected place where she'd been taken for lunch.

"I'm staying in a nice hotel on Viale Michelangelo. There are stunning views from up here."

"How long will you be there?"

"I don't know. A while … I think."

Suddenly, he was that young man again—the one who'd waited an entire summer for a girl he loved to decide if she would marry him. All that summer there'd been calls between Florence and Trent, just like this: homesick, longing, and maybe not entirely truthful.

"How was it? At the grave, I mean."

"San Miniato is special. It has a powerful sense of something ancient. But it was difficult to picture Angelica, to feel her there. It was clear—she's really, really dead. I said my prayers. I did my best."

"What more can you do?"

Again, there was a pause in their conversation. It seemed to Will that they were both reluctant to sever their connection, yet, resigned to its necessity.

"Take care of yourself." In her soft voice he heard the sound of a wife, lying close in bed, whispering in his ear.

"You too."

At eight o'clock, a car eased up the driveway toward the house. Will flipped a light switch and opened the kitchen door. Peering into the dimly-lit garage, he waved to his father, who smiled as he parked his Range Rover and got out.

"This is a pleasant surprise." Tom stepped up into the bright kitchen and grabbed his son in a bear hug. "You have a new car."

"We leased it for the business."

His father seemed impressed. "When did you get here?"

"Late afternoon." Will noticed how tired his father looked in the stark neon lighting. "How's everything at the hospital?"

"Kerry and the baby are fine. Dec is sleeping in the room with them." Just then, the telephone on the counter caught Tom's eye. "Is that 36 messages?"

"Reporters ... I've made a list."

"Jesus." Tom sat wearily at the kitchen table.

"It's why I'm here, Dad. I want to help."

Tom smiled, but said nothing.

Will couldn't stop thinking how old his father looked in this lighting.

"So, what do you think about this young man?"

Tom shrugged. "Dec's a nice kid."

"But what do you *think*?"

"You mean, do I think he's ..."

"*Related* to us," Will said, getting to the point.

"I have no idea. Neither does he."

"Have they asked you for money?"

Tom looked surprised by the question. "*No.*"

"I'm sorry, Dad." Will felt the spontaneous rush of shame. "Forget I said that. Do they have a name for the baby?"

"Kerry wants to call him Declan, but his father doesn't seem to like the idea. I guess they'll throw more names around tomorrow. Right now, they're safe for the night."

At least the edgy sound of embarrassment had begun fading from his father's voice, Will thought.

"I'm sorry about the craziness, Will. You've got better things to do with your time."

"Baloney."

"How *is* business? Must be pretty good if you're leasing BMWs."

"Business is good."

"And Nancy?"

"That's not so good. She's in Florence at the moment."

Tom listened for more.

"We're probably getting divorced; looks like we're *all* in the shit."

They stared at each other for several moments, uncertain of what to say next, until they collapsed in spasms of inappropriate laughter.

Finally, his father regained control of himself. "Is it possible things aren't as bad as you think?"

Will gravely shook his head.

"I'm sorry, son."

Deferring further discussion of love and marriage, Will informed his father of the nasty turn of events at Shelby College.

"That Maldonado is a piece of work," Tom said.

"She has to be dealt with."

"Be careful," Tom urged. "She's obviously crazy. It won't matter how elegant your PR strategy may seem. She'll still be crazy. That means dangerous."

"I know. I promise I'll be careful."

"Has Delia Radcliff pitched in for your mom?"

"Peg Harvey says it was Delia who got the board to hold off until Thursday."

"That's something, at least." Tom sighed. "We have to get your mom back home."

"Can you track her down? She has to really think about this board meeting."

"Right." Tom stood and placed his hands firmly on his son's shoulders. "I haven't had a shower in two days. I need one to stay awake."

"What if I make some coffee?"

"Good idea. I'll try your mother. Then, we'll talk about dealing with these reporters." Tom started toward the stairs, but paused. "By the way ... is there a Jack Daly from the *American-Leader* on your list?"

"He left four messages. Do you know him?"

"I've always known him to be fair. Apparently, he's friendly with the Maldonado family."

"Yes, Peg Harvey told me. His messages sound urgent."

"Okay." Tom reached the stairs and started climbing. "I'll call him when I come back down."

Forty-five minutes later, having made a pot of coffee and finished a cup by himself, Will went to the base of the stairs and called to his father. But there was only silence in the old house. Will climbed the stairs and found his parents' bedroom door half open. He knocked politely and spoke from the landing.

"Dad? Are you all right?"

There was still no response.

Gently, he pushed the door and stepped into the dimly-lit bedroom.

His father was stretched diagonally across the bed wearing a bathrobe, his right hand resting lightly on his chest, rising and falling to the rhythm of his breathing. A cell phone lay cradled beside him in his left hand.

Will leaned over the bed, lifted the cell phone from his father's upturned palm and checked the database. There'd been a 20-minute call to his mother's cell phone number during the past hour. Relieved for the moment, Will noticed his father's face had lost the aging effect of the stark kitchen lighting against angles and creases. In repose, it was the face of a younger man.

Will turned off the bedside lamp and crept out, taking the cell phone with him.

When he reached the kitchen, he poured another cup of coffee and reviewed the list of reporters on his laptop. There was still no formal press statement agreed with his parents; but he knew there was one call he should make tonight. He grabbed his own cell phone and punched in the number for Jack Daly at the *Connecticut American-Leader.*

Five

Waiting in the hotel garden, Nancy felt her stomach flutter each time a car passed on the boulevard. Violetta had invited her to visit the Antonini design studio this morning, followed by lunch—a gracious gesture. And though Gabriele's stern sister always had treated her respectfully, Nancy's heart wept as she recalled their shared secret.

"May I bring you a coffee, signora?" It was the hotel waiter, standing just outside the front door.

"No grazie, Vittorio," she replied from her bench. "My friend will be here soon."

"Molto bene." He vanished inside.

Minutes later, a shiny black Lancia entered the gate and moved slowly into the courtyard. Surprised to see Violetta driving herself, Nancy waved and started toward the vehicle.

Violetta lowered her window. "A beautiful morning ..."

"Gorgeous." Nancy crossed to the passenger side and got in.

"A family owned this villa many years ago." Violetta gazed at the manicured hotel grounds. "They sold it and moved away."

"Did you know them?"

Violetta smiled as she stared at the house. "I went to school with their son."

Nancy waited for more, then spoke. "You liked him."

"Yes." Violetta laughed softly. "I liked him."

"So what happened?"

"Love and fate are different things."

Violetta put her car in gear and glided back out onto Viale Michelangelo. They drove down the hillside to the river, crossed on Ponte San Niccolò, and continued north on a series of interlocking boulevards. The trip took them through several neighborhoods along the city's east end, past Giardino dell' Orticultura, a splendid park featuring elaborate, 19th Century greenhouses.

After 30 minutes of traveling across the valley basin, Nancy noticed they'd begun climbing steeply in a section of modest homes and commercial buildings.

Violetta glanced at her. "Do you recall this part of Florence?"

"Somewhat ... it's been 15 years."

"Of course." Leaving the main thoroughfare, Violetta sped halfway up a side street and turned abruptly at a small gate. She parked in front of a two story, stucco building with a red-tile roof. "Siamo arrivato."

They entered the building through a wrought iron door, whose amber glass panel was embossed with a gilded *A*. The stone floor of the hushed reception area reflected soft lighting from sconces and lamps. Antonini paper products were displayed on backlit shelves along two paneled walls, while, on another, there were framed letters of praise from famous clients. In one corner, a glass-enclosed bookcase held first editions of authors once published by the House of Antonini.

"I don't remember this building," Nancy said.

Receiving a stack of correspondence from a young female receptionist, Violetta turned to respond. "We didn't own it when you were with us."

"There *was* a lovely view of the city," Nancy said, as she followed her host into a dark corridor.

"From the other side of the factory ..."

At the end of the corridor they paused near a brace of wide, glass doors, beyond which some 30 crafts-people worked at slanted drafting tables beneath high-intensity lighting. It was a much larger studio than the one Nancy had visited years earlier.

"Shall we go in later and see what they're working on?" Violetta suggested.

"I'd like that."

"Good." Violetta pointed to a closed door on their left. "Gabriele's office is there," she said. "And this is me," she added, leading Nancy across the corridor and into a room filled with beautiful objects. "Make yourself at home."

Violetta placed her mail on an antique sacristy table that served as her desk. She tapped the mouse-pad on her sleek, silver laptop and stared gravely at the screen.

As Nancy waited for her host to settle in, she gazed around the spacious office. There were several sets of comfortable chairs and coffee tables, antique lamps, and a number of sculptures and paintings. One vast, wood-paneled wall was devoted to photographs showing generations of the family, many with notable figures from the political, literary and show business worlds—an international who's who extending from the mid-19th century to the present.

Behind Violetta's desk, southeast-facing windows brought morning light into the room. Fifty yards away, on a rolling green lawn, was the nondescript factory building Nancy remembered. In the distant valley, the city awakened.

"Come." Violetta indicated plush chairs near the wall of photographs.

As she sat, Nancy pointed to a particular photo. "That's a beautiful one of you and Gabriele, with your father."

"A long time ago," Violetta acknowledged, glancing at the wall.

Nancy's gaze moved on. "Is that the boy who lived at the villa?" She pointed to a photo of Violetta with a handsome young man. They looked to be 17 or 18.

"That is Roberto." Violetta stared at the photo, as if caught in a memory.

"Why did I never meet him?"

"He died … not long after that photo was taken."

"Oh. I'm sorry."

Violetta paused before speaking. "His father wanted too much from him."

"Do you mean success?"

"I mean that he was greedy. Having lived his own life, he wished to live again, through his son."

"*Two* lives," Nancy whispered. "That *is* greedy."

Violetta offered no response. Nancy moved on.

"I remember *those* … of Angelica."

"And there are several of *you*."

"I noticed. It's flattering to be included."

"You are a friend of the family."

Nancy felt a rush of uncertain emotion. "Marianna is in more photos than anyone," she said.

"And what do you think of my niece?"

"She's a sweet girl."

"Una tesora." Violetta spoke emphatically. "When she lost her mother, she carried her father's grief in her own heart." She paused. "It was a sin."

The young receptionist entered with a tray on which she carried a silver coffee pot, two china cups, and a small plate of biscotti.

"Grazie," Violetta said.

The young woman placed the tray on a lacquered coffee table, poured two cups and left without speaking.

"Gabriele told me what happened."

Violetta accepted this confidence with a brief nod.

"You were never convinced about Angelica."

"I thought she was ... not right for my brother."

"You disliked her." Nancy lifted her cup.

"My opinion is of no consequence. She was my brother's wife."

"Gabriele said she was unhappy."

Violetta sipped.

"Didn't he love her?"

"There are different forms of love. Are there not? Who can judge a husband and wife when only they know the truth?"

"Sometimes, even *they* don't know."

"Is the truth really so elusive?" Violetta smiled warmly. "I am no expert. But, in my observation, a lasting marriage is a kind of statement."

"Marriages that *don't* last are statements too."

Smiling subtly, as if impressed or amused by Nancy's refined concept of marital psychology, Violetta replied. "What do *those* marriages say?"

"If they're like mine, they say 'no.'"

"I'm sorry."

"So." Nancy spoke bluntly. "He didn't love her the way she needed."

"Her needs were ... *infinita*." Violetta's voice was tinged with emotion now. "Gabriele could never satisfy such needs. I doubt any man could."

"I understand."

"He loved *you*. Of that I'm certain."

Nancy stared into her host's intense gaze. "He thought he did."

"Even now, he does."

Nancy shook her head sadly. "He'd feel differently if he knew ..."

Violetta's expression remained calm.

"Angelica never told him?"

"I can't really say. I suspect not."

"She wasn't a vindictive girl."

Violetta accepted this assessment. "May we talk about something else?"

"Please." Nancy sighed in relief. "What should we discuss?"

"Family business ... I understand that yours is quite successful."

"My husband has had a lot to do with it."

"As Gabriele and *I* have collaborated. But ... as in marriage, perhaps, a family business must change if it is to last."

"This is why you're entertaining investment bankers?"

"Precisamente."

Kerry felt the ache of childbirth. Her new baby lay sleeping in a small crib beside her bed; her boyfriend was asleep in his chair by the window. It was just past sunrise and her makeshift family was safe for the moment. But if all went as expected, they would be discharged today from this pleasant country hospital.

The past few days had been filled with different forms of birth and rebirth, painful moments that had invited new ways of thinking about people. She could not deny that they'd been treated well here. Still, she was angered by this old man who'd taken them under his wing, confusing everything she knew of men—especially men like him.

How could he understand the world to which she, her good-hearted boyfriend, and their child belonged? How could he be so unobservant?

Several times this week she'd resisted an embarrassing urge to slap his face, to scream "wake up, for God's sake!" But life had taught her to be invisible.

"You can't teach men how to be men," her mother had warned. Of course, her mother had spent too much of her own invisible life waiting to be loved.

And this Doctor Coben—a kind enough woman—offering a professional version of motherly concern, hovering over Kerry during the long labor, Monday night into Tuesday morning, holding her hand, urging her not to be afraid.

Yesterday afternoon, when the nurses had brought the baby back from the neonatal unit and helped Kerry start nursing the little thing, Dr. Coben had stopped in again to check on them and say that all was well.

"Are you sure he's healthy?" Kerry had asked as the baby suckled busily at her breast.

"You have an extremely healthy boy," the doctor had said.

"A bruiser!" one of the nurses said as everyone laughed.

"He is, isn't he?" said Kerry, unable to resist a moment's pride, before her confession to the doctor. "I don't know if they've told you. We have no health insurance."

"Yes, dear, they told me."

"I'll arrange monthly payments with your office."

"It isn't necessary. Tom and Alice Winslow have taken care of it."

When the doctor left, a nurse informed Kerry that the Winslows were paying the hospital bill as well.

"They are?"

"It's what I heard." The nurse nodded gravely. "Are they related to you?"

"I don't even know them."

"You're a lucky young woman, then, aren't you?"

Stunned, uncertain of her feelings, Kerry glanced down at her nursing child. "When do you know if he's had enough?"

"He'll let you know." The nurse turned to leave the room. "Buzz me when you want help. I'll be right outside, or on the floor somewhere."

Now, as she heard the baby whimper in his bassinette, Kerry felt an indefinable joy listening to him fuss before he tipped back into deepest sleep again. She was proud of her growing expertise as a mother and of the baby's eager closeness when she nursed him. In some mysterious way, she realized, he'd been feeding her as well.

She looked again at Dec and suppressed a giggle at how deeply he slept in that uncomfortable chair. The poor guy had been up most of the night, she thought with affection, as the sun rose in the window above his head.

But soon enough, she knew, the facts of their existence would press in. She and her boyfriend and their baby were on their own, no matter what the motherly Doctor Coben and some nurse might think.

Edging her legs toward the side of the bed, Kerry felt the tenderness of her empty womb and traumatized birth canal, the urgency of a flaccid bladder. Resting briefly, her feet dangling girlishly, she decided not to let the old man bring them to his country house and put them in some shed. This whole idea she'd put Dec up to was wrong—she saw that now. The old man didn't even believe Dec was his son, and she refused to let them be anyone's church project, or the beneficiaries of some damned liberal guilt. She didn't even care that there was no other place for them to go. Dec would just have to figure something out for them.

Slowly, she stood. She shuffled gingerly across the cold tiles of the hospital room, and pushed at the heavy, wooden door of her private toilet. Stepping into the dark, hiking up her gown and sitting on the warm, plastic seat, she accepted that the masquerade was over.

Tom awoke from a dream in which Sally Hayes had been crying—refusing to look at him—as he'd tried to reason with her. They'd been in a windowless house at the edge of a desolate sea, and had spoken not in words but in thoughts freely understood.

"You left," she challenged.

"You should have told me," he countered.

"And make you hate us?" whispered another presence Tom sensed but couldn't see.

Sally finally turned to look at him with the face of an unknown woman.

He bolted up in bed and glanced at the clock. Its digital eye blinked: 4:32, 4:32, 4:32, 4:32—which meant an overnight power outage, a frequent country event.

His cell phone would have the correct time, he knew. But he couldn't find it in the folds of sheet and blanket. Hadn't he spoken to Alice last night while sitting here on the bed? Or had that been a dream as well?

He stood and moved unsteadily to the window, looking out on an overcast morning. He could barely see the shed in the dank meadow where a heavy mist drifted. There were clouds on the distant ridgeline. He decided it was still early.

Trudging from his bedroom along the upper landing to Will's old room, he found the door open and the bed made.

"Will?"

There was no response.

"Are you here?"

In overwhelming silence, he made his way down the stairs and into the kitchen where he found his cell phone and a note:

Dad—spoke to Mom this morning. As you know, she flies into Hartford tonight at 6:15. Her publisher is sending a car to the airport and they expect to get her home by 8.

Her agent wants calls from the major media forwarded to FSG. Their PR agency has crafted a statement and they'll deal with everything for the time being. I'll return those 36 calls today and give them FSG's phone number. In a few cases of local media, Mom suggests we also get the PR office at Shelby College involved. I've put phone numbers for FSG and the Shelby PR guy into your cell phone—in case you get any more calls.

There is one exception to all this—I spoke last night to Jack Daly from the American-Leader. You were right. He does sound like a fair man. We agreed to meet for breakfast this morning, so that's where I am right now. I'll see you later.

Love—Will.

Tom confronted himself with a sense of shameful ineptitude. It was much later than he'd thought—10 o'clock—and already Will was out there working on his mother's behalf. He, on the other hand, had slept for 12 hours and awakened just as tired as when he'd stumbled home last night. Fatigue was understandable, but everyone in the family faced crises this week.

Finding a bit of coffee left in the pot that Will had made earlier, pouring it cold and black into a cup, Tom opened the back door to feel reviving air through the screen. As he sipped and stared beyond the patio to the shed, a ray of morning sunlight filtered through the overcast.

When his cell phone buzzed on the kitchen table, he turned and grabbed it. Hoping it was Alice, he saw Dawn Harper's name and number on the screen.

"What a surprise," he said.

"I called you *twice* this morning."

"Sorry … I slept late and didn't hear the phone."

"I'm leaving for the airport." Her voice was urgent. "Teddy's very ill."

"Oh. No."

"I spoke to his wife. The cancer has spread more quickly than expected. He may not be with us long. So it seemed, I don't know, pointless, to keep carrying resentments."

"That sounds right to me, Dawn."

"His wife and kids are devastated. When I suggested I could fly out there, they picked right up on it. They seemed relieved actually."

"You're doing a nice thing."

"They're nice people, Tom. I just hope I can be of some help … and maybe have a chance to say goodbye to the man."

"If you can, would you give him *our* best?"

"Of course; now listen. I expect the limo any minute, so I'll make this fast. When you were here Sunday, I mentioned that neighbor of mine who'd read Sally's obit in the paper."

"I remember."

"I ran into him yesterday at the IGA. I made a point of asking if the obituary had mentioned her son."

"Yes?"

"Tom … he said it *had* mentioned a child, but not a son. He said it was a *girl* … a *daughter*."

Tom tried to comprehend the stunning news.

"Are you there?" Dawn asked.

"Did it give a name for the girl?"

"Kerry."

Tom felt his heart breaking.

"Does this help you?"

"It explains a few things."

"I see the limo pulling into my driveway. I'll call you when I'm back from Hawaii. Oh, wait! I almost forgot! I've seen some of this insane news coverage about Alice."

"It's a problem. We're dealing with it."

"Would you tell her something from me?"

"Okay."

"Fuck 'em!"

He laughed mordantly. Then, after thanking Dawn and wishing her a safe journey, he placed his cell phone on the table and began to weep. His body shuddered as memories washed over him like bursts of cold rain. He understood his troubled dream now.

Gathering himself, he pushed through the screen door and walked out into the meadow. He reached the shed, unlocked it, and stepped inside. Peter Harvey's refurbishment had been done years ago. But Tom kept the shed sealed most of the time, and so the scent of new building materials sweetened a stronger odor of decay.

No wonder those kids hadn't liked it, he thought.

After bringing them here Monday morning, he'd gone up to the house to call Alice in Chicago. Then, he'd tried working on his next column without success. Unable to concentrate, he'd paced the bedroom, gazed distractedly from the window, and observed the kids walking endlessly in the meadow.

"She's not hungry," Dec had told him when he'd gone down to get them for lunch. "She needs fresh air."

"It stinks in there." Kerry had looked pale, short of breath and heavy with child.

Examining the shed now, he saw the fresh, folded sheets still sitting neatly at one end of the sofa bed which they'd never opened. He estimated it would take an hour to haul the vacuum cleaner down from the main house and give the place a good going over.

He could also freshen the toilet and fix up the sofa bed. But would any of this make the place more inviting, make it smell less like a woodshed? And what about the baby, he asked himself?

Even before he remembered the locked file cabinet in the corner by the writing desk, Tom knew this cramped space with its single lonely window was all wrong.

Stepping out and re-locking the door, he hurried across the meadow toward the house. He wanted to reach Alice in Madison, Wisconsin, where she was scheduled to give a talk at the university before her flight back to Hartford. It wasn't that he doubted her concurrence about these kids. He just wanted to hear her voice.

Then, there would be plenty to do: vacuum and clean the unused third bedroom in the main house, drive north to Leicester Village, look for a suitable bassinette in one of the nicer stores there, pick up some roses—and finally, swing by the hospital to gather up his wandering children and bring them home.

Twice at home and again while driving north to Shelby, Peter had failed to reach Virginia Porter. His mission was sensitive. And he believed that disembodied voicemail messages caused misunderstandings. So not until one last call from the pickup, minutes from her house, had he let her system record his plea to speak on an "urgent matter."

He turned off Route 12, entered the gates of her estate, and followed a private blacktop road through woodland and across acres of meadow. As the house became visible on a distant hillcrest, he saw Virginia's landscaper, Jack Washburn, riding a massive mower several hundred yards to the west.

Peter parked on a white, gravel crescent in front of Virginia's 1840 clapboard home. The air was succulent with fresh-cut bluegrass as he climbed out of his pickup and noticed Jack's red truck and trailer parked discreetly near the barn behind the house. Waving in Jack's direction, getting no response, Peter hurried up the steps of the wraparound porch and pressed the doorbell button. He listened for footsteps inside the three-story house and pressed again.

Jack came closer now, less than a hundred yards away. This time, when Peter raised his hand, Jack returned the greeting, moving toward the house and shouting. "Is that you, Peter?" Jack stopped at the edge of the gravel crescent, killing his powerful engine.

Peter came down the front steps and crossed gravel onto lawn. "I need to see Virginia."

"Mrs. Porter went to Florida," Jack said, removing his Red Sox cap, wiping his broad, ebony face with a large, blue bandana.

"Florida!"

"Sarasota." They shook hands. "She's visiting her daughter, Beth, and the grandchildren."

Peter glanced at the silent house. "Is Marge Taylor around?" he asked, referring to Mrs. Porter's long-time housekeeper.

"Haven't seen her." Jack shrugged. "Mrs. Porter told me she'd be gone 10 days. Maybe Marge took some time ..."

"I don't think I have a phone number for Beth. Do you?"

Jack shook his head.

"She's married to a guy named Bill Alston," Peter mused. "There might be a listing for them in Sarasota."

"It's that urgent? Why not try at the campus? I'll bet someone in the president's office keeps all that detail."

"I'd rather not in this situation."

Jack wiped his face again. "Personal matter ..."

"Pretty much."

The men looked blandly at one another, then beyond each other—Jack staring up at the big, white house, Peter surveying the wide, green space around it.

"Well." Jack restarted his engine. "I hope it's nothing too serious."

"I just need her help on something!" Peter shouted over the engine.

Spinning his massive mower on a tight, balletic radius, Jack waved as he headed out toward an un-mowed area of roughly two acres. He ran his machine like a motorboat, bouncing the swales, cutting a wake through a thick green sea.

Peter felt the redoubled urgency of his task—an urgency fueled by affection for the Winslows, disdain for Cathy Maldonado, and a basic sense of justice. Yet more importantly, Peter had given Peg his word. Today, nothing in the world seemed more urgent than keeping a promise to his wife.

He jumped back into his pickup and closed his side window. He grabbed his cell phone, punched in the Verizon code for directory assistance and waited.

"Hello, Mr. Harvey." The operator, whose clipped speech had a South-Asian flavor, gave her name as Tessa. "What city?"

"Sarasota," he replied. "That's Florida."

"Of course," Tessa said. "What name, please?"

"Beth Alston ... I imagine it's listed under her husband, so ... Bill Alston ... or William."

"William Alston ..."

"Could be William and Elizabeth ... anything like that."

As he waited, Peter watched Jack skimming the green horizon.

"I show a number for Alston," the operator said. "William and Beth ..."

"That's it!"

"But it's unlisted," she added sadly.

"Oh no."

"I can't give it to you, Mr. Harvey. I'm sorry."

"There's nothing else we can do?"

"I don't believe so. Was there anything else?"

"No. I guess not."

Peter clicked off and tossed his phone onto the seat beside him.

Jack had finished cutting and was driving the mower back toward his truck and trailer. Peter watched him distractedly and realized what had to be done.

He turned the ignition key and drove his pickup around the gravel crescent, onto the blacktop, and away from the house quickly. It was already past noon.

In minutes, he'd crossed the long, open space of lawn and meadow around Virginia's home. Then, as the private road dipped into the wooded acreage buffering the estate along Route 12, Peter reduced speed and watched the foliage pass slowly on his right.

He was looking for an old riding trail that he and Virginia had used when they were in high school. The area was overgrown now, but something about the formation of oak, elm and birch trees began to touch his memory.

Abruptly, he hit the brakes. This is it, he thought, a path hidden in wild grass and shrubbery. Steering right, softly pressing the gas pedal, he drove his pickup into lush foliage between the massive, barrel-like trunks of two ancient elms. Hoping that his memory was accurate, he moved deeper and deeper into the cover of greenery, down a gentle slope toward a place where a brook would be.

With his foot on the brake, pressing and releasing as the pickup descended a few yards at a time, Peter rolled his window down and listened for the brook. Finally, he turned his steering wheel hard left and stopped completely. He turned off the engine.

He could see nothing of the blacktop driveway, which meant that he was hidden from view. And as he waited, listening for Jack's truck coming by, he heard faintly the sound of water gurgling around rocks and stones somewhere near the wheels of his pickup.

During their high school riding excursions, he and Virginia would stop here to let their horses drink while they kissed, excited by the innocence of erotic discovery. It was a pleasant, private memory for Peter, tinged with the sadness of years.

As he knew, riding out with her husband had been the singular joy of Virginia's married life. But Evan Porter had died 15 years ago. And soon afterward, Virginia had been thrown somewhere along this route by one of her favorite mounts, a gelding named Brandywine, who'd been spooked by a bobcat. The resulting injury to her back had forced her to give up riding. Now, the horses she kept in her barn were mainly for the use of visiting grandchildren.

"The strange thing about life," she sometimes said, "is how it takes away the things we love, one after another, and teaches us to survive without them. Sooner or later, we learn that this is the whole point … letting things go."

Though Peter generally agreed with her, he'd once offered a rejoinder, for argument's sake. He'd observed that there were people he knew who seemed to have reached their goals, attained their dreams, and seemed content in their gifts—Alice Winslow for one.

Virginia had nodded gravely. "We all know the price of our dreams."

And Peter had offered no argument to that.

Soon enough, he heard the rattling of Jack's truck and trailer. Peter held his breath as Jack drove past the spot where he'd entered the woods. Apparently, Jack didn't notice the freshly-made pathway of pressed foliage left by Peter's pickup. Or if he did, he ignored it. Finally, the sound of squealing brakes pierced the quiet woodland from down near the gates at the edge of Route 12. There, Jack paused, checking for oncoming traffic, before turning slowly onto the highway and driving off.

Peter waited a moment in the silent woods. Then he turned the ignition key, backed up a yard or two, and made his way up the slope to the blacktop driveway. In seconds, he was speeding back toward Virginia's house.

Craig McCall answered the phone in his University of Chicago office.

"Are you busy?" Alice asked him.

"No." He spoke cautiously, surprised to hear her voice. "Just making notes for my public policy class. Where *are* you?"

"Madison," she said. "I'm giving a talk at the university. Would you like to know the topic?"

Craig listened in confused silence.

"Writing Fiction in a Non-Fiction World," she said dryly.

Craig managed a chuckle as he leaned back in his chair. "Is Eileen with you?"

"She's at the auditorium. Making sure my book is properly displayed … reminding the campus press office that I won't take questions about Janet Mohamed. They've put me in a visitor's cottage. It feels like a safe house."

"Is it the one with the lovely garden?"

Alice laughed. "There *are* roses outside."

"That's the one." He paused to gather his thoughts. "We've been following the coverage. Janet feels horrible about it. She feels responsible."

"Tell her not to."

"I'll tell her. She'll worry anyway."

"Will is in Connecticut, now, helping with press calls. My publisher has taken responsibility for everything. There isn't much to worry about where media are concerned. We'll just let them play their game."

"I see."

"There *are* some people back at school exploiting the situation. I have to appear at a faculty board meeting tomorrow. I'm accused of bringing disrepute on the good name of Shelby College."

"Academic assholes ..."

"Some are."

"I suppose there's nothing I can do?"

"What do you suggest?"

"I don't know, write an Op/Ed on your behalf? I know some people at the *New York Times* who might run it."

She laughed again. "The last thing my publisher wants is another article about Janet Mohamed and Alice Winslow. Even my friends at school want the issue to go away."

Why has she called, he wondered?

"So, here I am." Alice sounded ironic. "Sitting in a university cottage normally reserved for dignitaries. I suppose being notorious is a kind of fame."

"Is it possible you really don't understand the effect of your novel?"

"I know a lot of copies have been sold."

"Your book is popular because it's an honest love story. It's about forgiveness."

After a brief silence, Alice shifted the conversation. "You're surprised to hear from me."

"I got the impression that you were uncomfortable ... when I came to your hotel."

"I was. And I'm sorry. I said some nasty things."

"I did too. I wouldn't say you owed me any grand apology."

"No. I think I do."

"So *that's* why you called?"

"Craig," she began. "Haven't you ever wondered why your mother disliked me so?"

"She didn't."

"She wasn't happy when I left Chicago."

"You'd hurt her son."

"I understand. But there was something more."

"You'd rejected her son, that's all. My mother came from a background where a lot of value was placed on form. She wasn't used to being told 'no.'"

"I gathered that."

"The truth is, she was a bit of a snob, my mother. I wouldn't worry too much about it. Is there anything more powerful than a mother's love for her children?"

"No," Alice observed. "Not even her judgment."

"Now *that's* something my mother would agree with."

"I hope you'll give Will a call," she urged. "He'd like hearing from you."

Craig glanced at his copy of *The Chastened Heart* on the desk nearby. "Do you really think so?" Opening the back page, he read Will's contact details in Alice's forthright script.

"He always liked you, Craig, and respected you. Which is … as it should be."

"Well …"

"I know what you did, Craig."

For a moment, there was silence between them.

"It was a noble, unselfish thing," she added.

"I'll call him," Craig promised, feeling an old flutter in his heart, an involuntary response to Alice's admiration. "By the way, has Eileen mentioned her novel yet?"

"She has a novel?"

"Oh, that foolish girl." He sighed. "She has a manuscript, not perfect, but pretty damn good. With the right editor, the right support, she could make something of it. I told her I'd publish it myself, but she refused. She didn't like taking advantage of a friendship."

"Maybe she wanted to be sure it *deserved* publication. That's important to some authors."

"I know it is, Alice. That's why I told her to speak to you."

After hanging up, Craig watched the street traffic passing along the edge of the campus below his office window. It felt as if decades had come and gone in the moments he'd spent with Alice on the phone. He placed his hand on her book as if on Holy Scripture. Then, with a small brass key, he opened a shallow desk drawer and removed a leather-bound photo album.

On its first page was the photograph Alice had given him when she'd lived here—a picture of Will, at age eight. Turning the page, he read a clipping from the June 27, 1993 *New York Times*, announcing the marriage of William Arthur Winslow of Trent, CT, and Nancy Clare Carlton, of Brookline, MA. It said the bride and groom were alumni of Harvard University, where Mr. Winslow had studied business and finance. Ms. Carlton had majored in American literature and art history. The bride's parents were physicians, at Massachusetts General Hospital, it said. The groom's father was a columnist for the *Hartford Chronicle*, his mother a professor of creative writing at Shelby College. The wedding had taken place at the summer home of the bride's parents in Wellfleet, MA.

Moving on through his clippings, Craig found a 1995 wire story announcing the launch in Boston of Winslow Public Relations. As the story explained, the firm was owned by "the husband and wife team of William Winslow and Nancy Carlton, and is located on the third floor of 175 Beacon Street."

Craig smiled as he re-read the wire story and perused clips from newspapers and business journals that had picked it up.

And then, there were clips of the couple's successes, starting with their first major client, Boston University, followed by the Harvard Alumni Fund, the John F. Kennedy Library, the Faneuil Hall Marketplace, two waterfront hotels and several investment banks headquartered in Boston.

Craig turned his album pages with mixed emotions—mainly pride, a bit of sadness, and even guilt—as he considered his role in this: he'd urged the chief executives of these institutions, all close friends of his or his parents, to consider the services of Winslow Public Relations without disclosing his connection. It was to the boy's credit, Craig thought, and the wife's, that these firms had ultimately given their business to Winslow and kept it there all these years since.

Closing the album, Craig shuddered with sorrow, remembering a conversation with his mother five years ago, just before she died.

"You've encouraged more of our friends to sign with the boy's PR firm," she said, sitting on the sun porch of their Lake Forest home, a *Wall Street Journal* in her lap.

"You mean the Chicago Opera," he replied.

As she nodded, he watched the sunlight on her pale complexion and pretended to ignore the Parkinsonian tremble of her hands. He could not overlook her age, her failing health, or her now frequent stays at The University of Chicago Medical Center.

"The opera company needs help promoting the summer tour," he explained. "Winslow Public Relations is a good, national firm. I made a suggestion, that's all."

"The boy still doesn't know about any of these ... recommendations ... of yours?"

"I hope not."

"You're a strange man, Craig."

"That's well established."

"I don't mean *that*. I just think it's odd. In all this time, you haven't once forced an issue with the boy's mother."

"First of all, he's not a boy. He's a grown man. And secondly, there is no *issue*. The Winslows are a family. They have their lives. We have ours."

She snorted and shook her head, a familiar sign of irritation.

"Mother, I'm grateful that you've followed my wishes about this."

"I think he's your son."

"You always did."

"Don't *you*?"

"It's possible."

"My dear boy, he looks just like you."

"It doesn't matter …"

"Then why play the role of secret benefactor? It's like something out of Henry James."

"It pleases me to be helpful. What more can I say?"

"It's her, isn't it? You're still in love with her."

"Is that an accusation?"

"Don't be ridiculous." She grabbed her *Wall Street Journal* and snapped it open.

He started getting up. "Shall I leave you to your reading?"

"No." She peered from behind the broadsheet and smiled oddly. "I should like very much if you stayed and kept me company." She pulled the second section of the newspaper out and handed it to him. "There," she said.

"Thank you, mother." He supplied his own smile, watching as she scrutinized the front page. "You know," he said. "Love is a permanent thing … if it's really love."

"I know that, son." She nodded primly as she read.

Craig emerged from his memories and checked his watch. There were still ten minutes before his public policy class. His instinctive thought, his habit, was to return his album to its place of safekeeping. But this morning, he didn't follow habit. He closed the empty drawer and gazed out on the busy streets.

Peter hid his pickup near the barn and walked quickly to the rear of Virginia's house, where he checked the ground-level windows and found them locked.

When he reached the old elm tree near the back entrance to the kitchen, he touched the gnarled bark of a massive lower trunk. Amazed by its girth, Peter estimated the tree was now a century old. From what he could tell, its upper branches remained strong and stable, but no limb was closer than 15 feet above the ground any longer.

Peter jogged back to his pickup and drove it slowly to the base of the elm. He climbed up on the roof of his cab from where he could just reach the lowest branch. Wrapping his hands around it, he threw one leg over and pulled himself up. Already, he was winded.

Sitting in the crook between limb and trunk, waiting for his breathing to normalize, Peter knew this wasn't something a 52-year-old man should be doing. But finally, he struggled to his feet and carefully scaled the ancient tree. When he reached a limb that extended close to the third-floor window of Virginia's old bedroom, he paused again, noting the initials, *PH/VS*, which he'd carved so long ago on the upper trunk.

Laying his palm flat against the window pane, he shook the sash and felt significant play in the casement. Relieved that the old flaw had never been repaired, he pushed in and up as the window sash rose six inches. Then with two hands, he lifted from beneath and opened the sash all the way.

From there it was a simple thing to get inside.

He was shocked by how dark and small her old room now seemed. There was no bed. The desk at which Virginia once did her homework now supported a big, old-fashioned sewing machine. In fact, the entire room had become storage space for sewing materials, with swatches of dressmaking cloth lying on the floor still attached to paper cutouts. Piles of worn children's clothing waited to be re-stitched. And on a table against another wall, numerous baskets overflowed with spools of thread.

Peter recalled that Virginia had worn her own handmade gown when he'd taken her to the senior prom—a night which represented both the highest and lowest points of his high school life. She had declined invitations from several of the most popular boys in school, the sons of her parents' friends, because Peter had asked her first. But when he brought her home that night, she announced that they couldn't see each other any more.

"I know your parents don't approve of me," he said.

As tears distorted her eye shadow and makeup, she kissed him in silent passion. Then, she gathered her crinolines, climbed out of his truck, and hurried to her front door.

Several nights later in the grip of adolescent madness, Peter scaled the elm to her bedroom window and tapped on the pane until she let him in. He stayed with her until just before dawn and then made his escape.

Summer came on. Their trysts continued until they made the mistake of oversleeping one morning—and Virginia's mother saw him from the kitchen window, as he clambered down the tree and hurried away through the meadows.

Virginia called and implored him to stay away because her parents were making things difficult for her, and were about to make things difficult for Peter and his family in their hierarchical little community.

For his family's sake, Peter complied. But soon after Virginia left for college, he made one last climb to the upper branch. He carved their initials where they could be seen from her bedroom window. Then, he opened the faulty window and climbed inside. He lay on her bed listening to the silent house, smelling the faint aroma of perfume on the pillow, imagining her lying with him there in the moonlight.

Eventually, he climbed back out, knowing he would never do this again. As he tried to close her window it squeaked sharply. Afraid that her parents would awaken, he left the window half-open and scrambled down from branch to branch, hitting the ground hard before running off into the night as lights came on inside the house.

Coming to his senses, Peter stepped through the sewing room clutter and out onto the third floor landing, quickly descending the elaborate stairway to the ground floor.

On a pad next to the foyer phone, he found Virginia's instructions to Marge Taylor about caring for the house and horses in her absence. There were contact details—including a phone number for Virginia's daughter in Sarasota.

Peter lifted the phone and dialed the number.

"Alston residence," said a woman with a Spanish accent.

"May I speak to Virginia Porter?"

"Who is calling, please?"

"Peter Harvey. I'm a friend from Connecticut."

"I'm sorry, Mr. Harvey," the woman said. "Mrs. Porter is sailing today."

"A *cruise*?"

"No sir. She's sailing on the bay with Mr. and Mrs. Alston and the children."

"Oh, I see."

"I don't expect them until dinnertime, sir. May I take a message?"

"Please tell her we need to speak as soon as possible. It's very urgent."

"I'll tell her."

"I wonder. Do they have a cell phone with them?"

"I'm not permitted to give that number."

"Perhaps *you* could call and deliver my message."

"They asked not to be disturbed."

"I beg of you ..."

"If they're far enough out, their cell phone won't work anyway."

"They must have a satellite phone or shortwave radio, for emergencies."

"I'm sorry, Mr. Harvey. I'll deliver your message as soon as possible."

After giving her his cell phone number and hanging up, Peter lingered in the spacious foyer. He felt his memories returning in the silence. He felt his reverence for old houses. And for a moment, Peter knew who he was again. But his confidence faded, replaced by a more familiar conviction—that he was, like most men, something of a fool.

In the kitchen, he found a door with a simple lock and went out that way, closing it after himself. He'd driven halfway to the Shelby River condo site before it struck him that he'd left the window open in the third floor sewing room. A fool indeed, he thought.

It had rained overnight in Trent, but not up here in this part of the state. There was no rain predicted here for several days. If Marge Taylor did her job correctly, she'd soon find the open window. She would tell Virginia immediately. And after some confusion, and suggestions from Marge that they inform the police, Virginia would realize what had happened. At least, he hoped she would. If so, she would assure Marge that nothing as dramatic as calling the police would be necessary. She might even lie to Marge and claim to have left the window open herself.

Checking the time as he drove, he saw that Peg would be teaching a class now, so he called her cell phone and left a secure message.

With a dozen roses cradled against his chest, Tom hurried through the hospital lobby and caught an elevator whose doors were closing.

A helpful young nurse stood near the button panel. "What floor?"

"Five … please." He was breathless.

The young woman pressed the five-button and smiled. "Pedes?"

"What's that?"

"Pediatrics," she said.

"Oh. Yes."

She looked at him doubtfully. "Your wife?"

"My daughter," he said.

The nurse nodded and stared intently. "Are you feeling well?"

"Just a little out of breath, why?"

"You look very pale."

"I haven't slept much the last few days."

"Of course." The nurse smiled as the doors opened on five. "Congratulations!"

Tom thanked the nurse and stepped onto the ward.

As he approached Kerry's room, he heard her voice inside and paused in the corridor. She spoke in a low, angry tone. Dec responded with frustration. Tom couldn't hear the words and didn't want to.

He noticed the name plate attached to the wall near her door— Kerry Beatrice—and only now recalled that Sally Hayes' middle name was Beatrice. How resistant he'd been to these events, he admitted.

"Bearing gifts, huh?" a passing nurse joked in a loud voice. "You can go in!"

"Thank you, nurse." He spoke loudly, too, giving Kerry and Dec fair warning.

He stepped into an abruptly silent room. Kerry sat alertly in her bed. Dec reclined with vague hostility in a nearby chair. Kerry noticed the roses and appeared embarrassed.

Tom held the flowers up—an offering. "I thought you might like these."

197

Kerry frowned. "We're leaving today."

"I know. I should have thought of it sooner."

She spoke without emotion. "We'll take them with us."

"Here he is!" said another female voice.

Tom turned to see a pediatric nurse enter the room with Kerry's baby in her arms.

"This little man is hungry," the nurse announced.

Dec jumped up and approached Tom. "Why don't we hang out in the coffee shop for a while?"

"Good idea," Tom agreed.

Kerry pointed to a small, bedside table and addressed Tom sternly. "Put them here."

Tom placed the flowers down and joined Dec near the doorway.

"Thank you," Kerry added.

Tom and Dec left the room and walked the corridor to the elevator bank. They waited in silence for the next car and descended to the lobby.

Once inside the hospital café, Dec spoke. "Coffee?"

"Sounds good." Tom glanced at the urns, reaching reflexively for his wallet.

Dec raised his hand. "I got it."

"Oh. All right."

As Dec fetched the coffee, Tom claimed an unoccupied table with a view of the hospital's steep front lawn and Leicester Village in the distance. He sat down and waited nervously. He had no idea how this young couple would react to his plan. Though they struggled to be polite, their hostility seemed always beneath the surface. His paying of the hospital and doctor bills had stunned them into mute anger. What would they say when he revealed his next idea?

"Just be patient," was Alice's advice, when he'd reached her in Madison two hours ago. "And honest."

Dec appeared with a small plastic tray which he placed on the table as he sat across from Tom. "Nice view," he mumbled, handing over a cup.

"Do you think she liked the flowers?" Tom asked.

"Yeah." Dec spoke with casual detachment. "I think so."

"I looked for a bassinette in some of the nicer shops downtown," Tom added. "But I couldn't find anything that I ... that I thought she might like."

Dec shrugged. "It's not your problem."

They stared out on the lawn.

Tom gathered his courage.

"Dec, I need to say something."

"Be my guest."

"You're *not* Sally Hayes' son."

The young man froze. Finally, he lifted his coffee and sipped. "No. I'm not."

"But Kerry *is* her daughter."

Dec sipped more coffee and nodded affirmatively.

"*My* daughter," Tom added.

"She made me call you. She wanted to know who you were. That time you and I were supposed to meet at the Starbucks in Bayview, Kerry was sitting at another table, waiting to get a look at you. The idea was ... you and I would talk for a while. Then, I would say, 'thank you very much, my mother was wrong, have a good life.'"

"I see."

"But you didn't come."

"So, she started calling every night. That *was* her, wasn't it?"

Dec nodded. "Things got screwy."

"I'm sorry I didn't come the first time."

"When you did show up at the Crow's Nest that Sunday, we didn't know what to do."

"I understand."

"She's pretty angry."

"I understand that too."

They went silent again, sipping coffee, staring at the lawn.

"She's a nice girl," Dec said. "Give her a chance."

"Give *her* a chance?" Tom laughed at himself. "She's got nothing to prove."

"It's hard when life keeps slapping you in the face."

"Maybe I can help."

"Mr. Winslow ... Kerry and I, we don't want to go live in your shed."

"That's fine, because I don't want you out there either."

"Oh."

"I've spoken to my wife about this. We think the three of you should stay with us, in our home, until you get on your feet."

Dec frowned. "That sounds impractical ... even nuts, maybe."

"I know people who might have some work for you."

"I don't know."

"I want you to help me convince her."

Dec smiled. "You don't know her like I do."

"That's why I need your help."

Dec stared at the lawn. "She wouldn't even give the hospital her real last name."

"You mean *my* name."

"Yeah."

After their coffee, they went back up to the room.

Kerry stunned Tom when she handed him the baby.

Sitting on the edge of her bed, holding his grandchild, Tom thought of Alice's advice. He said nothing. The baby fell asleep in his arms. Dec lay back in his chair, gazing at the muted TV. Kerry watched Tom for a while, then, closed her eyes.

Tom examined her face in repose. Without its stubbornness and borderline anger, it was clearly the face of Sally Hayes—with a bit of Will, perhaps, in the line of her nose, the shape of her chin.

Lost in his thoughts, drifting in the silent room with his grandchild in his arms, Tom eventually noticed his daughter's hand softly touching his knee as she dozed.

Alice and Eileen waited in the American Airlines lounge at Dane County Airport. Eileen's hop to Chicago was leaving Madison in less than an hour. Alice would have to wait almost two hours for her direct flight to Hartford.

"It's been an honor working with you, Mrs. Winslow."

"You've been wonderful, Eileen, under difficult circumstances."

"We had some moments."

"You're sure the Prairie Home Companion folks understand why we cancelled?"

"They do," Eileen assured her. "Whenever you'd like to reschedule, just let them know. Same goes for Weekend Edition."

"Will you work with me if my publisher sends me out again?"

"I hope so."

Alice touched Eileen's hand. "Why haven't you mentioned your novel?"

Surprise and embarrassment silenced her young friend.

"Craig told me you had a manuscript."

Eileen glanced at the Departures screen.

"Are you planning to publish it?"

"I haven't thought that far ahead."

"May I read it?"

"I don't know ..."

"You showed it to Craig."

"You're my client. I would never presume ..."

"I'd be honored to read it."

"Mrs. Winslow ..."

"And why can't you call me Alice?"

"I'm sorry. It's the way I was raised, I guess."

"All right, fine. What is this novel about?"

Eileen stared at Alice. "Love," she finally said. "It's about love, disappointment, hope."

"Okay."

"The main character is in her last year at college. She's involved in her first serious love affair. And she's conflicted."

"About?"

"Herself ... she's not convinced this man is right for her."

"Why not?"

"That's the thing, Mrs. Winslow. I've written the story. But, I'm not entirely sure why she's so confused."

Alice chuckled.

"They have great sex and enjoy being together," Eileen added. "She's confused by her expectations, I suppose. She feels her life opening up and, somehow, closing at the same time."

"Yes. I see."

"She thinks to herself, 'this man is lovely, but there must be other good men out there that I've never met. Is *this* really my life?'"

"And how is it resolved?"

"Her lover finds another girl."

"Oh!" Alice was intrigued by the dramatic reversal.

"He's been seeing the other girl all along, it turns out. He's been struggling with the same doubts as my main character. And he chooses someone else, almost as a way to make the confusion stop."

For several moments the women were silent. An American Airlines hostess came by and left them fresh iced teas.

"Your story sounds wonderful, Eileen."

"Do you really think so?"

Alice smiled. "I like your description of the man's motivation … wanting his confusion to stop."

"What about the woman's confusion?"

"It sounds like life made the decision for her."

"But now she's angry … and hurt."

"Which adds useful irony to the situation," Alice noted. "There's something very truthful in the way you've described their misjudgment of each other, and themselves."

Eileen nodded gravely. "What do you make of *her* uncertainty?"

"I haven't read it, remember." Alice paused, listening to the preliminary announcement of Eileen's flight.

"They'll be boarding in a few minutes." Eileen glanced at her bag.

"Your character is a woman I can identify with."

"Really?" Eileen sounded relieved.

"I imagine many readers would. Does she meet another man?"

"Not in the story. But she hopes to, I think."

"So, what has she learned?"

"As the story ends, she's caught between *two* realizations. On the one hand, she knows she was vain, and a bit presumptuous. On the other hand, it isn't just her pride that's been hurt. She's lost her belief in something that she can't even articulate."

"That's good. Very good."

Eileen laughed ruefully. "I told you she was conflicted."

"The heart learns from its own confusion. It *wants* to learn."

Eileen listened.

"Just don't let her heart become small and hard."

"All right." Eileen spoke softly.

Alice looked at her young friend and felt the deepest admiration.

The first boarding call for the Chicago flight came over the loud speaker.

Eileen gripped her bag. They stood up together.

Alice could see tears in her friend's eyes. "Do you understand what I'm saying?"

Eileen smiled bravely. "I do."

Alice embraced the younger woman and stepped back again.

"I better go," Eileen said, kissing Alice on the cheek.

"Send me your novel."

"I will."

Alice watched Eileen hurry through the lounge and out into the terminal concourse where she vanished in the crowd. The girl's flight number now flashed on the Departures screen, but her boarding gate was just down the concourse, so there was plenty of time.

Sitting again, sipping iced tea, Alice felt pangs of motherly affection for her earnest young friend. Once, her own heart had struggled with uncertain hopes. Now, her heart survived mainly on gratitude.

Alice watched the Departures screen until Eileen's flight had safely left.

An hour into her flight, Alice considered the tragic premise of Eileen's novel: that life is a tenuous balance of love and fate; that hope is a fiction made plausible by our choices.

Eager to be home and embrace her suddenly expanded family, her own choices, she felt armed against the madness she would face at tomorrow's hearing. She was a teacher—always would be—no matter what the board decided. If they couldn't understand her concern for Janet Mohamed, they didn't understand their own profession.

Staring from her window at the glorious afternoon sun above the cumuli, Alice recalled her awakening to the metaphysics of choice.

When she was 18, she'd applied to Boston University in opposition to her mother's lobbying for her own alma mater, Smith College—because BU offered the better creative writing program.

The application required two original writing samples—one in prose fiction, the other in poetry or non-fiction. Confident in her fiction, but feeling no special gift for the other options, she considered doing a non-fiction piece in the personal, improvisational style of the Beats.

Her mother was not easily impressed, but she smiled at the ingenuity of this idea.

"I still need a subject," Alice said.

Her mother mentioned the bookstore in Bayview, 20 miles west of Quakers Meadow. "They specialize in Beat literature. Jack Kerouac even lives in Bayview."

"Right."

"If you met him, and got an interview ..."

Alice laughed. "Kerouac?"

"Yes ... a perfect match of subject and style! You'd be the talk of Boston University."

"Oh, mother." Alice sighed.

"Let's visit the store and talk to the owner. I'll bet he can tell us how to reach Mr. Kerouac."

Alice nodded skeptically.

"If you impressed him, he might even give you a recommendation."

"It's supposed to be a *non-fiction* piece, mother. Your imagination is getting the better of you."

"Oh come, Alice." Her mother's Seven Sisters haughtiness flared. "We ahn't speaking of the President he-ah."

And so, on the following Saturday, they set out to find the elusive author of *On the Road*. Staring at homes and meadows as her mother drove west along Route 7A, Alice thought of her father's affection for Bayview which had reminded him of his southeast Virginia childhood.

John Goodwin had been a writer, briefly, for a Washington newspaper, before moving to New York after World War II. In short order he'd become the youngest partner in a large advertising agency, married Lucy Prescott from Brookline, Massachusetts, and purchased a home in the village of Quakers Meadow, Long Island.

Alice remembered the morning he died on the commuter train to Manhattan. Her mother had come to get her at the junior high school. And on the way home, Alice learned that a conductor had found her father slumped in a window seat with his *New York Times* on his lap. The train had reached Penn Station and the other passengers had disembarked. The conductor at first had assumed her father was sleeping.

Mrs. Goodwin turned off 7A and drove along High Street in the Chapel Hill section above Bayview Village. "Almost they-ah."

Alice nodded, wondering if her poor father had been surprised by his death. She'd always hoped he hadn't been afraid in those final seconds, that he'd known how much his daughter would always love him.

Her mother made the turn onto Main Street. "Day dreaming?"

"I was thinking of Dad. He liked it here."

"Yup." Her mother's clipped voice tightened on itself, as if anything more might reveal her loneliness.

When they saw Klein's Book Shop, they looked for a parking space along the street. But the town overflowed with shoppers and their vehicles.

So they proceeded to the waterfront and parked in a municipal lot near the harbor. As they got out and started back along Main, Alice resisted.

"I don't want to do this."

"Now, Alice, we've come all this way."

"But it's crazy."

"No." Her mother spoke firmly. "It's bold."

"At least let me do it myself."

"What do *I* do in the meantime?"

Alice pointed up the street. "Find us a place to have lunch."

Mrs. Goodwin frowned.

But Alice was firm as well. "I'll stand outside the book store when I'm done."

Mother and daughter parted company at Klein's. Mrs. Goodwin strolled on, examining windows, glancing back once. Alice stepped inside.

Several customers scanned tables where the latest books were displayed. Others browsed in three narrow aisles between the stacks that ran from front to back. And at the far end of the center aisle, a handsome young man sat on a wooden chair, intensely writing on a large pad balanced against his knees. Not only his handsome profile, but his self-possession, intrigued Alice.

Angry voices on the street drew her to the front window, from which she could see a man arguing with two boys and a girl who looked like college kids.

The older man wore tan chinos. The tails of his red-and-blue checked shirt hung free. The younger men sported droopy moustaches and afro-style hair. Their blue jeans were dyed, and their gauzy, Moroccan shirts were appliquéd with butterflies and flowers. The young woman's hair was long and straight. She wore a blue bandana around her forehead. Her brown trousers flared at the cuffs. And all three wore blue-tinted, wire-rim spectacles.

"No!" the older man said. "It's not about that!"

"Then what's it about, man?" said one of the boys.

The older man waved dismissively and nearly lost his balance.

They laughed at his inebriation.

"This is a drag," the girl said.

The older man lurched as he turned and reached for the book shop doorknob. But he'd miscalculated the distance. His hand swiped at the air and he stumbled again—this time, landing face-first against the window pane inches from Alice.

She was shocked to see the dark, dead eyes and once-handsome face of Jack Kerouac.

He peeled himself off the window and made another grab for the door knob. Now taking pity, his tormentors tried to guide him.

"Lay off!" he bellowed, flailing his arms like a stunned boxer.

"Come on." The girl pleaded with her friends.

They relented and slowly walked up Main Street with her, disappearing from Alice's view, as the author stumbled inside.

His sad eyes briefly focused on Alice. "Where's Klein?"

"I don't know."

"Klein! Reuben Klein!"

Alice backed away in fright. Two customers quickly left the store.

"Reuben!" The writer was bellowing again. "Where are you?"

"He went downstairs!" said the diligent young man at the rear of the store.

Kerouac appeared startled. "Who's that?"

"It's me. Tom!"

Alice watched from behind the poetry section.

"Tommy." The author sighed in relief as the young man approached. "Damn town is full o' hipsters ... using me to hang their theories on."

"Jack! Is that you?" An older man now emerged from an office doorway in back, hurrying toward Kerouac. "What's all the noise, Tom?"

"Mr. Kerouac was looking for you."

The author made a cryptic pronouncement. "The sky is empty."

"I know, Jack. I know." Mr. Klein put his arm on Kerouac's shoulders. "I have a coffee pot going in back. Come and sit down."

"That's all right." Kerouac waved his hand.

"I was checking deliveries. Tom was supposed to keep an eye on things."

"He *was*." Kerouac suddenly grinned.

"He's usually got his head in a book," Klein said. "Or something *he's* writing."

"Those aren't crimes." Kerouac laughed. "Not yet."

As the three men chuckled, Alice sensed their gruff affection for each other.

"How's business, Reuben?"

"We're selling a lot of your stuff, Jack."

Kerouac appeared pleased and surprised.

"I sell a copy of *On the Road* almost every day," Klein told him. "*The Subterraneans* and *The Dharma Bums* do almost as well. I don't think people understood *Big Sur* at first. But they're starting to."

Kerouac spoke with annoyance. "They're all parts of an ongoing narrative."

Mr. Klein smiled. "It takes people a while to understand serious writing."

Kerouac's mood darkened. "I need to get away."

"A change might be good, Jack."

"You know me, Reuben. I get sore and have to write." Kerouac began snapping his fingers, as if to a jazz riff only he could hear. "When I write, I got to move."

"Where will you go?" Klein asked.

"May swing out West for a while to see Neal. He's still hanging with Kesey. But then, I'm going to France ... for my next book."

"By the way, I read the proofs of *Desolation Angels* you gave me."

"What did you think?"

"Reminds me of the Jack I first met. There's some beautiful writing in that section about working as a fire warden in Washington State."

Kerouac nodded approvingly.

"When the book comes out we'll make some noise," Klein proposed. "Maybe you'll come back and read for us."

"Whatever you need, Reuben. You know that."

Alice shuddered when she noticed a large crowd gathering outside the store. The customers who'd left minutes earlier were back with their friends. They gaped and pointed at the storefront like visitors to a monkey house. The college kids were back.

"What's with these people?" Kerouac muttered. The crowd moved toward the door and he grew agitated. "Learn how to dream!"

Tom abruptly locked the door from inside.

"Don't be a dick!" someone in the crowd yelled. "Come out and talk to us!"

"I don't speak your language, friend!" Kerouac laughed wickedly. "Parlez vous Francais?"

The crowd looked annoyed and confused.

Tom offered an urgent suggestion. "I'll take him out the back way."

Klein pulled a set of keys from his pocket. "My car is parked on Soundview." He grabbed Kerouac's arm. "Go with Tom. He'll drive you home."

"All right." Kerouac was relieved for the moment. Then, the crowd began banging on the door. "I'm sorry, Reuben. It's not my fault."

"I know, Jack."

"Come with me," Tom said.

As the young man and the troubled author hurried to the rear and vanished, Mr. Klein spoke harshly through the glass panel of his front door. "You should be ashamed."

Someone in the crowd shouted back. "We just want to talk to him."

"If you're interested in books, you're welcome to come in."

The crowd grew silent.

"Otherwise, I can't help you."

Alice saw the three college kids walk away again. Several others followed.

Klein finally unlocked his door, allowing some 15 people to file in. He stepped behind his counter and watched as they wandered the stacks, grew bored and left.

Now, Klein noticed Alice standing near the poetry shelf. "Can I help you, Miss?"

"Oh, yes." She approached the counter. "I'm looking for *On the Road*."

"It's not poetry." He came back around the counter. "Would you like a signed copy?"

"That would be great."

Mr. Klein took a black paperback from a nearby shelf and handed it to her. Allowing her a moment to leaf through the front pages, including the first endpaper which the author had signed, Klein asked if there was anything else.

"Who was that kind boy?"

"What's that, Miss?"

"The boy who was writing in back … does he work for you?"

"You mean Tom. He's a kid from Bayview. He'll be a great writer some day."

"Oh?"

"He's very talented." Klein tapped his chest. "Has a lot of heart."

Alice placed her book on the counter and opened her purse. "I noticed."

Mr. Klein smiled as he rang her up. "He'll be back in a few minutes."

"I'm meeting my mother." Alice was embarrassed.

Mr. Klein nodded. His eyes were large and kind. "Are you from town?"

"No."

"Would you like to leave a name?"

"No. But thank you."

She paid him, picked up her book, and hurried out the door. Walking rapidly up Main Street, she was relieved to see her mother coming toward her.

"I found a lovely place for lunch," Mrs. Goodwin said.

"Can we just go home?"

"What about Kerouac? Did you find anything out?"

"I met him."

"You did?"

"We weren't formally introduced. I was just ... very close."

"I don't understand."

"I'll write it all down."

"You have something for BU, then?"

"Yes."

"Will he give you a recommendation?"

"I didn't ask him for anything." Alice spoke sadly. "He's a very troubled man, mother."

"I see."

All the way home from Bayview, Alice had felt her father's presence—as if his heart, and not her own, were beating in her chest. She had no idea why this would be, except that it was connected in some way to what she'd observed at the bookstore.

The pilot announced his approach into Hartford's Bradley Airport. Alice fastened her seatbelt, and looked out on the fields and highways and housing communities rolling underneath in the looming dusk. The winding river still glistened with fading light.

She remembered her non-fiction sample for the BU writing program. She'd started by addressing her father:

Today, I witnessed a sad thing and a beautiful thing in the same moment. I wish you were here with me, now, to help me understand them. I saw a man dying before his time, dissatisfied with what he'd once thought he wanted. I saw a younger man who tried to help him. He was a boy, really, respectful of the older man's achievements and aware, I sensed, of how those achievements had wrecked him. He was the sort of boy I might love, but will never see again. I know I'll always remember him, as I remember you. Everything I'd hoped my future could be seems held within a handful of memories.

Alice's application to BU had been accepted with stunning rapidity. She received a long letter from the program director who praised both her fiction and non-fiction samples. The director then telephoned and spent an hour talking with Alice and her mother about creative writing at BU. He said that everyone connected with the program thought very highly of Alice's potential, and expected her to bring credit on the school.

When she enrolled, the director took a personal interest, helping Alice get her stories published in literary magazines. He encouraged her to share her insights with fellow writing students. He secured a fellowship for her as his assistant.

By the start of her sophomore year when she met Craig McCall, whose family owned the well-known publishing group, life seemed to be arranging itself on her behalf. Then one night the following spring, at a party in a Boston brownstone, she and Craig had an argument so terrible he ended up leaving her there. Feeling stranded, yet relieved to be on her own in the crowded apartment, she was stunned to see the boy from Bayview coming across the room to introduce himself.

She couldn't help feeling drawn to him—nearly confessing her secret—until he mentioned Richard Fariña's modish novel. She called the book a rip-off of Pynchon and Kerouac, with nothing like the authentic power of either—"a clever college boy's experiment in literary vanity." He claimed it was a book that would live forever— "the record of a moment's change in American literature."

As it happened, she thought now, they'd both been right. The book was still remembered, though mainly as an underground oddity—a story as arch and self-referencing as the moment it had captured.

Alice said nothing that night, or ever, about her memory of Tom and Kerouac in the Bayview bookstore. It was a memory she'd felt the need to protect, even from him.

Six

Mid-morning sunlight glared on the granite crypt. The ripened heads of Nancy's red and yellow roses drooped in the vase where she'd left them three days ago. Marianna's white gardenias were a tangled desolation in the other vase.

Nancy removed her blackened roses and replaced them with fresh violets purchased in the square below.

"Fidelity … humility … chastity," she whispered as a prayer to summon the dead.

She remembered awakening in the stuffy apartment she'd shared with Angelica down near the river that summer. A tremor of nausea had rippled from her stomach to her throat. She'd run to the bathroom, fallen to her knees and vomited in the toilet.

Angelica stood in the bathroom doorway, watching. "Three mornings in a row."

Nancy glanced at her friend, then, tore off some bath tissue to wipe her sour lips.

"Have you told Paolo?"

Nancy stood and flushed the toilet.

"Have you?"

"*Stop*," Nancy pleaded. "It's nothing to do with him."

"He might not agree."

"I haven't *been* with Paolo for at least a month."

"It usually starts in the fifth or sixth week …"

"You're a gynecologist now?"

Angelica was confused by Nancy's anger.

"I *assure* you. It's not Paolo."

Nancy hurried back to her tiny bedroom with Angelica following her. Having forgotten to close the shutters overnight, she felt disoriented by sunlight on her dingy walls. It was incredibly hot. She lifted a latch and pushed the windows out, filling her bedroom with moist air from the Arno.

Angelica spoke earnestly. "What are you going to do?"

"Go home and marry Will. First, I have to deal with this." She stared at the river. "I hope that doesn't shock you."

"We're not little girls any more."

Nancy turned from her window. "I'm sorry."

"I can imagine how you feel."

"Do you think Gabriele's sister would help?"

"I can ask her."

"Just don't tell Gabriele."

Angelica paused before speaking. "Why would I tell Gabriele?"

Nancy looked at her friend in silence.

Spontaneous tears filled Angelica's eyes. "Why would you say that?"

Nancy gazed at the blanched face of Angelica's grave and felt the grip of oppressive heat on the mountaintop. She'd left her wristwatch at the hotel, but the sun's position suggested roughly eleven o'clock.

She heard footsteps.

A man's shadow passed over the crypt as he neared her. "I tried you first at your hotel," he said, as he sat with her on the stone bench.

She glanced at Gabriele. "I imagine you spend a lot of time here now."

"Less than before; I visit with Marianna."

"There's something shameful in us being here together."

"Actually, she imagined us together."

Nancy frowned.

"She said it more than once. 'If something ever happens to me ...'"

"You're keeping a promise to your wife?"

"There is no promise," he whispered, gazing at the crypt. "I have tried to bury my memories here, with her, and I think you should do the same. Do not go on thinking that every breath you take is another betrayal of your friend."

"It's not that easy."

"Angelica loved you, Chiara."

"Did you know I was pregnant that summer?"

"I did not know." He paused. "I may have suspected."

"Angelica and Violetta arranged an abortion."

He reached for her hand.

"They took me to a good doctor, but he was nervous," she explained. "He nicked my uterus. At least, that's what he told me. Later, back home, I learned how much damage there was. I had to tell Will there would never be children. He married me anyway."

"He loved you."

"I don't know why."

"There is no perfect love. A good man knows this."

Nancy glanced at the basilica behind them when she heard the faint chanting of the monks. "You make our sins sound like romance."

"Do you think we are not paying for our sins?"

They sat in the heat and stared at the silent crypt.

Finally, Gabriele offered a suggestion. "Shall we visit the church?"

She smiled wearily. "Another day."

"Lunch, then?" He stood, pulling her gently by the hand.

"I'd prefer one of Florence's famous peach iced-teas."

"Come with me." He pointed to the street below. "Just beneath the square is Café Michelangelo."

"Angelica loved that place," Nancy recalled. "There's a wonderful view."

"And the city's best iced-tea," he confirmed.

It took them fifteen minutes to descend the steps from San Miniato to the street, and to walk across into Piazzale Michelangelo, and down a winding walkway to the café, whose busy patio glittered with white umbrellas.

A waiter led them to an empty table overlooking the valley. After opening their umbrella, he invited them to sit, took their order, and hurried away.

"It is mainly for tourists," Gabriele said, a bit embarrassed by the crowd, and the American rock music playing on the outdoor sound system.

"I *am* a tourist."

Gabriele smiled warmly and stared out over his city.

Even beneath their billowy umbrella, Nancy felt the midday heat. Craning her neck to see the tip of the basilica on the mountain behind them, she sighed. "Il portale di cielo."

The waiter smiled as he placed their teas down.

Gabriele waited for the man to leave. "You were with Violetta yesterday?"

Nancy sipped her sweetened tea. "She explained the stock offering."

"As a 'public' company, Antonini becomes a truly global brand. The investment bankers tell us this is a good thing."

"She said you have doubts."

"We'll be incredibly rich." Gabriele shrugged. "My sister is an astute business woman. I have asked her only to consider what our father would want."

"To make your own decisions, surely ..."

"Perhaps." He sipped his tea. "Violetta must do as she wishes. She has given her life to this business. I must think of my daughter's future."

"Violetta asked my opinion," Nancy said. "But I'm a writer, not a business person. I oversee our clients' speeches and press materials ... media strategies. My husband is the finance and marketing expert. You should hire *him*."

"If you recommend it," he said.

She paused. "I've decided to sell him my share of our business."

"And *our* company will split." Gabriele stared into the valley as he spoke. "I've proposed an entity that retains a form of the company name, to publish books again."

"Oh?"

"Violetta and I will work this out with the bankers. I plan to re-issue the books my family first published. They will be well-crafted."

"Digital versions of books on reading devices ... that's the future, I'm afraid."

"We will make beautiful books for that market, and books of fine paper and bound leather for another taste."

Nancy nodded.

"I'll need an editor with an eye for new ideas," he added.

"I brought a book with me. It's a beautiful novel ... popular in the States at the moment. If the Italian rights are available you should buy them."

"What is this book? Do I know it?"

"It's called *The Chastened Heart.*"

"I saw a review in *The Herald Tribune.* I forget the author's name."

"Alice Prescott Winslow ... she's my mother-in-law."

"Ah." He nodded as he looked out on the valley. "Ché piccolo mondo."

She sipped her tea. On the sound system, Dolly Parton sang *I Will Always Love You* in a tearful voice that said she'd already stopped.

Nancy understood that Will and Angelica would be in her heart forever, sheltered by the memory of her failings. And this, she realized, was the answer to her prayer, a way forward that she could accept. She watched the silent river flowing into the heart of the ancient city in the wide openness of a sun-bleached valley.

"Do you think that you will stay with us, Chiara?"

Turning to answer him, she was struck by the beauty of his mournful eyes.

Tom eased himself out of bed at six o'clock feeling better than he had in days. He'd slept well with his wife beside him. Now, strong coffee would help him write his column.

He quietly closed the bedroom door for Alice and tip-toed along the hallway, glancing into Will's room, where the bed was empty. Creeping softly down the stairs, he welcomed the thought of an infant in his house again.

But as he entered the kitchen, he was shocked to find Kerry sitting near the window nursing the child.

"Sorry," he said. "I'll wait in the living room."

"There's no need. It's what babies do."

"Of course, but …"

"This is your grandson."

Tom laughed. "I know."

He stood very still, watching the back of his grandson's head, listening to the comforting sounds the little boy made as he drew sustenance from his mother.

"Have you seen Will?"

"He took his computer to your shed. He wanted to check newspaper websites and line up some phone calls."

"Oh, right." Tom remembered Will asking for the key last night. It now occurred to him that the shed would be a good place to work on his column in peace and quiet today. "How did you sleep in that bedroom?"

"We slept fine, didn't we?" she whispered, caressing her baby's head. "Dec was up all night though. That's why we came downstairs ... to give him a break."

"He's not comfortable here?"

"Oh, it's not that. When the baby fusses, Dec sits up with him. The baby loves falling asleep in his arms. And it lets *me* sleep."

"I see."

"But Dec *can't* sleep." She laughed softly. "He's afraid he'll drop the baby or crush it or something."

"He's a nice young man."

"Yeah, he is."

Tom stared into her eyes. "Are *you* comfortable here?"

Kerry smiled. "I like your son ..."

"Your *brother*," he reminded her.

"Yes. And your wife is very nice."

Feeling a puff of fresh air, Tom noticed the kitchen door was open. He could see the meadow beyond the outer screen. He looked at his daughter again.

"When we get past this hearing, I'll speak to a friend about a job for Dec. I hope something in construction is okay, for the time being."

Kerry stared at him. "My mother said you were a kind person."

Embarrassed, Tom glanced at the meadow again.

"Not perfect," Kerry added. "But who is?"

"What else did she tell you?"

"Not much; she didn't want me to build my hopes up."

"She could have contacted me about you."

"We girls have our pride. Didn't you know?"

"Come on."

Kerry shrugged. "You know what she was like."

"Loyal ... and stubborn."

"You got that right."

"I guess she finally *did* urge you contact me."

"At the end ..."

"The phone calls were a little bizarre. A therapist might call them passive-aggressive."

"I don't know what a therapist would say. Part of me didn't even want to reach out. I didn't know what to expect."

"I understand."

"I *tried* to make her talk about you." Kerry's voice grew edgy and the baby stopped sucking. As he twitched and stretched, Kerry put her hand on his head and pressed him back on her breast. She spoke more softly now. "When she got really sick, she finally opened up. I think *she* felt better. But then, I realized how angry *I* was."

Tom felt the sharpness of guilt in his heart. "I'm glad you found me."

"Couldn't stand the suspense any longer ..."

He liked his daughter's sense of humor. "I was going to make some coffee."

"I wouldn't mind a cup."

Tom opened the cabinet where they kept the coffee. "I make it pretty strong."

"Okay."

He turned to look at her. "I want to know more about you, Kerry."

She rocked as she rubbed her baby's head. "When things calm down we can talk."

"Ask *me* whatever you want."

"Don't worry."

Glancing out through the screen door, Tom saw Will emerge from the shed holding a cell phone to his ear as he came across the meadow toward the house. A flutter of pride filled Tom's heart—his children were home. Then, abruptly, Will stopped walking. Standing rigidly in the meadow, listening intently to his phone, he raised a hand to shield his eyes as the sun rose brightly.

Will didn't try to argue. He knew why Nancy had called and he let her speak.

She was staying in Florence indefinitely and wanted to sell her half of the business.

"To you," she said, "or any investor you prefer."

"Do you have a price in mind?"

"Whatever is fair. You know what it's worth."

"All right," he managed to say.

And then, after a long silence which tempted him to think she might still change her mind, she asked him simply to let her go.

Moments later, their trans-Atlantic conversation came to its awkward end.

Staring up at his parents' house through the morning glare, Will imagined he could see his father watching him from the kitchen door. But he wasn't certain. In sunlight this sharp, shining laterally into the meadow, it was difficult to be sure of anything.

Will turned and walked out beyond the shed into the farthest reaches of the meadow where the wild grass had been allowed to grow. His shoes and trouser cuffs grew damp. A rabbit darted past. Larks fluttered in the 12-inch growth. The rising sun baked against his back.

He couldn't help remembering a warm September morning 15 years ago, walking with Nancy in the same meadow. She'd come back from Florence two weeks earlier without letting him know.

"I've been staying at my parents' house on the Cape," she said when she finally reached him in Trent. "I should have called sooner, but, I needed time alone."

"I thought that's what Florence was about." He didn't bother to hide his irritation.

"You're right to be angry. But there are things I need to say."

"Say them."

"Not on the phone."

"Just tell me."

"No."

He sighed. "You want me to drive up there?"

"Let me come to you. Is that all right?"

"Whatever."

She came to Trent two days later.

After some small talk with his parents, they escaped to the privacy of the meadow. As they walked, she told him about a summer of affairs, the last one leading to an abortion before coming home.

Finally, she added what her American doctor had just told her—she'd been damaged by the procedure.

Will listened in disbelief until she stopped speaking.

"Are you in pain?" he asked.

This surprised her. "No, just disgusted with myself."

"You don't have to say that."

"It's a tawdry little tale."

"No. That's something our parents would say."

"Mine already have, believe me."

He nodded.

They walked in silence until she couldn't bear it any longer. "Say something!"

"I don't know what to say."

"Not even a question?"

"It didn't sound like you'd left anything out."

She stopped walking and stared at the ground.

"I'm sorry." He faced her. "There is one question."

She looked up, almost heartened by his willingness to engage her self-abnegation.

"Do you love me?" he asked.

She collapsed against him. When he wrapped his arms around her she sobbed.

Now, as he reached the western boundary of the meadow and stopped, he tried to imagine where his life could go from here. He'd never felt this futile or alone, not even as a boy enduring the despair of his parents' divorce. But maybe children are stronger than adults, he thought, their innocence another of those temporary immunities they carry into the world.

Just ahead he saw the rough stone wall that had marked the property line since the late 18th Century. On the other side was a stand of white birch trees, through which flowed the Bumble Bee Brook, a tributary of the Trent River. And beyond the birches and the brook was the town's 50-acre land preserve, on which a farm coalition was licensed to grow organic corn every summer.

Now fully lit by the sun, this vast preserve extended to the base of the Leicester Hills in the greater distance. The spacious land was a comfort in its silent readiness to be tilled.

Turning back and heading toward the house, Will accepted the truth with sadness. It had taken 15 years, but Nancy finally had forgiven herself. He was glad of that, relieved in fact, though he wondered how long it would take to forgive himself for having hoped this day would never come.

Alice stared into her closet as Tom sat on their bed. She lifted out a khaki summer dress and clutched it to herself. "What do you think?"

"I've always liked that one."

The garment's tailored cut did flatter her figure, but aroused her concern about making the wrong impression. She put the dress back with a sigh and stood in her underwear. "Why does Maldonado keep doing this?"

"Maybe she's jealous."

"That's what Judy Lavan said." Alice looked at her husband. "Will you be all right today?"

"*Me*? I'll be writing my column. I'll have the Rover if Kerry needs anything. *You're* the one we're all concerned about."

"I'm going through this hearing because I care about my job." She waved her hand as if impatient with the air. "I don't consider it a serious academic event."

"I *am* worried about Will," he said.

"He's devastated." She searched Tom's expression for a male reaction to her bleak assessment of their son's distress. "Kerry knew it the moment he came in from the shed."

"Did you notice how she put the baby in his arms?"

"I really like that girl." Alice fought an urge to cry. It was going to be a long day. "Do you remember when Nancy came back from Florence, and they walked for hours in the meadow?"

"Yes."

"I thought they were breaking up."

"They were."

"Then they came inside and told us they were getting married." She glanced again at the khaki dress. "We told them to follow their hearts. Was that the wrong advice?"

"No." His voice was heavy with sorrow. "They met in college, had trouble, got married, and stayed together 15 years. That's how it was supposed to go."

Alice tried to accept his philosophical speculation—that love has its own lifespan. Was it that simple, she wondered, afraid that it just might be?

"Then again ... look at us," he offered. "*We* were divorced."

"Oh, they're not going to do what we did. It's over ... period." Alice yanked the khaki dress from its hanger and turned toward him again. "You really think this is the right thing to wear?"

"It's perfect, Alice."

She held the dress up to the full-length mirror inside her closet door.

"*Really,*" he added.

Alice unzipped the back of the dress and stepped into it. She pushed her arms through on top and fussed with the way it hung on her shoulders and chest. Staring at the mirror, she thought of her secret. Then, she walked to the bed and turned so he could zip her up.

He stood and did his duty with a practiced touch, before kissing the back of her neck.

She faced him and smiled. "There's something I've never told you."

He eased himself down on the edge of the bed and stared at her.

"When you were a young man, you hung around that old book store in Bayview."

"Klein's," he said, looking surprised to hear his past coming back to him.

"I was there the day you saved Jack Kerouac from those celebrity gawkers."

He laughed nervously. "You were there?"

Someone knocked on their bedroom door.

"It's me, Mom! We need to go soon."

"All right," she called back.

"Could you send Dad out? I need his advice on something."

"I'll be right there!" Tom promised.

They heard their son's footsteps retreating on the stairway.

Tom looked at Alice. "You're saying that the night we met, in Boston, you already knew who I was?"

"I didn't know you, exactly. I just remembered how kind you'd been to that poor man. It touched me. I knew you were the sort of boy I could love."

Tom shook his head in bewilderment.

"Of course, things got confused," she added.

"That's an understatement."

"I knew when I married you that you'd been hurt … and I was partly to blame." She paused. "Still, it didn't matter how crazy or spiteful things got. That memory of you in the bookstore held me together somehow."

"Oh, Alice."

"I could never really believe that boy wouldn't find a way to heal his wounds." She laughed ruefully. "I even thought I could help him do it, right up to the day he sent me away."

"I should never have let you go to Chicago."

"I think that's how you survived, actually. But even then, I had to come back … to see if you'd healed yourself enough to forgive me. That must sound crazy."

"It was a second chance, Alice. We were smart enough to take it."

Now, she did weep. There was no controlling it. He hurried to their bureau for a clean handkerchief and she shuddered as she took it from him.

"We were just more fortunate than Will and Nancy," he said. "That's all."

"Our children are such good people." She pressed the starched white cotton against her eyes. "The way they deal with their losses helps *me* feel brave."

"Children give their parents courage," Tom whispered. "It's their gift."

She felt overcome by protective indignation. "Was your father being courageous when he killed himself?"

"Some parents throw their gift away," he said. "Some children take their gift back."

She touched his shoulder. "I'm sorry I mentioned that."

"It's all right." Tom shrugged.

"It's just … what he did to you was wrong."

"Have I done much better for *my* children?"

"We're all sinners where our children are concerned," she said. "But you haven't *betrayed* your children."

"I'm not so sure," he replied. "All I know is I can't judge him any more. He died believing he was unforgiven."

Alice kissed Tom warmly on the lips.

"It's getting late." He looked distracted suddenly. "I better see what Will needs."

Somewhere beyond the Harveys' screened porch a hawk cried out. Peter took a last gulp of coffee and glanced at his watch—it was nine-fifteen. Opening his cell phone, he keyed in the number for the Trent River condo trailer and left a terse message.

"This is Pete Harvey. I'm running late today."

Then he snapped the phone shut and contemplated the unthinkable—that Virginia Porter might not call back in time to help. If so, he'd failed his wife again.

Meanwhile, Peg had spent the better part of yesterday rallying Shelby professors and students on Alice's behalf. Late into the night she'd continued pressuring the few remaining holdouts with insistent phone calls. As a result of her efforts, a large group had agreed to meet outside the theater arts building this morning at ten-thirty—and then to march inside presenting a united front at Alice's hearing.

Peter heard Peg descending the stairs from their bedroom.

She joined him on the porch. "Are you sure Virginia got the message?"

"I assume she did."

Peg sat beside him in a wicker chair. "There's no other way to reach her?"

"I told you what I did to get the daughter's number." He stared at the woods behind their house, too embarrassed to look at her.

"Can you try her again this morning?"

"Yes." He heard the edge in his own sigh. "If I don't hear back soon ..."

"All right then." Peg stood abruptly. "I have to leave."

Peter looked at her helplessly.

"You'll call me if you hear anything," she said.

"Of course I will."

Peg nodded firmly and headed toward the kitchen to gather her school things. As her footsteps faded, he took a deep breath and got ready to call Sarasota again. But the phone startled him by ringing in his hand.

He put it to his ear and heard Virginia Porter's angry voice.

"Did you get this number from Dick Emerson?"

"No."

"You didn't get it from Marge Taylor. I spoke with her this morning and ..."

"I found another way."

"Dick and Marge are the only people who have my daughter's number."

"Did Marge mention the open window in your upstairs sewing room?"

"She mentioned nothing of the sort."

"I left that window open, by the way." Peter listened to Virginia's stunned silence. "Marge should close it before it rains."

Her silence continued for what seemed an eternity.

"Have you lost your mind?" she finally said.

"I had to reach you, Virginia. There's something immoral happening at Shelby."

"What are you talking about?"

"You haven't seen the news reports?"

"I'm on vacation, Peter. I'm supposed to be, anyway. And since I haven't been able to raise Dick Emerson this morning, I'm completely in the dark."

Peter described the situation in brief but stark detail.

"I dislike interfering with management of the school," she said.

"I know. But things have gone completely mad up there."

"Let's not be dramatic …"

"A fine professor is being railroaded."

"It does sound peculiar. I'm shocked that I knew nothing about this. Dick Emerson should have called me." She paused. "Cathleen Maldonado's family has suffered a terrible tragedy."

"We all have."

"Well, yes." She sounded surprised to be confronted on this topic.

"Unless you're suggesting that some people own 9/11, and the rest of us are spectators."

"That's a harsh way to put things."

"These are harsh accusations, Virginia. None of them remotely true, as I understand it. Peg and I have known the Winslows for 25 years."

"So have I."

"Alice protected a Muslim girl from a bunch of jerks. Most sane people would have done the same thing. But Maldonado grabs the wrong end of the stick. And you're saying we have to back off because of 9/11?"

"Is that really what I said?"

"*You* brought it up."

"All right, you've made your point." She paused again. "Even if we stipulate that your description of things is accurate, why would Cathleen do this?"

"Why would she make trouble for Peg over the Isaac Shelby diary? If you ask me, she's jealous of her colleagues."

Virginia listened.

"A self-righteous bully, and, quite possibly crazy."

"Did Peg suggest you call me? I know she and Alice are close."

"You're implying I'm prejudiced by my wife's friendship."

"No, I'm not."

"Then what *did* you mean?"

"Just that you're loyal," she said softly.

Now, Peter had no response.

"I remember a boy from high school," Virginia added. "He loved a girl in our class so much that even when her parents told him to stay away, he wouldn't listen. He climbed a tree outside the girl's bedroom window one night and woke her up."

"The girl let him in. That's what I heard."

"What girl in her right mind sends a boy like that away?"

Peter said nothing.

"I'll speak to Dick Emerson. If I can reach him, that is. I've tried several times this morning."

"*He's* not answering *your* calls. That's interesting."

"I could tell you stories." She laughed bitterly. "I'll try him again right now."

"Thank you, Virginia."

"Give my best to Peg."

When Peter clicked his cell phone off, he realized Peg was standing behind him.

"Will she help?"

Peter stood and faced his wife. "She's calling Dick Emerson now."

"You were very good."

Looking into her eyes, Peter was surprised by what he saw.

"Thank you," she said, kissing his cheek before hurrying out to her car.

Peter lingered on the porch, still astonished by his wife's girlish affection and the hope in her eyes. He heard her starting up the Nissan, pulling out of the driveway and motoring off.

Tom briefly admired a westerly view from the picture window Peter Harvey had built into the shed. Then, he opened his laptop and began writing his Sunday column. After an eventful week away from his Hartford office, he faced a deadline which precluded research or reporting. But Alice's secret memory had given him a subject that flowed from his heart.

The Day I Drove Jack Kerouac Home
By Tom Winslow

In the last years of his foreshortened life, Jack Kerouac was an angry, frightened man whose vibrant writing and handsome face had been ruined by booze.

I knew him in the mid-1960s when I was a high school boy hanging out at a Long Island book store that he frequented because he owned a home in the neighborhood. It was barely seven years since publication of "On the Road." But the 60s were becoming a decade of stasis for the hyperactive, ex-altar boy from Lowell, MA.

Shortly after arriving at Columbia University in 1940 on a football scholarship, Kerouac had dropped out, done brief stints with the Merchant Marine and Navy, and then commenced his life of travel and writing.

Though he made influential literary friends along the way, and invented a widely-imitated style, Kerouac always was set apart. He'd been born with the triple pedigree of a mid-20th century American outsider—the son of blue collar, Catholic, French-Canadians. And the sensibility of an outcast suited him.

Like Melville, Whitman, Twain, Hemingway, Ellison and Salinger, he produced a narrative style so unexpected and individual that it took the public some time to realize they were hearing the voice of the true America speaking.

"On the Road" did not extol the phony virtues of a fictitious nation. Its generous vision encompassed the beauty, goodness, disappointment and insanity to be found along the arterial highways of late-1940s America. But apparently, the journey took its toll. And at some point, Kerouac tried to get home and couldn't find his way back.

One day in 1964, at that little neighborhood book shop, he got into a drunken argument with some aggressive tourists. Behaving more like celebrity hounds than book lovers, the tourists had offended the unstable Kerouac who, after all, remained a mill workers' son raised to value politeness above all social graces.

To avert an embarrassing scene, the store's owner gave me the keys to his Buick so I could take Kerouac out the back door of the shop and drive him home. Once in the car and out of danger, Kerouac seemed to relax a bit in the passenger seat. And knowing I was a budding novelist, he asked me an interesting question.

"What would you say is the worst thing that can happen to a writer?"

I had no idea.

"Come on, Tommy. It's not a trick question."

"To be ignored?" I ventured. "Not to be read?"

He smiled, as if impressed or surprised by my response. Then he shook his head violently, perhaps to accelerate the self-lobotomizing effects of his daily drinking.

"That's not it. Any writer worth his weight can get himself read. The real trick is to be heard, man. To be understood, you dig?"

"You've done that," I declared, with all my high school certitude.

"No. I tried."

"Do you really think people don't understand your work?"

His initial silence suggested I'd stumped him. But he was still Jack Kerouac.

"I misunderstood myself. By the time I realized no one really heard the music, not the readers or the teachers, not the reporters or the TV hosts, not even my publishers, it was too late. And then, I didn't own my work any more."

"When a writer sells his work, should he expect to keep owning it?"

"You're too smart for me, kid. When I was your age, or even ten years ago, I might have had a good response for your cute little Thomistic proposition."

He closed his eyes and we traveled for several minutes in silence. Finally, as if responding to some inner sense of the road's pitch, he roused himself and pointed at a faded-white ranch house on a modest, tree-lined street.

"This it is, Tommy."

I stopped the car and waited as he got out and stumbled up the cracked cement pathway to the little house. As I put the Buick in gear and started away, I saw him on the front steps of the house with his hand politely raised.

Not long after that, I heard that he and his mother were moving to Florida. I never saw him again.

Five years later, working as a newspaper reporter on Long Island, I read a wire report about his death, at age 47, in the sunshine state. A moody silence fell on the newsroom. And when our shift ended that night, several colleagues and I went out to toast the author of "On the Road."

For most young men, especially writers, in that innocently radical time, Kerouac had been an inspiration. Late into the night, as drinks flowed, each of us was encouraged to offer some bit of personal insight and praise for his career, his literary influence, or the importance of this or that particular book.

At one point, someone asked if anyone in the group had ever met Kerouac.

None of my colleagues had, though each seemed certain of something about him.

"He was a real bad drunk," said one.

"Face it," said another. "He wrote the same damn book over and over."

"He only made a few thousand bucks from 'On the Road.'"

"Well, Warner Brothers had offered $110,000 for the movie rights. But his agent advised him to turn it down. They were holding out for a $150,000 deal involving Brando at Paramount. The deal fell through and Hollywood lost interest."

"Do you really think he wrote it in four weeks on a single roll of teletype paper?"

"I heard it was sheets of tracing paper that he glued together."

And it went on like that.

Finally, someone remembered that I'd been raised in Bayview, and that Kerouac had lived there during the early and mid-60s.

"Did you ever meet him, Tom?" he asked. "You must have seen him around town ... in one of the bars."

I waited for the laughter to subside, thinking of the disillusion Kerouac had confessed as I'd driven him home that day. I thought of his courtliness, the nervous grace with which he'd waited for his slow, alcoholic death. And I remembered the question he'd asked me, while suddenly realizing it hadn't been a question at all, but a word of advice, gently given: A writer's only purpose is to bear witness to mystery.

"Yes," I told my boisterous colleagues. "I met him a few times."

"So, what was he like?"

"Like anybody else, I guess, an average person plagued by doubt."

My colleagues were silent now.

"He didn't like people prying into his thoughts and feelings," I told them. "He wanted people to read his books and understand them as a journey, a record of self-discovery. He cared about beauty, seeking it, understanding it. Beauty was his word for love."

"I guess he never found it," someone suggested.

"Oh, I think he found it," I said. "It just wasn't what he'd expected."

Tom looked up from his work and saw Dec and Kerry approaching the stone wall in the far reaches of the meadow. Apparently, they'd gotten the baby to sleep and were having a moment to themselves. As Kerry moved in short, painful steps, Dec held her arm and guided her to a seat on the distant wall.

Tom's cell phone buzzed.

It was Jennifer Yi, sounding urgent. "They need your column."

Tom chuckled. "Is Bill Sanchez complaining?"

"Not any more. Carl Fervor let him go."

"What?"

"They've picked a new editor-in-chief. It's being announced today."

"Do you know who it is?"

"Rick McDougall."

Tom was shocked by the fact that this news didn't surprise him. He understood, now, why McDougall had talked endlessly on the phone in the days before Carl Fervor's visit—and had felt so free to come and go without explanation.

"Mr. Winslow?"

"Sorry, Jen … I've just knocked out a draft … about 1,100 words."

"Rick says he has space for 600."

"My pieces usually run 900," he said. "We can edit, but I can't see cutting it by half."

"Rick said take all the space you want for the digital version. We just need to keep it around 600 words, maybe 650, for the paper."

"What else is he running on that page?"

"Some advertising, I think."

"Can't we jump to a second page?"

"The Ideas Section is going down to a page and a half from four," Jen said. "Carl and Rick may fold it in with Entertainment. The paper itself is being reduced by two inches across and four inches down."

"Almost 25% ..."

"I've seen a prototype," Jen said. "It looks like a weekly shopper."

"The incredible shrinking newspaper ..."

"What's your column about?"

"Jack Kerouac ..."

"You mean the writer?"

"Yes. Have you ever read *On the Road*?"

"Maybe in high school ... I'm not sure."

"You'd remember."

"Un huh. What's the Connecticut angle?"

"It's a personal remembrance. I met Kerouac when I was a kid."

"Oh, a celebrity thing; I'll tell Rick."

"And I'll try cutting it, but 600 words is tough, Jen. If Rick has questions he can reach me on my cell. Now, what are *you* working on?"

"I'm kind of helping Rick at the moment." She sounded nervous. "But if *you* need me for something ..."

"It's all right. How's Lev doing?"

"He says everything's good with Carol and the baby. He starts paternity leave on Monday ... four weeks."

"Good for him."

Jen sighed. "Rick asked him to delay it or cut it in half."

"That's ridiculous."

"They were arguing in your office a while ago," she added. "Even with the door shut I could hear them. It got personal. Lev demanded the Shelby College assignment."

"City-desk is covering that hearing. My son talked to them yesterday."

"That was yesterday," she said. "Today, they're doing lay-offs. Lev heard they're so short-handed they want to go with a wire story. So, he told Rick to send *him*, and that's what started the argument. For some reason Rick didn't want Lev to do it." She paused. "Lev threatened to quit."

"Oh no."

"Rick gave in. Lev's on his way to Shelby now."

Tom made a note to call Will and have him look for Lev at the hearing and arrange an interview with Alice.

"I hope your wife's okay," she said. "What's going on at Shelby sounds crazy."

After clicking off, Tom scrolled through his draft finding two or three places to trim or end the column. Each solution would give his new boss the desired length, but produce a very different piece than he'd intended.

Think about it later, he told himself. It was just past ten, an hour until the hearing, which would be covered live on the Shelby College radio station.

He called Bill Sanchez at home, got no answer, and left a message. He repeated the process with Bill's cell phone. It was almost ten-fifteen now.

"Damn." He remembered that Will had spoken to Perry Miller, who'd promised to say something nice about Alice on his radio show. He set his laptop browser to the small, independent station that carried Perry's program. A moment later, the live web-cast kicked in. The show was in progress.

Perry's neighbor and frequent co-host, Vanessa Beasely, was speaking in the casual manner of a radio-wife. "I understand you spoke with Alice Winslow's son."

"His name is Will," Perry said. "Nice young man ... runs a public relations firm in Boston. He's helping his mom with media this week. In fact, he's been instrumental in arranging for Alice to appear on our show next Thursday!"

"I noticed he spoke for his mother in Jack Daly's article this morning."

"A pretty fair article in the *American-Leader*," said Perry, keeping the ball moving.

"I'd say it was *balanced*." Vanessa's tone betrayed a hint of discord. "Jack also quoted Cathleen Maldonado, the Shelby Dean of Students, and Delia Radcliff, the English Department Chair ..."

"Alice Winslow's boss," Perry said.

"So, yes, it was balanced in that way. Jack *could* have spoken with Richard Emerson."

"The college president ..."

"And maybe a few students ..."

"I know that Dean Maldonado is concerned about the school's reputation." Perry paused. "Do *you* think there's been damage?"

"I guess I do," Vanessa said.

"You may be right. I'm not sure it's Alice's fault."

"This morning's hearing will determine that."

"They'll try."

"Perry, I think the press coverage over the past few days, including Jack Daly's piece, has turned this into a question of sympathy for Alice Winslow. All about *her* rights, the unfairness of criticizing her."

"Yes. But don't you think the *first* few days' coverage, after Alice helped that young Muslim woman, went too far the other way? Some of it was frightening, Vanessa."

"I agree."

"Maybe that's how it's supposed to work. In an open society with a free press, every viewpoint gets its moment. In the end, people decide what's true."

"In theory ... but *everything* can't be true, Perry. Sometimes, there are hard facts staring us in the face."

"Do you concede that different people honestly see the truth from different perspectives?" he asked.

"They do. The question is whether they should. In my own writing, for example, I've been faced with decisions about what to emphasize, what to treat more lightly ... trying to find the *real* truth. Life is filled with ugliness and sin, but we're not obligated to wallow in that. There's a lot more to life than negativity. Our country is under attack and we don't have to attack it ourselves, even with things that may be technically true as facts. People need heroes and heroines. America produces plenty of both. *Uplifting historical fiction* … that's what I like to write about."

"And you do it very well, Vanessa."

"Perry, do you remember when the Isaac Shelby diary was published last year?"

"It was edited by Margaret Harvey. We had her on the show."

"She's another professor from that Shelby English Department." There was an edge to Vanessa's voice. "A close friend of Alice Winslow's in fact. Now, I know there was slavery in our country's past and in Connecticut's past. But that was one truth among many. It shouldn't define us. Did we need to be told an old Connecticut family, and the fine college they endowed, had been made rich through slave money?"

"It's the truth, isn't it?"

"It was something that people thought differently about in those days."

"I wonder."

Perry broke away, allowing the radio station to identify itself.

Tom checked the time—ten twenty-five.

Perry was back on air. "Thirty minutes from now, a disciplinary hearing at Shelby College will consider charges against Trent resident Alice Winslow, a Shelby professor of English Literature. Author Vanessa Beasely and I have been talking about ways of getting at truth through history and fiction. Now, Vanessa, you're not a great fan of Alice's new novel, *The Chastened Heart*."

"A very popular novel," she said. "But, no, I'm not a fan."

"Can you tell us why?"

"I found it depressing. Don't get me wrong. Alice Winslow is a brilliant writer. Her skills are fully on display in this novel."

"I should say so."

"But to what purpose? It makes love feel dysfunctional and cheap."

"Well, I found it human. With real insight into the truth of how men and women interact … how *lovers* interact."

Vanessa sighed. "The truth according to one novelist, maybe; it's a story of betrayals, disappointments, infidelity and alcoholism."

"But also compassion, transcendence and faith," Perry said. "Alice's characters take quite a journey to find the truth about themselves."

"It's not my kind of journey. And it's certainly not my truth."

Perry said they were out of time. He thanked his co-host, and told his audience he would be back presently for a final comment.

Tom glanced out at the meadow. Dec and Kerry had returned to the house.

Perry Miller was back to wrap up.

"Anyone who listens regularly to this program knows my views," he said. "I'm not one to criticize our country unfairly. I don't wallow in the negative. Nor do I admire writers who do. Vanessa Beasely and I agree on this. But we disagree on Alice Winslow's wonderful new novel. Vanessa finds *The Chastened Heart* unduly bleak. I find it unerringly true, stunningly beautiful.

"But I want say something about the charges Alice Winslow faces this morning at Shelby College. In my personal opinion, the situation should not involve questions of patriotism. Whether Alice's decision to help a young Muslim woman in Chicago was proper professional behavior … and I can't see why it wouldn't be … there certainly was nothing unpatriotic about it.

"Please tune in next Thursday morning, when our special guest on Book World will be Alice Winslow. This is Perry Miller saying goodbye for now!"

Alice reached for Will's hand as they approached a wall of faculty, students and reporters outside Shelby Hall.

"Just smile and keep walking," he urged.

A TV news woman shouted from the crowd. "What do you say to these charges, Alice?"

Another reporter jostled forward, thrusting a small recording device in her direction. "Do *you* think you're un-American?"

"How's the book selling?" asked another.

When the crowd parted, forming an avenue to the glass entrance doors, Will squeezed Alice's hand and took the lead. She felt grateful for his clear sense of what to do in this crazy moment.

Just then, Peg Harvey shouted from close by. "We're with you, Alice!"

The crowd roared in agreement.

Alice looked into her friend's eyes and forced back tears.

Will quickened his pace as they reached the doors and hurried inside, where clusters of students watched. Uniformed guards from the campus security force were stationed at each of three entrances to the auditorium.

"Let's go in."

"Okay." She smiled when several students raised their hands to wave.

Alice followed Will past the guards at the nearest door and paused at the rear of the auditorium. Not quite a week ago, she thought, this had been the setting of her triumphant book appearance—a night on which the community had turned out with affection, even admiration, to hear her speak about *The Chastened Heart*.

This morning, Cathy Maldonado had organized a sizeable crowd of her own—a group of about 100, already seated in the first ten rows, half on one side of the center aisle and half on the other. Standing at the base of the center aisle, with her back to the stage, Cathy spoke quietly to them. These were Cathy's neighbors and friends, people from her church, even a few members of faculty. Many were familiar to Alice from the Isaac Shelby diary fiasco last year.

Alice raised her hand in a greeting to Cathy, who responded with a formal nod and continued her quiet instructions.

On the stage, a dais had been set with 12 places. Each had its own microphone and a large white tent card with the name of a different faculty-board member in bold black letters.

Dick Emerson would be sitting in the center with Cathy Maldonado to his right. Phil Weintraub would be sitting on his left, suggesting Dr. Emerson's awareness of the PR damage this affair had caused.

And all the way down at the end of the dais, to Emerson's extreme left, was Delia Radcliff's seat.

For the first time since this madness had erupted, Alice felt the stark certainty that she would lose her job today.

"There's no seat for you," Will said, when he noticed no tent card with his mother's name on it.

"I think I'm supposed to sit there." Alice indicated a single, unlabeled chair to their extreme left—so far from the dais as to imply a decision had been made already.

"No, no, no." Will shook his head. "That's not right."

Glancing at the lobby, where people were beginning to gather, he guided Alice down the left aisle to the base of the stage.

"Wait here." He pointed to the empty front row at the extreme left of the orchestra. "Don't talk to anyone."

"Yes dear." She sat as he hurried up the aisle and vanished into the lobby.

Peg's group started filing in. Stationing herself halfway down the center aisle, Peg directed them into the dozen center rows immediately behind Maldonado's supporters.

Phil Weintraub came in with four TV crews. He showed them to the media platform at the rear of the auditorium. There, they began setting up tripods for their video cameras, while reporters plugged in their mikes and recorders.

And in the farthest corner from where Alice sat, the campus radio station, WSBY-FM, had unfurled its banner beneath a table at which a sound engineer and a commentator waited.

Visitors from the community filed in, taking seats behind Peg's group and along the sides.

Alice placed her bag on the seat to her left, saving it for Will, as the auditorium quickly overflowed. People stood in the aisles and crowded at the lobby doors. Alice began worrying that Will might not make it back through this mass of people.

It was ten minutes to eleven. Cathy Maldonado climbed the stairs below the stage on the right side and took her seat at the dais. Other board members filed in from the wings and found their seats.

Alice stood and looked over the throng, searching for her son, finally catching a glimpse of him near the center lobby door. He was speaking urgently with Delia Radcliff who nodded and disappeared. Will turned to look in Alice's direction. She raised her hand, and he began working his way down toward her. When he'd finally made it, Alice removed her bag from the saved seat as he stepped past her.

"What were you doing?" she whispered, as they sat.

"I asked Delia to fix the seating arrangement."

It was four minutes to eleven. Dick Emerson was seated, now, gesturing to Alice.

"They want me on stage."

"Ignore them."

"I don't know how much longer I can."

"Shush." He looked toward the center aisle. "Here she comes."

Alice looked right and saw Delia pushing her way through the crowded center aisle. She held something in her left hand. Two of Alice's writing students, Tim Sheehan and Florence Alvarez, followed closely behind Delia.

When they reached the base of the orchestra, they moved rapidly toward the stairs on the right and vaulted to the stage. As Tim hurried toward the unlabeled chair, Delia and Florence placed a new tent card down next to Delia's seat at the dais and made room for the chair that Tim now hustled to them.

"What do you think you're doing?" Cathy Maldonado bellowed at Tim, who ignored her. "I'm addressing you, Mr. Sheehan!" Maldonado stood and slapped her palm on the dais. "Stop this instant!"

"No, *you* stop!" Delia came quickly from her end of the dais to confront Maldonado. "This is a professional review, not an inquisition. Alice Winslow is a full professor in good standing here. She's a respected member of this faculty and community, and has every right to sit at this dais."

"And if Dr. Emerson and I don't agree?"

"You speak for Dr. Emerson now?"

"No one speaks for me, all right?" Dick Emerson cut the air with a sharp wave of his hand.

Delia calmly addressed him. "Dr. Emerson, unless Alice is given the respect her position deserves, this review proceeds without my support." She half turned and pointed at the chair and name card that now awaited Alice at the dais. "I dare say most members of the board agree with that, regardless of what they may decide today."

Alice listened to the awful silence in the crowded auditorium.

Cathy Maldonado appeared ready to continue arguing, but Dr. Emerson whispered something to her. Immediately, Maldonado sat down and leafed through her notes.

"Very well," Emerson said.

"Let's go." Will grabbed his mother's hand as they hurried to the stairs at the left side of the stage.

"I'll take it from here." She kissed her son's cheek, climbed the stairs and took her place on the dais.

Dick Emerson ordered security to clear the aisles in respect of fire laws. Most people complied with the guards' gentle coaxing and retreated toward the lobby. A few slipped away and found places to stand at the extreme left and right sides of the auditorium.

Next, Dr. Emerson asked security to close each of the three lobby doors, where people were gathered, straining to see the stage. But angry cries from the lobby forced him to relent, with a warning.

"If we have the slightest disturbance, I'll shut those doors and have them chained from inside."

Finally, Dr. Emerson called the hearing to order and addressed Alice.

"Professor Winslow, are you represented today by legal counsel?"

"A lawyer … do I need one?"

There were titters in the audience.

"Well, I just thought …"

"We all know each other here." Alice passed her hand across the dais. Several board members barely hid their smiles. "Are you recommending we postpone this meeting so I can hire an attorney?"

"No. I didn't mean …"

"Then fine. My son is here as my advisor."

"Very well, would you care to make an opening statement?"

"I didn't call this meeting." She stared at Cathy Maldonado. "I understand there are accusations against me."

"There are questions," Dr. Emerson cautioned.

"Very well, *questions*," Alice said. "Why don't we start there?"

Dr. Emerson glanced at Cathy Maldonado who leaned into her microphone.

"Professor Winslow," she said. "What is the purpose of a college?"

"We are a place of inquiry and learning."

"To what end?"

"I'm sorry. I thought those *were* the ends."

"No." Maldonado paused with a stunned smile. "The point of inquiry and learning is to arrive at the truth. Is that not right?"

"The truth, Dr. Maldonado, is not a thing one arrives at, as you put it." Alice wondered how far she ought to go with this, knowing she was already in danger. "The truth is an unfolding realization," she said, deciding not to be intimidated.

"Inquiry and learning are the work of a lifetime," she added. "The purpose of a college is to introduce our students to that life of inquiry. To encourage them, and equip them for that journey, and, I would add, to further our own journey toward truth, as teachers and administrators. We are a college ... from the Latin *collegium* ... meaning a community of equally empowered members, pursuing shared goals in a framework of mutual respect."

Several members of Peg Harvey's group started clapping. Dr. Emerson glared at them.

"So you don't believe in the idea of *truth*, as a finite thing," Maldonado said.

"If by finite you mean permanent and unchanging, then no," Alice said. "I believe in education, which I describe as the constant acquisition of new insights, the adjustment or even discarding of known facts, the testing and debate of all facts, and a sense of humility in the face of all that is unknown."

"Well, I'm sorry, Alice," Maldonado intoned. "You've clearly identified the problem many of us have with you ... your imprecise grasp of established values."

"Established values?" Alice's laugh expressed anger. "How dare you?"

The audience murmured.

"Truth, Professor Winslow, is a value. Patriotism, loyalty and faith are values. These things *are* fixed and permanent, or should be."

Sudden applause went up from the Maldonado supporters in the audience. As Cathy sat back in her chair, taking comfort in their vocalization, Dr. Emerson waited for the uproar to subside.

"We are teachers and administrators," Maldonado said with leering skepticism. "Not travel guides on some journey where everyone picks and chooses what to learn or believe. We're authority figures, professionals with a grave responsibility, to teach the core values of our culture and history, to uphold and represent those values, and the knowledge behind them."

Now, as members of Peg Harvey's group began to boo and catcall, Dr. Emerson tapped his gavel. "Quiet," he demanded.

"Thank you, Dr. Emerson," said Maldonado. "An influential professor and popular writer, who brings discredit on the college that employs her, doesn't deserve the backing of that college.

"I have difficulty understanding why a person who doesn't accept the notion of finite truth becomes a teacher at all. I guess I feel the same way about a writer. I mean, why would anyone put out a book, a serious book, if not to promote the values and ideals of our society?

"And when that professor decides to publicly aid and support a clearly malicious individual, determined to embarrass the country in this time of danger, something's wrong with her own grasp of who and what we are as Americans.

"I ask the faculty board this morning to censure Professor Alice Winslow. She has embarrassed us in public, brought negative attention to this campus, and betrayed her profession. In associating herself with a Muslim who flouts homeland security rules, and disdains the environment which made those procedures necessary, Professor Winslow has behaved in a gravely *un-American* manner."

For several moments the auditorium was as silent as a church. Then, it erupted in competing hosannas.

Listening to the WSBY web-cast, Tom was stunned by Dean Maldonado's vitriol and the audience reaction to it.

He heard Dr. Emerson shout over a rapping gavel and microphone feedback. "Security will clear the auditorium if there's another outburst!"

And then an urgent voice that sounded like Delia Radcliff's. "Dr. Emerson! Dr. Emerson, please! I would like to speak on behalf of the English Department."

"Very well, Dr. Radcliff" the president said. "But we'll take a five-minute recess."

Tom heard Emerson's gavel again, and the murmurs of an audience relaxing. The WSBY commentator broke in to recap the proceedings.

Tom's cell phone buzzed. It was Bill Sanchez returning his call.

"I guess you heard," Bill said.

"Jen Yi told me they're naming Rick McDougall."

Bill scoffed. "That prick; can you believe it?"

"I can believe almost anything at this stage, Bill."

"I don't know which is the bigger disappointment." Bill sighed. "That weasel, McDougall ... a kid I hired for Christ sake ... or Carl."

"You didn't see this coming?"

"I'm ashamed to say I didn't. I'd been talking to Carl for a month before he came to Hartford last Friday."

"Oh?"

"I even went to New York to see him, at his request. He showed me these charts and plans, and explained where Tri-Art was taking *The Chronicle*. He acted like I was going to be his right hand man. So, no, I didn't see it coming."

"You never mentioned going to New York. When we spoke last Friday, you made it sound like you'd only met Fervor that morning."

"Did I?" Bill sounded weary. "I'm sorry, Tom. I didn't mean to mislead you. I guess I just couldn't disclose certain things. And I was pretty distracted, as you can imagine, knowing Tri-Art's intentions." Bill laughed wickedly. "At least I thought I did. But again, my concern was getting you under budget and saving your jobs."

"It hardly matters now."

"No, I guess not."

"Will you look for another job?"

"Oh, I'll be fine. Tri-Art gave me a decent package. I have my *Chronicle* pension."

"You're still young."

"I'm 56, Thomas."

"Young enough …"

"Not the way things are *these days*. Anyway … Jessie wants to move back to LA. So, that's probably what we'll do."

"Los Angeles, huh?"

"She's got family there. I'll work on my golf game … and a tan … maybe teach some courses at UCLA."

Tom suddenly thought how the nastiness of campuses might shock even the coldest of businessmen. "I wish you luck."

"Jessie and I are meeting a real estate broker, to talk about listing our house. So, I better run. But we'll stay in touch, okay?"

"Let's have dinner soon."

"Good idea. And Thomas, watch *your* back."

Tom clicked off and put his cell phone down next to his laptop. It was almost noon. He still hadn't made any cuts to his column. The WSBY announcer was saying that the hearing was about to resume. Tom stared out the picture window and listened.

Waiting on stage, Delia felt like an actor in an absurdist drama. She was familiar with polite forms of campus thuggery, but this was something new, a mad reality show, scripted for the media and public, an entertainment with tragic consequences—the end not only of Alice's career but her own, and of any notion that Shelby College was a serious institution.

Dr. Emerson rapped his gavel. "Can we proceed?"

Several board members chatting in the wings hurried back to the dais, while Alice continued speaking with her son below the stage.

"Please?" Dr. Emerson tapped his gavel again.

"Sorry!" Alice clutched her son's hand before coming up the stairs to her seat.

Dr. Emerson looked down the dais. "Are you ready, Dr. Radcliff?"

"I am," she said, feeling Alice's hand against her elbow.

Delia stood and examined the stern faces of the other board members. Searching her heart for the right words, and the strength to express them, she recalled the urgent plea that Alice's son had made just before the hearing: "Miss Radcliff," he'd implored. "Don't abandon my mother."

Now, glancing briefly at Alice, Delia spoke. "If we believe in honest discussion … if we accept that our own ideas must withstand scrutiny … we may feel compelled to participate in something we know is false. This, my fellow board members, is precisely our dilemma today."

A chorus of boos floated up from the audience.

"Let me be clear," Delia added. "This hearing is a farce *not* because someone has expressed ideas I disagree with. I welcome disagreement. It strengthens my own ideas. Confrontation forces me to discard weak suppositions that poorly serve my own beliefs. What makes this forum so pointless is the fact that some participants don't honor its premise. They don't believe in scholarly debate or inquiry. They say we already know the truth."

Delia paused and looked down the dais at Maldonado and Emerson. "That *is* your position, is it not?"

Maldonado glared. Emerson was uncomfortable with direct scrutiny.

Delia continued. "So we're engaged in a charade … a mock debate. There is no serious doubt or question about Professor Winslow … her career record, her skill in the classroom, her stunning literary achievement. She's the standard to which the academic community should aspire. And yet, here we are today, ladies and gentlemen … pretending to seek some other truth, when our real purpose is to expel this honorable member of our community. Why? Because she's acted on principles that offend *other* members of our community."

As the audience buzzed, Delia sensed the fulcrum of her argument—the instinctive human dislike of unfairness. And judging from his expression, Dr. Emerson wasn't pleased with the abrupt mood-swing in the auditorium.

"Dr Radcliff," he said, tapping his gavel. "Thank you for your comments and opinions about this … *charade,* as you call it. We're academics, however, not theater critics. I ask that you present whatever argument you deem appropriate regarding Professor Winslow. We're ready to hear that argument, if you have one. If not … if you have nothing to offer beyond a critique of our sincerity, then, I politely suggest you sit down and allow *us* to proceed with our inquiry."

The audience grew quiet. Delia felt that she'd had them on her side for a moment, but had lost them again, to Emerson's show of authority. Desperately now, she searched her brain for anything that might keep her on her feet and delay the inevitable.

Just then, a cell phone chirped, sending waves of laughter across the theater.

Shielding her eyes against the stage lights, Alice searched the audience for the source of a ringing cell phone and a moment's comic relief.

"Sorry!" It was a woman in back. "I'm sorry."

Alice watched members of Peg Harvey's group turn in unison to gape at someone in their midst—it was Peg, Alice now realized—frantically digging in her bag.

Peg retrieved the phone and answered in mid-ring. "Why are you calling me?"

Another wave of laughter peaked and subsided, but Alice was alarmed. Will's seat was empty. She couldn't see him anywhere in the shadowy auditorium.

Dick Emerson spoke over the disruption with palpable annoyance. "Dr. Radcliff, is there anything more you wish to say on behalf of Professor Winslow?"

Alice smiled at her young friend standing in rigid silence beside her. Reaching for Delia's hand, Alice gently pulled her down into her seat.

"It's over," Alice whispered, as Delia wept. "I'm proud of you."

"Excuse me!" shouted Peg, causing another stir in the audience.

Squeezing out into the center aisle, Peg came swiftly toward the stage with the phone pressed to her ear. She stopped at the base of the stage, spoke softly to her caller, and addressed the dais. "Dr.

Emerson, this is a call from my husband. He's patching someone in who's been trying to reach you all morning."

"This is quite inappropriate," said Dr. Emerson.

"I have her for you now," Peg said, still listening to her phone.

"You have whom?"

"Virginia Porter!" Peg held the phone out toward him, then, brought it back to say something into it. The audience murmured as Peg climbed the stairs and hurried across the stage to the dais. "All right," she said into the phone. "I will."

Emerson shook his head in frustration, as Peg placed her cell phone on the dais.

"I've activated the speaker," she said. "Can you hear us, Mrs. Porter?"

"Yes, dear," said the disembodied voice in the phone. "I hear you all very well."

Alice glanced at Will's empty seat again before turning back in time to see Phil Weintraub grab Peg's cell phone and place it close to his own mike.

Now, Virginia Porter's voice was amplified in the sound system. "Dick Emerson? What is the meaning of this event?"

"I meant to call you back, Mrs. Porter." He leaned closer to the phone. "We've been extremely busy with the hearing." He spoke more politely than Alice had ever seen, but a signal drop lost Mrs. Porter's response. "Are you still there?" he asked.

Abruptly, the silence of dead air was shattered by a burst of garbled urgency. "… exactly my concern … this hearing … about … and why … was not informed!"

The connection kept going in and out, but it was clear that Virginia was not pleased.

"Mrs. Porter, this is Cathy Maldonado. We have serious concerns about the actions of a staff-member and …"

"Dean Mal … ado … wasn't speaking … you."

Members of the board were confused now, as if caught in their own dropped signals.

Peg reached for her phone.

But Cathy Maldonado grabbed it and turned it off, tossing it unceremoniously on the dais. "Enough! Why don't you take your seat?"

"Let me try to get her back," Peg urged.

"No," said Emerson. "Cathy's right. We've had enough. I'll speak to Mrs. Porter this afternoon. We need to bring this hearing to a conclusion."

Phil Weintraub spoke up. "Dr. Emerson, I move an immediate vote be taken on the proposition Professor Radcliff offered."

"What proposition?" Emerson's voice mixed surprise and contempt.

"That this hearing is a farce," Phil said. "I hereby move that we end this ridiculous inquiry on the basis that it is personal and improper."

Cathy Maldonado glared at Phil. "What are you trying to do?"

Phil ignored her. "Will anyone second my motion?"

"*I* will," said Delia.

"Thank you, Dr. Radcliff." Phil moved swiftly. "The motion before us is to end this hearing immediately, without prejudice to anyone, most particularly our colleague, Alice Winslow, whose patience and forbearance refute all claims against her fitness."

Alice glanced around the dais. The other board members were stunned by this unexpected maneuver. Emerson and Maldonado, who understood they couldn't stop a vote on Phil's motion, registered their own votes with silence. Alice watched the faces of the other members as they tried to read the disconcerting moment.

"Will the board signal its support of the motion with a show of hands?" Phil said.

Only three members joined him and Delia—five votes on 12-member board, Alice instantly calculated. Phil's brave motion had failed. Peg picked up her cell phone and headed back to her seat.

Relieved to see Jack Daly coming through the entrance doors accompanied by an attractive, dark-haired woman, Will hurried across the lobby to greet them.

"I'm glad you made it." He clasped the reporter's hand and smiled at the woman. "Laura?"

"Yes." Her own polite smile barely masked her nerves.

"I'm sorry we're late," Jack said.

"The board just blocked a motion that would have ended the hearing without prejudice to my mother. We may have missed our chance."

"I had to get my children to school," Laura said.

Will took her hand and looked into her warm, sad eyes. "I'm glad you came."

"My husband would want me to."

"All right then." Will glanced at the crowd between them and the jammed auditorium doors. "Shall we do this?"

He led them through the crowded lobby, working his way to the nearest door.

"Excuse us, please," he said with polite self-assurance. "Excuse us ... coming through ... please ... thank you ... excuse us ... thanks."

Will made it through first and stood just inside the auditorium waiting for Jack and Laura to come in behind him.

Now, all three were in.

"Ready?" Will whispered.

"Ready," they said.

"Dr. Emerson!" Will called out. His heart beat rapidly as he hurried toward the stage with Jack and Laura following. "There's another person who wants to speak!"

Will noticed several board members smiling. His mother looked confused. But the person clearly most surprised was Cathy Maldonado.

"You're Professor Winslow's advisor?" Dr. Emerson said.

"I'm her son. Yes, her advisor." Will addressed Emerson and the board from the base of the stage. "I'm William Winslow." Turning to his companions, he added: "Everyone knows Jack Daly, from the *American-Leader*. May I also introduce Mrs. Laura Bennett?"

"Laura Maldonado Bennett!" she said.

Cathy Maldonado finally managed a question. "Jack, why is she here?"

"Your sister wanted to speak," he said.

Dr. Emerson glanced at Cathy, looked along the dais for signs of resistance to another speaker, and found none.

"Very well," he said. "Would Mrs. Bennett like to come to the dais?" He glanced into the wings. "Can someone get her a microphone?"

Instantly, Tim Sheehan appeared from the wings holding a wand mike. He hurried to the edge of the stage, knelt, and placed the mike into Laura's up-stretched hand.

She thanked him, tapping the wand for signs of life.

Tim hurried back to the wings.

"Can you come to the dais?" Emerson repeated.

"No thanks." Laura walked toward the stairs on the left side of the stage. She climbed halfway and stopped, in full view of everyone on stage and in the audience. "This is fine," she said. "I appreciate the opportunity to speak, so, I'll be brief."

As Will and Jack joined several onlookers standing against the nearby wall, a young man smiled at Will and offered his right hand. "Lev Gellman, *Hartford Chronicle*," he whispered. "Hi Jack," he added, smiling at his fellow reporter.

"My husband would be appalled at this," said Laura Bennett into her mike. "He wasn't a man who liked making accusations about other people's patriotism. He always said it was wrong to make someone feel as though they weren't good enough, American enough."

Will's spirits rose as the audience stirred.

Laura continued. "My husband's family name ... Bennett ... was really Benedetti. That's the name his great-grandfather, Giuseppe, brought to America in the late 1800s. Back then, it wasn't always helpful to have a name like Giuseppe Benedetti. It wasn't always helpful to give an Irish name either, or a Jewish name, when applying for a job, or trying to rent an apartment. Real American names back then were English names, I guess.

"So, Giuseppe's oldest son, Carlo, changed the family name, to make it sound a little more American, to make it easier for *his* children to blend in. Carlo Benedetti became Charles Bennett, and so on …"

Laura paused and glanced over at Will and Jack. They smiled and nodded, encouraging her to stay on this theme.

"My husband's family was not alone in doing what they did," Laura said. "I wouldn't be surprised if some Middle Eastern people, the Muslim people coming here now and trying to make it as Americans, did the same. We all know they face the same problems our own families faced … suspicion and unfriendliness.

"Sure, the men who drove planes into those buildings in Manhattan, killing thousands of people including my poor husband, were from a certain background. And they claimed to believe in the Muslim faith. Frankly, I'm not so sure."

Laura paused and the audience grumbled. They were not in complete agreement, Will sensed, because the wound was still too raw. But Laura was gradually making her case.

"A hundred years ago, some people from backgrounds like my husband's, and my own, came here and reacted the wrong way to the unfriendliness they found. They became thieves, murderers, political conspirators, even a terrorist or two. Some of them made big names for themselves in a bad way. But they *never* represented the majority of hardworking, patriotic, fortunate Italians. When most of those people couldn't get honest work, they organized legal unions. When they couldn't get a landlord to rent them an apartment, they organized social action societies. And when the ugly prejudice and unfairness kept up, they ran for public office, to make sure something was done about it.

"And *that's* the American story. There's an Irish version and a Jewish version and a million other versions, just like the Italian version. And you know what? There's going to be a Middle Eastern version, too, a Muslim version."

The audience was entirely silent now.

"I know my sister, Cathy, has her own views on the subject," Laura said. "They're not my views. They weren't my husband's views. I don't think they're the correct views. And I'm just here to say that no one should support my sister's ideas, or her dislike of this professor, Mrs. Winslow, out of some well-intentioned but misguided sympathy for me, or what happened to my husband on 9/11.

"There's no connection between that horrible day, and whether or not Professor Winslow did right when she helped that woman in Chicago ... the Muslim woman. There's no connection between those Muslim hijackers and a young Muslim-American woman expressing her rights, taking something to the Supreme Court. That Court is there for all of us Americans. And if you ask me, she sounds pretty brave. My husband would have liked her. I'm sure he would have helped her. I know somebody should have. It ended up being Professor Winslow and, well, good for her. That's all I wanted to say."

Tom listened as Laura Bennett finished speaking to the Shelby Hall assembly. His heart swelled and the audience roared in approval as the board quickly voted to cease all inquiry about Professor Alice Winslow. The motion carried by 11-1. Dean Maldonado was the lone dissenter.

Tom closed his web-cast browser, revealing the open Word document that contained the draft of his column.

"Shit." It was almost one o'clock and his cell phone was buzzing—he could see Rick McDougall's name on the LCD screen.

He answered. "Hello, Rick."

"Hey, Tom, can we chat about your column?"

"I know you need cuts. By the way: congratulations."

"Oh, thanks. But listen, some space opened up on your page. So, I want the whole column. It's about 1,100 words?"

"It is now."

"Can you send it? Even if you're not finished, I'd like to take a look."

"Here it is." Tom saved the document and emailed it. "Jen said you had an ad running. I hope we didn't lose it."

"No, no," Rick assured him. "The advertiser needs more space. They're starting a new 12-month campaign with a full-page in the A-section."

"That's a nice piece of business."

"I just got your email. I'll read this ASAP."

"Who's the advertiser?"

"Bethlehem Mutual."

"They're becoming players in health insurance."

"That's what the new campaign is about, Tom. Health insurance could be the big domestic story of the year, and next year, and beyond. It's going to involve insurance companies, hospitals and pharmaceuticals. And with our aging population, the baby-boomers retiring, the whole political environment is focused on health care."

"It *will* be a big story."

"I'm pretty sure we'll get a Democratic president next year," Rick said. "The likely candidates have already made national health insurance their calling card."

"Luckily we've got Jen Yi to cover it for us."

"Actually, Tom, I want to move her out."

"Move her where?"

"There's an opening for a news writer at WCTC, the Tri-Art station in town."

"That's barely more than an intern's job."

"You just agreed that health care is a big story. I want someone with experience and industry contacts. I want a pro, Tom. In fact, I may finance a small reporting team to cover health care. But that costs money and money means advertising."

"You see no place in this for Jen Yi?"

"Jen's a great kid," Rick said. "We've had some laughs working together in the news room. But she's in over her head."

"That's ridiculous. She just had a public health-insurance story on page one!"

"It was embarrassing, Tom. A half-assed, socialist screed about public health options the Governor has already said will never happen." Rick paused. "It doesn't matter what the Legislature passes. She'll veto it. And Yi's piece made it sound like a *fait accompli*. If she'd talked to a few more insurance people, they would have told her that."

Tom laughed. "Did the Governor's office complain? Or was it your advertiser?"

"*My* advertiser? We all work for the paper, Tom. It's a business."

"This isn't the way it's supposed to work. When politicians and business people complain to an editor, it generally means the reporter did a good job. As editors, we take the hits. We protect our reporters. You do know that's how it works, right?"

Rick sighed. "You sound like a newspaper man in a Hollywood movie from 1948 or something. Now, I've made a decision. But since you hired her, I'm offering you the chance to teach Jen the facts of life. If she moves over to the TV station and does a good job, gets some seasoning, learns a bit more about our company, maybe we'll bring her back to the paper at some point."

"You just want me to do your dirty work."

"I'll do it, Tom. If that's what you want."

"No. I'll talk to her."

"I'm reading your column as we speak." Rick was enjoying himself. "I love it."

Bill Sanchez had it right, Tom thought. This guy is a prick.

"What about Lev Gellman?" Tom asked.

"Lev's a great reporter. He's a brilliant writer, but the jury's out on him."

"And what's *his* problem?"

"Attitude," Rick said.

"Are you fucking serious?"

"There's a new corporate culture," Rick said. "We better get used to the fact. Tri-Art is a media company that rewards profitable performance, hard work, and a mature, even-handed outlook on the news. No more sorry-ass, underground journalism, Tom. 'Attitude' comes off as uncooperative. That's the company's viewpoint. It's mine too." Rick paused, apparently to allow his warning to sink in. "Any questions?"

"No. I've got it."

"Good. And you'll have a chat with Yi?"

"I'll handle it."

"That's great." Rick sounded pleased again. "By the way: excellent column!"

Tom clicked off and tossed his cell phone onto the desk. His body shook with rage as he stared at the meadow and hills beyond the picture window. He felt the first rushes of an intense headache. He stood up and stretched, trying to relieve the cramps his back muscles had developed from hours of sitting.

For a moment, his left arm felt funny, a kind of weakness combined with dull cramping, as if the arm had fallen asleep. And then it was gone.

He sat down and composed an email to a friend at the *New York Times*. He told her about Jen Yi, noting a recent front page article about the politics of health insurance in Connecticut.

"Things are changing at *The Chronicle*," he wrote. "Jen's a bit dissatisfied with the track she's on, and she's looking to make a move.

"She's from Douglaston, Queens," Tom added. "I hired her two years ago out of Columbia J-School. She's got talent, initiative, and she learns fast. But *The Chronicle* doesn't have the logical next step for her. I hate to lose her, but I've brought her along as far as I can. If you're smart, you'll nab her before the *Wall Street Journal* does."

He checked his spelling, attached a link to Jen's health care article, and hit SEND.

"Damn." He stood again and stretched his cramping back. "I'm getting too old for this business."

Breathing deeply, he opened the door and let fresh air waft in. Even if it was hot air, coming off the meadow's sunlit stillness, it carried the living odors of real things—better than the dead air inside the shed. And from the open doorway, looking up at the house in the middle distance, he saw Kerry and Dec moving around in the kitchen, comfortably at home. That was a good thing, too, he told himself.

A ping from his laptop meant his email service had just received a message. He stepped back to the desk and leaned over to check his inbox. His friend at the *New York Times* had already replied.

Opening the message, he smiled at what he saw: "You're a mind-reader, Winslow! We're looking for a good young reporter to help cover Manhattan political news. Your girl writes good! And we'd like to talk with her. We've heard about cutbacks going on at *The Chronicle*, by the way, so don't try to finesse me about her salary, buster. Speaking of cutbacks, are YOU okay? Anyway, have her call me. And let me know when you and Alice are coming to NY."

Tom grabbed his cell phone and called Jennifer Yi.

Dusk descended as Tom grilled beef and salmon steaks on the patio. The voices of his family became a dreamy whisper until, abruptly, he felt himself breathing again in the soft evening air, relieved that his dizziness had subsided.

"Where did *you* go?" Will asked.

"Yeah, what happened?" Dec said.

Tom assured them he was fine.

"You don't look fine," Dec said.

"I inhaled some charcoal vapor and lost it for a second."

"Try *thirty* seconds," Will said.

Instead of protesting further, Tom offered a skeptical smile to hide his lie.

"You were seriously out of it," Dec said.

Tom nodded, turning the steaks.

"He's just tired." Will's voice lacked conviction. "I guess we'll all sleep tonight."

Dec sighed. "Now see, Will, that's where you're wrong."

A moment later they all laughed.

"What's so funny?" It was Kerry, standing at the kitchen screen door.

"Just some guy humor, honey," Dec said.

She repressed a smile. "The *baby's* sleeping."

The men snickered in delight.

"If you wake him up, he's yours."

The younger men barely contained themselves as Kerry glared.

"These are almost done," Tom told her.

Turning briskly, Kerry rejoined Alice at the kitchen counter. "They're almost ready."

"Would you toss the salad?" Alice replied, as the kitchen phone rang.

Another friend or neighbor, Tom thought, checking in to say "congratulations"—to assure Alice there'd never been the slightest doubt of her rectitude.

"Oh, hello," she said. "Yes. It was nice meeting *you* too. Hold on. He's right outside."

Alice came to the screen door. "It's Lev Gellman."

"I'll be right there." Turning over his fork, Tom instructed his young companions. "Take the fish off now. Give the beef another minute or two. Then bring everything in."

"Got it," they said.

Tom hurried in and picked up the phone.

"Am I interrupting dinner?" Lev asked.

"No," Tom assured him. "We haven't started yet."

"I've been trying your cell phone for hours."

"I was working in my shed today and left my phone out there."

Alice glanced in surprise. Tom smiled at her.

"I just want to say that I filed a story on your wife's hearing."

"I heard you and McDougall argued about it."

"Who told you that, Jen?"

"She said there was a disagreement."

"That moron wanted to go with an AP story," Lev said in disgust. "I told him *The Chronicle* should *lead* on a story like this."

"Of course."

"Your son arranged an interview with Mrs. Winslow."

"They told me. Now Lev, this McDougall is bad news. I didn't realize how bad until this afternoon."

"Never liked the guy … I thought you and Bill were too nice to him."

"Don't go picking fights," Tom urged. "My advice is to stay calm and find another job. I know some people at the *New York Times*."

"Jen said you got her an interview."

"I can try the same for you. I know people at *Forbes* and *Business Week* too."

"That's great. But actually, I'm working on a book proposal."

"Oh?"

"I have a month's paternity leave starting Monday. I'm using the time to write an outline."

Tom was impressed. "Can you say what it's about?"

"Banks facing a credit crunch," Lev said. "You can see it at your friend's condominium project, where the bank has ceased financing. The FDIC is going to take that bank over soon. But that's the tip of the iceberg. Banks everywhere are over-extended ... exposed to a weird new class of synthetic derivatives based on mortgages, including a lot of sub-prime garbage. They were originally conceived as hedging instruments."

"You mean risk insurance?"

"Exactly," Lev said. "The banks started re-selling them in a secondary market and made a lot of money in trading fees. But now, these things have been bought and sold and resold so many times, nobody knows who owns them or what they're worth. I suspect they're worth nothing. And it's about to hit the fan. It could take the whole banking system down ... not to mention the real estate business."

"What a story."

"As soon as I land a book contract, I'm quitting *The Chronicle*," Lev confided. "I'll spend a year or two writing the book and generating magazine work. And I can do most of it from home, which gives me the chance to spend time with Carol and the baby."

"It's the perfect plan, Lev."

"That's what my dad says."

Tom looked up as Will and Dec came in with the beef and salmon on a large platter.

"Do you have an agent?" he asked Lev.

"My dad put me in touch with a west coast agency. People he worked with in Hollywood. They do mostly show business stuff."

"You need a real literary agent. I can ask my wife to speak to Judith Lavan at Jeffords-Blaine. I *think* she handles non-fiction."

"I'd hate to impose."

"Nonsense ... I'll ask Alice to call Judy."

Lev sighed. "Thank you, Mr. Winslow."

"How *is* your father by the way?" Glancing into the dining room, Tom saw his family waiting at the bountiful table that Kerry had decorated with the roses she'd brought home from the hospital.

"Dad's good," Lev said. "Happy I'm leaving *The Chronicle*."

"Tell him I agree. And please give him my best. Carol too."

"I sure will."

For a moment, Tom sensed that Lev didn't want to hang up.

"My story should hit the website around midnight," Lev finally said.

"Can't wait to read it," Tom said fondly.

"All right, then. I guess that's everything."

Five minutes into their dinner, the Winslow family was interrupted again—this time by Will's phone.

"Oh, *hi*." His voice lifted subtly as he answered. "Excuse me a minute," he pleaded to his mother, getting up and walking toward the living room. "Really?" he whispered. "Thanks, Jeanie. I'll tell her."

Tom glanced at Alice. Her expression suggested that she'd heard the hopeful rise in their son's voice too.

Several moments later, Will returned to the table. "My assistant," he said.

"That was a work call?" Kerry was surprised.

"Jeanie Castro," Will said, embarrassed by his sister's question.

No one replied.

"She saw a good report about the hearing on the Boston evening news."

Again no one replied.

"Jeanie's more than my assistant. I mean … she's stepping up to account management."

Alice reached for his hand. "It was very nice of her to call."

There was more silence.

Tom changed the subject protectively. "Lev Gellman's working on a book proposal."

Alice turned to him. "What kind of book?"

"A business and finance thing … something about a lending crisis in real estate … a bunch of banks are about to fail, he says."

"Does he have an agent?"

"His father has some contacts in Hollywood. I'm not sure that's the best approach."

Alice nodded. "Would he like me to speak to Judy Lavan?"

"He'd be thrilled." Tom smiled sheepishly. "I kind of volunteered you already."

"I'll call her."

Just then Tom heard the baby starting to fuss in the guest bedroom upstairs. Kerry had heard it too and now glanced at Dec who understood his responsibility.

But Tom waved them off.

"I'll go. You kids enjoy your dinner."

Dec was halfway up. "Are you sure?"

"Completely," Tom said, as he hurried to the front hallway.

From the base of the stairs he could hear the baby crying in earnest. He climbed quickly to the second floor and entered the guest bedroom. Briefly, perhaps having heard footsteps, the baby stopped crying and started again.

Tom stood over the antique rocking cradle—an old gift from Alice's mother, purchased in Williamsburg, Virginia—which had served them for years as a living room magazine rack. Resisting the strongest impulse to grab the child and hold him close, Tom knelt beside the cradle and spoke softly as he gently rocked.

"Nothing to fear, little boy; you are loved."

It took several minutes for the baby to stop fussing. But gradually, he succumbed to motion and the sound of Tom's voice above his head. When Tom heard the baby's soft, regular breathing, he stopped rocking and stood up.

Outside a nearby window, the meadow was a blanket of shadows with the outlines of the shed—the faintest of shadows—in its center. The distant hills were invisible, though lights glimmered in the houses along the ridgeline. There was no moon, but a million stars shimmered in a silent sky.

Tom was pleased. All of his children were safe for the moment.

At first, he wasn't sure what was happening. He imagined seeing downtown Providence beyond the bedroom window, and then Main

Street in Bayview. He saw Alice as a young college girl walking across the meadow.

He felt dizzy, as he had on the patio.

His eyes strained to see the meadow, where dark shadows now were blanched by an all-consuming brilliance, a light so bright that it blinded him. He felt sick to his stomach. He was falling. Something slammed against the back of his head. The baby was startled and began to cry.

There were footsteps, muffled sounds—people calling his name, or saying "Dad."

Falling in darkness, now, Tom wondered if the blinding light had been a moment's illusion with nothing beyond it.

He felt people around him but couldn't speak.

The baby had stopped crying.

Tom felt Alice's hands beneath his head.

"Tom," he heard her say. "Please hang on. We've called an ambulance."

His chest was twisting inside itself, slowly suffocating him. Everything was cold—even Alice's tears as they fell on his face.

This is how it happens, he thought, already missing everyone.

Seven

May 2011

Though his firm had organized the premiere, Will was shocked by the turnout. Hundreds of people holding copies of *The Chastened Heart* lined 54th Street between Sixth and Seventh Avenues. Limousines paused outside the Ziegfeld Theater to drop off celebrity guests. Cameras flashed. He wished his mother could have seen this.

Four years since publication, her book continued selling in judiciously scheduled paperback editions. But the film rights had bounced from studio to studio, through the hands of several independent producers, and on into what had looked like Hollywood oblivion. Not until the Australian actress, Honor Cantwell, bought the option last year, commissioned a new script, and convinced British heartthrob Jon Lowe to co-star, had a film version of *The Chastened Heart* become reality.

Will's excitement rose as Honor Cantwell worked her way past the rope line into the busy Ziegfeld lobby. "There she is!"

"Isn't she beautiful?" Jeanie said.

Standing close between them, Lina tightened her grip on the latest paperback version, whose cover showed the film's stars embracing. "Do you think she would sign my book?"

"Of course," Will said, watching Jon Lowe follow Cantwell in.

Raising his hand, just as Cantwell glanced over, Will gestured toward Lina and pantomimed a writing motion. The willowy actress smiled and beckoned the star-struck girl.

"Go ahead," Jeanie said.

Briefly hesitating, Lina moved toward the actress as if in a trance.

Will and Jeanie watched as Cantwell wrote something in Lina's book, then, introduced her to Jon Lowe who inscribed his own message.

A small crowd encircled the actress—it included Cantwell's second husband, Kenny Simpson, the country singer, and the two adopted children from her first marriage to American actor Ted Castillo.

One member of her group broke away and approached Will and Jeanie.

"Ms. Cantwell would be honored to have your daughter sit with her family," the young man said.

Shocked and amused, Will and Jeanie glanced at each other, then looked at Cantwell who waited politely for permission. Jeanie waved and Cantwell smiled. The actress placed her hand on Lina's shoulder as she, her husband, and her children proceeded to their seats.

"They'll meet you back here after the film."

The young man hurried away and Jeanie pointed toward the lobby entrance.

"There's Delia."

Will waved to Delia Radcliff as she approached with her husband, John Woodward. Delia was President of Shelby College now. John was chair of the English Department.

"This is exciting!" Delia gushed.

"I love your mom's book," John said. "I'm anxious to see what kind of film they've made."

"They did a great job," Jeanie assured him.

"Cantwell involved my mother in the final script," said Will. "She and Lowe are wonderful together ... even better than they were in *Cold Harbor*."

Delia smiled at Jeanie. "How's the baby?"

"Alicia's fine." They embraced. "She's almost a year now ..."

"Ah!"

"She's at the hotel with our nanny."

"And Lina?"

"Sitting with Honor Cantwell's group!" Will said.

Delia beamed. "Is she thrilled?"

"She's 14."

"And nearly speechless," Jeanie said.

Everyone laughed. But, a moment later, Delia's smile faded. "I wish Alice were here."

Will nodded. "I know." Then, as Delia and John headed toward their seats, he sensed Jeanie's body stiffening. "What is it?"

"I'm not positive." She pointed to a gaunt woman near the entrance. "But I think Congresswoman Maldonado just came in."

Will saw a woman dressed in a navy-blue business suit that hung loosely on her emaciated frame. A brighter blue, silk scarf was wrapped around her head.

"Do you think that's her?"

"Yes."

He recalled Cathy Maldonado as a robust, thick-set woman. "She looks terrible."

"She's coming this way."

Indeed, the woman had recognized Will. As she pushed slowly toward him, he considered the changes that had come in the wake of the Shelby hearing four years ago—changes implemented so swiftly by Dick Emerson that observers assumed Virginia Porter had been their driving force.

Though Cathy Maldonado's position as Dean of Students had never been questioned, the transformational campus atmosphere had angered her. She'd resigned within the year, annoyed by Delia's promotion to Provost, a clear signal that she was on track for the presidency—a signal Emerson himself acknowledged by resigning in 2009.

Maldonado, meanwhile, had run for the congressional seat in northwest Connecticut. As a vocal member of the "Tea Party" wing of the GOP, she'd been elected in the House landslide of 2010.

Drawing near, she graciously offered her hand. "Hello, Will."

"Congresswoman," he said, feeling her bony fingers against his palm.

She smiled at Jeanie. "Mrs. Winslow ..."

"Ma'am."

"You're surprised to see me."

"In all honesty, yes," Will said.

"I understand."

"If we'd known you were interested, we'd have invited you."

Maldonado smiled at him skeptically.

"You *were* my mother's congresswoman ... for a month."

"I was saddened when she died. It seemed quite sudden."

"She'd been ill for some time," Jeanie said.

Maldonado looked surprised.

"Not long after the hearing," Will said, "she was diagnosed with uterine cancer."

"I didn't know."

"She'd been under a great deal of stress. There were family issues. Her book had just come out. The hearing didn't help." As he paused, Maldonado kept him in her steady gaze. "Of course, there was my father's heart attack."

The congresswoman nodded gravely.

"Mom decided to keep her condition private. She taught her classes almost till the end. Everything seemed fine, even this past Christmas. But just after New Year's she started feeling ill. And within a month, she was gone."

"February 6th," Jeanie said.

"I was in Washington when I read about it. It's a terrible thing. Perhaps it's obvious from my own appearance. *I've* been diagnosed with cancer too."

"I'm very sorry," Will said.

"Small-cell carcinoma … Stage Four. There is no Stage Five."

Will and Jeanie listened respectfully.

"Anyway." The congresswoman spoke over a rueful sigh. "I used my sister's invitation."

"Laura isn't here?" Jeanie scanned the lobby.

"Something came up with her oldest boy. He's had trouble since his father was … died."

"Then we're glad the ticket's being used," Will said.

"We'll make a note on the reception list," Jeanie added.

"You're both very kind."

"I hope it's nothing too serious with Laura's son," Will said.

"Teenagers are so vulnerable." Maldonado spoke wearily. "They need their fathers."

Jeanie glanced at Will. "Fathers are important."

"So, thank you both again. Maybe I'll see you at the reception."

"Congresswoman," Will said, as she started away, then paused.

"You know, Will, I always liked your mother."

He said nothing. He felt his wife's hand gripping his.

"I'm sorry the way things turned out," Maldonado added. "I've only recently read her book."

"Oh?"

"It's quite good. In fact, it's beautiful … a comfort. I should have read it sooner."

The congresswoman moved on.

"Hello, brother!" said a familiar voice.

"You made it!" Will hugged Kerry and shook hands with Dec.

"Who was *that*?" Kerry asked.

"*That* was Cathy Maldonado," Jeanie said, as she kissed her in-laws.

Kerry gasped. "*Noooo.*"

"She looks like death warmed over," Dec said.

"She's quite ill," Will confirmed.

"It's amazing she's here," Kerry observed.

"She just told us she loves Mom's book." Will was still a bit surprised.

"Isn't that something?" Kerry glanced up as the house lights flickered. A discreet chime rang twice. "Sorry we're so late."

"Traffic was horrendous," Dec said. "I hope the Harveys make it on time."

"I do too," Will replied. "Peg will *love* this film."

"Is Thomas settled in at the hotel?" Jeanie asked her sister-in-law.

"Oh, yes. Your nanny is the nicest girl."

The lights flashed again. The chime rang.

"You better go in." Will raised his arms in a gesture that encompassed his sister and her diligent husband. "Can you take them, Jeanie?"

"Of course."

"I'll be right there," he promised. "I need to check something."

Jeanie stared briefly before guiding his sister and brother-in-law to their seats.

Will hurried to the reception desk near the lobby entrance. Three young women from his staff smiled as he approached.

"How does everything look?"

A young woman named Anna spoke for the team. "It's a 90% turnout!"

As the other women checked-in late arrivals, Will glanced over Anna's shoulder at the master list, to which they'd already added

Congresswoman Maldonado. Most names had been marked with a red notation, signifying "present." He briefly studied the few unmarked names.

"All right, thanks everybody," he said. "I'm going in now."

"Enjoy the movie!" Anna said.

Will hurried across the lobby and entered the seating area as ushers closed the doors. The theater lights were going down. Jeanie stood at her seat waving. He hurried down the aisle and reached her as the opening titles appeared on-screen.

"Just in time," she said.

"The Harveys haven't arrived yet," he whispered.

"Anyone else missing?"

"A few people."

Kerry leaned over and shushed them in mock annoyance.

Will loved his sister and her husband. They were good people. He was glad his mother had left them the house in Trent, where they'd lived since his father died. His mother had relentlessly urged Kerry to enroll at Shelby. Now, Kerry was halfway through a bachelor's degree in psychology. Dec had been hired to work with Peter Harvey, who was Director of Facilities at Shelby.

And their little boy, Thomas, his nephew, was a precious thing.

The story unfolded on-screen. Will found it strange to hear actors speaking lines from his mother's writing—some of the words taken from the life he'd lived with her and his father. Though the words sounded true, he knew this was fiction, an artist's trick that bridged the past and the present with imagined coherence.

Had he not been his mother's son, her beautiful narrative, and the memories that flowed from its heart into his, might have been enough to explain his life to him. But none of it answered the simplest of questions: Whose memories were these?

As the film's sad voices whispered in the dark, Jeanie thought of Lina's father. Handsome, athletic and popular, Paulino Guerrero had been her high school boyfriend. She'd loved him from the moment they'd met, and had felt his love for her. When they made love that first time in their senior year, Jeanie was overcome with the joy of romantic assumptions. But Paulino reacted coldly when she told him she was pregnant. He shocked her by failing to suggest they marry.

She clung to him anyway, offering patience and compassion to a boy who seemed disoriented by abrupt changes in their lives. They moved into a cheap apartment after graduation, angering her parents, and forcing Paulino into a dull job at a neighborhood shoe store. When he started pilfering from the stock room and petty cash to support his growing drug habit, she prayed for him.

But her steadfast love was not enough; her once sweet boyfriend had lost all faith in himself. Then, one day, he hit her. Grateful for the gift of a rude awakening, she packed a bag, dressed the child, and left.

At first she lived with her parents, until their judgments became as unbearable as Paulino's anger. She found a studio apartment, got a job waiting tables at a hotel near Boston Harbor, and enrolled in junior college.

Paulino tracked her down and pleaded for forgiveness, begging her now to marry him. Jeanie wept at the sight of his beautiful face bloated by drugs and drinking.

"I *do* forgive you," she assured him. "But, it's too late for us."

"Don't *say* that." His anger flared. "Why are you saying that?"

"I'm not the person I used to be," she told him. "Neither are you."

Jeanie wasn't even sure where Paulino was now—probably living in some derelict part of Boston, she thought, abusing another woman. Or perhaps he was in prison being abused himself. Maybe he was dead.

For a time she'd blamed herself for the disaster of Paulino's life. But slowly, she'd found her own new faith—in work, in school, in raising Lina. And the unexpected gift of embracing a life with Will had seemed a natural part of her redemption.

Yet, since Alicia's birth, Jeanie had begun to fear that something was wrong in her marriage, that she and Will had made a mistake. And though there was no sin in hopeful intentions, she thought, to continue denying that her husband still loved his first wife would be a betrayal of herself—just as marrying Paulino would have been.

The film ended. Credits rolled beneath Rachel Portman's lush and tragic score. The house-lights came up to immense applause.

"Congratulations," Jeanie whispered to Will.

"We did it." His smile quickly vanished. "Are you okay?"

She squeezed his arm as they stood with the rising audience.

Will glanced across at Kerry and Dec. "What did you think?"

"Great movie," Dec said.

"It really captured the book," Kerry added. "I could actually hear them."

"It was almost frightening," Jeanie admitted.

Kerry slipped her arm through Jeanie's and spoke softly. "Are you all right?"

"I'm fine."

The couples pushed into the aisle and made their way back to a crowded lobby.

Jeanie searched the faces. There was no sign of Nancy or her husband, Gabriele, and the daughter, Marianna. Had they changed their plans and stayed in Florence after all? That would be ironic, Jeanie thought, after she'd been the one to urge their invitation. Will hadn't planned to include them—proof enough, she'd suspected, of his unresolved feelings.

"They *are* your mother's Italian publisher," Jeanie had reminded him.

In fact, the Antonini edition of *The Chastened Heart,* known as *Il Cuore Purificato,* had graced Italy's best-seller list for 18 months. Italian readers and critics were especially sensitive to an affinity with Dante's *Commedia* expressed in its characters' journey from disaffection to enlightenment, and in the strange dualism of its narrative voice. A noted scholar at the University of Florence now taught a popular course, based on her equally popular treatise, which explored the novel's dramatic use of key Dantean imagery: staircases, windows, mountains, rivers and bridges.

"I see the Harveys!" Kerry pointed toward the mezzanine stairway, from which audience members now descended.

Will waved to them.

"Let's say hello," Dec suggested.

"I need to wait for Lina," Jeanie said. "We'll catch up to you."

After a moment of concern, Kerry grabbed Dec's arm and followed him away.

Will moved close to his wife. "What is wrong?"

"*There* they are." Jeanie nodded toward the mezzanine stairs where Nancy, Gabriele and Marianna had just appeared.

"Oh." Will sounded almost surprised to see them.

Nancy wore a beautiful dress of crème-colored silk, with a splash of violet across the form-fitted midriff. Her husband was handsome in his tuxedo. The daughter was lovely—her white dress modest and full across her chest, flouncy and girlish from her black-belted waist to just above her knees.

"Go ahead," Jeanie urged.

"What about Lina?"

"If you don't go over and say hello to her ..."

Will was startled by Jeanie's edgy tone.

"Just go," she pleaded. "I see the Cantwell party."

Leaving him, Jeanie pushed toward the actress's group.

"Thank you, Mrs. Winslow," said the gracious actress. "We had a lovely time."

"I hope Lina wasn't a bother."

"Bother?" Cantwell laughed heartily. "We're all quite taken with her."

"You're very kind, Ms. Cantwell ..."

"Now tell me." The actress leaned toward Jeanie and spoke as if they were old, dear friends. "Did you like the movie?"

"Oh, what's wrong with me?" Jeanie gasped. "It was *wonderful*. We loved it. You were amazing!"

"Your husband was pleased?"

"Yes ... we both are."

"I'm so glad. I know how he feels about his mother's book."

"*You* gave it life."

As Cantwell beamed, one of her handlers whispered in her ear.

"All right." Her voice was suddenly business-like and hard. "My children are leaving for the airport," she explained to Jeanie. "I have some interviews. We'll see you at the party?"

"Of course." Jeanie reached for Lina's hand. "Don't let us keep you."

The actress smiled. "It's obvious where Lina's beauty comes from."

Jeanie was embarrassed by so direct a compliment.

"Now, Lina," the actress said, bending her long body toward the girl. "Don't forget."

"I won't, Ms. Cantwell."

The actress's husband quickly introduced himself to Jeanie, thanked Lina for sitting with them, and guided his wife and her children away.

"What did she mean?" Jeanie asked, watching two dark-suited men greet Cantwell near the theater entrance and hustle her children out to a waiting limousine. "Don't forget what?"

"We're invited to visit them, Mom ... in Tennessee ... with their new, little girl."

"Oh." Jeanie watched Cantwell's husband speak to his desolated wife, his hand a reassurance against her slender back.

"She's very nice and she really means it."

"She *is* very nice," Jeanie said, turning from her distractions. "I'm sure she means it."

"Let's tell Dad!"

Jeanie looked through the crowd and saw Will in conversation with Gabriele Antonini.

Nancy stood near them holding Marianna's hand and saying something to the girl whom Jeanie understood to be a year older than Lina. Jeanie observed a clear affinity between Nancy and Marianna, something almost spiritual, and even more striking than the stature, bearing and coloring the girl shared with her father.

Jeanie waved. Nancy recognized her and smiled.

Holding Lina's hand, Jeanie started across the lobby, thinking of all that Nancy had done for her, from the day they'd met in a tiny, third-floor office in a Boston townhouse—a day, Jeanie had always suspected, on which Nancy had convinced Will to hire her.

Lina broke away and hurried to embrace Will, surely telling him of her experience with movie stars, and the invitation to visit Tennessee. Will introduced her to Gabriele.

Nancy stepped forward to greet Jeanie. "It's so good to see you."

The women embraced; Jeanie found herself speechless.

Lina had already whispered something to Marianna, drawing a giggle, moving quickly out of earshot with a new friend. The men had resumed their discussion.

"I've been excited about tonight." Nancy stepped back. "And a little nervous ..."

"Nervous?"

Nancy smiled politely.

Jeanie began hearing loud voices outside on the street. "I was nervous too," she confessed. "I *am* nervous."

Nancy reached for Jeanie's hand and held it, gazing at it, as if reading Jeanie's fortune, but saying nothing.

"Are you enjoying your life in Italy?"

About to reply, Nancy was distracted by the shouting along West 54th Street. "Do you hear that?"

"I do." Jeanie looked toward the doors, then, at Will who'd been joined by his mother's agent, Judith Lavan, and the young PR woman from Chicago, Eileen Vachon, who had a novel of her own about to be published.

Gabriele came over to Nancy and asked what the commotion was.

"I don't really know," she told him.

"Marianna!" He spoke with warm urgency to his daughter, who stood at a distance with Lina. "Don't wander."

"I won't, papa."

As Nancy introduced her husband to Jeanie, the shouting outside became cheering. Suddenly, the lobby erupted in cheers as well. People stared at Blackberries and listened to cell phones.

"Oh my God." Judy Lavan gasped. "They've killed Bin Laden."

Will started across the old Tri-Borough Bridge watching for signs to I-95 and the coast. It was eleven on Monday. He hoped to reach the Connecticut-Rhode Island border by mid-afternoon and Boston by five.

Jeanie sat beside him staring down the East River at Manhattan's altered skyline. In back, Lina read her inscribed copy of *The Chastened Heart*, while Alicia slept in her ergonomic auto-crib between her big sister and Iris Perez, the family's 20-year-old, Nicaraguan nanny. A student at the Boston Museum of Fine Arts School, Iris had been with them now nearly six months.

"How do you feel?" he asked Jeanie.

"Fine," she said, as she took a last look at the city fading behind them.

He didn't believe her. In his opinion, she'd returned to work too soon after having the baby. Though, this morning, he nurtured his own desire to get back to the consolations of responsibility.

News of Bin Laden's death last night had evoked unexpected sadness. He suspected he wasn't alone in this feeling: that the mass murderer's demise, in a strange and distant place a decade after his crime, was somehow inconclusive, perhaps irrelevant—at best, a reminder of the disenchanted America his daughters were to inherit.

Jeanie closed her eyes and rested in her seat.

Will glanced at the elegant shape of her face with her hair pulled back. He welcomed a spontaneous thought of making love, something they'd done infrequently during the past year—what with the baby and all. But the changes between them had come to feel permanent. And he was running out of reasons to believe it wasn't personal, even if the briefest self-assessment in the rear-view mirror offered reason enough for her absent desire.

It had been a mistake, he knew, to have left the Antoninis off the first draft of the invitation list. His strictly honorable, if not quite honest, decision had betrayed a level of denial which aroused Jeanie's suspicions, only widening the distance between them.

Thus, when Gabriele graciously asked Jeanie to dance last night, Will immediately reciprocated.

It was Nancy who broke the ice as they held each other and moved, somewhat formally, to the music. "Are you happy?"

"I am." He said it without qualification. "You?"

She smiled. "Yes."

"I like Gabriele very much."

"I'm glad." She paused to watch her husband dance with Will's wife. "You know how I feel about Jeanie. She's such a beautiful woman. She's a good wife, isn't she?"

"She is. We've *both* noticed how Marianna admires you."

"She's important to me. She's certainly her mother's daughter." Will smiled.

"And you have *two* daughters now," she said.

"I'm very lucky."

They danced on for several moments in silence until Nancy spoke again.

"I'm reading the American galleys of Eileen Vachon's novel. I think we'll publish it."

"Good news for Eileen. You did a fine job with *The Chastened Heart*, and Lev Gellman's book."

"Those projects put our little house on the map ... thanks to you."

"*And* my mother," Will said, feeling his arm tighten around Nancy's back, as her fingers pressed down on his shoulder.

And perhaps to assert their freedom from the past, he thought, neither of them offered a hint of resistance to subtle familiarity.

"I guess everyone's where they're supposed to be," she proposed.

"It took us a while." He said it with irony meant as humor.

"Oh well," she said. And their dance ended.

Will heard the faint whisper of music from Iris's earplugs. It surprised him that the sleeping baby hadn't heard it, too, though perhaps the iPod's tinny voice had become a calming element of Alicia's little world.

Following signs onto I-95 at noon, he glanced in the mirror at Lina, who remained engrossed in his mother's book. And in the all-but-silent car, his thoughts again drifted.

Lev and Carol Gellman had said hello in the lobby right after the film last night. They were expecting a second child, and Lev's book about the banking crisis was still selling. An HBO film version was coming out in June.

Jennifer Yi, now a *New York Times* associate editor, had come to the after-party with her husband, and had interviewed Will for a story in the Style Section.

And having caught up with the Harveys, Will made sure to sit them at his table along with the Antoninis.

Peg now taught his mother's creative writing classes, and administered the Alice Prescott Winslow Fiction Prize, which Will and Virginia Porter co-sponsored.

Peter—rescued from bankruptcy by Mrs. Porter—now faced his first significant crisis as Director of Facilities at the college. The Bethlehem Mutual Insurance Company had stopped funding a campus library expansion.

"Dr. Emerson and Cathy Maldonado brought them in four years ago," Peter explained last night. "Bethlehem had pledged $35 million for exclusive rights to market student and faculty health plans. When Delia was named Provost, she looked into the arrangement and discovered the policy excluded abortion coverage. It even made contraceptives hard to get."

"Apparently, that's a trend," Will said.

"When Delia took over as President, two years ago, she got Bethlehem Mutual to end those restrictions. But in the process, she discovered Dr. Emerson had been named to Bethlehem's board of directors after leaving Shelby."

"I'm not surprised."

"Virginia wasn't any more comfortable about it than Delia was," Peter said. "So, Delia renegotiated the Bethlehem contract. She worked out a five-year grace period, after which any insurance firm would have the right to compete on campus. Six months ago, Bethlehem told us they couldn't continue funding the library. Three months ago, they stopped offering policies."

"That's a shame."

"We have several insurance companies offering health plans now. But the premiums are expensive."

"Have you looked into self-insurance? It's the best way to control what you cover. And it can save you money in the right circumstances."

Peter seemed skeptical. "No insurance companies?"

"You can do it yourself, or in partnership with an insurer to help you manage everything. It may not be the right approach for a smaller institution like Shelby, but it wouldn't hurt to find out. One of my clients is a British insurer looking to expand in the States. I could put them in touch with you."

"I think Delia might be interested," Peter said. "Would you mention it to her?"

"Okay," Will said. "So, what's happening with your library?"

"Virginia writes a monthly check to keep construction going. Delia and I are talking to banks, but the credit environment is tough."

Will frowned. "I know."

"We've started a corporate campaign. Maybe one in ten companies we talk to pledges some money."

"I could arrange to have you speak with my clients about your library."

"You're being so generous to us, Will."

"Isn't that what my parents would want?"

The men clasped hands. Then, Peter wrapped Will in a spontaneous embrace. "I miss them, too."

Moments later, Peter grabbed Peg who laughed girlishly as he spun her onto the dance floor.

Briefly watching the Harveys enjoy themselves, Will smiled as he observed Lina and Marianna engaged in a plan to monopolize Jon Lowe's dance card. Finally, he realized the Gellmans were standing near his table with urgent expressions.

"There wasn't enough time at the theater," Lev said.

"Please. Sit down." Will pulled two empty chairs from a nearby table.

"I wanted to say … your dad meant the world to me."

"You *miss* him," Carol Gellman said.

"That's right." Lev agreed. "I do."

"He knew how you felt. He'd be thrilled about your book … and the *movie*."

Carol Gellman smiled as she rubbed her husband's back.

"I have a framed copy of his last column," Lev said. "The one about Kerouac."

"A beautiful piece," Carol added.

"Why didn't *he* publish a book or two?" Lev asked. "I'm sure he *could* have."

"He wrote half a novel at college. He worked on it for a while after graduation, mainly at my mother's insistence. But he wanted to be a journalist."

Carol looked skeptical. "He couldn't do both?"

They all stared at each other, listening to dance music.

Finally, Will spoke. "Would you like to hear a story about my dad?"

Intrigued, Lev and Carol sat back in their chairs.

"He had a track scholarship to a small college in Providence," Will told them. "In his junior year, he and three teammates got into a dispute with their coach. It was early spring of 1968, the height of Viet Nam. There were rumors of college deferments being rescinded."

"We had more than half a million troops in Viet Nam by 1968," Lev said. "Almost 17,000 American soldiers were killed that year alone."

"The track coach called my father and the other boys into his office. He lectured them about the war, patriotism, responsibility to the country and the college ... the whole nine yards."

Lev glanced at Carol. Will continued.

"The coach said he had it on good authority, from the campus ROTC commandant, that college deferments *were* being eliminated. Young men like them would soon be classified 1-A. It would mean they could be drafted right out of school. Of course, it would cripple the team since they were his four top runners."

Lev's eyes narrowed in distress.

"But the coach offered a solution: sign up for ROTC on campus."

"What a solution." Carol sighed.

"The coach said it would guarantee they could finish out their junior years. And then their senior years, without any problem."

"And the day they graduated," Lev said coldly, "they'd have one-way tickets to Saigon as Second Lieutenants."

"My father asked why they should believe the commandant. 'It's his job to recruit for the ROTC,' he said. Well, the coach started screaming. 'That's a friend of mine you're talking about.'"

Lev frowned. "Ugh."

"The coach claimed they'd be in breach of responsibility to the team and the school unless they joined ROTC."

"That's *legal* wording. Was he threatening their scholarships?"

"Absolutely," Will said. "The boys were smart enough to say they'd have to speak to their parents. And they got the hell out of his office. But later that day, before they'd really thought things through, a sports reporter from the main Providence newspaper contacted them. He said he'd heard about what was happening at the school and wanted to get their side of it."

Lev was incredulous. "That crazy coach called the newspaper."

"Based on how things turned out, I'd say he did," Will acknowledged. "The reporter convinced them he was sympathetic. He said it was outrageous for a coach to be 'pressuring kids' like that. They were afraid of losing their scholarships, concerned about publicity for themselves and the school. They just wanted to get back to running. So they told him they'd rather not do an interview. But the reporter told them he was doing an article one way or another … and it would be best for them to air their side of the story."

"Right," Lev said, recognizing the classic journalistic ploy.

"So they met him and answered his questions. Next day, the story appeared. They were all quoted in ways that made them seem ungrateful and unpatriotic, a bunch of brats who'd been catered to by the college. And the coach, well, he was the hero … hard-working guy, Marine veteran … just trying to protect his team, and the college, and the whole damn country."

"Naturally," Carol whispered.

"The story went national on the AP," Will said. "*Sports Illustrated* did a sympathetic profile of the coach a week later. The college more or less sided with the coach, allowing him to cut the boys from the team. They *wouldn't* let him vacate their scholarships."

"Well, that's something," Carol said.

"The following term, the coach got a raise."

"Unbelievable," Lev said.

"I'll tell you the worst part. Visit the athletic complex at Aquinas College today, and you'll see an entire wall devoted to the track team's trophies, medals, championship certificates. But look closely and you'll notice an odd, four-year gap between 1965 and 1969. Not one reference to four of the best runners who ever went to that school, some of the best runners in the history of New England track and cross country."

Lev shook his head in disgust.

"Where were the parents?" Carol asked. "I'm surprised there wasn't a law suit."

"The students agreed not to sue, in exchange for keeping their scholarships," Will said. "The parents were embarrassed by the negative press and told their sons to keep quiet."

"It wouldn't happen that way today," she said.

Will agreed. "I used to think my parents' generation was … overly dramatic. That whole rebellious, 60s thing, and all the anti-establishment stuff … their skepticism toward authority. It just seemed over-the-top, self-indulgent. But when you hear a story like this, it makes you think."

"So what you're saying is, your dad came out of this experience wanting to be an honest reporter with a sense of justice," Lev suggested. "Fair enough … that's what he was. It still doesn't explain why he didn't finish that novel."

"Did you know my dad had a drinking problem when he was younger?"

"He mentioned something about it."

"I think he felt he'd wasted too much time on his own sorrows. That he'd been too self-involved. And just decided to pursue different goals, a life devoted to his family, and the people who worked for him." Will paused. "That's how I read the Kerouac essay."

They were silent for a moment. The party swirled around them.

Finally, Lev nodded, as if to say he understood. "Carol and I just put *my* father in a nursing home."

"How old is he?"

"He's 81. He was always such a strong man, but in the past year he's been … slowing down. He needs constant care now. We wanted to hire a nurse and keep him with us, but he refused. So, we picked out a home together and he went in. You know, he really liked your dad. They only met once, but it made an impact on my father."

"I didn't know."

"He asks about your dad every time we see him."

"He knows my dad passed away, right?"

"We told him when it happened." Lev shrugged. "He keeps asking."

"Oh. I see."

The Gellmans thanked Will for speaking candidly. He assured them that his father would have approved. But as they left, smiling politely, Will had the sense of something not quite adding up for them in what he'd shared. Then again, he hadn't shared everything.

The baby's crying roused Will from his distraction. It was just past two.

Jeanie suggested they stop for a restroom break and something to eat.

"I think we passed one of those rest stops a while ago," he said sheepishly.

"We *did*." Lina's terse reply was unexpected.

"Sorry." He glanced at her in the mirror.

"Middleton," Jeanie said, reading a sign for the next exit.

"There's a nice, old hotel in Middleton." Will slowed and left the highway. "It's on the water."

Iris lifted Alicia from the auto-crib and handed her forward.

In her mother's arms, the baby stopped fussing briefly, then, started again. "She needs a change."

"We'll try the hotel," Will said. "They'll have a clean bathroom … experience dealing with children."

Jeanie nodded and stared from her window as she held the baby close.

"Good idea, Dad." Lina was discernibly annoyed and not just with him.

Driving south, they quickly reached a stoplight at Main Street, which ran east-west through Middleton.

"Nice town," Iris said. "A bit like The Hamptons."

Will looked east at the shops, bistros and art galleries along Main Street. The art cinema's marquee advertised *Company Men* and *The Conspirator*, while *The Tree of Life*, *Midnight in Paris* and *The Chastened Heart* were coming soon.

"Southampton, maybe ..." He turned west on Main, and made a quick left at the first light, heading south again toward the beach on a tree-lined, residential street. "As I recall ... the hotel is down this way."

"I see water." Lina pointed to the blue space into which the street vanished far ahead.

"These homes are lovely," Jeanie said.

And they were, Will thought, looking left and right as he drove slowly within the local speed limit. There were old, white Colonials, on generous parcels of property, with great green lawns and wide, circular driveways. There were gabled, grey Victorians, on somewhat smaller plots, but equally attractive. And there were a variety of newer capes and ranches, all well-tended, painted in beachy pastels. Finally, as they neared the edge of the Sound, the street narrowed in a community of screen-porch cottages.

"There's the hotel." Lina indicated a four-story, wood-framed Victorian guarding the beach at the road's end. "Are they rebuilding it?"

"Looks that way." Will saw contractor vans and pickups parked along the street, and building materials stacked below the hotel's front porch. "I'll just check."

He pulled in next to a van, turned off his engine, and got out. Shading his eyes against the brilliant sunlight, he called to the nearest workman.

"Pardon me! Is the hotel open?"

"Partially." The man paused to hook his thumbs on his carpenter's belt. "The guest rooms are being redone. They'll be ready in a few weeks."

"I see."

"The restaurant's operating." The workman frowned as he glanced at his watch. "They stop serving lunch at two."

"Oh." Will's voice sank. He glanced at the new clapboard on three upper levels, and the Tyvek insulation around the bottom level awaiting its new facing. "We've got a baby that needs changing." He nodded toward his family in the car behind him.

"The owners will help you out," the workman said. "They're good folks." He pointed to the wooden staircase leading up to glass entrance doors with their Marvin window labels still showing. "Just watch your step."

"We will. Thanks."

Back at the car, Will opened the driver's door to lean in and explain.

"I'll change the baby and see if they'll give us anything to eat," Jeanie said. "Iris, will you come with me?"

"Of course, Mrs. Winslow."

Jeanie got out, cradling Alicia in her arms, and proceeded with Iris toward the hotel.

Will watched them climb the porch stairs. Then, he glanced at Lina, who waited nearby with his mother's book held tightly under one arm.

"I'll stay here," he said. "I guess."

Lina responded to the deflation in his voice. "Don't be angry with her."

His daughter's earlier annoyance had vanished, replaced by an empathetic manner, which made her seem older than 14.

"I'm not angry."

"No?"

"It's been busy these past months. Things are busy at the firm. We're all busy with the new baby. Things are just … well … it's life, Lina."

"I know what life is." He heard that other sound in her voice again, the clipped displeasure of a teenage girl. "Don't lose it, Dad."

"What do you mean?"

Lina held the novel out with two hands. "Like your mom says … love is precious. It doesn't always come when you want it to come. It doesn't always stay when you want it to stay. You can't take anything for granted."

He admired her so. "You're right."

"You and Mom *really* love each other."

He laughed. "You think?"

"Everyone can see it. Why can't *you*?"

Embarrassed now, he glanced out to sea.

"I've known her longer than you," she said. "She gets crazy sometimes, and needs to be in charge of everything. It's the good part of her, but it's also the bad. It can make her seem …"

"Frustrated?"

"I was going to say bitchy." She laughed. "*Your* word's nicer."

"Yours might be more accurate." Now, he heard the edge in his own voice.

"And *you* can be overbearing and obtuse." She paused. "It's just fear."

He laughed to hear such truth-telling, but caught himself, seeing confusion in her eyes. "I'm not laughing at you, sweetheart."

She nodded warily, putting her arms around him for a moment before hurrying away.

Will watched as she scaled the stairs and vanished into the hotel.

Overbearing and obtuse, he thought, marveling at the clarity of youthful assessments.

It was a beautiful day, at least, with a high warm sun and a slight breeze off the water. They were still about an hour from Rhode Island. It had been the perfect place to stop.

As he walked past the hotel toward the sand, he saw 50 yards of beach extending to the calm waves of Long Island Sound. And in the extreme distance, Long Island itself, a thin, blue line on the horizon.

To his left, another residential street ran parallel with the beach. It was lined on its north side by grand, old Victorian homes—their wide, beveled windows glistening in the sunlight, their generous front porches open to the street and the beach.

He had the clearest memory of his mother, and himself as a young child, spending days like this at Long Island's eastern end—usually in North Fork harbor villages like Mattituck and Greenport, which his mother had preferred to the jazzier South Fork beach towns. Those were sad days during his parents' first marriage, when his mother struggled against hopelessness, and he struggled with a jumble of guilt and relief over being rescued, even briefly, from his father's bleak undertow.

On those daytrips, his mother invariably described his father as a sick person. Will didn't understand what that meant—then. It took him years to comprehend illness of spirit, to learn that lives encounter crises of faith in themselves, that every form of love, perhaps like art, requires compassion and a willing suspension of disbelief.

His cell phone buzzed.

It was Craig McCall. "I'm sorry, Will. I just couldn't make it last night."

"What happened?"

"Got tied up here in Boston ..."

"You're in Boston?"

"It's where I normally stay when I come east. I'm on those committees at Harvard."

"Yes."

"I have friends here, old classmates ... one of whom is a constitutional lawyer. We met and discussed Janet Mohamed."

"Oh."

"Time just slipped away. When I realized how late it was, I knew there was no sense racing out to Logan to catch the shuttle. How was your premiere?"

"It went well. We're all star struck now."

Craig chuckled. "Is the movie any good?"

"They did a great job. My mom would have been pleased."

"Can't wait to see it. What did you think of the Bin Laden news?"

"I don't know." Will sighed. "Does it change anything?"

Craig paused before answering. "The world was changing *before* 9/11, Will. *That* was the wake-up call. The important thing, now, is to face the changes rationally."

"So, you're still pushing the Janet Mohamed case?"

"Truthfully, I'd rather not be. We exhausted the federal court process in Illinois. The Supreme Court decided it wouldn't consider our brief after all. But, I feel an obligation to her."

"It's a tough environment for what she's doing."

"We lost in Illinois on denial of religious expression," Craig said. "There's another way to approach it: unlawful search, failure to observe due process."

"You'd think it wouldn't be difficult to show you were being profiled. Especially if you look and dress like Janet Mohamed."

"We're *all* being profiled, Will, the moment we buy a plane ticket. That's Janet's point."

"Most people seem willing to accept it," Will suggested.

"Well, the Constitution exists whether people like it or not. Anyway, there's a Boston firm that might take the case and try it in federal court here."

"Why not try it in New York?"

"Too many interest groups ready to demonize someone like Janet, and turn the trial into a spectacle."

"You're thinking of the mosque in lower Manhattan."

"Exactly," Craig said. "There'll be opposition here too, of course, but less extreme."

"Until some terrorist plants a bomb at Fenway or along the Marathon route."

"Don't even joke about that, Will."

"I'm not joking."

"Oh." Craig sounded distressed. "Anyway, Janet's willing to move east for the case."

"And you're paying for this?"

"Not all of it." Craig paused. "Janet put her book royalties in escrow. There's talk of movie rights being sold."

"I'm sure you're picking up most of the tab."

"Janet's already paid a heavy price. Her husband's had it with trials, publicity, criticism from family and co-workers, not to mention death-threats. He didn't want her royalties diverted to the case, apparently. So, he's filing for divorce. They have a two-year-old child and he wants sole custody. He claims she's unfit."

"What a disaster."

"I've urged Janet to think about what's happening to her life. She says 'if I quit now, because my husband has lost faith in me, what sort of marriage would I be making?'"

"I hope she knows what she's doing," Will said. "I can't help thinking some new technology may come along and make airport body-scanning a moot issue anyway."

"You could be right," Craig said. "And I've told her I'm not supporting a new case unless she works out a settlement that's fair to her and the husband. We'll just have to see."

Will had mixed feelings about Janet Mohamed. He agreed with her constitutional arguments, but believed she'd been given a good shot at the American court system. And yes, her husband sounded unsupportive and bitter, but who can judge another's marriage? Her real obstacle, Will thought, was the country's determination to confuse fear with wisdom.

"How's business?" Craig asked. "When we spoke at your mom's funeral, you mentioned a bit of a slowdown."

"We had zero growth last year. *This* year, so far, is a loss."

"Are you losing clients?"

"One or two, but revenue is steady … more or less. It's this loan I took, to buy Nancy out. It's cut our margins. I may have to start laying people off."

"I told you three years ago I was willing to buy Nancy's share."

"It's too much money, Craig."

"I'd be making a good investment. Can you give it some thought, at least?"

Will sighed. There was a long silence between them.

"*What?*" Craig finally said.

"I was just imagining how Winslow & McCall would look on a letterhead."

"You wouldn't have to do that."

"No, Craig. I'd insist."

"I'm happy to be a silent partner."

"You deserve more."

A briefer silence.

"You were always good to my mom," Will said. "You've been nice to Jeanie and me these past few years. You were kind to me when I was a little boy."

Craig still didn't reply. Will sensed the other end of the connection being muffled.

"Craig? Are you there?"

"Yeah." He was coughing. "Yes."

"How long are you in Boston?"

"A few days, to see this law firm—did you want to meet?"

"We have a nice box at Fenway."

"Your mom and I used to go to Fenway." Craig was wistful. "A million years ago."

"The Sox *are* in town. We could talk some more … about … everything."

"I'd like that, Will. I'd like it very much."

After ringing off with Craig, Will started back toward the car. He could see the girls coming down the hotel steps. Iris carried Alicia now. Lina clutched her book. Jeanie lugged a picnic basket.

"What nice people," Jeanie said, as the family reunited outside the car.

She explained that the hotel keepers had loaded the basket with sandwiches and deserts, because their restaurant was closed until 6pm.

"They're fans of your mom's book." Jeanie smiled broadly. "When they saw Lina's copy, and realized she had autographs from movie stars, they were *very* excited."

"That's when I told them Alice Winslow is your mom," Lina said.

"They couldn't do enough for us," Jeanie added.

Will looked to the sky and called out. "Thanks, Mom!"

Everyone laughed as they loaded themselves into the car.

Alicia, fast asleep again, was gently placed in her auto-crib.

Jeanie gazed at the hotel. "This was a good choice."

Will hit the ignition, backed away, and slowly turned, facing north again. Jeanie told everyone to wave to the owners who stood on their porch watching them leave.

"We should stay here sometime," Will suggested.

"It's a nice idea." Jeanie opened the basket and riffled through the neatly wrapped sandwiches. "Who wants ham & cheese?"

They reached Providence, and Jeanie checked her watch. "We're making good time."

"We'll be in Boston around five-thirty," Will said.

"And hit rush-hour traffic." Jeanie noticed a sign for Aquinas College and turned to Lina. "Do you want to see it?"

"Can we?"

"See *what*?"

"Our daughter would like to make a brief stop, Will … at Aquinas."

After some confused silence, he responded. "Sure."

"Exit 23 … State Offices," Jeanie reminded him.

"Right."

"It's highly ranked among private, New England colleges," Lina said. "Of course, your dad went there."

Jeanie smiled nervously as Lina's commentary continued.

"They have an excellent literature program and women's soccer team."

Now, Jeanie laughed. "She's been reading their web-site."

Will nodded. "You should have mentioned this before."

"It's *one* school she may consider." Caution seemed the wisest course to Jeanie. "Decisions are a long way off."

"It's good we're thinking about it," he said.

The exit ramp off I-95 brought them to a neighborhood of bodegas, loft-buildings and modest, two-family homes just north of the Capitol. An Amtrak commuter train glided beneath the ramp. Farther north, a system of freight-rails cut through a complex of red brick factories.

Will drove west on a four-lane thoroughfare of retail businesses and cafés that reminded Jeanie of the Fenway and parts of Beacon Street on a smaller scale. Then, quickly, the thoroughfare became a peaceful, tree-lined street of Victorian homes—some clapboard, others fieldstone. This was Shelby Avenue.

They passed a sign for the Lyman Shelby Historic House located two miles northwest.

The street was climbing a long hill at this point. Lincoln Park consumed a square block on the left. St. Dominic's Hospital sprawled across several blocks to the right. And Shelby Avenue became Exton Street as Aquinas College emerged at the hillcrest several blocks ahead.

Jeanie knew that Will was skeptical.

She'd visited Aquinas with him in February, after his mother's death, to see the athletic director and the track coach. They'd discussed his father's accomplishments at the school, and broached the idea of bringing the performance records of Tom Winslow and his three teammates to light.

The meetings had been cordial, though the track coach had been skeptical of the boys' achievements—notwithstanding the file of news clippings Will had brought along with a box of his father's trophies and medals. The coach and athletic director barely looked at the materials, and declined Will's offer to leave them behind for review.

Jeanie had her own doubts. Aquinas was a Catholic college, and she'd ceased being an observant member of the Church after feeling its institutional pressure to accept Paulino back. On the other hand, her education at secular Boston schools had evoked its own skepticism.

She understood that many private colleges had been founded as religious schools. But, in her opinion, their spiritual heritage had faded—devolved in some cases—to an empty pretense of elitism. Jeanie wanted her daughters to develop something more than a sense of entitlement. Any college that helped make them educated women of independent mind and generous spirit was fine with her.

Will turned in at the main gate and drove along the landscaped entrance mall leading to a four-story, gothic edifice—the school's original building at its 1907 inception as a men's college.

"This seems very nice," Iris said.

"There's more than 100 acres," Lina replied. "On the highest point in the city."

Jeanie listened closely to her daughter and observed—as she hadn't in the austere chill of February—a campus that blossomed with beautiful, purposeful young women.

Beyond the imposing, gothic building, they found a space in the visitors' parking lot.

Jeanie conferred with Iris about the baby.

"She looks so comfortable in her tiny capsule," Iris whispered.

"Do you mind staying here?"

"No. I brought one of my art books."

Will suggested that Iris keep some windows open.

"I will." She pointed to a row of benches along a shaded walkway leading to the library. "If it gets too stuffy, we'll sit over there."

"Call me if there's a problem," Jeanie said. "You can always catch up to us."

Iris smiled. "We'll be fine!"

Moments later, Jeanie, Will and Lina found themselves on a wide pathway from which the busy campus, sections of the surrounding neighborhood, and even the distant city, were visible.

Groups of students and professors moved among the campus buildings, talking and laughing. Young men in pin-striped uniforms strolled toward the baseball field. Young women dressed for field hockey, carrying sticks on their shoulders, hurried down the slope toward an open pitch next to a large stadium. Inside the stadium, the women's soccer team conducted spring practice, while separate groups of men and women worked out on the track around them.

"Let's go down and watch the women's soccer team," Will suggested.

"Okay." Lina smiled broadly and held up her copy of *The Chastened Heart*. "Then we'll check the library and see if they have your mom's book."

"I'm sure they do."

"And the bookstore?"

"It's probably there too," Jeanie assured her.

A group of female students came by and smiled at Lina.

"Great book!" one of them said.

"Isn't it?"

Jeanie felt warmed by her daughter's spontaneous joy. "It's so friendly here."

Halfway down the grassy slope, they met a young woman in soccer gear coming back up.

Jeanie noticed that she walked with a limp. Her soccer cleats were hung by their long laces over one shoulder. And on her white-stocking feet, the girl wore what appeared to be elegant, Italian loafers.

"Is practice over?" Will asked.

"My knee's acting up." The young woman grimaced as she paused to speak. "Most of those girls are trying out for next year's team," she said, pointing down into the stadium. "They've got another 40 minutes to go."

"I hope your injury isn't serious," Jeanie said.

"It's a chronic thing. I'll miss the national-team trials in June."

"Are you a senior?" Will asked.

She smiled. "I graduate in two weeks."

"My name is Will Winslow. This is my wife, Jeanie."

"How do you do. I'm Kate … Adams."

"And this is our daughter, Lina," Jeanie said. "*She* wants to play soccer, maybe here."

"It's a great game," Kate said. "Are you on your high school team, Lina?"

"I made freshman squad this year."

"Very good. And you're reading *The Chastened Heart.*"

"Oh, yes!"

"Don't you love when he takes her up to the 20th floor of the unfinished building?"

"It's my favorite scene!"

"It happened here, you know. She gives a different name for the school. But it's Aquinas all right."

"How do you know that?" Jeanie asked.

"*Everyone knows.*" Kate spoke with charming certainty. "If you want, I'll take you to the actual building."

Will waved her off. "You must be very busy."

"Not really." Kate smiled. "I have one more final, and I'm done with soccer, so, I'm pretty much free. I'm off to the Cape right after graduation, for my summer job. Then grad school in the fall." She laughed. "But, right now, I'm basically loafing!"

Jeanie liked this girl. "Where are you going for grad school?"

"Northeastern ... I'm studying American literature."

"Lina *loves* literature."

Kate nodded thoughtfully. "Come with me to Beatrice Hall. It's my dorm. I'll show you the exact spot on the 20th floor that inspired that scene in the novel."

With no pressing reason to continue resisting, the group followed Kate back up the hill. As they walked, Kate engaged Lina.

"You have a new paperback edition," she said. "It's tied in with the movie."

"We saw the movie last night."

"You did?"

"We met the actors." Lina handed the book to Kate. "They signed my copy."

"*What*?" Kate opened the first pages and read the inscriptions.

Will explained the family's connection with Alice Prescott Winslow.

"Alice Winslow is your mother?" Kate seemed awe-struck.

"And his father was a student here," Jeanie told her.

"You mean *Tom* Winslow. He was a great runner."

Will nodded. "How did you know that?"

"Everyone here knows that. There's a reference to it in the novel. Of course, it's fictionalized. But we know the basis of it. A group of us went to see the A.D. and the track coach, oh ... almost two years ago. We'd done a Google search of old meet results, newspaper articles, archives of other colleges ... we asked why there's nothing about Tom Winslow in our own school history. We know he had that nasty dispute with his coach, but he's still *part* of us. His medals belong in our trophy cases."

"There were three *other* boys," Will said, as they approached Beatrice Hall.

Kate held the door open for her guests and followed them into the lobby, directing them toward the elevator banks. "Yes, we know about those boys."

They crowded into the elevator and rode to the 20th floor in polite silence. As the doors opened and they filed into the hallway, Jeanie spoke up.

"Will and I visited the track coach last February."

Kate called out to the floor. "Male visitor!"

Two young women emerged from a lounge. "Hey, Katie," they said, hurrying past and jumping into the elevator ahead of the closing doors.

"I'm sorry." Kate smiled at Jeanie. "You were here in February?"

"Yes, but they weren't interested in revisiting old records ... not even when we showed them medals and trophies."

"People get locked into a version of the past, Mrs. Winslow."

"I suspect it's political."

"What happened to those boys was *definitely* political." Kate was pensive. "But at this point, I think, it's just embarrassing. After all this time, it's easier to forget."

Kate directed her guests past a stairwell door toward a large window with a southeast view that clearly matched the stunning description in *The Chastened Heart*.

"Isn't it the way she describes in the book?" Kate stood close to Lina and pointed at the distance. "There's the Capitol. There's the Biltmore. There's Narragansett Bay."

"Oh ..." Lina sighed.

Will stepped closer to the window. "It really is."

"Did your father ever ask the college to look at his records?" Kate asked him.

"Not that I know of. I'm pretty sure he didn't."

"He must have had his reasons."

"You're probably right."

Jeanie glanced at her husband. "Facts are still facts."

Again, they all stared at the vista.

Jeanie broke the silence. "What are your plans after grad school, Kate?"

"You've been talking to my parents." The young woman laughed at herself. "I hope to write ... and teach."

Will smiled. "That was my mother's life."

"I can't tell you how many times I've come out here to read her book," Kate said. "I let her beautiful voice live inside me. And it all makes sense." Kate looked directly at Jeanie. "So when you ask what I'd like to do with my life, the real answer is … to write a doctoral thesis, and maybe a book, about *The Chastened Heart.*"

"And what would you say about it?"

Kate pointed to Lina's copy. "That novel is a love letter to a shattered boy. At first, I thought the story was about how strong you need to be, how much you have to sacrifice, to succeed … to reach your goal, your dream. There's so much in the story about how the husband failed to follow his own dream, failed his early promise."

"He finds a *new* path to follow."

"It took a while for me to see that, Mrs. Winslow. After several readings, it began to dawn on me that the story is more about love than success. It's about how the husband overcomes the things that nearly killed him when he was young.

"And he does that by giving his unfinished novel to his wife," Kate added, turning to look at Will. "She writes *hers* from *his*. And so, *The Chastened Heart* is a story about art as love. Those two characters in your mom's novel essentially collaborate on the wife's book, which becomes the story of their life together. Each contributes something unique about that life to a single, finished work … a novel with so much more power than one author could put on a page."

Jeanie admired this young woman's sophistication.

"It's a novel about a promise two young people make to each other," Kate said, "and how they keep their promise." She paused to examine the faces of her guests one by one. "I'm sorry. I get carried away."

"No, no." Jeanie touched Kate's hand. "You have wonderful insights about Alice's book. If you knew her, you'd see how close you are to who she was."

"I wish I *had* known her. When I read her book, I feel she knows me."

Jeanie stared at Will intensely, until he understood and nodded.

"I'll have to speak with my sister," he said to Kate. "But Jeanie and I would like to offer you access to my father's papers ... for your graduate work."

Kate listened with a stunned expression.

"We've been trying to decide what to do with his papers. They include a beautiful, half-written novel that might help you with your thesis." He paused. "There *is* an uncanny similarity between what my father was writing many years ago, and my mother's book. His manuscript and her book tell the same story about the promise you described."

"Mr. Winslow, I don't know what to say."

"You'll need to study my mother's papers too. Those are at Boston University."

"I've been to that file," Kate said.

"What you really should do is read the drafts my mother wrote on her way to the finished version of her novel. Then read what my father had been writing."

"I've read her pre-publication galleys. I didn't have time to examine all her drafts. Are you saying they're actually *based* on your father's manuscript?"

"Yes." Will nodded. "My mother finished a story that my father wouldn't. Of course, she did more than simply finish his story. She added her own vision to it, and made it something new. In each of her drafts, the story moves farther into a new realm. And yet, the essence of my dad's story is there. She even captured his voice."

Kate gasped. "Does anyone else know about this?"

"Not outside our family."

"Now I understand that sense of duality you get in her narrative," Kate marveled. "It's a story of *two* poets on a journey together, a pilgrimage, as in Dante's *Commedia*."

"Two *voices*, woven together," Jeanie replied. "'A story about art as love,' I think you said."

"May I give you my phone numbers for Quincy and the Cape?"

"Of course." Will opened his cell phone. "And we'll give you ours."

"We should exchange email addresses," Jeanie added.

"I'll get my phone!" Kate was excited. "Lina, would you like to see my room?"

"Yes!"

Jeanie reached for Will's hand and watched the girls walk down the quiet hallway together.

"She understands your mother's book, Will. She'll do a great job with your father's material."

"The Gellmans were so touched when I shared some of Dad's story last night," he said. "You don't think Lev's a better choice?"

"Lev would do a great job. So would Jen Yi, Peg Harvey, the Vachon girl from Chicago … any of the people we've discussed. I just think Kate is the *perfect* choice."

"You know what? I do too. I hope Kerry agrees."

"She will. Leave it to me." Jeanie turned toward the window again. "There really is something magical about this view."

She felt Will's arm around her waist.

A moment later, there was music from the open door of Kate's room—a familiar, old recording of *Heart Like A Wheel*.

As they listened to Linda Ronstadt sing of un-mended hearts and sinking ships, the sun's lengthening rays settled on the city and the watery distance beyond. Jeanie glanced at her husband and saw a tear coming from his eye. She felt his body move in a subtle, nearly imperceptible shudder, as if a painful burden had just lifted from him. And now, the weight of her own doubts began to lift.

"It's kind of amazing, when you think about," he whispered. "To be standing here."

Her cell phone buzzed. She fumbled in her bag for it.

"It's Iris," she said, looking at the call number and answering. "Is there a problem?"

"No problem," Iris assured her. "We're over at those benches."

"The baby's comfortable?"

"Couldn't be happier." Iris giggled.

"We shouldn't be much longer."

"No rush. Half the women's track team is sitting with us. They're all in love with Alicia. We're chatting … having a great time."

"That's wonderful."

"This is such a friendly school, Mrs. Winslow."

Will could see the glow of Fenway Park in his old neighborhood across the river—no game tonight; just the field-crew prepping for the Baltimore series—while headlights glided over Harvard Bridge between the Back Bay and Cambridge where he lived now.

It was nine-thirty. They'd been home for an hour. Jeanie was downstairs in Lina's bedroom no doubt talking over their exciting Manhattan trip, and their sojourn in Providence, which had included dinner in the Aquinas student center as guests of Kate Adams. The baby was deep in sleep. Iris was with her boyfriend at the Museum School, checking the installation on which they'd collaborated for an exhibition.

Smaller than the office he'd shared with Nancy in that old, Beacon Street townhouse, this little room was a builder's afterthought—a walk-in closet with a south-facing window. A large, master bedroom and a long hallway consumed the greater part of this quiet, third-floor.

On the desk in front of him were his father's unfinished novel and a simple, manila folder containing a faded newspaper clipping from the now defunct *Long Island Press*. The clipping was dated December 27, 1968; its headline read: **Bayview War Hero Laid to Rest.**

The article recounted Colonel Arthur Winslow's military exploits in the South Pacific and Korea, his subsequent teaching position at West Point, and his staid retirement on Long Island, where an eventful life had ended tragically. Colonel Winslow was said to have been highly-regarded among his neighbors and fellow parishioners at St. Matthew's Roman Catholic Church on upper Main Street in Bayview.

A photo of the Colonel in full military dress, with brass and ribbons, highlighted the article. But the newsprint had oxidized and looked like rotting parchment from an archaeological dig, the record of an ancient warrior prince.

Two weeks before her death, Will's mother had given him a key and told him to look in a file cabinet in the shed behind her house.

There, he'd found the manuscript and the obituary locked together in the same drawer.

Several days later, on an afternoon when his mother felt a burst of energy, she gathered Will and Kerry and Jeanie in her bedroom.

"Did you find the manuscript?" she asked her son.

"Yes."

"Have you read it?"

"It's beautiful."

Alice smiled at Kerry. "What do *you* think?"

"I'm reading it now," she said. "It *is* beautiful … and sad."

"We also found a newspaper story about his father," Will added. "I always suspected suicide."

"It plagued your father for years."

"He never talked about it."

"No."

"And his mother never said anything."

"She was an odd woman." Alice's voice was hoarse, but her tartness was apparent. "More remote, in some ways, than the Colonel …"

Will nodded. "What's the connection between the manuscript and the obit?"

"Why do you assume a connection?"

"He kept them together," Kerry said. "It seems like they were connected for *him*."

"Well," Alice whispered. "I suppose all betrayals are connected … in some way."

She told them about the 1968 incident, involving the four boys and the track coach, at Aquinas College.

"Ironically, your father might never have gone to that college," Alice said. "His father had pushed for him to go to West Point. During his senior year in high school, they'd visited the Academy several times for meetings with the dean and the athletic director. Your father worked out for the track coaches, and they were impressed.

"The head track coach advised your father to go through regular channels, which meant applying for an appointment with his senators and congressman. But if that didn't work, the coach said, he would seek a Superintendent's Appointment for your father."

Kerry was impressed. "That's pretty spectacular."

"He *wanted* to go to Yale," Alice said. "He'd only gone through the motions in this West Point thing for his father's sake."

"It's still a good college, though," Kerry said.

"Yes." Alice agreed. "But it's an engineering school and, of course, a military academy. He never wanted those things. He was waiting for a final letter of commitment to study literature at Yale. The letter never came." Alice paused and looked upset.

"Are you all right, Mom?" Will leaned over her bed and held her limp right hand. "We should let you rest."

"No!" she hissed. "I'm running out of time."

Will sat back in his chair and glanced at the stunned faces of his wife and sister.

Alice started again.

"Your father applied for congressional appointments to the Academy, and took one of the tests, but then stopped. He was stalling, waiting to hear from Yale, and it reached a point of having to proceed with the Military Academy, or find some other college quickly. He was such a noted running prospect that there'd been plenty of schools ready to accept him. Many had offered scholarships earlier in his senior year. But now, it was too late. Most of those schools had turned to other applicants. And though some were still interested in having him, their scholarships had been distributed."

"Oh gosh," Jeanie whispered.

"A parishioner at St. Matthew's in Bayview, an alumnus of Aquinas College, put your father in touch with the track coach there. Apparently, the coach had counted on a recruit from New Jersey and another from Maine, both of whom decided to go elsewhere at the last minute. So, he was desperate. He had a full scholarship available. Your father accepted it."

"I suppose it might have been worse," Will said.

"Oh, it *was*," Alice replied. "There *had* been a letter from Yale, with a generous offer of financial assistance. But your father wasn't told at the time."

"What do you mean he wasn't told?" Jeanie snapped.

"Tom's father had intercepted the letter. He'd read it and held it back, so Tom wouldn't be led off the path to West Point."

Will was shocked. "Are you kidding me?"

"The summer after Tom's first year at Aquinas, he went back to visit his high school track coach," Alice explained. "As they were talking, the coach said something odd: 'It always confused me, Tom, why you never picked up on that Yale invitation.' Of course, your poor father had no idea what the man was talking about. The coach was mortified … and nervous. He apologized and told Tom to speak to his parents about it."

Kerry sighed. "Oh, my God."

"So, Tom went right home," Alice continued. "He told his father what the coach had said. 'Was there a letter from Yale that I never saw?' he asked. His mother said nothing, as usual. His father was embarrassed and evasive. Then, he was angry. 'You should have gone to the Academy, like we planned.'

"'Like *we* planned?' Tom said. 'I wanted to go to Yale. You knew that!' His father tried to leave the room. Tom followed him. 'Where's the letter?' he demanded. 'Do you still have it?' His father shouted at him. 'It's gone!' Tom was stunned. 'How dare you?' he said. 'You would have lost your faith at Yale,' his father told him. 'My *faith*?' Tom said. 'In *what*?' Then, he stormed out of the house."

Visibly shaken by her narrative, Alice paused briefly and began again.

"Things were never the same between Tom and his parents," she said. "Eighteen months later, the ROTC incident happened. The following December, his father killed himself on the cross country course at Deep Meadow State Park."

"One last attempt to control his son," Kerry speculated.

"Everything I've told you comes from your father," Alice said. "His mother confirmed it to me before she died."

In the silence that followed the telling of this bitter tale, Will recalled his father's imprecise answers to questions about his grandfather, and the family's rare, stilted visits with his grandmother in Bayview.

"Dad's been dead almost four years," Will reminded his mother that day in her bedroom. "Why have you waited so long to share this?"

"I didn't think the time was right," she said. "Maybe I was wrong. I don't know any more." She looked upset again.

"It doesn't matter," he assured her, seeing her pain.

"It really doesn't," Kerry added, getting up and reaching for Alice's hand.

Alice nodded at Kerry and took a painful breath.

"Whatever I've said, or haven't said to you children, has been with good intentions," she confessed. "I hope you'll believe that."

"Mom, stop," Will urged. "You don't have the strength for this." And in an effort to change the mood, he changed the subject. "We heard from Craig McCall the other day."

"Oh?" Alice wiped her eyes with a silk handkerchief pulled from behind her pillow.

"He called to ask how you were feeling," Will said.

"That was nice of him."

"He's been staying in touch with us, ever since you ran into him in Chicago."

"He's a nice man," Jeanie said. "He sends a card on Christmas ... remembers Lina's birthday."

"And has good advice about the PR business," Will said.

His mother gazed deeply into his eyes, and he had the strangest feeling that she wanted to say something particular about Craig. But the rigid concentration in her face softened, replaced by something more doubtful—something to do with age, he thought at the time.

"I'm glad you've been speaking with Craig," she finally said. "He was a good friend to us. I expect he'll always be a friend to you children." She paused. "*I* should have been a better friend to *him*."

Now, looking out on the Charles River, in the glittering night, Will had no doubt of his mother's best intentions—or her love—expressed in a million ways over the years, in her choices, words and silences. She'd led him in her subtle way to his father's manuscript and an understanding of it. Yet more subtly, he now realized, she'd led him to Craig McCall.

Will heard soft footsteps on the stairs. It was Jeanie. She gently pushed the half-open door to their office and approached him. After kissing his cheek, she stepped back and settled into her seat at their partner's desk.

"You have the manuscript out," she said. "Are you reading it again?"

"Just thinking; how's Lina?"

"Her head is spinning."

Will laughed with affection and glanced out on the river.

"Are you happy in this life?" Jeanie asked.

"*Our* life?" Will turned to look at his wife. "Of course I am."

"You're sure?"

"Jean," he said, purposely using her formal name. "I put a lot into that first marriage. I tried to make it work. I wanted it to. But there was nothing more I could give ... nothing more I could do."

"And seeing Nancy last night wasn't difficult for you?"

"It made me feel free," he whispered. "You were right about inviting them. Whatever was there before isn't there now. That's something from another time." He reached for her hand and held it tightly. "*This* is my life."

His wife stared intensely at him. Will feared she might begin to weep.

"This is my life," he repeated.

"All right," she said. But a moment later, her troubled expression returned. "I need to tell you something."

"What?"

"I didn't know until tonight."

"What is it?" He could feel her urgency.

"Lina has gotten my parents to help her locate Paulino. And now, she wants to meet him. Actually, she's already spoken to him on the phone. They've made a date to meet next week at the restaurant where he works."

"So, he's working," Will said with interest.

"And sober, apparently." Jeanie nodded. "He goes to NA or AA ... maybe both ... I'm not sure. He's married and has two little boys."

"You learned all this from Lina?"

"Yes."

"How do you feel about it?"

"How do *I* feel about it?" She sighed. "I don't know. It's a bit shocking, I guess, to learn he's even alive. How do *you* feel about it?"

"It's natural for her to be curious about her father."

"She thinks of *you* as her father, Will. This is just …"

"Why did she kept this from us?"

"She was afraid I'd be angry," Jeanie said. "That *your* feelings might be hurt."

"She doesn't have to worry about me," he said.

"I don't know what he expects … after all this time."

"Maybe he doesn't expect anything."

"Lina asked me if you would go with her," Jeanie said. "To meet him."

"Of course. We'll *both* go."

"No." She frowned as she shook her head. "Not this time. Lina wants *you*."

"Oh."

"Are you sure this doesn't hurt you? She's concerned about your feelings."

"It really doesn't," he said. "I'm impressed with her initiative. Don't you think it's quite mature?"

"I do," Jeanie said with affection. "I think your mother's book has made a profound impression on her … as it has on all of us. Just remember. You're still her father."

"Oh, Jeanie," he said. "She can have *two* fathers if she wants."

Jeanie touched his hand.

For a moment, they enjoyed the comforting silence of their tiny office.

"I was checking P&L sheets last week," she finally said. "I know we've discussed layoffs. But … we can't do that."

"No?" He spoke gently.

"Our people depend on us. They've made *us* comfortable, and now it's our turn. *They* have lives too. They have husbands, wives, children many of them. We have to find some way to get through this without layoffs."

"Any suggestions?"

"We don't need to be driving around in a leased BMW," she said. "And *I* don't need a salary for my work."

"You're right about the car. But you're *not* forgoing your salary."

"Let *me* decide that," she said firmly.

"There *is* another option. I spoke with Craig McCall today. He's in Boston this week."

"Oh?"

"He repeated the offer he made three years ago."

"What did you say?"

"That we'd have to make him a partner ..."

"Of course we would. For that kind of money, it's only right."

"Do you think it's a good idea?"

"If it allows us to keep our staff intact," she said. "It might be."

"That's what I was thinking."

"He's a decent man, Will. Your mother thought so."

"They nearly got married at one point."

"I know. She told me."

"She went back to my father ... with *my* encouragement. But, I always liked Craig."

"*He* likes *you*," Jeanie said. "So, we'll meet him while he's here."

"I thought we might take him to Fenway," Will suggested.

"Good. And we'll have him to dinner."

Will watched his wife as she appeared to contemplate their plan.

"I'm not sure what it is," she said. "But something about him reminds me of you."

"What do you mean?"

"I don't know. It's just ... something."

Will glanced at the manuscript and the manila folder on the desk.

Jeanie stood and kissed him again. "Will you come to bed?"

"Yes." He jumped up and held her. "Let me put these things away."

"Don't be long," she whispered as they kissed again.

Jeanie left their little office and made her way down the hall to their bedroom.

Will carefully placed the manuscript and the folder into a drawer on his side of the desk. He pushed the drawer a few inches and stopped, distracted by the darkening river beyond the window. The lights had dimmed at Fenway and bridge traffic was sparse now. The city was going to sleep.

He thought about the story his father had been working on as a young man, a story of college love, heartbreak and betrayal, written with innocent irreverence—a smart college novel set to the mood of its time. It told much the same story as *The Chastened Heart* until a point at which the narratives diverged. From there, his mother's version soared. His father's abruptly ended.

On the day before she died, briefly alone with Will in her bedroom, his mother had mentioned the manuscript again. She spoke with nervous agitation, as if something more forceful than time, or death itself, were collapsing down on her fading life. She no longer used the term, "your father."

"I always liked Tom's version of the story," she said that day. "It was honest and funny, until it went off the rails, and just … stopped. Like his own life back then."

"That's a good description, Mom."

"I knew Tom would never finish it," she said. "Even though he'd promised me he would."

"I think his father's betrayal, and the suicide, were too much to deal with."

"I think so too. He felt he couldn't write about those things as honestly as he should. And he saw no point in writing a different version. I never stopped trying to get him to change his mind. And finally, maybe to get me off his back, he gave me his story. He encouraged me to make it my own, and asked only that I make it beautiful." She paused. "I did my best."

"So," Will asked. "Which is the more truthful version?"

"Truthful to what?" she gently scolded. "Tom said my version of the past was better than his." She stared into Will's eyes. "I hope you find it in your heart to agree."

Will turned off the desk lamp sending the tiny office into darkness. There was no window now—only darkness inside and out. Everything was night.

He thought of what Kerry had mentioned several months ago, the fact that some children of suicidal parents inherit a death wish. Surely that impulse lurked in the pages of their father's manuscript, especially in its culminating scene at the top of the unfinished high-rise. In his version of the story, there was no doubt that the young man had climbed the skeletal building in despair, planning to leap.

Kerry believed that their father's unfinished novel represented a choice to stay alive. And that the newspaper story about Colonel Winslow's death had been his grim bookmark, a way to remember where someone else's version of his life had ended, and where his own might begin.

If his sister was right, Will decided, their father had done more than survive. He'd banished the ghosts of his past and imagined a life of his own. Tom Winslow had finished his novel after all.

Pushing the drawer all the way in and turning from his desk, Will accepted that his parents' version of the past was true enough for them. But he knew the answers to his own questions weren't there. The past is not a life; it is a dream that belongs to the dead.

The things he wanted to know about himself lay only in the future. And so, he thought, hurrying down the hall to the bedroom where his wife waited, he would find his own path to love. He would be his father's son.

Author's Note & Acknowledgements

The Chastened Heart was conceived as a modern expression of Dante's timeless theme—the pursuit of enlightenment in the mysteries of love and art. But as I developed the novel into its final form, I found that my admiration for another great writer, the trans-Atlantic author of *The Portrait of a Lady*, had subtly influenced my version of Dante's quest.

This should not have been a surprise.

The typical Henry James story turns on an unanswered question. The marriages in his stories harbor secrets; his characters withhold information. Anonymous gifts and unspoken alliances, when revealed, imply presumption or deception. Outright betrayals assume the guise of friendship. James was a master of literary fiction that renders human love in all of its psychological ambiguity.

Dante was similarly interested in the guises and aspects of love. *La Commedia* is an epic contemplation of love in every imaginable form—as something irreparably lost [*Inferno*], as something physical, and thus, confused and imperfect [*Purgatorio*], or finally, as something enlightened and salvational [*Paradiso*].

But Dante Alighieri (1265-1321) and Henry James (1843-1916) had *several* things in common. They were artists in exile who spent their adult lives traveling far from their birthplaces, writing about home with an authority that only distance provides. And they owed a similar creative debt to Florence.

The city in which Dante was born, from which he was banished in 1302, but which had introduced him to his Beatrice, also gave Henry

James his Isabel Archer. Having assumed permanent residence in London by 1876, James commenced writing *The Portrait of a Lady* during a six week Florentine holiday in the spring of 1880. The window of his 4th floor room in the Hôtel de l'Arno offered just the right perspective from which to imagine a spirited American girl making friends in England and Italy.

Then, there is the issue of choices and consequences.

Dante came to feel that his misguided ambition and numerous infidelities—the political, artistic and personal vanities of youth—were responsible for his disastrous exile from home and family. Recall the famous opening lines of *La Commedia*, probably written at a friend's villa in eastern Tuscany, high in the mountains of the upper Arno Valley with Florence far in the distance below: "Midway along the journey of our life / I woke to find myself in a dark wood, / for I had wandered off from the straight path."

Throughout *La Commedia* Dante contemplates the spiritual consequences of self-deception in human choices. Sometimes the consequences are revelations; sometimes they lead to confusion and doubt. But always, sooner or later, choice leads to enlightenment, a realization that love has been betrayed or misunderstood. Even the accursed souls of *Inferno* understand what they have lost forever through their own choices.

In some of James' greatest novels—*The Portrait of a Lady, The Wings of the Dove, The Golden Bowl*—choices lead to a mature understanding of what hadn't been known before. In recognizing their false assumptions, James' characters come to see the loss of their innocence. They learn that friends, and supposed friends, have acted dishonestly. They realize that motives, including their own, have been imperfect, that graciousness has masked self-interest, and that what had seemed to be love was something less.

Above all there is a very clear idea, in both Dante and James, that sin has some connection with imperfect love, and that evil is the absence of love.

I should mention several other sources of inspiration and guidance in writing this novel:

Marilynne Robinson's 2008 interview in *The Paris Review* (The Art of Fiction, No.198) helped me enormously, particularly her reference to Albigensian themes in *La Commedia*. I was guided further by A.N. Wilson's *Dante in Love* (Farrar, Straus and Giroux, 2011). I am also indebted to *Dante Alighieri's Divine Comedy: Inferno, Purgatory and Paradise, Italian Text with Verse Translation, Notes and Commentary* by Mark Musa (Indiana University Press, 1997, 2000 and 2005).

My copy of *The Portrait of a Lady* is a rare Modern Library volume, published by Random House in 1951, based on Henry James' 1906 revision (the so-called New York Edition) of his original text, which had debuted in serialized form during 1880-1881 and as a book in late 1881.

Finally, I learned much about James' creation of this marvelous novel from Michael Gorra's informative study, *Portrait of a Novel: Henry James and the Making of an American Masterpiece* (Liveright Publishing Corporation, 2012).

* * * *

I wish also to acknowledge the insight and encouragement of novelists Eileen Charbonneau and Vinton Rafe McCabe, literary agent Susan Schulman, and my wife Angela Crooke.